REALM OF SHADOWS

Thea Atkinson

Chapter 1

I was drifting off from exhaustion when they finally came, hours after Stone's footsteps had faded into the darkness of the fae dungeon he'd left me in. The monster hunter in me raged at my impotence, and somewhere deep inside, the woman who had dropped her guard long enough to trust the dark fae was sick at her naivete.

Three of them trooped in: Stone; One of the guards from before, with sheepish hands tucked neatly at his hips as he avoided my gaze; and another man. Large. Powerfully built. He looked like a bull-mastiff, handsome in a way but so very fierce. He was the one who commanded the most space.

"Do you know who I am?" he asked in a higher-pitched voice than I expected for such a large male.

I lifted my chin, but didn't get up. I wasn't sure I could if I wanted to.

"You're the boss." My voice so deadpan from exhaustion that I half-expected him to take it as an insult.

His expression never wavered, even thought the politeness in his voice grew tighter. "In your language I might be called Don Sidhe," he said. "But my intimates call me Terran." His eyelids narrowed as he scanned me with disapproval. "Though everyone pays me proper respect."

He inclined his head at the guard, who moved so quickly to heft me to my feet that my hand snapped out in reflex. I caught the male in the groin, and I cupped and squeezed until he doubled over with a whoosh of sour air. At least his reaction told me the fae shared the same weakness as human men.

Even before the guard staggered back, Stone appeared beside me in a blur of unseen movement that was nothing but a trail of light and color, a disconcerting effect that left me staggering until his hand beneath my armpit buoyed me. He leaned down, his height curling downward so he could help me to stand on my own. Gentle, tender prodding that kept me barely on my feet.

I tried to hate him for it.

A tight, very brusque voice that held a note of interested humor, halted his attentions. "Seems my son has taken a fancy to you, Ms. Ashe."

My head snapped up in surprise as I stood on shaking legs in Stone's hold. "Son?" I said, unable to cage my surprise behind closed lips. My gaze lifted to his pinched face, then to the Terran. *His son.* Stone was the boss's son. A snort of disbelief fled my lungs because, really, I just couldn't believe my luck.

Here, I'd thought his blood oath was to mere organization when it was truly an oath to family. Not just a cartel. A bloodline. I'd been so foolish.

The realization of just how tight that bond was between them made the leash of hurt I held onto go slack in my grip. But it was still difficult to stand. The shock of the realization paired with the pain that lingered after the beating, the stiffness in my joints and muscles, the fear of broken bones, made it a struggle to get to my feet.

But standing was critical, I knew. This wasn't a mere predator sizing up prey, even if this boss was doing so in a very mortal-looking suit. Armani, I thought. Or Brioni. The situation were more insidious than that.

Terran was no simple violent fae with a lust for power. Optics were important to him. No doubt he saw things others passed over. A tremor in an eyelid. A wobble in the knee. He'd see me balancing on the fulcrum of strength and fear and would measure which side I'd likely fall on long before I teetered off.

And that quality made him more dangerous.

I had to be crafty, not brash. I needed him to see me as strong enough to stand up to him, but too weak to do his bidding. Because while a wounded assassin was useless, a sassy bitch might get her sister killed.

It was too late for me, I knew, but not for Kit, and this was all to protect her. My knowledge was a liability. A thread left uncut. Images of concrete shoes and fishes swimming around my face flitted through my mind like a kaleidoscope. But I was used to laying my life on an uncertain line. I'd accepted that the moment I took up the hunter's mantel.

But my sister? That was different. She was ignorant of this fae realm and this fae court. If this bastard could respect my strength, he might only remove me and leave her untouched. So long as Stone hadn't already insinuated her to his father, she might remain safe. Traitorous bastard though he was, I needed him as an ally.

Keeping her face in my mind's eye, I swiveled my gaze toward Stone, the burn of Terran's scrutiny razing every inch of my body.

I forced out a harsh, humorless laugh. "The boss's son," I said. "And here I thought you were just some anonymous soldier, when all along you were so deep in the bowels of the organization, you sprang from its very cock."

Stone had the grace to shuffle his feet. He'd have no idea what kind of favor I was doing him with my cavalier attitude, calling him out like I didn't care, like we hadn't exchanged a single tender moment. It was the least I could do for him after he'd killed that nasty prick of a guard.

To his credit, he held the intensity of my gaze better than most men could. I had to respect that.

"Some oaths are bound by more than the letting of blood, Ava," he murmured.

I sucked the back of my teeth. "Oh, I understand," I said, inflecting all the truth I felt into the words so Terran would sense it and maybe decide that whatever had been between Stone and me was over. For Kit's sake, I needed to preserve anything that might be left, and the last thing I needed was for the boss to think we were chummy. Best to deflect that little chance while I still could.

"Those guards weren't stepping outside their jurisdiction at all, were they?" I asked with heat in my voice that I didn't need to fake. I'd had a lot of time to think and

I was pretty sure no lowly soldier would take it upon himself to hurt me, not knowing I was an asset to the Shadow Court. "Someone sanctioned my beating."

An unexpected growl from the darkness caught everyone's attention, a sound so low and threatening, without so much as a clear, human-like vocalization, that it raised the hair on the back of my neck. On her side of the cellar, Jasmine let go a low, hopeful moan.

Confused at her reaction, I stared hard at the poisoned vines draped over my own door, trying to see through to her cell and catch her eye. *Jasmine.* An innocent in all this, caught up because she was kind to me. An indentured human from the tavern Stone and I had portaled into from Blade's apartment. She sat in the corner of her own cell across from me with her knees propped up, arms wound so tight around her legs. It was hard to see her face above them. But I could see she was naked. No doubt torn from the fae tavern when I'd been abducted and dropped here to torment me. Her weeping had drilled into my solar plexus.

Hearing her sound so hopeful at a noise from the shadows was the same sort of gut punch, especially when Terran's gaze flicked to it as well. His mask didn't slip long, but I knew from that instant that he was uneasy about what lurked there in the shadows.

If whatever was there could make this powerful fae uneasy, then I was most assuredly screwed.

But at least now I was standing, weaving, but standing, and I had a better sense of my surroundings. I narrowed my eyes, lids going half-mast as I reconsidered Terran as he stood beside Stone. His energy was strong, masculine, violent. But there was another sensation of energy coming from outside the cell, and it too was violent. Angry, even. I might not be fae or magical, but I knew the way air shifted in a space in the moment before violence erupted. I'd made a study of it in order to stay alive.

Whatever lurked outside the cell was feeding power into the room hard enough that it was grazing my skin with little shocks that felt almost like a bee whizzing by. I compared that energy to the one surrounding Terran and I shrugged my shoulders back. Arrogant. Confident. Whatever I had to show him in order to stay alive…whether I felt it or not.

"The question, Don Sidhe is why you would sanction the beating of an unarmed mortal woman you hired to kill a king."

His posture never shifted. Not a smile, cold, hard, or otherwise moved across his face. He simply regarded me with that expressionless face, but I saw something move in his eyes. He was amused. Not because he enjoyed my pain, but because he saw my bravado as the teeth of a gnat chomping into a lion's paw.

"Terran," he said, correcting me. "And after what you've endured at my soldier's hands, I'd think we can be more casual, Ava. I may call you Ava, may I not?"

"I don't care what you call me," I said.

It was all I could do not to drop onto my backside on the flagstones. I was having a devil of a time remaining upright, even with Stone standing close enough that I could lean ever so slightly into him and hold myself up. My knees wanted to buckle. My spine all but collapsed on itself, curving out despite my best attempts to keep it ramrod straight. The boss watched me, the loose skin around his eyes moving as he blinked. He was amused, it seemed. A sort of angry humor that would indulge me until it wouldn't. I knew that sort of look, too.

He adjusted his cuffs as he regarded me, such a human gesture that I almost forgot what he was until he said, "You are not what I expected in an assassin."

I leaned against the wall, a way to hold myself up as my knees buckled without letting on I was about to collapse. "Neither are you."

His bottom lip pressed up into his top one and his jaw ticked. "My son told me you were better than the hunter we originally arranged to do this job."

"Is that why you had me beaten?" I asked him. "To see what sort of torture I could take?"

Another growl from the dark, primal enough that Jasmine started whispering in hushed, secretive tones that I noted made Stone's ears perk up. She had to know they could hear her, but whatever she said was lost to my mortal senses. Maybe she was begging someone for her life. I hoped so. It was obvious by now I was in no position to help her.

Terran folded his hands over his hips and cocked his head at me. "That wasn't torture," he said with a feral grin. "Just an unfortunate misunderstanding."

My ass. Stone might not have realized his father had ordered it, but I did. That I was left alive had to mean Kit was safe for now, because otherwise, that beating would have been fatal.

The relief was so acute, I slid down the wall to my haunches, laying my back against the cold stone, propping myself up. *Safe.* For now. It was the best I could hope for, and I'd take it. I'd take it and rejoice.

I licked my lips, realizing I was thirsty. Life-threatening kind of thirst.

"I prefer my misunderstandings to be of a liquid sort; a miscommunication about whether I ordered tequila or mezcal, a glass of water instead of wine." I swung my gaze to Terran's. "You don't have any of those sorts of misunderstandings handy, do you?"

Terran stood over me, and the way he looked down at me, I knew he hadn't enjoyed the joke. Not at all.

"Are you looking for a drink to celebrate your survival or your bravado?" he said. "Because at the moment, that survival is hanging by a thread."

I blinked up at him. "Ask Stone," I said. "He's the one who dragged me here."

"Because of your skills," he said dryly. Not a question. A bald, unimpressed statement.

I nodded anyway. "Seems so."

He studied his nails and seemed to find enough dirt in one of them to dig at it with his fingers. "A skill I've yet to see in action," he said. "My son had to take out one of your guards for you."

Except it had been at least two by my reckoning. If he wanted to doubt my skill, he should at least get his math right.

I shrugged. "Hard to kill in a jail cell when you're outnumbered three to one, but do tell your men to come at me two by two like civilized brutes, and I'll give you a demonstration."

It was bravado, all of it, because it was also just as hard to kill a man when sitting on one's ass on cold stone because you were dancing up to the state of shock. I had no more ability to resist than I did to brush my teeth, and he knew it. He merely pressed his lips together and sighed through his nose.

"This is no jail cell, Ms. Ashe," he said finally. "We don't hold people here for extended lengths of time the way they do in the royal dungeons." His teeth showed, a large bank of white with the tiniest sharpest points. "We don't find it a profitable endeavor to keep our prisoners very long."

Not long. Just days. Well those days had given me plenty of time to mull over exactly how and why I found myself in a dank dungeon cell at all. I'd gone from thinking it was the witch's fault, to Shea's, and straight along a razor's edge to the fae male who had shown up at the tavern after Stone left me there.

Flint, Jasmine had said his name was. Well, he certainly seemed flinty. Blackly clad head to toe with an equally black demeanor.

He wasn't some random male who had ambushed me in the witch's lair. He'd been sent because he was part of the Shadow Court. And if Stone and Flint were both in the organization, then they were both made-fae.

I'd already put together what that might mean after Gideon had used the term. A made-fae was very much like what the human mafia called a made man, sworn by blood oaths and initiated into a violent life they couldn't be discharged from except through death.

My jaw ticked to the side. "If I'm here at your behest," I said, "then why put me here at all? I thought you ordered me to complete a hit."

For a moment, I thought Stone would interrupt, but Terran put his hand up, quieting him. He took a step closer, and he was already standing pretty close. That one movement ate up the inches between us, close enough that I could smell moss and forest on his boots. He made me think of a dog running through the woods after a rabbit. I didn't need a lesson to understand which of us he thought was the hound.

Terran tilted his head thoughtfully. "Funny," he said. "It almost seems as though you have forgotten that order. Have you misunderstood who you are working for?"

"Walmart?" I quipped as I sagged to the side, almost all of my energy taken up by the bravado.

He didn't smile this time, but his mouth worked as though he were chewing over the words he wanted to deliver to separate them from the ones he wanted me to hear.

"You'll see when my enforcer reminds you exactly who is your boss, Ms. Ashe, and just who holds your life — and your sister's—in his hands."

I leveled my gaze toward Stone, who stood rigidly by, his face struggling to hold back emotion. He wouldn't meet my gaze. Blood oath or not, he had a lot to answer for no matter what side of forgiveness I landed on. His explanation for abandoning me at the tavern and stealing the cursed objects from me that I'd taken from Lilah was that he had no choice.

"You think Stone is going to hurt me?" I asked, a sort of dry disbelief flaking from my voice. "Just hours ago, he killed one of your guards for doing just that."

While Stone's aqua-colored eyes flickered over me sympathetically, he squared his shoulders in a way that made me think he was bracing for something. My brow furrowed as confusion swam over me. I shifted my gaze back to Terran. His eyebrows merely climbed to his black hairline.

"Stone?" he barked. "You think Stone is my enforcer?"

He laughed, and I was left to gawk at the way he gave his head a short, dismissive shake. "Stone may be my son, but he's not the dark enforcer. Oh, no. He's nowhere near as violent as that."

Not as violent? My mind replayed the things Stone had done to the fae guard and reminded me that it had looked impressively violent. If that wasn't enough for this stylized mafia don, then his idea of violence and mine were vastly different. A prickle of dread began to climb my spine, and long before it reached the back of my neck, where the hairs were rising, Terran waved at someone outside the cell, standing out of sight in the shadows. A faint waft of cinnamon began to bloom in the air, and I realized whoever Jasmine had been speaking to in such a hushed, intimate voice, hadn't just been the ravings of a frightened woman.

The guards moved first, parting slowly as if it was a scene in a movie meant to incite tension, and I had to crane my neck to see around them. The ringing in my ears went dead as I caught sight of him shouldering his way past, strolling into the cell the same way I'd seen him prowl into the bathroom of the tavern.

Even catching a glimpse of that broad chest and ridiculously gorgeous face, I wasn't prepared to hear his voice when halted in front of me and pinned that steely gaze to mine.

"Blade," I said through clenched teeth.

"Hello, Ponytail."

CHAPTER 2

IT HAD ALL STARTED with the witch. As a monster hunter turned reluctant, would-be assassin; turned captive prisoner of the fae mafia, I could blame my imprisonment in this hellhole of a jail cell to just about anything. But if I really thought about it, I could trace my path from my first steps across Lilah's property to this moldering dungeon, and know my decision to kill her was where this entire mess had all begun.

Or maybe it had started with Gideon. Or Shea. Because if my mentor's new lover hadn't come traipsing up my steps to tell me she was worried he might do something rash and, unlike him, I'd never have tracked him down at his favorite bar. I wouldn't have stolen his stupid goblin-spelled shirt. And I wouldn't have used it to hunt and kill Lilah the dark witch in the first place.

And I wouldn't be here. After years in the game, a gal knows when an important piece has been moved into play, and I knew it now.

Days, maybe hours earlier, I had made the mistake of ignoring the warning tingle in the small of my back that told me Blade was something more than just an irritating fae. Now, as a coppery light flashed in his eyes, as he shuttered all emotion from his face, I understood just how grave that role might be.

With dread lodging itself deep in my marrow, I watched Terran shift one foot to the other before he laid a hand on Blade's shoulder in a fleeting sort of touch that suggested he was nervous being in close proximity with the 'dark enforcer'.

"I find disobedience a most loathsome thing," he drawled. "And find very painful punishment an effective deterrent." He pulled his arm back to his side and rubbed the palm of it against his leg as though to wipe away the taint of touch. "But I don't have quite the same affinity for delivering pain as Blade. No one does."

My spine crawled at his tone. It was the sound of a man who might want to watch the violence, not just order it. "Good thing for me then, that the only disobedient child here is Stone."

His nostrils flared and panic sparked in my belly. I was already aching from the beating the guards had given me. I wasn't sure I could take more.

I lifted my chin. "I've done everything I was told," I said, a wheeze sounding in my chest as I panted out the words.

Terran began prowling the cell, and I began to hope Blade's presence was more posturing. A way to cower me. But then he pivoted sharply enough that it looked like he twisted his ankle. Except the only one who winced was me.

"If it wasn't already getting too late to find another assassin," he said. "I'd put you in one of the brothels, maybe sell you to The Kennel in the Shadow Bazaar."

There was that mention of the Shadow Bazaar again. I held his gaze despite the way my stomach was twisting into knots. I had no idea what The Kennel or The Shadow Bazaar were, but I understood the threat well enough.

"I'd kill the first man who touched me," I said, liquid nitrogen in my voice.

He examined his nails. "I'm sure you would," he said. "Which is why I've decided on a different punishment. The kind I reserve for my disobedient bootlicks." He flicked his hand toward Blade.

I didn't see Blade move. A blink of time, maybe, before he stood in front of me. A waft of cinnamon brushed my skin like a lazy summer breeze. The heat radiating from him felt much the same, an invitation to stretch out, to arch into it, and despite my fear, I felt my body straining toward it. Every inch of my being was greedy for heat regardless of the source. I was so cold. I'd not realized it till that moment just how cold I was.

But he was there to hurt me, not heat me and we both knew it. I sucked in a shaky breath and squared my shoulders. Terran grossly underestimated the limits of mortal bodies if he thought he could merely torture me a bit after what I'd already suffered. I already ached all over. Every ounce of my being was cringing at the thought of enduring another blow.

The only solace was the thought that he'd likely be forced to seek out a new assassin after all, and that thought curved my lips as I eyeballed the granite façade of the fae who stood in front above me.

"Does Jasmine know you're a bastard?" I rasped out, my head hanging back like a broken doll's neck.

I didn't expect an answer, just clung to the last vestiges of bravado that had kept me going in this business in the first place. I wasn't sure if Jasmine could hear me from her cell, but I hoped so. She should know what was happening in here. She should know the kind of monster she was in love with.

Blade's hand snaked out so fast, I'd not realized he'd leaned toward me. I tried not to flinch when it gripped my elbow. A surprised movement of his eyebrow indicated I'd failed. For a moment, I thought his fingers softened around my tissues the way a man sometimes does when he's playing with a lover and forgets the force of his own strength. The regret that comes with an unexpected bruise.

But then, the moment evaporated as he let go a huff of exasperation. He tugged then, a silent order to get to my feet when he could so easily have forced me to stand.

It took an effort of will to worm my way up the wall instead of using the leverage of his weight to gain solid footing. I stood on legs that threatened with every breath to buckle beneath me, and I had to lean against the wall to remain upright. The wounds inflicted by the guards delivered hateful jabs into my back with every muscle that rested against the stones.

Even so, I held the dark enforcer's gaze with all the courage I could muster. "I wonder if Jasmine really know the sort of monster she's fucking?"

"Careful," he said in a gritty voice.

"I'm always careful," I said. "But is Jasmine?" I fluttered my eyelids at him and hoped it didn't look like it felt, which was more like trying to blink away a gob of goo than flirtation. "I do hope she isn't carrying some miniature monster in her belly."

He swallowed hard, and I thought he might backhand me, but Terran, obviously realizing I was trying to goad Blade into striking me, ordered one of the guards to fetch him a chair. It was enough of a diversion that I relaxed unintentionally in the enforcer's grasp. Standing in front of a roaring fireplace couldn't have felt more bone-warming.

But as a respite, it wasn't much.

He peered down at me, measuring each breath I took with shuttered eyes, and I did my best to breathe without showing that every inhalation was like driving shards of glass into my lungs. Something silent and intimate was going on between us, the sort of bonding that happens between two opposing forces in the moments before a strike, when the victim knows there's no way out and the abuser anticipates the satisfaction he'll feel when he releases his energy.

And by the time the chair was delivered, I felt like I knew every seam of his face and neck, the power behind his shoulders, and he knew every small inch of uninjured terrain. Almost out of periphery, I saw Terran turn the chair so that the ladder-style back faced me. He sat on it, legs splayed out to the sides, while I did my best to keep from collapsing.

The guards huddled closer together, each one vying for a spot at the back of the cluster, while Stone stood silent. His fists clenched at his sides. I didn't dare look at him too long.

"You might have noticed the sparseness of your accommodations," Terran said, and I was so surprised at the banality of the statement that I swung my gaze to his.

His expression was a blank a mask as Blade's. But behind his eyes was a calculation that told me he had a masterful command of his emotions. I all but held my breath as he continued.

"We have to keep such a place for those who aren't quite so compliant as we might need. Mind you, we've not had to use this place as often anymore." He chuckled to himself. "Most would rather die than face Blade." He crossed his arms on the chair's back as he studied my face.

I stole a glance at Blade, whose lips had pressed together tightly even as his gaze moved to lock on the wall behind me. His hands slid behind his back like a soldier. A good soldier, willing to do whatever he was ordered. And yet, when Terran followed my gaze, I felt a slight movement of his shoulders, angling away from the dark enforcer if only slightly.

"He's ruthless," he said of Blade. "Quite terrifying, even for me. I'm not disappointed that I've had to use him less and less over the centuries. But he does get restless." The short glance he gave Blade pulled a thoughtful sound from his throat, and when he turned back, I saw the expression that he tried to hide. It owned his expression in that flash of time when he'd turned away from Blade to face me, but I recognized it immediately. Revulsion.

It was enough for me to realize he feared Blade. He might even hate him. More importantly, he didn't want me to know the truth about either of those things.

I ran my gaze over the guards' faces and saw the same. I eyed Blade with renewed interest, recalling the loathing Stone showed him, the deference of the tavern patrons. I badly wanted to lean to the side to see if Jasmine was watching because I'd not seen an ounce of disgust in her reaction to him. The dichotomy of it was perplexing.

What I did was drop my head back against the wall. I regarded Terran with as casual a glance as I could muster and said, "If you have such a ready-made, terrifying killer in your midst, why do you need me? Surely he could assassinate your king."

The surprise on Terran's face seemed genuine. "Blade is a killer, yes, and quite terrifyingly good at it, but that's not his true specialty." He ran a scalding look over the dark enforcer, and a curl stole over his lip that suggested whatever Blade's specialty was, it did not endear him to the organization. "Besides, I believe my son explained that we need distance from this hit."

"Right," I drawled, digging my head into the stones to keep focused. "And what does it matter if everyone knows the Shadow Court killed the king if he's dead?"

He shrugged. "That's no business of the assassin doing the killing," he said and propped his elbow on the back of the chair. Cupping his chin, he watched me, a most casual, unassuming, innocent looking posture. Purposefully, I thought.

"Do you know where you are?" he asked. "This safe house of ours? It's in the City of the Dead."

"Is that anything like calling a chihuahua Killer?"

Terran's eyes narrowed, but he ignored my jab. "The city is a living thing. Like many parts of Fae, it possesses its own unique magic. A magic that needs to be fed."

"I'm guessing its favorite dish isn't Eggs Benedict."

Those eyes narrowed even further. I thought he might soon lose all ability to see through the slits. "You have a smart mouth," he said. "I'm sure some find it endearing. I don't. What I find endearing is obedience."

He dropped all pretense of appearing conversational and leaned on those elbows, the tension in his shoulders a knot that looked like tennis balls beneath his suit. "What the city enjoys most is death. But it will accept pain if offered."

My fingers twitched at my sides out of instinct, moving for the karambit that wasn't there. He noticed and his smile lengthened, showing all his teeth. A cold bead of sweat slid down my spine.

"The city that straddles this plane possesses a unique power rooted in very dark magic." He brushed the arm of his suit. "It heals as well as harms. Isn't that fantastic? Even here in Fae, it's a wondrous Janus-faced coin. When I first discovered it, I didn't understand how it could be possible, but then I realized it works like most magic, giving and taking in a sort of balance." He leaned forward slightly, threateningly. "The power to heal, the power to harm. The drive to take balanced with the gift of giving. It's a serpent swallowing its tail."

"You do look a little like a snake to me," I said agreeably. "You might be careful you don't choke on your own dick when it goes down."

He chortled good naturedly, but it was a sound that made my skin try to shudder off my bones. "Indeed, that would be make things difficult, wouldn't it? Luckily for your sake and mine, the city chooses only certain fae to wield it." He swung a nonchalant eye toward Blade. "Those with the greatest gift for violence are given its boon of healing."

My gaze jumped to Blade automatically, and for a second, he met me look for look. We locked eyes for a heart-stopping moment before his narrowed and dropped again. This time to my pulse. He was reading me, I realized, and I willed myself to breathe in slow and steady to calm my heartbeat.

Terran watched it all with quiet interest. But his eyes never left me. "You tried to warn the king," he said to me after a moment.

Ah, the reason I was here finally. I shrugged because I needed some deflection from the trembling that started moving through my core.

"Courage," he said, tilting his head as if in a bow. "Normally, I would respect that, but at the moment, it's as foolish as your bravado. I know you tried to warn the king whether you confess to it or not. I own the Captain of the Guard."

The information didn't truly surprise me. Just annoyed me more than anything. "If you own the captain, maybe you should get him to do your dirty work for you," I said to Terran. "Like I told your son, I'm a hunter. I kill things *like* you. I don't kill *for* you."

He eyed me as he gestured with one hand without uncrossing his arms from the back of the chair. "It's because Stone thinks you are the best assassin for the job that you are alive still." His gaze flicked to Blade, who stiffened visibly. "The city hasn't had a good death in a while. The power might get greedy for it. I do hope it gives back enough magic to heal you once my enforcer gets to work."

My fists clenched, and I rammed them into my thighs to keep them from shaking. "For a mafia boss, you sure do a lot of talking," I said.

He sighed. "Oh, don't worry," he said. "I've lingered here long enough. But just in case you might need an additional bit of motivation once your punishment is delivered, I have one more thing to show you."

He held out his hand and one of the little guards passed him a mirror. Without a further word, he passed it to Blade, who held it toward me, his gaze still on the wall behind my shoulder.

With a dry throat, I dragged my gaze from Blade's face to the mirror. I couldn't know with a certainty what I'd see in the mirror, but I had a feeling that somehow the reflection would be my worst fear. Even that minute suspicion wasn't enough to prepare me for what met my eyes.

Kit stood on the street outside her apartment. I recognized the flower garden with her prized dahlias hedged in by a little copper cage and framed by a black flagstone path. Behind her, a concrete gnome with a bright yellow hat had tucked his nose into one of the blooms. I'd bought her that gnome for her birthday years earlier. A tight pain lanced my chest at the thought she still had it.

I couldn't hear her, but I knew she was talking to someone. Her hand kept moving to her smokey ginger hair, sweeping it over her shoulder. Whoever she was talking to, she wanted them to like her. The fact that Terran possessed a tool to show me her face so clearly made my stomach clench.

"Where is your bravado now?" Terran asked, and I pulled my gaze away reluctantly from Kit's face.

"You made your point," I said through clenched teeth.

His eyebrow lifted. "No," he said. "I don't think I have."

CHAPTER 3

THE THREAT IN TERRAN'S voice was all I needed to know that whoever Kit was talking to was dangerous, and my throat went tight. With a nod at Blade, Terran bid him show me more in the reflection. It took effort to watch the picture pan out without letting go a single gasp of nerves. Because the image within the glass revealed a fae male I recognized well.

"Flint is a good son," Terran said of the male reflected back at me. "He'll do as I ask. But he hates the mortal realm, and he wants to come home very badly. Do you know why he stays in your world when he could be home in his own?"

I barely recognized my voice when it broke the long silence. "Because he's tailing my sister."

Terran chuckled. "Tailing implies distance and a modicum of safety. No. Flint will be your sister's constant companion. He's very good at creating shadow out of nothing. Most times, she won't even know he's there.

He'll watch her sleep. He'll watch her dress. He'll watch her fuck the neighbor out of boredom."

Terran stood then, and spun the chair around, offering it to me. "Flint will be there every waking moment with her, waiting for my signal that he may come home," he continued when I shook my head, even though every muscle was screaming at me to take my rest.

At that, Flint turned to face the mirror, as though he could hear every word we spoke. His reflection stared back at me and winked. In that second, my body recalled every blow he'd delivered back at the tavern. Cell memory is long, and it's almost sentient. I knew the glee he'd taken in each punch, kick, and bite. I knew exactly what 'coming home' meant, and I knew he wouldn't just kill my sister, but would make her suffer.

I tried to remain calm, but my hand trailed to my neck, trembling a bit, giving away my fear as easily as the shaking note in my voice. "You don't need to remind me," I said.

"Don't I?" Terran shrugged as he reached out for the mirror. He looked into it for several long moments before he tucked it into his suit jacket. I didn't need to be told that mirror once belonged to Lilah. One of the cursed objects I'd retrieved, and that Stone had taken from me. When Terran turned his gaze to mine once more, I had a feeling he liked what he saw in my face.

"Flint has his orders and you have yours. I'm guessing I can trust you now," he said.

I nodded, thoroughly miserable.

"Good." He knocked his palms together, wiping imaginary work dust from his hands. "Now. Let's get the rest of this business done." He nodded at Blade, who stepped forward with a resigned sigh.

I sucked in a breath and held it as I faced Blade, and as his gaze locked onto mine, something visceral moved through my belly, like a snake cracking through its shell to slither free.

Everything faded from my vision except his eyes. If my brain registered the way the guards stiffened uncomfortably, or the slight shift of Terran's head, angling itself away from me, it was only a subconscious thing, stored somewhere in my mind that only nightmares could reach. All my focus, all my energy was coiled in my muscles, waiting for the blow I knew would be coming. And I'd have to let it happen. For Kit's sake, I needed to show submission. Vengeance could come later.

The entire room tunneled down to the space surrounding the Shadow Court's enforcer and my own body as it quivered beneath the tunic. He leaned in close. A waft of cinnamon rose to the air and I had to will my arms to remain at my sides. If I fought, it would just prolong the torture, and I needed to get out of this cell. What was a bit of pain to my vengeance? What was a trifling of agony next to Kit's life?

And yet, the moment that green-eyed gaze roamed my body in ways far more intimate than a lover's, I knew I didn't have the courage to restrain myself if he attacked me. As it tracked the hollow of my belly, the spaces between the muscles where the least resistance would lie, my fists clenched. Instinct flared as those eyes traveled my throat and my clavicle where it showed over the tunic. A dozen blocking moves flashed through my mind, half a dozen retaliatory responses strained through my muscles.

Except. Except his gaze stayed locked on my shoulders, where I was sure one of the guard's lashes had broken the skin. I had the insane urge to yank the garment up, to cover up the shame and humiliation of being beaten when I was powerless to fight back.

"They hurt you," he whispered in a rasp of sound that reminded me of sandpaper on wood. The cinnamon and clove scent of him rose and fell. I didn't understand the pain in his voice. Was it because he felt robbed of the chance to break me? Did he want to be the one to bruise and bleed me?

"Hurt but not broken," I rasped in challenge.

"I might argue that point," he said, and the way he scraped me with his gaze, I thought he saw through the bravado to the trembling I couldn't control.

The moment strung out between us even though no more than a heartbeat filled the gap. I thought time was standing still while those shoulders tensed into bands of hard muscle, as his jaw clenched down around the space after those words, so white I thought it would light up the gloom of the cell if someone didn't move soon.

And then, he did move. His powerful hands clamped down on my arms, fingers tightening, violence coiled into the knuckles, a palpable thing, and of course, I reacted. I couldn't stop myself. Instinct borne of hundreds of hours of battle kicked my foot up and out, launching into his groin with all the strength I could muster. Thick flesh rolled and shifted aside. A solid hit.

He let go a soft whoosh of air and a quiet grunt. I expected him to recoil and jerk backward.

But his nads must have been made of some numb lump of clay because he only inched closer, his nostrils flaring like he was taking in my scent. I froze, captured by the gaze that touched down on me again. It skimmed over my clavicle to the raw wound, and as it roamed, I felt the itch of skin gathering together, the warmth of blood pooling beneath my skin. The blood on my body tingled as it dried and flaked away.

I stood there in a quaking puddle of frail humanity as his eyes traveled my skin from top to bottom and that itching, gathering sensation tickled over my flesh.

By the time he dropped his gaze to the flagstones beneath his feet, I was blinking in stupefied confusion. Unbelievable as it was, my wounds and contusions had knit together or smoothed over. Where my skin had been raw against the tunic, there was no pain. Where my bones ached from bruising, I felt mobile. The pain, the bruising, all gone.

This was the Shadow Court's enforcer? I almost laughed in relief. It was Terran's voice, smug and husky that kept me from doing so.

"Are you surprised?" he asked, his lips thinning into a cold and calculated smile.

I didn't dare speak. I wasn't sure I could even croak out a word if I did.

"I told you the city's power was special." Another nudge, the tone of a man who had just pulled a dove out of his ass and discovered no one had noticed.

I offered him a nod. Because that was all I could manage. Because I wasn't about to insinuate a single hint of gratitude for a monster. Instead, my eyes drifted to the dark enforcer's, morbidly curious about what his gaze might suggest, and caught the movement of that serpent coiling around his irises, swallowing the silver that rimmed the green in his eyes.

In front of me, Terran grunted, dissatisfied with my lack of awe, when all the while I felt it so keenly I couldn't manage a single movement of my tongue.

"You feel well?" he asked. "No aches. No pain."

I swallowed. Nodded one more time.

"Good," he said, standing from the chair. "Now, perhaps you can carry out your task without further interference from your morals. Do as asked, and your sister—Kit, is it?—" he asked so conversationally he might have been extending his hand in a soiree somewhere, meeting upper crust society. I nodded my response, although he knew full well what her name was, and he continued with a curt dip of his chin. "Then Kit will be just fine."

"Thank you," I said, stuttering around the words. If I'd managed to assuage this violent bastard's sense of authority, I'd not look to risk more than a show of gratitude.

I looked up through the fringe of my hair to see Blade staring down at me. He hadn't moved an inch and the hard muscle of his body against mine was a block of immovable granite. I remained corralled behind it. The intensity of his gaze was a brand scorching over every inch of my face. For one second, it left my eyes to the decade-old rope burn on my throat. His eyes narrowed to slits as they lingered there, and I had to fight not to tug the collar of the tunic higher.

I remained still. Stoic. Despite the hammering of my heart against my ribs that I was now sure he could hear.

It was Terran's movement that freed us both from that intense scrutiny. At his motion, the guards beside the wall finally sagged into a normal stance. Some shift in energy wavered over the chamber and I had a sense that whatever magic Blade had brought to bear, it had relaxed. Blade, however, showed no sign of softness. And neither did Stone. A glance at the male who had blackmailed me into Fae proved he was just as rigid as the dark enforcer. The way he looked at Blade could have lit the flagstones on fire around his feet.

"Ms. Ashe?" Terran prodded so politely, I had to drag my eyes from Stone's tense form to Terran's face. Lost in thought, I'd not realized he was still talking to me.

"Yes?"

"Are you ready for your punishment now?"

"My punishment?" I said in a small voice. My stomach dropped like a boulder into my intestines. "I thought…I mean…"

His eyebrows climbed. Blade swallowed hard as he dragged his eye back to mine. The muscle fluttering beneath his earlobe went white.

"You thought a threat to your sister's well-being was your punishment? That I would order your wounds healed because I care about your welfare?" Terran shook his head, feigned disbelief crowding the bullishness of his features. "Good gods, we haven't even begun." He held his hand out, a motion that might be construed as an olive branch proffer but that obviously was a command of sorts.

"Are you ready?" he asked the dark enforcer.

Blade nodded agreeably even though a muscle twitched in the corner of his eye, a tic that came and went so swiftly I doubted even he knew it had even marred his perfect face.

Terran leveled his chin at me, and all the last remnants of warmth in my body evaporated. "Then you may begin."

I felt a tremor move through Blade's body as he strained even closer, our shoulders touching in a way that suggested he wanted me to feel every quiver. His mouth descended to my neck in a movement so languidly slow that it felt almost sexual.

Something within me shrieked that I shouldn't just be allowing whatever was to come. That I should be fighting. Tooth and nail and elbow and feet.

But I didn't move. I couldn't. The moment that Blade's lips brushed my skin, I felt them alter from something soft and unexpectedly lush to something coarse and hard. Despite the years of training, the primitive instinct of a prey animal to remain perfectly still beneath the notice of a nearby predator held me captive.

Hair scraped my skin. A cold, wet nose pressed in deep. His thighs that held me pinned, grew thicker still with corded muscle.

When I reached out in reflex, my fingertips grazed what felt more like haunches than legs. Canine or lupine or something *other*.

Every inch of me not already coiling into fight or flight was shrinking into itself, making the decision that my brain couldn't. I could swear I felt my veins burrow deep into my flesh, preparing themselves to protect my vital fluids.

As his fingers transformed to claws, they dug into my skin, hooking me like a landed fish by the elbows.

I'd fought monsters in my day. Lots of them. I'd fought men too. Each battle is different. Each opponent wants to win, and you know that fact going in. You know that the weaknesses of your opponent are based on the desire to be the winner. You knew death was inevitable. For someone.

But most monsters, even vampires deep in the throes of craving, have some strategy. Primitive though it may be, instinctual and filled with nothing but lizard brain survival, they would kill or be killed, and that instinct would give over to whatever plan meant they weren't the latter.

But I'd seen plenty of hunters go to water when facing a rabid dog or a werewolf. Somehow, that primal fear of a canine slashing its teeth into your skin, tearing and thrashing its way to a kill, raised the flight instinct higher than the fight.

And what faced me now was not a man or a Fae. It was a hellhound.

CHAPTER 4

AND I RECOGNIZED THE beast immediately. Impossible as it was, I knew this creature. The self-same hound that had hunted me all the way from the witch's house to Gideon's stood before me now. My mind flashed to the corset I'd dropped, the clothes that had fallen from my saddlebags and disappeared from Lilah's property. I thought of the blood Blade had tasted when I'd portaled into Fae, Stone's comment that he'd marked me, that he could track me...

And then it all made sense.

He'd have known who I was the moment I showed up at his apartment—corset or no. He knew me in the tavern. From my scent. From the blood that marked me.

And he was the mafia's dark enforcer, which meant it probably hadn't been Stone at all who had alerted Flint and his cronies that I was in the tavern. When he'd interrupted Stone and I in the room, when he'd drawn the guards to the suite, when he'd pretended to get arrested. All that nasty bit of business had been his doing.

Blade was a big man, standing shoulders above the guards and at least an inch taller than the boss. But as a hound, he was massive.

No wonder the guards were so repulsed by him. It wasn't a strange aversion to torture and killing unless it was by their own hands. It was that primal fear of the predator. In his male Fae form, Blade might wield magic or a weapon to instill fear and injury the same as the guards. He might take his time with torture. He might love or lust. He was no different from the Fae he worked with, in the end.

But as a canine, there was nothing left save the instinct to go straight for the soft insides of the belly. Not the arm, the face, or legs. He'd want the mush of the unprotected viscera. And that horror was what amped up the fear in a victim with no more than a growl and the threat of thrashing, slashing, mindless violence.

I felt that terror down to my very primal monkey brain's dendrites. Reflex made me cower against the rock wall even though I had years of hand to hand combat experience.

Because this wasn't just a dog. This was a hell-hound. Massive enough to stand with its muzzle at shoulder length, its haunches filling the cell behind it. Its massive chest and shoulders radiated enough heat to be a blasting furnace as it barred escape.

Only one other hunter I'd ever met had taken one on. His photo took up an honored spot on Gideon's memorial wall.

I felt Blade's nose skim along my throat, heard his inhalation, deep and shuddering against my skin. I thought of Terran's sharp canines, a familial match to Flint's and Stone's, and I imagined that the fae of the Shadow Court were all predators of a sort, built to devour. My eyes squeezed shut as I waited for the hellhound to bite down. Every rapid beat of my heart whispered to my mind that this was punishment, not death. I'd survive this. I had to hold firm.

But it was agony to wait. My heart pounded in my ears until I thought it would deafen me. My chest ached to inhale. My bowels cramped. Fear, palpable and visceral was taking over my will to hold steady.

His muzzle tucked into the hollow behind my earlobe. That thick, fleshy mouth pressed down an inch below where my carotid thrummed with frenzied life. A low, guttural growl loosed from him, rumbling up my skin to my earlobe. Cinnamon cascaded over my cheek as he spoke into the soft shell of my ear, a rasp of syllables struggling to sound like language in a throat meant to emit only howls of rage.

"Scream," he whispered.

I didn't need the coaching. I obliged him whole heartedly and without hesitation. For a moment I thought I'd pass out from lack of breath as the scream tore through its fuel. Beneath the fear, the underbelly of tension that cloaked the cell, I heard the guards scrambling backward, but the realization that they were afraid too, evaporated as Blade's massive paw flattened onto my chest.

This was it. This was the moment I'd suffer. I sucked in a shallow, pained breath. Every inch of my body went rigid.

But by the miracle of physiology, shock is a greedy mistress. It robbed the violent action of pain the way a thief grabs for a woman's purse. All I felt was a brief tug of pressure zippering across my chest. No burning sting of pain. No icy hot zing of nerves being severed. And yet, I didn't need to look down to know his claws had sunk into the skin around my clavicle and dragged down between my breasts. A sob shuddered free of me as images of him slashing through my torso and raising a spray of blood flooded my mind's eye.

Pain would come, though, eventually. Even if I felt nothing in the moment but the rusty swing of an antique weathervane in my throat as I gathered one more gust of air. I might not even feel its icy advance as I shrieked so hard my throat hurt, but it would descend, and I'd be helpless in its razor-winged embrace when it finally did.

The anticipation had me cowering into the gaps of space as my body did its best to hold onto survival. Blade pulled back, just enough to lock his eyes on mine with a keen intelligence that told me he was not a mindless predator. He was completely sentient. He knew exactly what he was doing.

The look in his eyes made my hands fly to my chest in an instinctive, panicked survey. There was nothing. Not even the razor thin line of injury I'd felt him slice into my chest. Befuddled, I looked down. Blood smeared my chest and pooled into the scraps of linen that had been rent open at his touch. His muzzle was coated with it. The floor felt sticky.

Nausea bit into my stomach. This wasn't illusion or glamor. This was real. Shock held me in its velvet-robed embrace, and I threw up a prayer of thanks to God, Hera, Buddha and any other religious icon known to man and Fae for it because it didn't just steal my pain away, it took with it the fear, leaving me in a cushion of numbness.

I felt myself swaying on my feet, the adrenaline fleeing the tissues it had flooded. Something steadied me, a warm, fuzz of muscled shoulder sliding between my legs and bracing me against the wall.

I caught Blade's eye, his intelligent, sentient eye. Swallowed. Nerves thrummed the strings of my veins like a guitar strung too tight.

A subtle shake of his head, the way someone does when they're trying to send a message of warning. His gaze, held fast between a man's and a beast's, narrowed.

Scream, he'd said. As though he wanted everyone to hear how much pain he was inflicting on me. As if he wanted them all to know how brutal he was. And I had. But it wasn't enough. I'd held back like a hunter might, trained not to alert the predator of my fear. The sentient glimmer in the hound's gaze suggested I needed to trust him.

So, I screamed again. This time from the pit of my bowels and straight up to my lungs, letting it tear free at a decibel that hurt my ears. I sobbed and the tears that squeezed a stinging trail from my eyes were as real as the snot that mingled with them. The sound trolled in the hellhound like a decoy.

And still there was no pain.

I bled, and my fluids coated him, and then the wounds healed. I felt them stitching up as quickly as they were inflicted. At one point, I could have sworn the same wounds he delivered to me opened up on his body, closing shut again so instantly that I doubted the evidence of my own eyes.

I don't know how long it went on, but I sensed exhaustion in the hound's body long before Terran's voice cut through the air.

"Enough," he said.

At his words, my knees bottomed out and I would have collapsed if Blade's body, still half hellhound, wasn't holding me upright.

I ran a trembling arm over my face. The swipe of it coated my skin with fluids. But the moment of respite, the sensation of being held upright, gave me the strength to lock my knees.

Seeming to sense it, Blade backed away. Two steps and no more, his expression like his gaze, shuttered. He was covered in my blood. My tunic was wet with it.

"You see how the city gives to me?" Terran asked, and I nodded stupidly because I didn't see. I didn't understand one thing past the fact that I was standing in a prison as helpless as a turtle on its back. But I was standing at least. I wasn't dead. I blinked. Then again. Water squeezed out of my eyes and I swiped at the moisture angrily.

"No matter how much harm he inflicts, the city will heal you, so the enforcer can do it over and over again. It's a brilliant symbiosis, really." His voice was liquid with awe and satisfaction.

I swallowed hard, nodding still. "I see," I said, although confusion still muddled everything but the ability to form the words Terran seemed to want to hear.

I sank to my haunches, my back against the wall as Blade retreated into the shadows of the cell. The guards moved away from him when he shuffled into the corner. His transformation to fae again was quick and soundless. His green eyes blinked through clumps of blood, but he did nothing to wipe his vision clear. Just stood there. Silent. Brooding. Watching.

I noted he kept his face steered carefully, purposefully away from Terran.

Ignorant of the tension gathering in the corner where the dark enforcer lurked, The Don Sidhe prowled toward me and lifted my chin with his finger. He leaned down, staring into my face. His was a breathtaking visage, perhaps even more beautiful than Blade or Stone's, but the malice, the quiet rage behind every smooth inch of his face made him ugly.

"I need you whole and hale in order to complete your task. But I wanted you to know — really know—what is coming next. I want you to be awake and aware and fully understanding when the real punishment is dealt."

Bewildered, I stared at him. Was he trying to terrify me even more? I was already a sopping mess. Blood coated me from top to bottom. Shivering from the violence of the attack. Adrenaline pounded on my heart with such force it made the small bones of my ears vibrate, smothering all other sound. I had to watch his lips to make out his words.

"Do you understand, Ava?" he asked.

I nodded.

He canted his head. "I don't think you do." He looked over his shoulder at Blade. "I think we're done with her here."

My gaze clawed its way to Blade, and I knew my eyes were so wide with panic I must look like I could see in the dark.

Blade wasn't the least bit breathless. He was deadpan, an automaton on a recharge cycle.

"It's time," Terran said.

At that, Blade's head jerked toward Terran. His arms twitched at his sides as his eyelids shuttered down half way. He didn't move.

Terran nodded toward the door. "It's time," he said again.

One long blink and then Blade finally showed evidence of motion. This time, he didn't transform fully into the hound. This time, only his hands and jawline changed. Razor-sharp claws, pointed and strong-looking teeth. His stride toward the vine-covered door and into the hall left a cooling gap in the chamber that tore a sigh of relief from me even as dread climbed my spine to replace it.

I couldn't imagine he was just leaving. That it was over. Dread climbed my spine as I found the courage to speak.

"Where is he going?" I dared ask. I tasted the fear in my throat like bitter and unripe limes.

"Get up," Terran said, ignoring my question. "When I order a show, I expect it to be appreciated."

One of the guards yanked my elbow, trying to pull me to my feet.

I shrugged him off. "I don't need help," I said through a throat tight with rage and fear. "I can get up on my own." I wasn't remotely sure it was true, but I would make it happen.

He glared, but let me stand on my own. With shaking legs, I forced myself every step toward the door where Terran was pointing. The vines were still pulled aside, hooked on large wooden pegs.

Jasmine's cell too was wide open, but Blade filled the space so full I couldn't see her inside at all. He looked back over his shoulder and waited for a signal. My throat closed up. I couldn't even squeak out a warning. An icy hand of dread curled itself around my voicebox.

Terran waggled his index finger. Wrap it up, that gesture said. Get on with it.

I yanked on Terran's arm in a panic. "Don't," I shouted. "Please don't. I told you I would do what you say."

Terran rolled his shoulders out of my grip as casually as if I were a child asking for candy an hour before supper. Surprisingly, he didn't strike out in retaliation, just spun on me, his expression hard.

"This is as much for my guards as it is for you," he said. "It's been ages since they've seen the dark enforcer work. They forget why he is the monster in so many of our bedtime stories."

A movement of one of the guards drew my gaze. He was hugging himself. The others crowded together, vying for spots that might obstruct their view of the cell across the way. The feeling of dread lodged in my stomach grew to a clump of black, sodden earth.

"Watch," Terran said and there was no give in that voice. It would be obeyed.

I dragged my gaze back to where Blade towered over Jasmine.

He'd angled so his body was sideways enough that I could see her face clearly. Strangely enough, it wasn't fear I saw in her face as she looked up at him. Just. Confusion.

He peered down at her without speaking. His arms with the curved claws so reminiscent of a grizzly's hung by his sides, but even I could see that his shoulders were a knot of tension.

"Are you going to kill me?" she asked in a quiet voice.

My heart squeezed. My stomach tried to twist itself inside out. Every muscle in my body strained to act, to do something to protect her, but even as I considered raising my hands to wrap around Terran's throat, one of the guards bear-hugged me immobile.

Even if I did free myself, I knew it would be too late to stop Blade. I kept telling myself she'd feel no pain. What Blade had done to me hadn't hurt. And it had healed instantly.

His hand snaked out so fast it made me suck in a breath. By the time his hand with its sharp claws had circled her neck, yanking her hard against him, the guards beside me had started to retch. Even then, I believed everything would be fine.

It took his muzzle descending to her throat, his canines descending to her skin, her outright look of shock and terror for my feet to finally uproot themselves from the floor.

Everything stopped then. The lights didn't flicker. The air didn't move. I thought I saw Blade run his lips over her ear the way it had mine, before descending once more to her throat.

I didn't have to fight to be let go after that. The guard had already released me and was puking on the floor behind me. The stink of it rose to my nostrils and made me gag.

The others were hunched over, those hardened made-Fae, struggling and losing the battle to keep their stomachs down. The noisy puking of their failure followed me as I raced for Jasmine's cell. I had to do something. Had to stop him.

By the time I made it halfway, Blade was already thrashing her back and forth. She was a rag doll in his teeth. Her empty gaze staring back at me told me I was too late. She was gone. There was nothing left inside the shell of her body to save.

The quiet trickle of her blood hitting the floor shouldn't have risen above the growling and crunching Blade emitted as he took hold of her shoulders to keep her body still as he savaged it. But it did. Somehow the sound of it caught my ears, and I stared at the droplets as they sprayed outward and down to the flagstones.

My own gorge rose, acrid and sour and stinging. Sweat broke out all over my body.

For a second, Blade swung toward me, Jasmine's limp and crooked body hanging from his jaws, and that coppery flash moved through his eyes again. That one instant and I was held immobile by what I saw in those depths. I thought I heard a quiet whimpering in the corner where the shadows were too deep to see through. At the sound, as if it surprised him, Blade released Jasmine from his hold.

She slumped to the stone floor, a mess of flesh and blood that was only recognizable by the flashes of fairy paint on her skin. She'd said they'd washed it off, that it had taken her power to look lovely.

She was wrong, and she was right. The paint still colored her skin, but it was a body that was so unlovely that I knew it would haunt my nights for years to come.

I meant to hurl myself at him, rage infused, terror-stricken, but in that instant, I too lost the battle with my stomach, and I buckled over, my hand going for a support that wasn't there as spasms turned my stomach inside out. The violence of it left me sodden like a wet rag. Without anything to hold me up, I sank to my knees on the cold stone, squeezing my eyes shut, breathing so fast through my mouth that the residue of bile dried on my lips.

I'd waited too long. My hesitation, believing something good of him for that moment, cost Jasmine her life. I might have blacked out.

After a time—I wasn't sure how long—a hand fell to my shoulder. I craned my head to look up at Terran, whose face was grim but nowhere near as apologetic as the words he chose to say. Ludicrous, ridiculous syllables that meant nothing.

"I'm sorry you had to see that, but it needed to be done."

He didn't sound the least bit sorry.

"She did nothing to you," I mumbled, still trying to make sense of the useless show of violence, the sickening feeling that I was in over my head.

I couldn't look up. I didn't want to see any more. Least of all, I didn't want to catch sight of Blade or Jasmine's body. "You didn't need to do that."

Terran sighed. "You're wrong," he said. "I did need to do that. This is a deadly game we are playing, and all of us need to be on the same page." He made a weird line with his mouth. "Is that how you mortals phrase things like this? Deadly game."

"We frame it as murder," I said in a tight voice, shaking my head as though it was a willow leaf in a tornado.

He smiled, a thin, cold movement of his mouth that somehow looked worse than the grim line it had been.

"I expect to be obeyed without question." He passed the mirror to Stone, who stuffed it into a soft-looking velvet bag with golden laces. I recognized it easily as the one from Lilah's lair.

"I can easily find another assassin," Terran said. "But my son seems to believe you are the best choice for us." He sighed theatrically. "And so you live."

He pointed toward the dark room where Jasmine's screams still echoed against the walls. "That woman paid the price for your disobedience. Next time, it might be your sister, and you'll not know it until after your task is done."

I felt the blood leave my face. I wanted so badly to tell him that if that happened, I'd come for him. Him and his entire cartel. But what I said was, "Then how can I trust you won't just kill her outright, anyway?"

He shrugged. "I expect you to hate me. I am used to hatred, the way it looks, the way it sounds. I don't care how you feel about me. To that end, I don't care how you feel. I just care what you do. And so all you have to trust me with is my word. I'm no different from any other fae in that my word is my bond, whether for good or ill."

"A devil's bargain, then," I muttered, and he crouched in front of me, his knees snapping with the sudden movement.

"Some fae may be forged from the pits of Hades, but my line, I assure you, is pure. More pure, even, than the bastard king's." He straightened up, arching his back as though he had put in a hard day's work. I heard his spine pop. "Tell me your word is also your bond, hunter, and I'll trust you to do as asked, no matter how much hatred I see in your eyes."

Miserable and too keenly aware of everybody within the space to do more, I nodded. As I did, I surveyed the cellar. Terran above me; Blade standing stoically at the door of Jasmine's cell, guarding the carcass within like a rabid hyena from what and for what I didn't want to even guess; the guards clinging to the walls and doing their best to recover from their nausea.

Stone…wherever Stone was, I imagined he was as sick at it all as I was. He was the one who had betrayed me. I couldn't forget that. I'd thought he was the one good thing in all this mess. But he'd let this happen. Even if he hated it, he'd let it go on.

Everything started to shrink down to the surrounding space about me. My body vibrated with quiet rage and shame.

Terran mistook it for acquiescence. "You will commit yourself whole-heartedly to the task ahead?"

"Yes," I said, not bothering to hide the loathing in my eyes as I regarded him. I was careful, ever so careful, to answer perfectly.

"I commit myself to the task of murder in order to protect my sister from harm."

It wasn't a lie. If I'd learned anything at all in my time with the Fae, it was that they always told the truth and took vows very seriously. In that, they were different from humans. But they were the same in at least one conspicuous thing: the monsters were truly monsters. Oh no. I meant every word of the vow.

I let my eye linger on his, holding his gaze with an intensity that should have made him backhand me.

Because what else was there for a monster hunter to do but hunt and kill them one by one until there were no monsters left to threaten humanity?

I wasn't going to take out the king. I was going to take down the whole damn mafia.

CHAPTER 5

THREE DAYS THEY LET me stew in the cellar. Three days while I waited and worried and growled to myself, mourning a girl who had done nothing but be kind to me.

I kicked at the stinking bale of hay Terran's henchmen had provided me as a bed after they all left me, the guard's parting jab that I should spread the straw around on the cold stone floor if I needed to sleep. They'd smirked at me and left me nothing but the hay and the linen tunic I wore. The garment stiff with my dried blood. Buckets of stale water were shoved through the vines once a day. A hunk of moldy cheese and bread sat on the stones at one point, a gift I'd not noticed until I had to fight off a rat to acquire it.

To be fair, I did sleep, but I didn't do so on scattered hay on the damp stone floor. I'd propped the bale into the corner and laid back into the crevice with my legs splayed out in front of me. If someone decided to come for me, I wanted to see them. They'd see my face when I fought them like a cornered wolf.

Snatching bursts of sleep kept me from hallucinating or losing consciousness when I least wanted, but it didn't replenish my energy. Instead, I felt snarlier than a honey badger. Pacing took more energy than I wanted to expend, but I'd grown restless as I stared at the poisonous thorns on the doors growing and growing until I began to think the walls were moving inward to crush me.

It took an effort of will to remain calm when the sounds of other prisoners in the dungeon echoed through the cold, dank air. Despite Terran's insistence that the Shadow Court did not hold prisoners because it wasn't profitable, I heard their muffled cries intertwined with the suffocating silence, and knew he was feeding the city with suffering. He might not hold them long, but he certainly did use their pain. I didn't want to think what he might do with the magic the city gifted him in exchange.

All I knew was that the noise was a constant reminder of the suffering that permeated this forsaken place.

Frustrated, I gave the bale a kick. My bare toes grabbed onto a splinter of straw, catching it beneath my nail. It bit into my skin like an asp.

"Damn lice-ridden thing," I muttered, my voice blending with the distant clanging of chains and the occasional moans that escaped the lips of my unseen companions. Heaving an exasperated sigh, I sank down onto the bale to inspect my foot and contemplate for the hundredth time just how I was going to convince Terran I meant to make good on my vow when a promise hadn't seemed to do the trick.

No doubt the Don Sidhe wanted these last three days to be filled with quiet, shame-soaked contemplation.

All it had done was fuel the fire of my rage as I contemplated the betrayal of the Fae who had brought me here. Stone. I'd felt drawn enough to him that I'd very nearly let him screw me into a state of happy forgetfulness. Now, I just wanted to screw a couple dozen nails beneath his eyelids.

With the stick of hay pulled out from beneath my nail, I wiggled my toe, testing. To commit myself to the task of murder in order to protect my sister from harm. That was my promise to Terran. And I meant it. First Stone. Then Blade. Then Terran. Flint. One after the other, they would die at my hand. And I wouldn't just do that for Kit, but for Jasmine.

Peering down at my foot, I noted just how filthy it was. Grime clung to me like static. I'd not showered in at least four days. Three here in this god-forsaken cell and the day before that when I'd rousted out the witch and run to Gideon's to gloat. I needed a shower most badly. But the stench of armpit sweat and the taste of my own unbrushed teeth was not the only stink that came off me in waves.

Blood kept the rest of those aromas more than company.

I brushed at the dried blood on the tunic that barely stretched to mid-thigh and pursed my lips. It wasn't that I was afraid of blood. I'd drawn my share as a hunter. It was just that the thought of killing someone innocent hollowed out a space inside me that was already pretty gaping. Hunting had been something I'd taken up to fill that hole, not turn it into a dark cavernous crater.

Many of us, like those in Joy Shape's Hunter Network, hunted monsters for altruistic reasons. Some—like Hale Saint—did it for money. A few went rogue and killed monsters for other reasons: trauma, excitement, redemption. The rare hunter, like me, would never admit to why they did it, let alone give much thought to the drive behind the job. Too much pain there. No good could come from stewing in it.

But the one code we followed was that we fought and killed monsters. We did not lurk and murder innocents. Even rogue hunters followed that code. It was what set us apart from mercenaries and assassins.

I squeezed my eyes closed, exhausted at more than just a physical level. Kit was an innocent in all this. She might have cut me out of her life, but she didn't deserve to die because of me. And neither did the king. As far as I knew, he wasn't a monster. I'd not seen enough of Fae to believe every one in it was a fierce and brutal killer.

I had to believe that at some point, Terran would tire of leaving me in his dungeon and usher me out into the land of Fae to become his merry Iron King killer. Until then, I would wait. I'd grab sleep when I could, splayed out over the hay bale in a ball of my own sweat and sit in a meditative state, cross-legged when I was awake. I'd imagine all the ways I'd make them pay. And if I felt eyes on me from outside the vine covered door, I'd pretend I could see exactly what shadow the gazes hid in just to keep my mind active.

Which was the state I was in when someone finally came into the dungeon.

Boots that indicated mid-sized feet pounded out a hapless rhythm as this someone strode toward my door.

He was petite, this little male they sent to me. A mafioso dressed in what looked like boiled leathers and a midnight black cap with no brim. I noted he carried my combat boots in one hand.

"You're to be brought above," he said, and with a wave that spoke of some runic language writ on air, the vines covering the bars peeled away to hover around the sides of the door.

The thorns that had stood out so painfully sharp against the greenery retracted into the foliage. I'd not tested the doors after Jasmine had informed me that they were poisonous. A truth that seemed to bear out when none of the Shadow Court soldiers charged with watching me these last days dared to touch it.

Now the male grasped the handle and wrenched the door nosily open. He stood aside with a scuff of his boots on the stone floor, expecting me to merely sweep past him without incident. He tossed my boots at my feet, careful not to get to close.

"I thought you fae were allergic to iron?" I said, testing for knowledge like a snake licking the air.

His soft note of surprise indicated he thought it should be something I knew. "It's not iron. It's black-steel. A metal wrought from magic and no taint of human hand."

I could strangle him with my very human hands and make short work of the body, except I wanted to be brought above ground and out of this stink of detritus and poisonous greenery. Down here, I was not accomplishing anything. Down here, I was impotent.

I pulled on my boots and gave him a long look that he returned for far too long before he finally dropped his gaze to his feet, unable to hold my unflinching study.

"I apologize for not bringing you a slop bucket," he said in a soft voice. "I wasn't allowed."

Something in me cracked just a bit. He was young, this male. With a brush of fine hair over his chin. It was the first time I'd met him, so I wondered when or why he might have petitioned for such a thing for me. Even so, I didn't bother to look at the mess in the corner of the cell. If they couldn't bring me a place to contain it, they'd just have to clean it. I didn't feel the least bit guilty.

"What's your name?" I asked him, thinking I might create some sort of ally as I slid out of the cell like oil and edged out of his reach. I had no idea what sort of magic he possessed, but distance was one thing I could do to protect myself.

"You may call me Steaphan," he said. "It's not my name, but close enough that I'll answer to it."

I inclined my head as politely as I could and peered ahead of me, avoiding the cell opposite mine. I smelled nothing coming from Jasmine's cell. No blood, no rot. But I imagined they'd cleaned it up at some point.

I'd shoved my feet into the boots without stopping to lace them, and so I stumbled now and then. The sloppy, awkward fit gained me precious seconds here and there for survey of the landscape. Mincing along slowly to make up for the slack fit of my boots, I clomped along ahead of the little fae silently, my eyes taking in everything they could and lobbing them into a storage closet in my mind.

Various rooms branched off from the narrow hall below us. Between each cell, torches emitted a creepy purple light, flooding the space with enough illumination that I could see that half the area had once been a wine or liquor cellar. Dusty accordion style wooden racks lined one wall of the room we entered that owned a staircase that wound up to the first level.

I noted several places that could be breached if opportunity arose. The most promising was a dark alcove that leaked a line of light in the shape of a small door. The cellar door. Probably an ancient entry where wine casks and liquor barrels got hoisted through. Cobwebs threaded themselves over the space in a blanket that suggested no one had used that exit in a very long time. Steaphan jerked his chin in the direction of a winding stone stairwell.

I lifted my chin and pushed myself forward, taking the first step cautiously. After that, it was easier, a scuff of boots over worn grooves in ancient granite. Nothing dangerous.

I traced the seams in the rock wall as I climbed, noting several sconces filled with a pale light that seemed barely able to light the stairwell. "Where is Stone?"

His steady pace behind me indicated he followed me closely. The glow ahead of me flickered with each step. My shadow seemed hunched and tired. I straightened my back and looked over my shoulder.

"Well?" I asked again.

"I don't know who you mean by Stone," he said without blinking. "But I was told someone would attend you in your suite after you've showered."

"Showered, huh?" I muttered, hating the anticipation that flared in my chest and waved a white flag of hope. A shower boded well. Maybe I wouldn't just die in filth after all.

I ached to be clean even more than I longed for a good rest. Despite being exhausted, I hadn't slept more than an hour at a stretch, waiting for someone to come for me when I wasn't expecting it.

We climbed three levels, with males just as silent as I was falling into step behind us, trailing my heels as though they were concerned I'd attack Steaphan. Smart, considering I would if given the chance, but with those sets of boots—three, I thought—I knew any sort of escape attempt would just endanger Kit more.

It occurred to me as we stopped at the door situated in the middle of a short hallway that my escort had mentioned someone would attend to me in my suite. Suite. Meaning a bed along with that shower. Maybe some food. Food meant weapons: forks, knives, glasses. My stomach did a somersault. That faceless impending arrival was nothing to the thought of peeling off the wretched linen tunic.

With a strangely reverent bow, Steaphan opened the wooden door that faced us and sent me a tight smile.

"You'll like it," he murmured. "It's warm and comfortable."

I had the awkward sense that he was waiting for a tip, but then, with a shrug, he turned his attentions to those who had come along behind us and who started lining the hall on either side. Burly males. Hairy-looking Fae with corded muscles roping their necks and shoulders. I huffed and thanked Steaphan with a genuine smile and was rewarded with another tight smile.

"They won't hurt you unless you do something foolish," he said.

My left eyebrow lifted an inch, and I had to struggle not to roll my eyes at the comment. I was at a disadvantage, certainly, but I'd not lost all my senses. I knew any move against them now wouldn't just be foolish, it would be a waste of energy. I wanted Stone. Terran. Blade. I repeated the names in my mind like a prayer as I crossed into the room, and when the door closed behind me, I checked to make sure I was alone before finding a plush wingback chair made of fine brocade and collapsing onto it.

I stared down at my feet and toed off one combat boot, then the other and hurled them across the warm marble floor to thud against an ornately carved mahogany dresser. They bounced back as though the wood had been insulted. Maybe it had.

My toes stared back at me through the grime they'd gathered from the dungeons. A flash of pink nail polish winked at me from my big toe, the result of a moment of weakness when I wanted to wear sandals to the beach and was ashamed of the callous state of my hooves. The sight of it reminded me of Blade. He wore color on one nail.

Blade. The name made me clench my teeth. I repeated the mantra that had kept me going in that cell: Stone. Terran. Blade, as I ran my gaze over the splash of acrylic. Seeing the girly shade now put an ache in my stomach that would not go away. Kit would have ribbed me raw over the polish, accusing me of going soft.

Resolving to stuff that pain into an already overflowing mental bin for later, I bit down on my lip and looked around the room I sat in, worlds and weeks away from a moment when I'd stroked a pink-blushed brush against my nails.

I realized with clarity that what I did in the next few days would decide whether she could ever speak to me again.

I was stooping to gouge a flake of polish away from the nail when a knock sounded on the door.

My hand froze with my fingers wrapped around my instep. The young fae had told me I was brought up to shower, but there was no way I'd been released long enough for that to happen.

That could only mean one thing.

They weren't going to wait for me to do something foolish. They were going to instigate it.

CHAPTER 6

I WAS IN TROUBLE and at a disadvantage, but I braced myself nonetheless. Let them come. I'd give them a run for their money and show them what a trained hunter could do when pushed to shove. I scanned over my shoulder, searching for a weapon. Chairs, a bed, desk, bureau. Nothing met my gaze that I could lift and heft and hurl.

Just a bedroom. Pretty as it was, with everything neat and tidy, the lack of movable objects suggested it was a luxurious prison.

Weapons or not, I wasn't going to let them take me without something in my hand to fight back with.

I had hands and feet. I had teeth. I had my boots, for shit's sake. Leaning over, I scooped the nearest one off the floor and was gathering it to heft over my shoulder, preparing to let it fly when a shout came from the other side of the door. A shout. No more.

'Get cleaned up,' it said. I had ten minutes.

Letting go of my air in a hiss, I stared at the door, trying to decipher the sound of the voice. It wasn't Steaphan. It was too rough and gravelly. But it wasn't Stone's either. Or Blade's.

It also didn't suggest with its staccato and clipped notes of command that it wanted a reply. I dropped the boot with a thud to the floor and pushed off the chair.

"I need more time," I said to the door, creeping toward it on mouse-soft treads.

"Ten minutes."

My jaw ticked to the side as I laid my ear against the wood. I didn't care about the time. I wanted more samples of the voice. More sounds from the hallway that might indicate who and how many there were out there. Was the young Fae still there? Had he left with the majority of those thugs or had they all stayed behind?

I eased away from the door a few inches, just enough to make it seem I hadn't moved, that I wasn't going to break through the door and do something 'foolish'. Lifting my chin to allow for more air intake and to throw my voice just a little, I said, "It's going to take more than ten minutes to clean up the mess you all made of me."

A grunt came from the other side, bored. "Ten minutes or you'll see what else we do to you."

Definitely not Steaphan, but enough movement out there that it could be two men. I could take two men. A quick snapping punch to one that tossed him into the other. But even if I did get to suss out exactly where they were and managed the maneuver, what then?

With a huff, I stared at the wood, hoping it would give up more secrets than it was able.

"Nine minutes," the man said.

I gave the door one final slam with the butt of my fist and pushed off to whirl on the spot, facing the room. Threat lingered in the air like a bad smell no matter how pretty the décor.

And it was pretty. I spied the bathroom to the left, just down a very short hallway I'd not noticed when I'd entered. Not really a full room on its own, but more like an extension separated by a sliding mirror door that was pushed aside to show a bath area the size of my entire apartment. The bedroom and bath suite itself took up as much floor space as the first floor of the brownstone apartment building.

These Fae were wealthy. Judging by the amount of henchmen lurking about, the Fae mafia, or Shadow Court as Stone had referred to them, I would never make it out of the building and off the property by cutting through them one by one. Someone would stop me long before I got them all. I wasn't even sure I could get to the top three on my list before someone took me out. And knowing nothing about the magics any of them possessed lowered the possibility that escape from brute violence was possible.

And they knew it. Part of me wondered if letting me see and hear so many faces and voices wasn't just a ploy to prove to me the futility of escape. The breadth of the manse, with a basement big enough to have multiple cells and still have space left over for a wine cellar, suggested the property would take hours to get clear.

They'd not brought me up from the dungeons via a public staircase, that much I knew. I'd not caught sight of any servants or even the three Fae I most wanted to see. I still got a wrenching feeling in my stomach when I thought about Stone.

I lingered beside the bathroom for several long moments, running the scene from the cellars over in my mind again, sorting through the strangeness of it now that I was days away from the event and could think clearly. Now, staring at the shower stall, I focused on the details, not the fear. Stone hadn't made a move to stop Blade, but he'd been angry over it. And what of Blade? I shut down any thought of his attack on Jasmine and concentrated on mine, a bit of violence that seemed to be a deviant play of theater meant for Terran, not for the guards as Terran wanted.

My eye darted to my chest, where the tunic was so stiff with my dried blood that it slid along in chunks of fabric instead of folds when I moved. No matter how much blood I'd shed, there wasn't a single scar on my body to prove I'd been hurt at all.

Scream, he'd told me, and I'd done my best to sound hurt, thinking I was doing a hell of a job of it until I heard Jasmine's shrieks of pure agony moments later.

That was when I knew I'd done a piss-poor job of pretending. That was when I'd realized the differences in the attacks. One was real. The other a show.

My biggest question now was why he'd spared me when he hadn't spared her. And why Terran believed both acts were equally violent. He'd either trusted that Blade hurt me, then healed me with the aid of the city's magic, or he hadn't cared.

Something was off about the whole ordeal. I was just feeling as though the explanation was within my grasp when the guard called out to me again.

"Five minutes," he growled.

Five minutes. I could do a lot in five minutes under different circumstances. With the right tools, I could take out one guard and be working on the second, maybe even a third, if the guards weren't battle-trained soldiers. No doubt they were scrappers or they wouldn't have a place in the Shadow Court, but just how experienced were they?

I leveled the door behind me with a fixed gaze. What would happen when that time ran out? Would they come for me then? Send the dark enforcer? Send Stone? I was ready to sell my soul for a weapon.

"I need more time," I said, throwing my voice. "But I have no idea why my being clean will matter if I have to put on the same bloody clothes."

A shuffling past the door. Murmuring. I counted three different voices. I waited, eyes narrowed in thought as footfalls faded down the corridor. One of them was leaving. I might be able to rush the door…

"Four minutes," the first one said, and I scrubbed my face with my hands.

"That's not enough," I said.

"Then you better hurry."

I turned around and headed back to the door, slamming my palm against it. "I don't have anything to wear," I said.

An irritated sigh from the other side. "Check the bathroom. You'll find your clothes there."

My clothes. Between stripping me of my own filthy things and forcing the tunic over my head, someone had collected my clothes. Brought them along when they'd taken me. I rushed to the bathroom, praying he was right. My clothes. Oh, what I could do with my clothes.

There. Right there, all my things. The duster jacket, my pants, and tank top. My underwear.

I'd assumed when they'd stripped me that they'd destroyed my things. I prayed as I skidded to the marble tiled floor that they'd not ran their hands through my pockets.

As I fell to my knees in front of the toilet bowl, I ran my fingers over the jacket. It took several paces of burrowing fingers and hands to discover my karambit was gone. They'd found it and taken it.

Disappointed, I sank back onto my haunches on the cold floor, tossing aside the corner of leather of my jacket. A chunking kind of thwack sounded against the bowl.

The inhaler. Sweet Jesus, had they left the vape pen full of Bloodmist?

As a mentor, Gideon had been good and bad in equal measure. As a lover, he'd been alternately doting and indifferent. But the one thing I always appreciated was that he trained me to think any edge was appropriate if it led to a kill of a monster that might hurt a human—or me. He'd never held anything back that he thought might keep me alive to fight another day.

He'd introduced me to Bloodmist to give me that edge. And when Stone had blackmailed me into following him to Fae, Gideon had given me this duster to wear, and conveniently placed a fresh vape in my pocket.

He knew the risk I was taking in Fae, and despite my addictions, he'd thought it necessary to arm me with a full vaporizer. My mouth went dry as I stared at the jacket.

More than once, I'd found myself on the bathroom floor puking up blood and sulfur as the magic wormed its way back out of my body. Each time, I'd told myself the come-down was worth it. If I could walk that tightrope between using and coming down, my reflexes would be faster. My eyesight, better. Senses as keen as a vampire's. I'd hear a bead of sweat trailing down a monster's ball sack.

That was the kind of edge I needed if I was going to go up against creatures who owned their own magic. To be short: I wasn't anywhere near Kansas anymore. A little bit of wicked magic might level the playing field.

With a speed I didn't think I possessed, I had my hand into the pocket, burrowing through until my fingers curled around the inhaler. I pulled it out with a sort of reverence, and when I opened my hand to stare at the canister in my palm, my mouth flooded with water. A Pavlov dog reaction that had me hearing the tinkling of bells somewhere in the back of my psyche.

The liquid inside glowed and sparked as though its light was a serpent coiling within the fluid. I knew the feeling it would give me. The taste of it threatened to prickle my tongue like the contemplation of biting into a fresh strawberry. I realized I wanted it. Bad.

But was now the time? I had no weapons, no knowledge of where they were bringing me. I had no plan. I very well might waste the hit.

Swallowing hard, I curled my fingers curled back around it, closing the inhaler off from view. With the feel of it in my hand, I didn't think I'd ever wanted the drug more than I'd wanted it right then. My teeth bit down on the inside of my cheek.

I was just uncurling my fingers when another thudding knock sounded on the door. The voice that came through the wood this time was Stone's. I felt the thrum of some emotion—rage? excitement?—in my throat as my heartbeat ratcheted up.

"Ava?"

Stone's voice, I thought, but I didn't care. All I could think about was the drug right in my clutches. My neck itched. The vape slid between my knuckles and I let it play over each finger, sliding in and out like a magician's parlor trick. The knocking on the door grew more insistent.

"Ava, my father said…well, he said you'll either come to dinner or you'll be dinner."

Chapter 7

As much as my throat ached at the sound of Stone's voice, I shoved down the desire to race for the door and cut his throat with my teeth.

"Am I to gather from the comment that you fae eat human flesh?" I asked, and part of me coiled into a tight ball as I waited for the answer. My breath hitched as the silence drew out between us.

"At one time, yes," he finally said. "Some of us did. Some still do."

An even longer pause while I stared at the liquid in the vaporizer. I thought it caught the light in very strange ways, so peculiar it had all my attention for the moment.

"But you know," he went on. "Any eating I do of mortals now usually ends with a cigarette." He put a note of inflection on the last words, a playful tease, as though he hadn't just betrayed me.

"I'd tread lightly, if I were you, Judas," I growled in the direction of the door.

A long sigh sounded on the other side of the wood. "You're mad at me for leaving you at the tavern."

I snorted as I stared down at my clenched fist. "Mad is an understatement. I should let you in just so I can cut your throat."

A soft chuckle. "You could try, and I'd deserve it, but I happen to know you have no weapons on you."

My fingers uncurled. The insides of the inhaler winked at me. "I have my fists, feet. I have teeth," I ground out.

His silence suggested he was contemplating the threat seriously. I waited. Not sure if I wanted him in or out, and if I did let him in, what exactly I planned to do with him when I heard him draw his palm along the door. "I didn't just leave you," he said. "Trust me. The last thing I wanted was to be yanked off by father's henchmen and dragged in front of him with my butt still hanging out like drawers on a laundresses clothesline."

"And the cursed objects?" I said, aiming my gaze at the door. "They just walked off all by themselves and found their way somehow into your father's clutches, I suppose."

I heard the doorknob twist and in seconds, I was across the room, slamming myself against the wood. "Don't you dare," I hissed. "Don't you dare try to come in here."

I braced myself, feet planted, back against the door, but it was for nothing. He didn't try to push back against me. Disappointment sagged my belly. I wanted him to try, dammit. I wanted a reason to unleash holy hell. I closed my eyes against the sight of the inhaler poking out from between my fingers and thumb.

"I'm sorry, Ava," he said. "It was a betrayal, no matter how you slice it. I didn't want to. I would have done anything to avoid it. But my father—"

This time I sucked the back of my teeth. "Abandoning me at the tavern after stealing something I put my life on the line to acquire is a betrayal. Dishing me up to your father to assault and imprison in your disgusting dungeons is a death sentence."

"Would it help if I told you I could explain?"

"Fuck you," I said.

He sighed, long and heartily, as if he expected no less from me, but was still annoyed that I'd not given in already. "Why don't you just let me in and I'll let you have at me."

"Is that another one of your weak-ass innuendos?" I asked with grit in my voice. "Because I'm not feeling the sexual tension right now."

A pause. One where I thought he might be smiling, and I slammed the back of my fist on the door.

"OK, OK," he said from the other side. "I get it. You're right. All of that was an unforgivable offence the likes of which I shall have to answer for by any means you suggest—and I'm sure I will once you get the chance. I apologize for suggesting a little sexual humor might lighten the load of bullshit I slung your way. It was uncalled for even if all I was doing was trying to I gave up the practice of eating my lovers centuries ago. You can trust me."

I felt my eyebrows climb and decided I wouldn't touch that comment.

"Are you going to let me in?" he asked. "They really are waiting, and I'd rather not make my father angry. Not right now."

This time, I snorted at the words. "Why should I care what you'd rather not do? Let him wait."

"Maybe I didn't phrase that exactly right," he said. "What I meant was you don't want to make him angry."

"Is that another threat, Stone?" I asked.

"Hell no," he said too quickly, and I had an image of him trying to decide whether he should try the doorknob again. My whole body tensed until he spoke again. "I don't threaten, Ava. I act. I do what I'm told."

"Like a good soldier." Even I heard the bitterness in my voice. Exactly what had I expected from the fae who'd forced me into this mess?

"Yes," he said, his voice laced with enough resignation that it made me pause. "Like it or not, I am a soldier. Just in a different sort of army."

I took a beat to consider how things had gone down. I'd all but melted into his arms at the tavern. That hadn't been an act. He'd wanted me and I'd wanted him. I knew the look of desire. That much, at least, had been genuine.

My mind flashed to the rage in his eyes when he'd seen me being whipped by the guards, the sick look on his face when I'd realized he was Terran's son.

I clenched the vape just a little tighter. Things would be easier if I could just hate him. He was a traitor. But he had also killed for me. My emotions were a revolting mire of confusion.

"Who is down there?" I asked, because my entire brain was short-circuiting as it tried to sort everything out, and I so did not want to feel sympathy for him. He was not a victim in this mess.

A skimming sound came from the other side of the door, his hand running down the wood. "Just a few of father's closet allies," he said. "And me." This tacked on as though it was a bonus.

I stared at the inhaler again, past my bare arm where the tattooed script blazed a trail in ink down the inside of my forearm. *Fight like you're already dead.* Well. There were other ways to fight besides physically.

"And Blade?" I asked, feeling the itch to pluck the vape from its spot and use it right then. I might be conflicted about Stone, but I most dearly wanted a piece of that prick. I was already deciding which tooth I'd take from him and which plaster cast I'd use to hang it on my trophy closet.

One very long, tension filled pause before he said, "Blade is not welcome here."

"Unless he's doing some uncommonly horrible thing, I take it," I said, feeling the disappointment in my bones.

"He's always doing some uncommonly horrible thing," Stone said. "Not always by order. Now, come on; let me in. You must be starving."

I was. I cast a long look at the pile of clothes visible on the bathroom vanity from where I stood. This wasn't about clothes. It was about gaining some semblance of control.

"My clothes are filthy and stinking," I said. "And the nightshirt is bloody. Which do you think is the more appropriate for a sophisticated dinner with the head of your army?"

A long pause, and then a sort of whispering before another light rap sounded on the wood, a gentle request, not an urgent demand.

"Let me in," he urged from the other side of the door. "I'll show you."

I turned around and placed both hands on the door, one fist still clenching the inhaler. The vape was close enough to my face that I could see the sparks of magic inside the tube. I slid my hand back and forth, sweeping the surface of the door, feeling the polished smoothness of the grain against the heels of my fists.

I could let him in. He certainly deserved to be betrayed the same way he had me, with a quick clothes-lining elbow to the throat as he entered, and a kick to the stomach so he could experience what it felt like to let your guard down for once and receive a blow to a soft belly. Steal his knife. Shred his dignity along with a few cords in his neck.

It was tempting. The way the inhaler was tempting.

"I'm naked." I said, even though it wasn't true.

"Is that supposed to dissuade me from coming in?" he asked in a tight voice.

My cheeks grew warm despite my rage. "What should dissuade is what I might do to you when you come in."

A sigh from the other side. "I understand. But if you won't let me in, at least get dressed and come out. There's fresh things in the closet."

I blew out a long breath as I dropped my fist with the inhaler in it. Eyes closed for a short moment, I took three deliberate breaths before dropping my head back. This wasn't the time to give in to the siren call of the Bloodmist. I'd just waste the hit because even if I did take down Stone, all those cronies in the hall and below would no doubt overwhelm me. I was good, but not that good. And I didn't relish another night in the cellars.

I tucked the fist with the inhaler beneath my armpit. It was hot from my hands. "I'll check the closet," I said, conceding for the moment. "But I'll need more time."

A rustling of fabric made its way through the wood between us, and I guessed he was backing away.

"Fine," he said, conceding his own piece of territory…for the moment. "I'll stall them for another ten, but I'll be back. I won't leave you to face them alone." After a moment of tense silence, during which I refused to respond, he said, "Take that shower, Ava. Then you'll feel more like eating."

I grunted out an answer, thinking it didn't matter what they fed me. I knew the food would stick to the roof of my mouth like a communion wafer and would taste about as flavorful. But the shower? That did sound like heaven.

"Thanks," I mumbled, not sure if he was still there to hear it or not. With one lingering brush of my fingers against the stub of the vape that stuck out from my fist, I put it back in the pocket of the duster jacket and forced myself to walk to the bathroom. Sans drug.

I stripped the tunic off as I crossed the room. If only it was as easy to shed the memories of the cellar the way it was to peel away an article of clothing, but I wasn't sure anything would be able to erase the horror of Jasmine's screams. Just dancing up to the edge of that memory made the hairs on my arms rise. Once more, I tried to will myself to bring Stone's face to mind, to remind myself he was ultimately to blame, but it was Blade's face

I saw, tight with fury. And I had to stop and catch my breath.

I was in the bathroom when I realized how huge the suite truly was. The chamber with its gilded walls and creamy porcelain was half the size of the sleeping area, but it still took up at least a dozen square yards. Lights came on automatically, illuminating the vanity sink and clawfoot tub. In a fit of curiosity, I leaned to see exactly what sort of claws the feet were made of and drew back sharply when I discovered they had talons, and clutched in each foot was a golden orb etched with runes. Testing, I touched one with my toe, half-expecting the carved copper to come to life and grab my foot.

To my relief, it remained inert. At least things were as they seemed here. No glamor or tricks of illusion. Saved, no doubt, for the creatures that inhabited the realm.

The faucet turned on and off automatically as well each time I slipped a finger beneath and pulled it out again. For a world that eschewed technology, the fae certainly enjoyed their luxury.

It was the outright luxuriousness of the walk-in shower that actually helped shove the memories of Jasmine and Blade and the cellars back into their moldy trunk where they belonged. With tiled walls of black basalt that were warmed from beneath either by device or magic, the entire shower felt warm and tropical even before I turned on the three shower heads to stream hot water.

I stood there for several minutes and let the blood rinse from my body. My hair spilled around my shoulders as the water cascaded over it, releasing enough dried and caked in blood that the water roiling around the drain held a distinct tinge of rust for at least two full minutes. I watched the eddy with a numb sort of feeling, as though I could pretend it wasn't real until long after it ran clear. With a hand on the wall, I watched the eddy of the shower circle the drain, my hair hanging in curtains down my cheeks.

As the steam rose around me, I realized that what I needed was to recover. Get my strength back. I was no good to anyone in this state. Recovery meant a full belly, a good rest. A keen eye waiting for evidence of a good opportunity to present itself. Because it always did.

Once the water finally ran clear, I soaped up quickly, rinsed off, and then switched off the faucet.

For a long moment, I stood in the stall naked and shivering with my palms on the wall. Considering the magnitude of taking out an entire cartel dropped a weight onto my shoulders that bowed me over to stare at the drain.

Trapped in a realm I didn't understand, without any real weapons except my wit and determination, I knew I was in over my head. I couldn't just use my typical in and out, get it done hunting mentality.

Perseverance was never my strong suit. I didn't even like drawn-out foreplay, for heaven's sake. My entire M/O was a quick strike, whether it was screwing or killing. Bowl my way in, bully my way through, and take down everything that came at me.

From the corner of my eye, the tattoo I'd had inked into my forearm the night Gideon finally told me I was ready to be a fully fledged monster hunter stood out as proof of that. I'd had it put there where I could see it.

Not in some inconspicuous place only another set of eyes would see.

Fight like your already dead.

I ran my fingers over the lines of ink before each hunt because I wanted the reminder that once a monster was engaged, the only way out was death. I had to act like I had nothing to lose or the death would be my own and not the monster's.

I ran my gaze over it now, considering this, the longest hunt I'd ever taken on. I might succeed and still end up dead. I had to be careful. One false move, one wrong word and I might not just lose my own life but risk Kit's as well. Trekking meekly down the stairs to whatever surprise Terran had in store for me seemed the most logical, but man, did it stick in my craw. I wanted vengeance for Jasmine. I wanted safety for Kit.

I wanted badly to just take Stone by surprise when he came back to the room for me, grab his weapon and rampage into the dining room. I dreamed of slicing my way through the cartel one by one, all hopped up on a blast of Bloodmist to fuel the rampage, but that would only serve to liberate me. And I knew liberation and living were not the same thing.

And this wasn't about me. It was about Kit. For her sake, I'd have to do what I wasn't good at. I had to play a long game. Only then could I take them out. One by one, if I had to.

My head drooped lower, and I let go an exhausted sigh. I could do this. I had to do this.

I was tired of letting myself be led by the nose just because the cartel threatened my sister. It was time I let them think I was being led. I'd lull them into thinking I'd do their bidding, but instead of the king, I'd make sure it was Terran who died at my hand. And then Flint. And then Blade. Stone was a bit of a grey area, so I decided not to think about what I'd do to him.

Watch. Learn. Wait for the opportunity that always came if a hunter was patient enough. Gideon had taught me all those tricks. It was time I put them to use.

Even if I had to die to do it.

Chapter 8

Death had always lurked in the shadows, waiting to thrust its homemade shiv into my ribs. Expecting and planning to die was not a strange notion for me. So deciding to take out the cartel, even if it killed me, that was a no-brainer if it meant saving someone who deserved to live. And Kit deserved to live.

She'd always told me I had a death wish. Gideon had often said the same. Even the witch who had spelled a cache of cursed objects had suggested it when I'd stormed her house to kill her. Sister, mentor, and enemy all on the same page.

Maybe I did have a death wish, but it wasn't for the reasons they thought. I just knew my life was a waste of breath. So I used what breath I had to kill things that would do harm to the innocent, and if I died in that pursuit, then maybe…just maybe my living wouldn't have been a waste of time.

I reached for one of the white towels hanging on a peg out of reach of the spray. It was still warm from the heated stone it had rested against.

Such luxury. Whatever Terran wanted to kill the king for, it certainly couldn't have anything to do with money.

I didn't linger to enjoy the feel of plush warmth on my skin. But I did take the time to think about the impossible decision I'd made in those cellars. Killing the heads of the cartel was not going to be an easy task, and if I was honest with myself, I wasn't sure I could manage it on my own. These weren't ogres or werewolves or even vampires. These were men of a sort, and they had a power that single monsters didn't possess. Hunting groups of things was never easy. Add to it magic I didn't understand, and I was way in over my head.

But what choice did I have? Escape would be knowingly abandoning my sister to a killer.

And these fae, though they resembled human men, were monsters. I'd be doing the Fae world a favor, let alone the innocent king they'd tasked me to murder. The smart thing was to bide my time. Take them out one by one with stealth and wits. I already knew Blade and Stone hated each other. It might be easy to get rid of one and blame it on the other.

Besides. Likely there were more chinks in the armor of the cartel that I could exploit. It wouldn't be like monster hunting, where I blustered in and took out a baddie with much violence and pain. This would take cunning and planning the likes of which I'd never done before.

Brushing the towel haphazardly over my body, I dried most of the water before wrapping my hair into a turban. With a renewed sense of determination, I trod from the bathroom to the suite and headed for the closet. I had to admit to being curious about why they wanted me to go down to dinner when they'd spent three days nearly starving me in a cell without so much as a slop bucket.

Quite a turn around from a couple hours earlier. I worried the inside of my cheek thoughtfully as I walked the layout of the house in my mind. In the short time I'd been in the house proper, I'd taken in everything of the layout that I could.

My guess was that if the house wasn't a mansion in the human sense of the word, then it was most likely a small castle. That dank basement with its dungeons and cells and wine cellar revealed more information now than it had then. I didn't know much about Fae, but based on the Velvet Boar's décor of distinctly mid century Europe, castle would probably be the appropriate term for the building. The dank flagstones and rock walls of the cells reinforced that.

A castle had battlements and spaces to hide in. It had an armory. And if it had an armory, then it had weapons. Maybe even explosives, though I shuddered at the thought of setting off blasts in a world I didn't understand. Explosives were tricky as a plan on the best of circumstances. But as finicky a method as it was, I wouldn't rule it out entirely. I would do whatever it took to protect Kit, and if it meant wadding bombs into the seat of my pants, I'd do it.

My best bet was to use the lack of technology to my advantage if I could. Stone himself had said the Fae didn't enjoy technology. Too much cold iron. Steaphan had suggested the metal in this realm was made of blacksteel. I'd have to find out exactly what that meant. That information could also be useful. Just knowing that I'd not have elevators or cars or cabs would shift how I approached things.

A rap on the door cut through my speculations, reminding me that I didn't have much time left to ponder. I grabbed whatever my hand laid on, and by the time Stone's voice drifted through the door once more, I had pulled out a long, crimson gown from the closet made of the softest fabric I'd ever touched. A familiar scent drifted out at me, and it felt so comforting, I nearly closed my eyes as it wrapped around me. For a moment, I tried to place it, but Stone's voice halted that.

"It's time," he said, his voice nearly muffled by the wood.

I ran my eye down the silk garment, and near choked at the low cut of the bodice and the narrowness of the skirt.

"You've got to be kidding," I muttered.

There was barely anything to the garment. I started to shove the dress back into the closet, but Stone opened the door, causing me to swing around, splaying the material over my naked breasts and hips out of reflex. It was by the grace of sheer will that I didn't drop the garment and come up with fists curled.

"Oh," he said. "Oops."

He had donned a suit for dinner. An unbidden and hated reflexive breath caught in my throat. I was mad at him. He'd betrayed me. I would not ogle the way his body looked in that suit. I would treat him with the disdain and anger he deserved.

But fuck, he was gorgeous. With his hair slicked back to show off the bold angle of his jaw and the intensity of his eyes, he looked like Michelangelo had just cut him from marble and stepped back to let me admire his work. He had shaved. I thought the stubble was a much better look on him, and almost said so, except his gaze dropped to my throat and sunk lower, and I remembered I was damn near naked.

My chin lifted as I raised one, challenging eyebrow. "Oh?" I said, more than a little annoyed at myself for the way it sounded all strangled and throaty. "Is that all you have to say when you break into a girl's room? Oh, oops."

His gaze darted to my throat. "To be clear, this isn't a girls' room," he said. "It's where my father keeps his mistresses."

I might have blushed a thousand shades of red except monster hunters like me, who'd seen some pretty horrendous things and heard worse, did not blush. Even when she suffered an immediate and visceral memory of his hands on her skin, with gauzy curtains of a tavern room billowing into the image. My fingers tightened over the fabric in my hands, and I was certain the way I clutched at it drew his gaze directly to my chest.

He cleared his throat. "That dress will be perfect for you. Dinner is…well, it's a fancy thing." He waved at the armoire, but his eyes remained locked on my chest. "Whatever you pull from there will be perfect, actually, because the armoire is spelled to match what my father wants. But the red. Well, the red is right. You should wear it."

His cheeks flamed about the same color of the dress, and I had the feeling he was remembering the same moment I was. And it pissed me off.

"I'm guessing red is perfect because it disguises the color of blood?"

He had the grace to look uncomfortable. Good. He should feel far worse, but I waited for a moment more to see what he would do.

When he didn't turn around to give me some dignity in getting dressed, I gave him a long look with narrowed lids. So we were going to play it that way, were we? Well, I wasn't some shy virgin, and he couldn't possibly be either. Let him see how unfazed I was by that damned suit and the way his hair curled just so around his ears.

Holding his gaze, I dropped the gown over my shoulder and shook my hair free of the towel. Watching him swallow, I twisted the locks into a coiled ponytail that I tied with strands of my own hair. Then I slid my hands into the folds of material till they found the hem, and I gathered the material to hoist the dress in the air. My arms slid under the skirts as I lifted the gown over my head.

I heard his sharp intake of breath a moment before the material slid down over my head and draped over my hips. Because I had hips. Boobs too. Gideon's protégée Shea wasn't the only one who could fill out a Lara Croft tank and tights.

I took a second to spin to check the fit in the floor-length mirror behind me. He was right. It was perfect. Almost as though it had been made with my measurements in mind.

When I lifted my gaze to his face in the looking glass, it was to see his eyes were locked on the way my nipples stood out against the fabric. Even Gideon hadn't looked at me like that, and I wasn't sure I could speak through the tightness in my throat, but I had to. I had to break the tension.

"Everything is filthy," I said. "Including my bra. I'd say I'm sorry about the nipples, but silk isn't very forgiving if a woman wants to disguise her unmentionables."

Planting my hand on a cocked hip, I let him take it all in, and some part of me felt as though I was doing it for another reason. I shoved that thought stubbornly aside. I just really wanted him to see how terrifically he had messed up by betraying me. Like, he could have had all this and more. Many times over. So, screw him.

He swallowed, and I noted with satisfaction that his fists were clenched at his sides.

"Sports bras are the devil anyway," he said in a strangled voice, and without looking away, he gestured at my dirty clothes. "The maids will sweep those things into the laundry for you. You'll have them for the morning."

I stuck my toe out from beneath the hem of the gown, feeling awkward as hell. "And shoes?" I asked. "I mean, I can tramp around like a hippie, but I gather that wouldn't be à propos to whatever your bully of a father has in mind for me."

I headed for the wingback chair where I'd toed off my earlier footwear. "Of course, there's always my boots—"

"God no," he exclaimed, jumping like a startled rabbit and jabbed his chin in the direction of a trunk at the foot of the bed. "The chest has shoes."

With a shrug I hoped showed a nonchalance I didn't feel, I strolled over to pull open the bottom drawer. Inside, three pairs nestled next to each other like a reckless drunken threesome. One looked like a pair of moccasins, another had all the appearance of a pair of rubber boots, and the last could have been pulled off Mary Magdalene's feet. They were leather and worn in places so much they barely held themselves together.

"The sandals," he said with a confident air from somewhere behind me.

"Mary Magdalene, it is," I muttered beneath my breath as I scooped them from the trunk. If he thought ratty old leather sandals were the thing to wear with such a gorgeous dress, then who was I to argue.

I was straightening up when I heard him behind me. Close. Enough that it was his breath on the back of my neck, hot and wet, that alerted me to the fact that he was there.

Some hunter I was. That I didn't even hear him move did not bode well for my plan to rampage through the lot of them. If they could move like a liquid breeze over a hard-packed and petrified forest, then I was going to have a hell of a time killing them.

CHAPTER 9

KILLING WAS NOT WHAT the fae behind me seemed to have in mind.

"Here," he said in a throaty voice. "Let me."

It took an effort not to grapple Stone's wrists together and kick him in the crotch as he plucked the straps of the sandals from my grip and used them to gesture toward the bed. I'd already decided to do what I could to set these fae against each other, and for now, I needed an ally.

But keeping my emotions out of the deal was more difficult. My temper, my anger, my sense of betrayal was not one I could forgive easily and my body knew it.

"Sit," he said.

When I didn't move, he smiled briefly, uncertainly. "Please."

My lips twitched back and forth as I struggled to get my body and mind in concert with each other. "You're a bastard," I said through gritted teeth, but I did edge closer.

His guiding touch on the hollow of my back was infuriatingly gentle and fleeting, even in the face of my ire. His fingers were there and gone in a millisecond, a moth's kiss on my skin.

"I'm sure my mother would be quite displeased at being called a whore," he said in a soft voice as he aimed his chin at the edge of the bed.

My hands smoothed over the curve of my belly to catch onto each other. His mother? I hadn't thought about his family outside of Terran, and felt immediately sorry for "I didn't call her a whore."

His eyebrows raised delicately, teasingly. "You called me a bastard."

"That's more a commentary on what I think of you than her," I said, but the unexpected playfulness in his voice bagged my knees.

"I'm sorry," I said, and meant it.

He flashed half a smile before it disappeared, replaced by a wistful sense of grief. "She died centuries ago."

I thought of my own mother, gone too soon. Gone because of me. I had to clear my throat and say something or the memories were going to flood through all the careful dams I'd constructed. I was already feeling like I was treading water too icy to survive.

"Nothing can replace a mother," I muttered, because no one could love like a mother, and few people would need that unconditional love more than people like us. Hard. Violent. Unforgettable.

So when his hand splayed over the small of my back, urging me ever more gently to the bed's edge, I told myself it was that sense of mournful companionship that bid me allow his touch. I told myself that small bit of comradeship was the reason I let him angle me onto the mattress and kneel between my legs.

I looked down at him there, that black hair so civilized and slicked back, a strange contrast to the wild abandon of the curls that normally rioted over his head and let him shoulder my knees further apart to accommodate his width.

"My dad tried to replace her," he said amiably, standing back while I perched my ass on the edge of the mattress. "We had a parade of women enter the house, trying to trick us into liking them."

I was aware he was probably trying to wrangle sympathy from me as a way to worm himself back into my good graces, but the comment was too curious to let go.

"Trick you?" I asked. "Why would he do that?"

He shrugged. "My father is wealthy and powerful, and while it may not look like it, he loves his sons. Well, most of them." His gaze fixed on a spot behind me on the wall for a long moment before he shook free of whatever thoughts held his attention. It was so unexpected, this vulnerability that for a moment I forgot I hated him.

I started to tense my thighs in an attempt to squeeze him out of range, but he gently resisted, picking up one sandal in his hands and flipping it the right way to slide onto my foot. My breath caught at the sight of the top of his head bobbing about as he slid the skirt up over my knees, slow, languid, a sensation made even more so by the exhaustion grazing my consciousness, lowering my defenses.

I wanted so badly to lie back and grip his hair that I almost choked on the realization. I snapped myself back to reality, my voice a bit more grating than I expected.

"You're taking an awful risk putting your face close enough for me to kick you in the teeth."

"It's a risk I'm willing to take," he murmured without looking up. I thought he might be afraid to.

"You know what Blade did to me in the cellars," I said. It wasn't a question.

A long, leaden silence.

"I know," he said.

"You know what he did to Jasmine?" This, too, was a statement.

He sighed without looking up. "I'm sorry for what happened…in the cellars," he said. "There are things at play that even I can't control."

His breath grazed my instep, making parts of me coil and tighten.

"You may hate me if you need to," he said. "I can't explain away what my father—what Blade—did below, and to even try to make an excuse is an even more hateful thing." At that, he did look up and his face was so damn earnest that it was a struggle to hold onto my anger. "But if you could…just for the next couple of hours…agree not to attempt to make pate of my liver, I'd be most grateful."

It wasn't an apology, not a plea for forgiveness, and I appreciated that. And he'd shown himself to be powerful enough, fast enough, that he could thwart my attempts at attack. And yet, he showed this disarming vulnerability. It was a surprise. And a gift.

I watched his eyes flare with blue ice. There was sincerity within those depths, regardless of whether I wanted to see it or not. In all my time hunting, I'd never not trusted my gut, and my gut told me now that he was telling the truth.

I sucked in a long breath, willing myself to let go some vestiges of my anger.

With a tight jaw, I said, "I prefer my liver fried with onions."

His entire face beamed as he ran his gaze over my features, trying to discern if I was being coy or honest. I tried to smile back, encouraging him to see the truth for what it was, because we'd found some neutral ground that could carry us both through this ordeal, and even this small spate of time when things felt normal, I could see as a blessing, a way to retrieve some part of myself that had whimpered in that cell and forgotten who I was.

And with the tension gone, he began recanting short tales of his childhood, little ditties of cute moments that showed him as a mischievous boy and not the raw, masculine power kneeling between my legs. But the whole while he talked, churning melted butter into his words, I couldn't ignore the scent of him, the caramel fragrance that swept around me, or the way his palms felt on my bare legs. I couldn't ignore the fact that he was close enough between my thighs that I could hook him over the shoulder and wrangle him in.

Seeming oblivious to the heat skimming its way over my body, he lifted my right foot and rested it on his shoulder as he fiddled with the straps of the shoe. My ankle crooked in reflex and I had to stuff the desire to grab hold of his ears to the back of my lusty brain as

I imagined hooking him in. I fought the urge to close my eyes, feeling the whole while that he could hear my heart hammering against my ribs.

And then, his hand ran absently along my ankle to my calf, smoothing the skin in a possessive gesture, and for one second, his eyes met mine.

And fuck. I knew he was imagining the same thing I was. A lazy session of meaningless but enjoyable sex that would strip away the last of our nerves. A way to forget everything that was going on and chase a different high for a while, a different sort of death.

For a moment, we hung there, suspended by a desire that might have been borne from different needs, but that was equally palpable. My breath hitched. His hand flipped over, the backs of his fingers brushing my skin the way feathers might whisper over air as a bird takes flight. One move, that would be all it would take. A shift of my thigh, a palm on his cheek—

"The boss says time is up," came a gritty voice from the hallway.

I jumped, my legs tightening, and a shutter came down over his eyes. "Time to get going," he said and slid the sandal over my other heel with less finesse than I expected after the drawn out moments a few seconds earlier.

Immediately, the sandals became golden, high-heeled gorgeous things with glitter enough to make Cinderella jealous.

"Holy fuck," I said with an appreciative whistle, then I cringed at the sound of my own voice, so out of place, so crass when everything about my physical appearance in that moment was so sophisticated.

He chuckled softly. "Well said."

One last, lingering whisper of his calloused hands on my calves and he stood, letting my skirts fall back down. He looked me over lazily, the smolder in his gaze lingering in places that warmed my belly, and as he surveyed me, I felt like a chasm had closed between us, lined with the tiniest seam of gold.

"The shoes all have a glamor embedded in them. Being able to inject glamor into fibers is a unique natal magic passed down the way you might inherit blue eyes from your father or blonde hair from your mother." He grinned. "None of us has it, but I tell myself my mother might have had the power."

He extended his elbow and with a tight throat, I took it. I doubted the glamor was a passed down trait at all based on the secrecy hard-wired into the realm. More likely he'd used mention of his mother to hold onto the tenuous truce between us a little longer. A suspicion that proved itself when he patted the hand I curled around his biceps.

"Friends?" he asked, and I chewed my lip in thought. Could I blame him for trying any means to keep me docile?

"Impossible," I said. "But at least I don't want to kill you anymore."

"That's enough for me," he murmured, his voice carrying a tinge of regret or grieve.

With my throat feeling like I'd swallowed a lump of oatmeal too big and too sticky to go down, and my chest fluttering, I squared my shoulders. I needed to bring back the real Ava. The one who knew how to stomp out the flares of emotion. That Ava was the one who would survive here. That Ava needed to wake the hell up.

Only once I felt her click solidly into place like a canister of Bloodmist into an inhaler did I let Stone lead me across the room to the door.

The Fae standing in the hallway barely looked at me. His balding pate caught the light as he turned to avoid Stone's eye.

"Has Flint arrived yet?" Stone asked him.

Still no glance at us, as though he was afraid to meet Stone's eye. "He's in the dining hall."

My heart skipped as I realized Kit was alone, that the bastard sent to tail her was here in Fae and not in the shadows of her home, ready to plunge a knife into her stomach. If he was here, she was safe. And that was when it dawned on me that with Flint in Fae, every single monster who threatened her might be in my reach, leaving no one to retaliate against Kit if I took them out. Stone. Blade. Terran. Flint. All of them here.

The stumble that overtook me as I realized I'd be facing them both made Stone slip his arm around my waist.

"Are the heels too high for you?" he asked as he peered down at my feet. My toes curled to hide the flash of chipped polish.

My eyes pinned to the curve of my instep, not sure I could look at him and not show my thoughts. "I'm usually in combat boots or running shoes," I admitted. It was true enough. He might buy it.

"Just hold onto me," he said. "I won't let you fall."

As though I was a damsel of some sort. But I let it go. This subterfuge was difficult when I was more used to quick, tactical take outs. I was still caught in the fantasy of slicing through every single monstrous throat when his voice cut through and drew my gaze to his face.

"One last thing." He halted mid step and used the arm slung behind my waist to spin me around like a dancing partner, expertly, smoothly. An image of him kneeling between my legs flashed through my mind, and my breath caught unexpectedly, hatefully, causing my knees to tremble, just a little.

"I need to frisk you," he said. Matter of fact. No emotion in the words. "Make sure you aren't carrying."

As though there were any weapons available to conceal. I snorted, grateful to be relieved of the unwanted image of him between my thighs. "Unless I've suddenly gained the ability to hide a Bowie knife in my cooch, I'd say you all are safe from me."

He didn't so much as smile. No problem. I hadn't meant to be funny.

"Lift your arms please, Ava."

I gestured wildly at each wall. "The room doesn't have so much as a spoon in here," I protested. "What would I conceal?"

His expression didn't shift. He really was going to just stand there until I complied.

Lips pursed tightly, I raised my arms over my head, breathing loudly through my nose in irritation.

The whisper of his touch ran over my wrists first before sliding down to my shoulders. The straps of the gown slid down an inch, and he hooked one of them back up, lingering there for a full second while I watched his throat tense and let go.

"So?" I intoned. "What do you think? Are my guns dangerous?" I meant to be flippant, but I was mortified to hear how husky my voice came out.

He said nothing, making the moment even more electric as he stepped closer, leaving a whisper of breath between us. When his gaze caught and held mine, his hands whispered down my ribcage, lingering at the curve where my inhalations swelled my chest. My throat tightened as he dropped his gaze to my lips.

"My father will ask me if I checked you for weapons," he said, looking down at me between my arms.

I noted his voice was equally as husky as mine and my legs tensed together in traitorous reflex.

His fingers trembled against my skin. "I have to be able to answer without lying."

"Fuck," I said and the one word was full of everything I was feeling: the rage, the impotence, the sudden confusing blast of lust. It was so thick with emotion that I had to cover it up with a forced laugh. "I'm not some Mata Hari or Bodicca. Just tell him you saw me naked. It's true enough."

Holding my gaze, he said, "I'm not done." A bob of his throat as he swallowed, then his palms moved down along my hips and gathered the silk enough to slide his hand between my legs. A shiver of touch over my inner thighs and I hissed in a sharp inhale.

"Ah," I said in a long breath. "Now you've found my real weapon."

There was a moment when his fingers skimmed the flesh where my legs curved into the folds of intimate skin and I thought he might linger there. My breath caught. I thought I grew slick. And then his hands continued their journey down my legs and disappeared, leaving me straining toward him like some silly teenager.

"Clean," he said in a thick voice.

I tried, really tried, to come back with something sassy and smart, but all I could think was how badly I wanted him in that moment, and how hard it was going to be for me to kill him.

Chapter 10

I WAS HEADING INTO a room full of fae mafia with nothing to defend myself. My skin itched with threat even though the arm guiding me down the corridor to my doom rested against my waist so gently I might have been a piece of delicate China.

Daring to steal a glance sideways, I noticed Stone's mouth had pressed itself into a thin line. His jaw was white. Something had him on edge.

My senses went into high gear then, and I wished I'd taken the hit of Bloodmist while I'd had the chance. A hit would have levelled the playing field a bit more, sharpened my senses, sped up my reflexes. It could give me a boost of everything I needed to take on four very powerful fae, and my mind swirled with plans on how I could isolate each of them from each other. I ran through ways I might be able to fight two of them at a time, and which might make the least powerful pair. I even began to imagine ways I could bring down the whole entourage of them at once and stay alive lone enough to make sure no one survived.

But as I minced my way through the halls along side Stone, who was far too intimately close to me as we walked, I realized it might be more difficult than simply taking out a couple pairs of powerful fae. Guards of every shape and width lined every wall and lingered in clusters around the exits. A glance at Stone and his clenched jaw suggested he might fully aware of the threats around us, and perhaps my own silent machinations and how they might affect him.

And the place was massive. As we turned a corner to another hallway, I decided I'd been slipping in and out of consciousness when I'd been brought up from the dungeons. I should have remembered every twist and turn. The hunter in me would have memorized the layout if I could. But I didn't.

We came to a halt on a portico of sorts that over-looked a grand room. Lined by an oiled railing that drew our gaze down the sweeping staircase, I felt like a belle being delivered to a Southern cotillion. So sweeping was the space, that it opened up on the other end to an even greater chamber.

The manse was far bigger than I'd imagined.

That could create a problem if I wanted to kill and run. It would create a problem if I wanted to run at all.

"I don't remember this," I said.

"That's because you weren't brought to the third floor this way..." Stone cleared his throat and his eye dropped to the carpeted treads. "You were led up the servants' staircase."

That explained a lot. I nodded quietly and stored that information away as my eye drew a line directly to the stunning crystal chandelier that coated the entire expanse below us with a warm, ethereal glow. Sconces lit the stairs and lined the walls below.

That same purple light as I'd seen below in the dungeons spilled over every surface as it emanated from the sconces, but instead of lending a sort of unnatural pallor to the things it touched as it did in those stone chambers, it made everything here come alive, as though the light streamed from within them instead of merely catching the glow of the chandelier.

Several conversational seating areas dotted the space at the bottom of the staircase, with plush chairs and small tables scattered in intentionally intimate proximity to each other. The way they were arranged seemed meant to draw your gaze deeper into the gallery to the magnificent area beyond, like bread-crumbs from a child's nursery tale.

With a deft touch, Stone angled me toward that space, aiming me toward a large dining table with enough seating that I couldn't count the number of dishes and cutlery and crystal glasses filled with a sparkling drink that were set out upon it. Everything on the table winked in the purple light, and beyond it, a bank of large windows lined the farthest wall, offering a view of manicured gardens. Even at this distance, I could make out ages old cedars and red-woods lining a garden so lush, it would take dozens of gardeners to care for it.

Luxurious looking damask curtains the shade of blood were clawed back from the windows by tiebacks that appeared to be carved from bone into the shape of a hand.

"That's a pretty big dining room," I said, hoping the prompt would bring me far more information than what my eyes could take in alone.

I felt his shrug as he aimed me away from the stairs and toward the dining gallery. "This was once a fae lord's castle. Father won it in a bet centuries ago."

The way he said 'bet' indicated it had been nothing of the sort, but I kept my tongue as he continued.

"The dining gallery was once a ballroom. Father uses it now to impress those he thinks can further his interests."

My mouth twitched. Surely, I didn't warrant such treatment. There was nothing I could do to further his interests that he hadn't already forced on me. Whatever he had planned, it had to be more than just sending me out into the Fae world to hunt down and kill a king.

I clamped my mouth closed, doing my best to map it all out in my mind because if this staircase led to the dining room, and I'd been brought to the suite via a servant's staircase, then there were multiple exits.

Multiple exits meant multiple entrances, and I resolved to find each one of them.

I took note of the number of steps we'd descended. Thirty-four. And I noticed when we reached the bottom that a long corridor snaked off to the left that revealed the face of a massive fireplace and a broad, wooden table laden with fruit and braised meats. Roasted vegetables crackled in pottery platters and sent an aromatic steam trailing down the corridor toward me.

The kitchens, I realized, releasing fragrances so savory and sweet that a fully stuffed gourmand would salivate.

Exactly what did the cartel want from me that it would put out such a spread after nearly killing me in the dungeons? I was glad Stone wasn't holding my hand because both of them grew suddenly cold and damp.

By the time we made it past the first seating area, where several surly looking males sat drinking a blood red liquid, Stone's grip on me tightened, and I felt a tremor in his hand that surprised me enough to go rigid.

"Don't catch their eye," he said under his breath. "If one of them looks at you, look away."

The comment just made me want to look, but despite the burning desire to peer at the males, a desire created by the warning that I shouldn't, I kept my eyes downcast as we walked. When I did lift them, it was to let my gaze travel to the walls as Stone led me through the maze of chairs. The males sitting in them grew silent as we trekked through.

I felt eyes burning into my back as we weaved along, me thinking the whole time that it was nothing like the sensation of a man's eyes following the backside of a beautiful woman in a sexy gown. The feeling of those eyes on me felt distinctly feral. It prickled along my arms and made my fingers itch to hold a blade.

Not for the first time, I mourned the loss of my karam-bit and my decision not to take a hit of Bloodmist.

It wasn't just the men's eyes that I felt following me. Several large paintings dressed the walls that lead to the galley. One of the hunters I knew was a visual artist who had told me once that it was easy to get a painting's eyes to follow the viewer if you knew the right tricks. But the eyes on these really did move, following our progress in a way that lifted the hairs on the back of my neck.

Even the intricate moldings seemed to darken and lighten as we passed, not from our shadows, but from some sort of innate magic that made them look as if they were lighting the way like a landing zone. I imagined dropping breadcrumbs like Hansel and Gretel, even though it was a straight line and I couldn't possibly get lost along the way.

By the time we breached the threshold of the dining area proper, I was a wreck of nerves and tension, battling my instincts to turn and face the threats I felt all around me. I heard the men behind us in those chairs rise from their chairs and sofas, and their footfalls prowled toward me.

If I wasn't already on edge, the way the footsteps echoed through an otherwise creepily silent room made my spine feel like it was crawling up through my skin.

"What in the hell is going on?" I said through gritted teeth.

"They're what you mortals might call my father's capo-sidhe," he said and led me around the table toward the place setting at the head. "Whatever you do, keep your eyes on me, your plate, or my father. They won't take kindly to being scrutinized."

Or remembered, I thought as I nodded my acquiescence. When Stone halted behind a place setting without cutlery, I looked up at him, curious why he would guide me there when it was so obviously not a seat.

He offered me a tight smile. "You have to earn your utensils, I'm afraid," he said.

"Earn them?" I was about to follow the disbelieving comment with a stream of curses that in no uncertain terms would show what I thought of the ridiculous order when a seam in the wall the size and shape of a door lit with that same purple glow that emanated from between the sconces.

My fingers gripped the back of the chair tighter as it yawned open and Terran stepped through.

Another escape, I thought, eying the way the door closed and sealed shut behind him. The light pulsed once and was gone. If I looked hard enough, I could just make out the outline of the door, so it wasn't a portal of any sort. Just good, old-fashioned carpentry magic.

I was aware of the males who had been in the chairs strolling forward to surround the table, taking their places behind chairs, waiting to be given permission to sit. Capo-Sidhe. I guessed the term meant under-bosses like in the human mafia.

I wondered about the hierarchy. Someone here was undoubtedly the advisor. I already knew Blade was the enforcer. Terran was the big boss. I needed to get a bead on how big the court was, and why they wanted to kill their king when they obviously already possessed power and wealth.

My hands gripped the chair back so tightly my knuckles went white. The wood beneath felt like it was fraying splinters into my palms. With one nod from Terran, the capo-sidhe pulled out their chairs.

Stone nudged me as he pulled out his beside me. Looking around, I noted a dozen place settings, including mine, Stone's, and Terran's. So in all nine additional bosses. Terran, the head honcho sat at the head of the table. Stone to his right, with me beside Stone. The man sitting beside me smelled of juniper and pine.

"The soup will come first," Stone said beneath his breath, and I found myself wondering how in the hell I was going to eat soup without a spoon.

I was the only woman in the room, and I felt the eyes of the others on me like ants crawling through honey. I desperately wanted to eyeball each of them, but I did as Stone warned and kept my eye on the silver charger in front of me, the crystal glasses filled with water, and some sort of greenish liquid that fizzled like soda.

I felt naked in the dress with those gazes running over me in such an electric fashion my hairs lifted from my skin. By the time several servants scuttled in from the kitchens with several tureens and plates of herbed bread, I was at my breaking point.

Terran pulled a napkin from the table and draped it over his lap. Just like a gentleman. A gentleman who not three days earlier had ordered the horrific death of a human just because I'd attempted to warn the king.

That truth in mind, I almost snorted at the way he smoothed his napkin with such genteel pickiness over his lap. But then, someone on my left nudged a green drink toward me, and I understood I was supposed to drink.

I reached for the stem, feeling very much like a landed fish, and was about to pull it toward me when I noticed that no one was doing the same. All eyes had traveled to a raggedy-looking child who had materialized from thin air beside Terran. Even Stone sat silent and immobile with his hands on his lap.

I peered sideways, trying to catch sight of the rest of the crowd without appearing like I was looking. Juniper guy fiddled with a long wooden pipe beneath the table, placing his fingers purposefully over small holes dug out of the wood.

The child, a boy with hair on his knuckles and bare feet and wearing a white tunic, dipped a wooden spoon into the bowl that sat in front of Terran and lifted it, dripping with broth, to his mouth.

His eyes were wary and frightened, and my heart clenched at the sight. I'd seen looks like that before in children terrorized by bogymen. My heart did that little squeezing thing it did when I didn't want to think about something. My hands flew to my lap, where they clenched and unclenched into balls of knotted fingers.

With eyes on the spoon, the boy slurped noisily. Then he took a hunk of bread and dipped it into the broth and chewed silently. He inhaled slowly, his eyes rolling back as though his palate was combing through the fragrances and nuances of the soup.

"Anise seed and fennel," he said. "No sulfur. No salt peter. No arsenic. No poison of any kind mortal or magical."

He stepped back and put his hands behind him like a soldier at ease. Only then, did Terran lift his spoon, and in almost perfect unison, the others did the same. The sound of the cutlery scraping along the table grated the back of my teeth. The breaking of the bread and tasting of the soup seemed to crack through a spell of silence then, and Terran began talking to the assembly of mundane things. Answers came swiftly. Succinct. Like a general or a king being briefed.

All the while, I sat there waiting for someone to bring me a spoon. My stomach growled loudly enough that, at one point, Terran glared at me.

"You may eat," he said.

A retort sprang to my tongue along the lines of lapping the broth with my tongue like a cat, but the fae sitting across from me spoke before I could.

"Perhaps her belly is too full of treachery and she has no appetite for soup, Don Sidhe," came the comment and it was said with such loathing that before I realized what I was doing, I snapped my gaze to the face across the table and glared back into the eyes that peered back at me. Flint.

I must have gone totally rigid because Stone grabbed my thigh beneath the table and squeezed in warning.

But his hands, warm and strong though they were, could not keep my tongue from dripping the acid absent in the soup. I faced Flint with a curl riding my lip, the hatred spilling over. "A belly full of treachery is better than one filled with iron and steel," I said. "Because I do have an appetite for making that happen."

Silence dropped over the room like a shroud.

"Are you threatening me, mortal?" Flint asked with so much heat in his voice he could have boiled the soup.

"What I'm doing," I said. "Is wondering how in the hell I'm supposed to eat without cutlery. Am I to drop my face into the bowl and lap it out?"

He shrugged. "A bitch does what it must to survive."

My jaw ticked sideways as the entire table went even more silent than before. I couldn't even hear Juniper Fae fiddling with his pipe. I picked up my bowl with both hands.

"While you might know a dog's nature intimately," I said. "In the mortal realm, we don't fuck the pooches."

His face went white, and every inch of his body tensed. There was no way he was going to let that insult slide and I knew it.

Once, on the playground when I was ten, a bully had pulled a girl's hair for no other reason but to see what I'd do. The larger girl had picked on me mercilessly for days until I'd beaten her back with my water bottle. She'd limped off, seeming to give up, only to select another victim who was smaller than me.

This had that vibe. A challenge. A moment where one tests the mettle of another.

All my ire balled up in my stomach, the rage at what had happened to Jasmine, the fury that I was here involuntarily, the thought that they believed they could steamroll me without so much as a peep of protest.

I heaved the steaming contents of the bowl across the table.

CHAPTER 11

I KNEW THE INSTANT the soup splashed over Flint's suit and sprayed sideways onto Terran that I was as good as dead. All the chairs around the table scraped back as the guests pushed to their feet. The sound of blacksteel whisking out of sheaths everywhere sliced through the air.

Every inch of my skin came alive with awareness, and yet everything slowed down to a painful crawl.

Stone's hand left my leg, and my skin felt cold and clammy where the palm had once rested. The sizzling sort of pop as the child disappeared from view was the last sound I heard before that of a crystal shattering against wood.

I looked down to realize I'd grabbed the nearest glass, the one someone had nudged toward me, and had smashed it against the edge of the table. Shards had flown everywhere. A spot of warmth wet my cheek. Blood, I knew, without even lifting my free hand to check with probing fingers. A shard had flown back and caught me just in front of my ear.

Terran nodded and the room erupted into chaos. The distinct scent of woods and juniper intensified along with the electric feel of static, and I knew magic of some sort was being gathered somewhere close.

With a deft dodge sideways, I avoided Stone's grapple for my arm as I swung the shattered glass, jagged edges facing out, toward him. He was the boss's son. I could use him as leverage for my own safety if I had to. If I couldn't, I'd slit his throat. One down, so to speak.

I aimed the glass, shattered end forward. The shards would have caught Stone in the throat if he hadn't dodged in time. No matter. I didn't want him. I wanted Flint. I moved on him, laughing out loud.

They were all here, I kept thinking. No one was lurking over Kit, threatening her life. If I died right in the room, there would be no need to hold her existence as hostage. The thought gave me more courage than a hit of Bloodmist. I couldn't believe I hadn't realized the truth of that before. Without me in the picture, Kit was safe.

Without me. I almost laughed at the simplicity of it.

"You think I'm a bitch?" I asked Flint with deadly calm in my voice. "Then let's see what you do with a rabid one."

I knew he was a fighter. I'd seen the way he'd prowled toward me the night I'd taken on the witch. I'd known he was fae, too. But what I hadn't known because he'd done no more than talk and threaten me on that night, instead electing to dispatch the hellhound, was what his magics were.

The man whose lips curled back now was still a male, but with panther-like qualities. I inched backward, the broken glass in hand, holding it out like a knife. Perhaps, like Blade, he could shape shift. Maybe Terran could as well, and if Terran could, then most likely Stone too.

But what would their animals be? Something powerful, for certain, but without knowing exactly what I dealt with, I was at a disadvantage.

Perhaps I needed to encourage a species reveal.

"What are you waiting for?" I demanded, letting my gaze flick toward the table. The dare, the challenge was a technique I'd learned foes of some ego couldn't resist, and I needed…really needed to distract him long enough to find more than a broken glass as a weapon.

What the others were waiting for, I had no idea. I was acutely aware of them lurking around me. I knew the moment I swung for Flint, the rest of them would lunge. I had to be smart about the attack.

But in the moment, no matter how hard I tried to reason, I saw Flint in my mind's eye lurking beside Kit. I saw him talking ever so cheerily to her the whole while waiting on his father's signal to do her harm.

The corner of my eye touched on the winking of a carving knife just to the side of my vision. The blade was black and shining and if I dodged left and low, I might grab it in just enough time to stab forward as Flint launched across the table.

Because he was coming. I saw it in his eyes.

I coughed out a challenge. "I'm waiting, you bastard."

His long incisor teeth caught on his lips as he smiled. I watched the muscles bunch in his shoulders, an indication that he was about to move.

I braced myself, mindfully measuring the distance to that knife and imagining my fingers curling around the handle. The leap I needed to make played out a dozen times in the microseconds that hiccupped between us.

As Flint launched himself across the table, I could feel the power emanating from him. Dishes and glasses and cutlery smashed in his wake. The others backed away. I could hear their movements even if I didn't dare avert my gaze from the Fae coming at me. I followed suit, taking several steps backward.

All my attention was on Flint, who had somehow cleared the table and was stalking toward me. His eyes glinted with a dangerous light, and then, in a flash, his hand shot out, furred and clawed. Only my reflexes saved me from getting swiped by his claws.

I stumbled back, but he charged at me, incisors elongated and bared. I dodged to the side once more, lurching for the blade. The dress tore at the hem as I leaped, zippering into a long slit that gave my legs much freer rein.

My palm slapped down on the table right about the time he swiped at me again. I rolled, using the touch down as leverage to thrust myself toward the knife. My fingers scrabbled for its handle. I felt the brush of it against the pads of my index and thumb.

I couldn't hold on to the glass and reach for the blade and keep my footing all at the same time.

An instant of consideration flew to my muscles with barely a whisper through my brain. Dropping the glass with a crash to the floor gave me what I needed to heave myself for the knife. In my mind, I knew the exact way

I should toss myself toward it and my body followed the order.

I hit the edge of the table with such force, the wind knocked free of my lungs.

There was no time to relish the feel of the leather handle in my grip. I spun over, not truly knowing if the blade would come with me or not. Just trusting it would.

I'd already decided if I didn't come away with it in my grip, I'd rake out with my nails.

Flint was already there, his jowls elongated, his mouth gaping and paws groping.

I punched out. Right. Left. I felt like I connected with something hard. Something fleshy.

When I hauled back my left hand, it came away with a splash of blood. The knife dripped beads of it into my eyes.

I didn't wait to see how badly I'd hurt him. Waiting, checking, watching, that was for rookies. Never hesitate.

Instead, I hoisted my knees upward, bringing the soles of my feet to bear with the thought that I could create enough thrust with the movement to aid in the swing of my head. Forward. Hard. Never holding back a fraction of the force gained from the legs.

My head plowed into his with enough power to buckle my legs and send stars shooting behind my eyelids.

I might have dropped the knife.

Blind, I tried to regain my footing, but everything was a black canvas of twinkling stars. My feet rolled sideways as I fought the buckling of my knees.

Flint was on me in an instant. His teeth grazed my shoulder as he brought his head down. One second more, and they'd be burying themselves into an artery. I should just let it happen. I should just let go and leave Kit to her life as I died.

But a decade of fighting ingrained the instinct to punch back until I couldn't punch anymore.

Left with my back pinned against the edge of the table, I had nothing to spare. I just knew I wasn't going down. Not this soon. I had an entire room to take out, and I'd not made it through even one of the bastards.

With a roar, I swung my head toward his. As my mouth closed, it clamped down on his shoulder. I ground my teeth, giving my all to meeting them through the tough flesh of muscle. My fingers clawed into his ribs, scratching as though I too had claws.

He pulled back, howling, obviously not expecting my reaction. Over his shoulder, I caught a glimpse of Terran standing in the corner of the room. He was watching the fight with an amused expression, clearly enjoying the spectacle.

It made me sick to my stomach. I knew that if I could just get to him, I could end this once and for all. This time when I brought up my knees, they collided with Flint's belly, and I shoved hard as I flexed them straight.

He stumbled. Not a lot. Just enough to give me room to slide down the table to my haunches. The dress split even more as I rolled onto my hands and knees and crawled beneath the table.

I came up on the other side, my chest heaving, eyes straining as they scoured for another knife, glass, plate, anything I could use to tear through whatever came at me.

I wasn't human in that instant. A flash of primal rage told me I was all lizard brain and adrenaline.

Something caught my attention. Something audible and not visual. My name. I thought I heard my name.

But then the juniper man stepped in front of me, his own magic radiating off of him like a thick fog. I could sense his power. I heard a rustling sound behind me. I turned to see him with his pipe between his teeth, the notes dancing on the air. With one hand raised to the ceiling, spinning in its own dance, power coiled about him in an aura of faint green light.

In an instant, vines and branches snaked out from the walls and floor. I saw them slither toward me as he merely stood, watching me, the unearthly sounds of his flute trilling to the cells within the greenery.

Whatever his intention, whatever his powers as a Fae, he'd not stepped forth until this moment. None of them had. They'd let me rage and rampage, with the distance of a video gamer, watching, learning, studying.

For a moment, I hesitated, weighing my options, and that one second of pause gave the magic what it needed to surge toward me once again. I knew the awful truth then.

I'd not chosen my moment to attack. I'd done so impetuously and without planning. I'd barged in when I should have jimmied in with the stealth of picking a lock. I bit down on a sob, because I'd not just lost, I'd lost any chance I had of taking them by surprise.

With a heavy heart, I lowered my fists. The vines and foliage immediately shrank back.

For a moment, I thought it was over. But then I caught a glimpse of Terran standing in that corner, his greedy eyes taking it all in with a cold detachment. The lizard brain nudged the rational, human brain back into action.

I took a step toward him. My chest was still heaving with effort and adrenaline, but I was far from done. I was a dervish without plan or thought of penalty. I wanted him dead. I wanted them all dead.

Whatever Terran saw in my face narrowed his gaze into hard slits.

"Enough," he said, his voice echoing through the room. "Sit down."

At the words, everyone in the room scraped toward their seats. I stood there unmoving as they assembled, Flint included, around the wrecked buffet. Soup had sloshed everywhere. Glass, pottery, and bread scattered the floor.

"Sit," he said again and this time the tone of his voice froze my legs in their advance.

"I want a damn spoon," I countered with a growl.

His eyebrows scaled his forehead, but without another word, he jerked his wrist. There was a flurry of movement and some pallid looking young woman scurried into the room, carrying a fistful of cutlery. She handed a spoon to me without a word.

I took it from her, curling my fingers around the handle like a cave woman. I inhaled slowly, aware that the dress had torn and was all but hanging off me. I didn't care.

"Thank you," I said and quietly picked up my chair from where it had fallen, keenly aware that Stone was already sitting in his place and was leaving me to arrange my chair. Not that I was a diva who expected such courtesy, and I'd probably have refused it, but I noted it all the same.

Terran waited until I pulled my chair up close to the table, a polite host awaiting his honored guest's decision to tuck into a lovely meal. With the adrenaline still shredding holes in my breath, I propped my elbows on the table and steepled my fingers as I eyed him. Calm. As though I hadn't just torn up the dining room and threatened to stab one of his men. It took all the last vestiges of my will to do so, but I managed it.

Once it looked like I was settled, he turned to his men in turn.

"The game has changed," he said. "It's no longer enough to hire an outside assassin and have her take out the king before the new century." He leveled each Fae around the table with a brooding look, ignoring the surrounding chaos. "My Consul advises me that the king has shifted the balance, changed the chips."

Stone cleared his throat and adjusted his cuffs. "We've discovered he has spelled the grand ball room as well as the throne room."

I fixed my gaze on his face. He was Terran's consul? So higher than mere son and loyal soldier. He was the boss's Second. My throat tightened like a rope had been pulled around it. It was a struggle to keep my focus on the information drifting around the table so freely.

"And this spell," Flint began. "What is it meant to do, exactly?"

Terran tapped his spoon on the table. "It's meant to protect him," he said. "In effect, any instrument lifted against him with the intent to do harm will turn on the holder."

"Fuck," I said, because while I didn't know much about magic, I knew that the force I'd use, the speed I'd put behind any sweep of my karambit to take out the king, would end with me dead in seconds.

The burly Fae, the one who smelled of juniper and pine, laid his hand on the table between his plate and mine. "You're saying that for the duration of the Endowments, no one will be able to attack him without bringing to bear all that violence back against themselves?"

Terran lifted his spoon and balanced it on one finger. "Not exactly."

I pinched the bridge of my nose. I kept trying to see the positive in it all, that I'd be relieved of the impossible and Kit could be safe and no one would even know the Shadow Court tried to take out their own king. But I remembered the violence in the cellar and I knew it wouldn't be so simple as that. They'd come to far to halt the operation now.

"Then what, exactly?" I asked.

Terran swung that calculated gaze to mine. "My consul thinks if we can convince the king to somehow commit the violence himself, then the wards shouldn't fire."

"And if they do, the end result will achieve what you wanted in the first place," I guessed.

Terran smiled. "I didn't get to this position believing in chance and magic."

Strange thing for a fae male to say, but I narrowed my eyes, trying to sort through exactly where I might fit now.

"You don't think it's possible," I said.

He ran his tongue over the inside of his mouth, skimming his teeth thoughtfully. "I know I don't take chances when I can't guarantee results," he said. "I still think the best attack is a frontal one, but because I trust my son and value his advice, we will try it his way first."

I echoed that last word with a note of suspicion. "First."

He nodded. "I have a backup plan for when his fails."

"You say that like you expect it will," Stone said, and Terran nodded.

"It has to fail because our monarch is already in-credibly nervous and on edge. He knows he's not safe until he has received the magical blessing of the demi and low Fae and the new century has begun. He has a long week of anxious appearances, contests, and galas to attend, and he and his guards will be on the alert."

"Then why wait at all?" I asked. "Why do it during the festival? Do it now. Do it after. Just do it." I didn't want to wait. If I was to be used as a weapon, best get it over with while there was still a snowball's chance in hell of it working.

Terran gave me a long look that suggested he was working out whether I should be involved in the details, and I held his gaze because I was damn sure I needed to be involved. Just in case he didn't get that, I said, "If you want me to succeed, you can't withhold information that can help me."

His sigh was one of resignation. He eyed the males around the table and only seemed to consider giving me information when they remained silent.

"In the Iron Court, the King's powers wane over the century. Once a century, the low fae and the demi-fae can transfer the magics they cannot access to the king for use as he will. For that century, he is the most powerful in our court. But at the tail end of that century, he is at his weakest."

I didn't want to think about the sort of power a fae might possess if others were willing to give him more.

"And what do they get out of it, these demi and low fae?" I dared ask.

His mouth worked as he considered the question.

"I need to know," I said. "If I'm going up against a king who can take the magic of other fae, I have to know why they would do such a thing."

Stone's hand touched mine on the table. "They get a chance to wield their magic for an entire year. One hundred of them."

I leaned back in the chair, watching Terran's face, not Stone's. It was the truth, I realized. I remembered Jasmine and that gilded token.

"If that's true," I started, my palm laying flat against the table top, "then that number is frighteningly coincidental."

Stone pulled a glass of green liquid toward him. "The tokens," he said. "There are a hundred of them. Whoever bears a gilded token may ask a magic boon of the king, and he cannot refuse to grant them any of the magics he possesses that are granted to him, or that he is gifted. For one year, a fae with a gilded token may wield magic."

I skimmed the table with my gaze, letting it trail to where Terran sat with his arms folded. "I'm guessing those tokens don't grant boons to high Fae." Otherwise, I was sure Terran and his gang would find a way to usurp the power.

His silence was answer enough. But it also told me more. It explained the small window of opportunity when a mortal assassin such as myself could take out a king, and in case the window closed unexpectedly, they did not want to risk a Fae life. I suspected there was more to it that he wasn't telling me, but that small tidbit was enough to reveal one important thing.

"You expect the assassin to fail," I said.

Terran sighed heavily as he toyed with the spoon next to his broken plate. "I think based on your performance here, you may have been able to complete the assassination with enough luck and circumstance. But with the magical wards set to counteract such violence, it's best if we create an additional opportunity."

Creating opportunities. He sounded like Gideon. I noticed Stone squirmed in his chair at the comment, and I eyed him from beneath lowered lashes as I cast a sidelong glance his way.

"It sounds like you have no use for an assassin," I said, deciding that maybe this wouldn't have to end so badly after all, and looking for a way out. I sent a meaningful look in Flint's direction. "This opportunity you plan to create makes me useless."

Terran pointed the spoon handle at me. "You've proved to be anything but," he said, waving the spoon around to indicate the mess. "A bit of a nuisance in some ways, but fierce enough. I just don't like to leave things to happenstance. We need a failsafe."

A failsafe. Meaning a rip cord in case I didn't make it. Something that would fire even if my life was forfeit. Fine. I didn't care if I lived through it but I did care about one thing.

"And if I fail," I said, tapping the end of the spoon on the table. "Then what happens to my sister?"

He drew a long breath. "You won't fail, because you are both Plan A and Plan B. We just need to make sure you're well-trained to execute them both."

"I've been training since I was eighteen," I said. "I can handle any opponent with my foot in a cast. Just get me alone with him."

"A single opponent, perhaps, as I've seen you do here. But the reality is he is Fae. A powerful Fae, even if he will be vulnerable for a short time. Stone has devised a wonderful Plan B and it uses the king's own weakness to our advantage, as well as allows us to attempt plan A." He beamed at Stone, who pressed his lips together, a sure sign he wasn't pleased his father mentioned it was his idea.

I glared at Stone as Terran went on, my chest burning hotter with each word.

"The king has an unhealthy appetite for human women," he said. "They pose no threat to him. Insipid, royalty-loving fools that they are, and he ruts with them because he is a coward who dares not open himself to a fae woman with power of her own. He keeps a harem of women, and one by one, he goes through them like you mortals do a bag of chips."

Everything in me rankled at the insinuation that all mortal women were insipid fools, but I held my temper in check. "And that should matter to me because?"

"Because you will be a gift for that harem."

CHAPTER 12

I WANTED TO CURL up in a corner. I'd started the day thinking I would be a killer only to end it discovering I would be a prostitute. Nice. Whatever hunger I felt when I entered the dining space was gone.

With a gritty feeling in the back of my throat, I laid a trembling hand on the table, fingers pressing down until the knuckles turned white. The spoon had left my hand at some point and clattered to the floor. Stone's gaze was pinned to it.

Terran's words left me gawking at him. I would have laughed in his face if he didn't look so damned serious.

"Boy do you have the wrong chick if you think I'm some sort of Pussy Galore." I inched backwards, my hand feeling for the back of my chair as I swung my gaze toward Terran. "I'm a killer," I said. It was a terrible, sickening echo of the words I'd said to Stone when he'd suggested a hunter like me could become an assassin.

"I take out nasty creatures. I do not seduce them."

Terran's sigh came out hard and irritated. "The Iron King has a weakness for mortal women," he said. "You are a mortal woman." His eye drew a line from my throat to my breasts. "Unless, of course, you have fooled my son and are male, in which case, the king won't care." His grin was diabolical.

My hand clutched at my chest as I flung my way off the chair. "Come see," I said in a hard voice. "I invite you to test how feminine I am."

When Stone stood with me and touched the back of my arm, I whirled on him, and struck his chin with the heel of my hand, snapping his head back.

So. Rage then. I could work with that. My lips were curled back from my teeth as I glared at him.

"Bastard," I said. "I'm no one's bitch."

Terran must have thought I was going to strike again because he nodded to Juniper man who wrangled my arms behind my back.

I blamed it on the blinding fury that I hadn't seen him come up behind me. He pulled my arms taut enough that I let go a grunt of pain. My breasts strained against the remnants of fabric, and Stone peeled off his jacket and draped it over my chest, tucking the sleeves behind my head. Like I was indecent.

"Fuck you," I said and like a gator, I thrashed in the fae's arms until the jacket slipped away and puddled at my feet.

I glared at Stone. "I might as well look like a whore if I'm to be one," I ground out.

Juniper Fae leaned backward just enough to put leverage into my arms and make me sag from pain. Defeated, I sighed. "Alright," I said. "Alright. I won't struggle."

All while Stone stood there with his hands crammed into his pockets and balled into fists. All while Terran watched with a narrowed gaze. While Flint leaned back on the back legs of the chair, his face a mask of unmoving expression. Bastards. Every one of them.

Once more, my resolve to kill them all rose like sour bile in the back of my throat. It must have shown on my face, because Terran sent a hard glare in the Juniper Fae's direction.

"We are not done here," he said, and waved his hand at Juniper Fae. "Eldric is overzealous. He wants to climb the ladder and is too quick to act, thinking I need his aid."

Eldric released me and stepped aside to sit in his chair. He angled it away from Terran, and like Flint, he leaned back and watched me. They all did. My jaw hurt so much, I was sure everyone could hear me grinding my teeth.

I pulled in a long, bracing breath. "I'm not going to fuck the king," I said, and noticed at the words, Stone flinched as he stood next to me. I dragged my gaze to his face. "That's what you expect of me, right? To fuck him to death?" A harsh bark of laughter escaped me. "Boy, have you got the wrong chick."

Stone held out his hand over the seat of my chair. "It's not what you think, Ava," he said. "Please. I wouldn't do that to you."

Terran snorted and Stone's jaw whitened. He gathered his composure before anyone but me could see the twitch of his mouth.

With a long sigh, I sat primly on the edge of my chair. My gaze raked the table, from the shards of glass to the heavy plates and bowls that I wished I'd broken instead, and I laid my wrists against the edge of the table. The fabric of the table cloth was slick and soft in places, a stark contrast to the stickiness of the green champagne that pooled over the white linen.

"If it's not what I think," I started, "then what, exactly is it?" I swiveled my gaze to Terran, whose eyes lit up with a dark humor. "What exactly do you expect of a seductress if not to roll around in satin bedsheets?"

"For a hunter who didn't want to be an assassin, I would think this would be much more preferable."

"Forgive me if I'm not leaping for joy."

This time it was Flint who snorted and my lip curled back before I could stop it. He picked up a fork and tapped the table with the butt-end as he watched me.

"She's right about not being the right woman," he said, running his eye over my face and down my chest. I felt naked at his glance but I held myself rigid. "Ferranus prefers a more docile female. Not to mention she isn't nearly pretty enough."

From beside me, Stone flew across the table, and even though he was a large man, the surface was too broad for him to reach Flint, and both knew it. It all happened so fast, I was left gawking as Stone stabbed the table with his carving knife while Flint just sat there, confident that he was out of range.

Seeing Flint's bored expression, Stone's face went white with rage. "I hear she looks a lot like her sister," Stone said, planting his hands on the table and shoving aside dishes and cutlery noisily. "And you seem to think she's pretty enough."

It was subtle, but something crossed Flint's face. His gaze dropped to Stone's fingers splayed on the table cloth. But I didn't miss it, and neither did Stone. When Flint rose from his chair, and leaned over the table, close to Stone's face, his mouth working as though he was trying to find something to say to deflect from the obvious nervous tick that had taken over his forehead.

"I admit the human sister is on my mind a lot," he said. "I spend most mortal realm nights imagining what she'll sound like when I flay the skin from her face."

The clump that formed in my throat at those words, the incredible effort it took to swallow it down long enough to speak again, those things put razors in my chest. Enough that I knew that no matter how many fantasies I might entertain about killing this man, Kit would be the one to suffer.

When Flint gave me a loaded stare, I grabbed for Stone's sleeve. My ego wasn't worth fighting over. Not right now. I pulled him backward to his seat.

"I'm not here as a beauty queen," I told him. "I could care less if he thinks I'm hot or not."

Flint's gaze raked over me. "You should care. Your sister's life depends on the king finding you irresistible."

I was aware that the others around the table seemed to be waiting for something. Stone hadn't moved. He still glared at Flint and for his part, Flint had plucked the knife from the table and was inspecting the edge as he watched me.

My jaw ticked sideways as I squinted at him, but before I could say anything, Terran stood, gathering the attention of everyone at the table.

"We have much to get done. My guests have all come a long way to discuss the unexpected issues presented to us these last couple of days." He smoothed his palm along the table, giving Flint time to take his seat. Only after everyone had folded their hands neatly on the table, amid the rubble of food and dishes, did he speak again, this time, addressing Eldric.

"Before we can even consider if this human is worthy enough of Ferranus's interest to train her as a courtesan, we must first discover what wards are on the castle. Exactly where they have been placed, and if they can be removed."

Eldric leaned out around me to look at Terran, who was busy adjusting his cuffs again. "My woman in the kitchens says he paid a Fae sorceress from another realm to cast the protection spell. It's bonded with her blood and only upon her death will it be removed."

Terran sighed and pushed his bowl aside. "We have no witches who can counter the spell?"

Eldric shook his head. "Witches are very canny. They hate each other, but they stick together. Who knows if this sorceress can. I just know she won't."

Stone spread his palm over the tablecloth in one of the few places clear of mess. "Do we have time to find this sorceress? Convince her to counter the spell? Surely, the right coercion can encourage a sorceress for hire to do what we need."

He sounded so much like a *Godfather* character that I had to take a breath.

Eldric shook his head. "My men cannot find the witch. She has gone into hiding somewhere in the human realm."

"Maybe she's dead," I said, thinking of Lilah.

Terran slid his eyes to me. I had the feeling he wasn't pleased at my interruption, but I just stared back at him, holding his eye. "What makes you say this?"

I shrugged. "If she's in the human realm doing nasty things, a hunter might easily have neutralized her already. It's what we do." Without acting smug, I slung my arm over the back of the chair.

He huffed as though my comment meant nothing. "A Fae witch would not so easily be snuffed out by a mere mortal. They are cunning and more magically inclined than our mortal kind."

That there were Fae witches at all surprised me, but I kept quiet.

He pointed his fork at Eldric. "Keep your men on it. If we can find her, it would be easier to have our assassin finish her job directly than to pin our hopes on a seduction she is incapable of carrying out." He eyed me as he said this and his gaze traveled to my nipples.

I had to resist the urge to pull the bolts of fabric over my cleavage. Instead, I steeled my spine as I said, "Is the king a breast man?"

With a flinch, he dragged his gaze to my face and smiled. Cunning. Nasty. He'd ogled my chest on purpose. "Unless we find the sorceress, you'll discover what sort of man he is soon enough," he intoned.

At that, he clapped his hands and several servants swarmed the room and began to clear the table. The boy who had popped into view earlier and tested the soup appeared again. This time, he wore a brown tunic and held a silver tray with a thick, wet towel. Terran plucked it from the tray and began washing his hands with it.

While the rest of the guests waited, and I steamed, he ran the cloth over his neck and face and passed it back to the boy. Only when the table had been completely cleared and his setting was replaced did he speak again.

"Ferranus's peculiar penchant for mortal women can work in our favor," he said, looking at me. "He has suffered that particular affliction for centuries. He'll think nothing of a woman presented as a gift. I expect several other High Fae to be doing the same. So you must stand out. We must test your skills."

"I thought you already did that," I said, and the moment the words exited my mouth, I realized with horror what he meant.

"Sweet Jesus. You can't mean what I think." I gripped the edge of my chair, willing myself not to jump up again, not to do something foolish.

"What else would I mean?" he asked. "We have a lot at stake here. You have a lot at stake."

"If anyone of your disgusting men touches me, they will be shitting their balls out the next morning."

"That's just it," he said. "It's not just any male who will touch you, Ms. Ashe. We have too much at stake to just trial you with any fae."

Sour bile rose to sting the back of my throat. "I'll kill anyone you send to me."

His eyebrows arched. "I'm quite sure you'll try," he said. "Which is why I had to select the right partner for the tests."

I'd given up my virginity at eighteen to Gideon. He was easily ten years older than me and with his sexy day old stubble that never seemed to fully get removed, he'd had more than his share of women. Kit hated him the moment I brought him home, and as she'd screamed at me later, giving me the worst ultimatum a guardian can give a loved one, I left without looking back.

I moved in with Gideon and stayed there for three years, training, hunting, loving.

So, I was no shrinking violet. But the thought of being assessed for my skills in seduction drained the last of the blood from my face. My cheeks felt cold and clammy.

"I beg your pardon," I said, hating the timid sound that underpinned my voice. "Did you say you have someone in mind to teach me how to seduce a man?" I panned my gaze toward Stone, firing off knives from my eyes. He had the intelligence to look at his hands instead of me.

Terran leaned forward, placing his forearms on the table. His eyes glinted with a malicious pleasure. "That is indeed what I'm saying."

I pushed to my feet, my stomach tightening into knots. "You've got to be kidding."

Terran stood as well as he faced me. Maybe he didn't like the feeling of me looking down at him.

"Do I look like I kid, Ms. Ashe?"

I whirled on Stone, and my throat was so tight I could barely get the words out.

"You suggested this?" I growled. "This was your idea? Don't tell me you think you're the one who believes he can teach me a few tricks."

I snorted, thinking of how Blade had characterized the Fae Consul's skills.

Stone looked miserable. "I volunteered, yes," he said. "But it was not my idea."

Terran cleared his throat, his palm skimming the table in the same motion. "My son is a good adviser, but he knows nothing of true cunning. Not to the level we need here."

I sucked the back of my teeth. "Are you serious right now? You think he can teach me a thing or two in bed?" I barked out a laugh and sliced my hand through the air. "Forget it. I don't need instruction."

"Fae males like things that perhaps you mortal women don't understand," Terran said, picking up the steak knife that interfered with his hand's progress across the table. "It would be useful for you to receive the schooling."

"I don't care if he eats tuna with peanut butter while he rams his dick into some poor hapless wretch. I am not going to agree to be tutored this way." I sliced the air with my hand. "I agreed to kill him. Not fuck him."

"You won't have to…" Terran cleared his throat with a look at me that suggested he hadn't expected me to be so crass. I noticed the other males busying themselves with their cutlery. "You won't have to go that far. I'd expect if you get that close, you can finish him off." He cocked his head at me, a glint in his eye that indicated he'd not expected the Freudian slip but found humor in it.

He flipped the knife over, tapping the point on the table. "Even so, you need to know a few things about the king's proclivities that will enhance your chances of getting close to him. And use that to your advantage."

My shoulders sagged as I gave him a sharp, narrowed look. "I don't need to know more than his weaknesses," I said.

He shrugged. "I'm telling you his weakness. If you can't take him out at the gala, you'll need to be placed in his harem so you have a reason to be in the castle. And then it's up to you to use that placement to get close enough to him to complete your task. I don't mind later than the gala," he went on. "But you'll only have a few days after that to get to him before it's too late."

The tension in the room at his last words ratcheted up significantly. So. Now I knew my time line for finishing the real job. Sounded like I had a couple of weeks.

In the end, I supposed it didn't matter. I was just biding my time until I could find a way to kill them anyway. If I had to agree to eating a live goldfish while I stood on my head, then so be it.

"Fine, then," I said and sent Stone a resigned glance. I could do worse, I supposed, than trying out my feminine wiles on a gorgeous, darkly dangerous man with a body like his. "Stone can come back with me to my room. We'll get this lesson over with. Then we can move on to getting me those weapons I might need to finish the job."

"I said I needed someone I trust," Terran said. "And while I trust my Consul implicitly, I need to know you can impress the unimpressionable. Someone who isn't already interested in your feminine wiles and likely to give in without much urging."

He sent me a withering look that indicated exactly what he thought of those wiles before continuing.

"Stone is already too invested in your welfare to be of use in this case." He sent Stone a scathing look that had him pressing his lips together. I noticed Stone dropped his gaze to his hands.

My stomach dropped at the possibilities. "If not Stone, then who?" I asked through gritted teeth. I hoped it wasn't going to be Flint. Please don't let it be Flint.

Terran leaned back arrogantly. "My dark enforcer. My Blade."

CHAPTER 13

THE BASTARD EXPECTED ME to bed down with a monster. Even if it was just a test, even if it was just an insinuation, I was not going to do that.

"No," I said, and discovered I was backing away from the table. "I won't."

"You will," Terran said. "He's the only one I know I can trust to keep this quiet, and it will be a challenge to ingratiate yourself with someone who disgusts you. Because the king will disgust you. Trust me on that."

At his words, Stone shot up from his chair. "Really, Father. Blade? You know he'll take it too far. And then where will we be." He paused, darting a look at me. "She'll be dead within the first ten minutes."

"Nice vote of confidence," I grumbled, but was grateful to have someone on my side, even if it did make me look like a shameless damsel.

Stone's hand snaked out toward me. When his fingers sought the tips of mine, I almost snatched my hand away, but then I noticed Terran had followed the movement of his son's hand and his expression had hardened, and I left it there. Spiteful.

"That's exactly why you can't be the one to do this, Stone," he said. "Now move away from her. It's going to be Blade. If she can't hold her own against him, she isn't right for the task, anyway."

"It's not that she can't hold her own," Stone said, turning away from me and more toward his father. "It's that she'll try to kill him."

Terran shrugged. "If she can take out the dark enforcer, then we'll know we have the right assassin."

Stone's sigh indicated he'd already given up. I scrubbed my face with both hands, ending with a skim of them over the top of my head. Hairs pulled free of my ponytail and caught in my fingers.

"What would you have done if you'd used Gideon?" I asked. "Would you have tossed him into the harem too?"

With my hands folded over each other on the back of my neck, I stared at Terran, waiting for an answer.

He held my stare while his mouth worked quietly. Finally, he said, "Ferranus has been known to enjoy a mortal male now and then."

I had to work to wrangle the image of Gideon and the nameless king getting it on out of my head, and only managed it when Stone spoke, interrupting my thoughts.

"Please, Father," he said, trying one more time. "Let me do this for you. We don't have time to search for another assassin. You know you can't trust Blade."

Terran shut him up with a look. "It's done. She will start tomorrow. We have precious few weeks before the window of opportunity opens and Ferranus is vulnerable. We can't waste time with her trying to bed someone she already lusts after and who lusts for her in return."

Past the thought that my feelings for Stone were stated so baldly in front of him, I felt sick to my stomach at the thought of what Terran was suggesting.

"I'm not a prostitute," I spat out. "You can't just offer me to whomever you please."

Terran waved his hand dismissively. "Oh, how easy it would be if you were," he said. "Our human prostitutes have far more natural wiles than you do." He shrugged one shoulder. "If you're not up for it, then Flint can make a quick visit to your sister's house. I hear her plants are doing quite well because of his suggestions. She might want to thank him."

Kit again. Flint. The threat was clear. I nodded somberly without letting my gaze trail to the monster who had already taken a good few blows at me, and who no doubt would jump at the chance to do so to my sister. At least, with him here in Fae, Kit was safe.

With a subtle gesture, Terran dismissed me, and Stone took my elbow to guide me back the way we'd come, my stomach growling the entire time. I heard the mass of capo-sidhes shuffling out of the dining room, Terran suggesting they move to the kitchens for the remainder of the meal, and I realized they'd never truly expected me to dine like a lady with them. Terran had been testing me in front of his capos, seeing how I'd react.

The journey to my suite was a silent one. I was too angry and too contemplative to make chit chat. Plus, I'd seen the way Stone had looked at me when Terran suggested I lusted after him. My skin still felt hot at the thought of it. Hot and nauseous at the same time.

Each step I felt the air currents move over my thighs and down my back. How badly I'd torn the dress I didn't want to contemplate. I had to keep clutching the panels of the bodice together to keep my boobs from bouncing right out into the open, and that made me grouchier.

By the time we arrived at the door of the suite, I was too exhausted and hungry to do more than wave him away as he lurked at the threshold.

"I'm tired," I said when he tried once more to apologize.

"I just want to be sure you're OK," he said.

"Listen," I said. "I get it. I agreed to do this. I'll do it. But you need to leave me the fuck alone right now."

Stone tried to speak again, but I pushed him further down the hall. I was surprised he let me.

"Just tell me that bastard isn't coming tonight," I said. "I need to sleep."

He reached for me, thought better of it, and then dropped his hand to his side. "I don't think he will come tonight. He's… occupied."

I lifted my hand, unwilling to even imagine what could keep the dark enforcer busy. "Don't tell me what he's doing. Just warn me when he's coming."

He shrugged. "Blade does not live by anyone else's time line. He does as my father asks, but not always the way he asks it. When he'll come is anyone's guess." He inched closer again but halted when I shot him a warning look. His sigh seemed dragged from the pits of his soul then. "You need to be careful with him, Ava," he said.

"No shit."

"Really," he said. "He's not called the dark enforcer for nothing. He has no scruples."

"And you, who caught me up in all this in the first place, you do, I suppose?"

"I guess I deserve that," he said. "But Blade…well, you haven't seen just how brutal he can be."

I lifted one eyebrow in a sarcastic lift and he responded by nodding. "Yes. I know," he said. "You've seen some of the horror, but trust me when I say that wasn't the half of it."

I snorted. "Trust?" I groped the edge of the door so hard my knuckles hurt, and it still didn't relieve the adrenaline pumping suddenly through my body. "You betrayed me, made me think you were just a soldier in the Fae cartel. You're the freaking adviser to the boss." I made to slam the door, but he held it open with his foot, with enough force that it pushed back against me, yawning open. The sight of the gap in the door filled me with rage.

"You abandoned me at the tavern, stole the cursed objects, then let me ROT in the dungeons, and you think I should trust you?" I barked out a hateful laugh.

He took the rant without shifting his expression one bit. Instead, he leaned closer, his voice going soft.

"I've seen and done things you can't imagine in my lifetime. Horrible things you would kill me for without batting an eye. But Blade is what Fae mothers frighten their children with. He's what my father uses to keep his capos in line. Blade works for my father under his own conditions and for his own reasons, but no one likes him. No one trusts him. My father is the only one who can get him to do anything. Except..." he shook his head when I lifted my eyebrow in question. If the dark enforcer had a weakness, I wanted to know what it was.

"Except?"

"My younger brother, Mica. He can twist Blade around his finger."

"Younger brother?" I said despite myself.

He nodded. "I told you I have brothers. I have three. Mica is the youngest. Flint is older than him." He tried again to push through the open door, but I blocked the gap with my body.

"Ava," he said. "Just be careful with Blade. His reputation is not an exaggeration."

I leaned on the door frame. "Be careful," I echoed. "You mean, when he comes to my rooms on orders to let me try to seduce him, that I should be careful how far I go?" I waited for a beat, just to see if I'd get any reaction before I said, "Or be careful not to get too close when I do so? No shit, I should be careful, Sherlock."

I let go of the door and spun around to face the interior of the room. I pointed at the corners, the locked windows, the torn dress I wore, my voice gaining fury like a wind gathering leaves.

"I'm a prisoner in a world I don't know how to escape and ordered to kill the most powerful Fae with nothing but a fucking lace corset and my decidedly unfeminine wiles, and your best advice is to be careful." I snorted. "I hate to break it to you, but you're a little late to the party."

Air whistled out of his nostrils, and I thought he was doing his best to remain patient. Well, bully for him. He wasn't the one who had to demean himself by using stupid feminine wiles to get close enough to use the very real skills he'd been training for, for over a decade.

I made my voice even and calm as I faced him. "Understand this, Stone. I'll do your dirty work for your father, but I'm not going to let that bastard touch me."

"I know," he said.

"Do you?" I asked. "You just said he can't be trusted. Jasmine trusted him and look what he did to her." My voice broke at the memory trying to worm its way through my defenses, and I had to shove it back down so I could continue. "You expect him to act like a gentleman when he comes with permission to be 'seduced'?"

His face paled at the insinuation. "I'll post soldiers outside the door. I'll make sure you're protected the whole time."

I blew through my lips. "I don't need your kind of protection," I said. "I drive that bus."

He shook his head. "You don't understand," he said. "Blade does not come to Fae for just anyone or anything. He prefers the mortal realm to Fae and we're happy to keep it that way. My father keeps him on a short tether by allowing him to come and go as he pleases, but it's a false sense of security and he knows it."

"Just leave me my karambit. I can protect myself."

He eyed me with a narrowed gaze for a long moment, and I thought he was going to tell me it was long gone, melted down or given to Terran as a trophy. But then he slid his hand behind his back, reaching for something. He came back with my karambit in his grip.

I tried not to show too much excitement as the light winked off its surface. I had to force myself not to grab for it, but my mouth nearly went dry with the thought

I'd have it in my hand once more. My knife. My means to finishing this for real.

"I won't tell anyone I have it," I said, crossing my hand over my heart. I supposed I could be forgiven for the note of relief in my voice.

He leaned down, something odd tightening his features even as his gaze went soft. "I trust you, Ava. I know you feel like I betrayed you, but there is more going on than you can know. What I did, I did to protect you. I know you're doing this for your sister, but I hope there's something more here. Between us."

My throat ached at the gentleness of his tone. "Just leave, Stone," I whispered.

He nodded quietly. "I understand."

He held out the karambit, handle first, with his fingers splayed over the rubber grip in a way that made room for my own. It nestled in my palm the way it always had. Mine. Not a glamored object offered as a Trojan horse. Mine. My karambit.

For a heart-stopping second, my biceps tensed in reflex and instinct. My mind's eye played out the entire act of slicing sideways, cutting through Stone's stomach in an instant and tucking back along my forearm as I ran headlong through the halls and down the stairs to where we'd left Terran and Flint. I fantasized throwing myself at them and just letting the primal rage that swelled in me loose.

But then I inhaled. The vision left me like a fog clearing. I was out of my depth here, and I knew it. A land of magic that I didn't understand, with creatures who wielded magic like breath. One single woman, no matter how skilled a fighter, with one single blade, could not take down an entire cartel.

At least not today.

Because first I had to make sure my sister was safe. And then I'd take them down.

"You should know Ferranus is not vulnerable to cold iron the way the rest of Fae is," he said. "His line can wield it without worry. It will take more than a slice across the throat with steel to take him down."

Stone's arm dropped back, and he shoved his hand in his pocket, offered me a nod, and then turned on his heel. He looked back at me once and gave me a tentative smile.

I didn't smile back. I couldn't. All I could do was close the door and trace my steps to the bed. Every cell in my body was screaming for sleep and yet, I was afraid the moment I closed my eyes, that I'd see Jasmine's face behind my eyelids and that Kit's features would overlay them until I stared into the darkness too terrified to do more than breathe.

But I had to at least try. Without bothering to peel out of the now ruined gown, I padded to the bed, tucked the blade beneath the mattress and fell onto the king sized bed face first.

The next I knew, a sharp rap on the door woke me. A puddle of wet fabric stuck to my cheek. I'd not moved an inch except to adjust my head so I could breathe.

The rap came again, and I called out to it, wearily, still struggling to find my way to full consciousness. "I'm coming."

For a moment, the remnants of sleep held me there in its safety net, like swinging in a hammock on a hot summer afternoon. Then it all came flooding back in on a torrent of hard, icy rain.

My body came awake all at once, but not fast enough to get out of the way of the sweeping gaze that raked over me the moment the door swung open.

Too late, I realized I wasn't ready. I wasn't ready, and the dark enforcer stood in the yawning doorway.

Chapter 14

I DIDN'T GET A chance to roll out of bed before Blade stepped into the room. But I did have time to grab for the clock on the nightstand. I hurled it at him, all the remembered fear and residual adrenaline firing the instinct for defense.

He ducked neatly, not that he needed to. I'd aimed too high in my haste, and it struck the lintel. When it crashed to the floor, its innards sprayed everywhere.

"Shitty aim," he said.

"Lucky for you, I wasn't aiming."

My heart fluttered from the sudden dump of adrenaline. I had dropped to a crouch when I'd slid to the floor, automatically making myself smaller so I could assess the situation when the door opened. My hand had slid beneath the mattress to search for the handle of my karambit. I swept side to side, searching for my knife.

He pulled the karambit from behind his back and held it out. "Looking for this?"

I glared at him.

"You sleep like a child," he said as his gaze dropped to my throat. "Arms and legs splayed out everywhere. Out so hard a battle could wage under your nose without you waking. It's strangely endearing." His flash of smile indicated he thought it anything but.

"I thought Fae couldn't lie."

He shrugged. "Which statement do you think was a lie? The one where you lay drooling like a baby or the one where the big bad monster hunter had no idea I sat on her bed watching her sleep for several moments before deciding to leave so I could enter her room like a gentleman?"

The blood washed out of my face at the realization he'd been in the room with me without me knowing. That wasn't like me. The only time I'd slept like that, my parents had been alive. Kit and I had shared a bed. I'd been safe. Probably the last time I'd ever felt like that.

I swallowed down the ache of that memory along with the horror of knowing I'd been inches away from danger and not known it.

I crawled to my feet, pulling my hand out from beneath the mattress. My knees caught on the dress's skirt and I realized I was still wearing it. At least partially. A glance down showed me that the panels covering my boobs had slid aside to show both my nipples. The long tear in the skirt had got higher and now reached my mid thigh.

It draped back around me as I stood. Reaching for the scraps of material left to me to cover my breasts, I tugged them back into place with as much dignity as I could muster.

"It's all the adrenaline and endorphins," I said. "They knocked me out."

He advanced into the room. "I know the feeling."

I looked up at him and had to brush the hair out of my face to see him clearly. It was probably standing on end from sleep.

"Don't do that," I said.

"Don't do what?"

"Try to make me feel like you understand me."

"Maybe I do."

I laughed. "Right. Been in my position a time or two?" I let all the anger and disgust I felt for the last twenty-four hours leak into my tone. I guessed I wasn't too tired to be furious.

He chuckled, a strangely warm and dark sound that reached out toward me like radiant heat from a fire on a cold night.

"You don't think I've spent my adult Fae lifetime working for the Shadow Court and not felt the after effects of adrenaline and the icy danger of threat in the air? You don't think I've fallen asleep when my subconscious knows things aren't normal, that someone might be trying to kill me?"

I eyed him. "Forgive my insensitivity for a man who tears a woman's throat out at a single word from his boss."

The sound he made deep in the bottom of his throat gave me a shiver. When his lips pressed tightly together, I took an involuntary step backward, but I couldn't make the words on my tongue do the same. The thought of Jasmine and the things he'd done to her still burned in my mind like acid.

"Did you enjoy doing that to her?" I asked, dropping my grip on the dress and letting the material fall where it may. I didn't care what he saw of me because I was sure every inch was tense and knotted with anger.

I preferred to prowl toward him, near-naked and unashamed, so he could see each and every muscle of my body that I'd trained to be a machine of death, a body comprised of muscle. I might be all but powerless without magic here in Fae, but I wasn't useless, and I wasn't afraid. I wouldn't *be* afraid. Any predator would think twice before taking on a honey badger.

That was what I was. Minus the honey.

I wanted him to see—really see—the scar on my throat that proved I'd looked death in the eye and spat in it.

"Your boss wanted me to hear her scream, didn't he? Well, I did. I noted each cry of pain, just like every scar I've taken on my body. I marked them and I vowed to avenge them." I halted, my gaze hard enough that I felt my jaw clench as I drilled him with hate. "Are you still willing to come to me and see if I'll lay a seductive hand on you?" I asked in a low voice.

I watched his Adam's apple plunge. I waited, expecting him to attack.

But he pivoted on his heel with a curse that put the hairs on the back of my neck at attention. Before I could take another breath, he barreled back through the door and out into the hall, a low hum of growling vibration in his wake.

He could easily have torn my throat out like Jasmine's. My hand went to my throat as I reminded myself that he'd been sent on Terran's orders. He wouldn't have killed me. But he wanted to. I knew that. The tightness of his expression as I'd goaded him was a strong enough indicator of that.

Suddenly spent, I sank into the chair. My heart tripped over on its next beat as I let out a strained hiss of air. Whatever had just happened, I was sure the reprieve would be brief and the return, violent.

It took several long breaths to bring my heart rate back to normal. Even ticking along at a slower pace, my breath still felt ragged, so when Stone peeked his head around the corner a few moments later, I jumped, more startled at seeing him than Blade.

"Good morning," he said, without a hint of notice that I'd nearly leaped onto the table top. "Are you hungry? I brought Fae toast."

I blinked and tried to process the sudden shift of circumstance. The noise that rumbled through my belly was enough answer for either of us. Except for a bit of moldy bread and cheese, I'd not eaten a proper meal in days.

I waved him in, not caring who the heck was carrying food. I just wanted it.

"I don't care what Fae toast is, but if it's edible, bring it on."

With a smile that seemed almost fake but very welcome considering who could have entered my room, Stone swept in, carrying a tray filled with fare that released such aromatic deliciousness that my mouth started to water.

So excited at the prospect of filling my aching stomach, I found myself standing and clutching the edges of the dress together chastely.

I lifted on tip toe, fabric gathered in my fingers to see the entire expanse of the tray. "That looks delicious."

A pile of thick, fluffy something that resembled a bedding of cloud rose above a single plate. Coffee steam rose above a carafe as it sat close to a pitcher of thick cream, companioned by a single bloom of black hyacinth peeking above a squat urn-shaped vase. Three lumps of brown sugar trimmed a saucer holding a glass pitcher of syrup. To the side, a bowl of berries and cinnamon threatened to fall off the edge of the tray.

I smiled up at him, all the while thinking I was some piss poor monster hunter. Charmed by a tray of food and coffee. I decided that if I ended up dead by the last bite, at least I wouldn't die hungry.

I picked at a plate of what looked like custard-soaked bread. He tapped the back of my hand lightly, scolding me for my rudeness.

"I don't know how you do it in your world, but here in Fae, we don't use our fingers to eat," he said in a matronly voice, and I narrowed my eyes at the comment coming so soon after the disastrous meal the night before. He held up a fist filled with cutlery as though he were brandishing the holy grail.

He pointed the ends of the forks and spoons at the adjoining room, where the small table and chairs tucked into an alcove space overlooking the country-side was covered with odds and ends. I'd never given it much thought in the time I'd been here, too concerned about showering, sleeping, and surviving, I supposed. But the lovely view it granted of the lush meadows filled with flowers and trees, already put me at ease.

"Shall we sit at the table?" he asked. "You know, like civilized Fae?"

I huffed out a sigh through my nose. "I'm not fae, but I think I'd like that."

He headed toward the table, looking over his shoulder at me in that endearing way he had that made my heart tumble about like dice. "You go put on something that makes you feel more comfortable," he said in a husky voice. "I'll set this out for us."

So thoughtful. So kind. He must be really trying to make up for the ratty way he'd treated me. Well, I was happy to let him try. The smells of the food and coffee were making my mouth water.

It was hard remembering he was my enemy, watching him move as he began setting out the food. The sinews of muscle as he cleared the table of bric-à-brac and then arranged the food, dishes, and carafe had a grace that could be equally at home with a domestic chore or arcing brutally at an enemy on a battlefield.

I wanted to see him fight for real, I thought. Wanted to stand back and admire the play of muscle as it moved beneath his skin. The image of both sent a hum along my spine and I had to force myself to turn around and head for the armoire because no good could come from thinking about anything except food right then.

As starving as I was, I found myself raking through the clothes inside in a rush to get dressed. Last evening, the closet had been filled with gowns. Today, I found my own clothes, all clean and hung neatly without a single gown to be seen.

I yanked off the remains of the dress I wore and let it puddle to the floor as I reached for my underwear and bra.

I felt the prickle of eyes on my back as I did so. He was watching. I wondered what he'd say about all the scars on view. Would he care, or would he just enjoy the sight of my ass and glimpse of side-boob like any red-blooded human man would?

Terran had suggested that what Fae males enjoyed might not be something a human woman would consider. That had my mind conjuring all sorts of horrors while I slept, and vestiges of the dreams waved at me from the corners of my mind, flutters of gauze that crumbled to ash when I tried to grasp for them.

Whatever they enjoyed, I wished I could ask Jasmine. She would have known, surely, since she'd worked The Velvet Boar in her fairy paint for what seemed a long time. Her experiences would have been useful, and it was short-sighted of Terran to have her executed.

My heart squeezed a bit as I thought of her. There would be no way to ask her now. I wasn't sure who I was angrier at: Terran or Blade, and I found my teeth grinding together as I contemplated the reasons for that.

With a flush of low-grade temper cresting over my chest, I had to remind myself that Stone would know those things too, and if I was smart, I'd use him while he was here so I wouldn't have to endure Blade's company as he tutored me in the arts of seducing a male fae. The situation was a pricker bush of thorns beneath my nails. I was a hunter, for Pete's sake, not a harlot. The mere thought that this was the backup plan had me all sorts of grouchy.

But the quicker the charade was over, the quicker I could get home. I was willing to do whatever it took. For Kit.

Plus, it didn't hurt that Stone was hot as literal fuck. His gaze on my spine was electric. It warmed me in ways it really shouldn't. He might look like a boxer, with his misaligned nose and thick, corded neck, and he might be the son of my enemy, but he wasn't Blade. Another bonus.

The truth was, I liked the feel of Stone's gaze on me, and I knew it. Terran had been right. I did lust after his son. I wanted to take him down a peg, have him begging on his knees. I wanted to control that hard body and make it putty in my hands.

So I took my time. Let him look. I had a good body. Gideon always said so. Not entirely soft and feminine like a Victorian lady, but round and firm where it mattered. My breasts should have been smaller, with all the muscle I trained into my core and pectorals, but they weren't. The muscle just made them high and taut.

When I turned around, fully dressed, his eyes were back on the plates in front of him. The warm nutty smell of expensive coffee tickled my nostrils and drew me to the table. I fell on the mug with both hands before I even sat down, curling my fists around the belly of porcelain and drawing it to my nose. The fragrance was like a warm blanket on a cold night. A brief thought that it must have been so inviting that it disguised his own, caramel scent ran through my mind, but I let it go as a sigh of contentment escaped me.

One moment. That's all it was, but it was enough to remind me life could return to normal. So long as I did what was asked. Seduced a king. Killed a king.

I was still working my way through the heat that swarmed up my spine when he smiled up at me from his chair and spread his arm over the table.

"Sit. Eat." A flash of something moved in his eyes, and for a second I hesitated.

"You're starving," he said, prodding me. "You said so already. At least face the day with a full belly."

My jaw clenched, some forgotten or unrealized danger coiling in the muscles, but then he yawned, putting his hand over his mouth in the most normal way, and I ended up pulling out my chair. He was heaping the custard-coated bread onto my plate by the time I reached for a fork.

"Yetta makes the best Fae toast," he said, pouring what looked like homemade strawberry sauce over the top of the stack. "She used to make it for me when I was a boy a thousand years ago, it seems. It's my favorite."

He shot me an earnest look that gave him a boyish quality, and I dug into the pile without hesitation. It tasted like sugar-coated, fruit laden clouds. "Sweet Jesus," I said, and didn't wait for a response before I plowed through the rest of the stack.

To his credit, he let me sit and eat without further comment. The custard that enveloped the bread tasted faintly of vanilla and maple and was pillowy soft. I ate the entire plateful and was sitting back with the coffee held in both hands before he spoke and ruined it all.

Chapter 15

"You have to face Blade soon," he said.

I leaned back in the chair, studying him. The coil of coffee fragrance hadn't diminished despite the carafe being nearly empty. "I know."

"You know, but are you ready?"

I rolled the fork over on the table, tines pointing down. A smear of syrup coated a small circle of cloth and the tackiness of it held the fabric in place against the wood beneath while the rest of the material puckered around it.

"Are you ready, Ava?"

Peering across the table, I said, "You made it pretty clear to me just how much of a monster Blade is," I said.

His eyes shuttered. "Indeed," was all he said. No more a word than a low-throated hum.

"Indeed," I echoed and waited for him to argue or deny or even expand on his comment. Earlier, he'd been railing at me to understand just how horrible Blade could be, and now that I was indicating my acceptance of that fact, he was playing coy? I held his gaze with more intensity than I might have needed, but he merely stared back just as intensely. Enough to make the small of my back itch.

"What I saw in the cellars was a monster," I said, breaking the silence. "And I know monsters. Knowing them and killing them is what I do. So, yes. I'm ready."

"Seems to me a monster hunter would have expected such violence, been prepared for it, even," he said, and a copper light coiled through his eyes. "She should have expected to see a monster and not been surprised when it showed itself."

I sucked the back of my teeth, stung by the comment but unwilling to show it. "Monsters like you are different," I said through a clenched jaw. Was he really going to argue this with me?

His gaze dipped to my throat. Despite myself, my body heated up. That just made me angrier. My fingers clenched around the fork.

"You let me believe Blade was just some Fae who owned a tavern with a portal to this realm. You knew the night he tracked me to Gideon's place who and what he was." A snort of harsh laughter escaped me. "You even let me believe you have the power to control beasts. You left me at his mercy in the cellars, and let me sit there and hear Jasmine's agony. And despite being able to control beasts, you just let it happen. That's a worse monster, I think. I think that's— "

"I told you I had the power to control beasts?" he asked, cutting me off mid-rant.

I gaped at him, mouth still open. It wasn't just confusion that hung my jaw. He knew this already. Why was he even questioning it?

"Of all the things you could have latched onto, you care about that?"

He shrugged and his gaze flicked ever so swiftly to the door and back again. "I just find it interesting that I trusted you enough to tell you about my natal magic."

Interesting turn of phrase, I thought. My jaw ached with the tension so much I couldn't finish. It took me a moment to gather control of my emotions. All the while, that coppery light moved in the depths of his gaze, and it was enough to drive me to my feet. I didn't want to see him struggling with whatever emotion bestirred itself in his Fae heart. I had let his pretty eyes and perfectly chiseled body distract me for too long.

"You are the boss's son," I said, looking down at him through my anger. "You stole the dark objects from me. You sent Flint after my sister. You let Blade…" I paused to swallow down the revulsion and emotion thickening my throat and when I spoke again, I could barely hear my own voice. "You let Blade do that to Jasmine when you could have left her out of all this. That makes you a worse monster, even than Blade."

He stood slowly, like a panther rising from a siesta as it spied a bit of prey flickering through the foliage. Everything in me wanted to back up, fingers searching for my karambit, but Blade had taken my knife with him when he'd left. It was just me and my fists. I instinctively knew that wouldn't be enough. And I instinctively knew I needed more. Something had shifted in those last seconds. I might not be sure what, but I knew the change like I knew the back of my own eyelids.

I would fight, sure, but I wasn't sure I'd be able to hold him off for long.

I needed a weapon.

My eyes locked on the heavy pewter carafe. He caught the direction of my glance and just like that, shot up from the table, blocking me from reaching for the heavy jug.

My hand moved in response to his movement with the swiftness of a snake, curled into a striking head.

The punch struck the flat space of his jaw. At first, I was surprised I'd landed it, and I pulled my hand back quickly, shaking off the pain slicing through my knuckles to brace for another. He'd shown me already how swift he could be, so for that moment while the echoes of bone on bone crawled through my elbow, I thought it was all part of the play. I danced back, instinct buzzing through my body with commands my mind wasn't even getting a chance to process. I thought I was heading for the door. Maybe I was searching for a weapon.

Whatever my subconscious had in mind, I didn't manage it.

He was blurringly fast. Faster than I'd seen in any creature I'd faced. Faster than I'd known he could move. My arms were pinned to my sides in less than a heartbeat, with his massive hands curled around my wrists.

He pulled me close, holding my arms at my sides. A single foot hooked me behind my heels so expertly, I fell into him before I could take in a sharp breath of shock or react to counter his movement. For a moment, I almost sagged into him, the pheromones of sleep and good food and the sultry waves of heat coming off him almost teasing me into thinking this was something different than aggression. But then I stiffened. Because it wasn't. I couldn't be that stupid.

"Fuck you," I said through the heady scent of cinnamon that coiled around me, shoving aside the smell of coffee so sharply it might have been a line drawn with a razor on skin.

His gaze locked on mine and it took several seconds of focused breathing to realize his entire body was filled with the same sort of tension as mine. The moment I realized his erection was pressing into my hips, I discovered I was straining into him as well.

"Well, fuck," I said, the words slipping free as disbelief rocked through me. "You're kidding me right now."

I wasn't sure what I meant…whether it was his desire or my own that surprised me, or if I was just so damned upset that after everything, my body could still respond to his. My head dropped back, annoyed with myself as I closed my eyes. I had to defuse this bomb pronto.

"Let me go," I said in a flat voice. "You don't get to be excited after all this."

"Don't I?" he said, but didn't let go of his grip. Rather, he pulled me closer, letting his thighs corral me between his legs.

My throat ached. Damn the traitorous thing. That fragrance of spice coiled about me like a satin thread. My senses searched for that caramel smell but all I could register was the hint of cinnamon and clove.

"You black-mailed me into the Fae realm, and then abandoned me there in that tavern to fend for myself," I said, reminding myself once more why he was so wrong for me.

His eyebrow cocked upward. "I did?" he intoned. "How cowardly of me."

"Where are the cursed objects you took?"

He shrugged. "Where do you think they are? If Don Sidhe wanted them, he must have them."

I studied his face, noting the subtle fluttering of muscle in his jaw. "So you just passed them over after you stole them?"

Again, a subtle shrug that could mean anything. "I'm not sure that's an accurate portrayal."

My lips pressed together as I considered the answer, which was no answer, I decided. That meant he didn't want to tell me, but didn't want to lie either.

I gave him a shove with the heel of my hand. I needed space between us to think. But when my palm met the hardness of his chest and felt a shudder move through him, my resolve…melted. I sucked in a sharp breath and struggled in his embrace, desperate now to get away. I did not want to melt now.

In turn, he grappled for my wrist and held me even closer. Tighter.

The heartbeat beneath my palm was rapid and forceful. A different, more masterful Stone than I'd nearly bedded in that damn tavern.

"You want me," he said, his nostrils flaring. "I can smell it."

Oh fuck me sideways. It was the expectation in his voice that I minded the most. The entitlement. That he believed I wanted him so badly, I would respond to aggression.

And the worst was that he wasn't wrong.

"You're smelling adrenaline," I said. "And if you don't let me go, you're going to be smelling blood."

He canted his head sideways, and a slow smile moved his mouth. The coppery light sparked in his gaze. "No," he said. "I know adrenaline. This isn't it. Yours is the scent of arousal. Although, I must admit, the promise of blood does thrill me, too."

At that, he flipped me around so easily I realized with horror just how powerless I really was. About as strong as a butterfly. He could have pinned me to a board already any moment he'd wanted to.

With my back against him and my arms expertly crossed over my stomach so I couldn't do more than twist in his grip, it took me precious seconds to adjust and fire up the reflexes to fight for real.

By then, he had me man-handled across the room and pushed into the wall.

CHAPTER 16

EVERY HORRIBLE RAPE SCENARIO I'd ever seen in movies played out in my mind in a millisecond.

The moment my chest collided with the wall, the air went out of my lungs. My cheek jammed against the patterned plaster as he wrangled my hands with one of his massive ones, leaving the other free to roam my ribcage. Which it did. All the way up to my neck.

He swept aside my hair and dropped a thumb onto the worst part of the scar, the place behind my ear where it bulged like a worm for a quarter inch. The way his thumb caressed it, holding me so tightly I couldn't do more than strain to look at him over my shoulder, and even then, it didn't look like Stone. The harshness of his jawline from the corner of my eye put iron into my spine.

There was no denying how strong he was. How immovable, despite my struggles. The hard length of him felt like cement against me except for the breath that whispered over my neck as his mouth lowered to skin. He traced the line of scar with his lips, brushing them the way an archaeologist might move a layer of fine sand from the surface of a sacred relic.

My heart seemed to freeze mid pump. The moment I felt a prick of teeth grazing my neck, I didn't dare move. Something was wrong. Very, very wrong.

"Who did that to you?" he said, his voice a rasp of fury that didn't make sense. He'd seen the scar before. Why was he asking now?

"I asked you a question," he said, and the tone and anger in it made me feel small and ashamed as memories flooded from their dark little corner of my mind and out into the pale open of my consciousness. Like a stream of boiling water, they scalded their way through and bubbled into a mist that wet my eyelids.

"Fuck you," I ground out and tried once more to squirm out from beneath his hold. Damn him for making me think about that night.

"I think that's the intention, is it not?"

"If I remember correctly," I spat out. "Your father expressly forbid it."

One long pause drew out between us, charging the air with electricity. I barely breathed as I waited to see if he'd release me.

His mouth whispered at the back of my ear. "And just who do you think is about to plunge his fingers between your legs, Ponytail?"

At that, I did freeze. My brain wouldn't even process the horror of that instant. I felt the gears inside gum up and try to move, getting stuck again on a wad of thick resin. Sweet baby Jesus.

"You're not Stone," I said in a tight voice.

"No, I'm not," Blade said in a husky voice. "But judging by the way the lust is all over you, it does seem as though you might not like his vanilla flavor of Fae after all."

He pulled my back higher, arching me more sharply into his torso. Rage lit little red dots behind my eyelids. I would kill him. Once I was free. I'd hunt him down first and scoop his balls out with a melon baller.

"Let me go," I said.

"Believe me, Ponytail," he said. "I'd love nothing more. But we are here to prepare you for what awaits you at the Iron Court, and you need to understand that vanilla is not what you'll get with Ferranus. What you'll get with the king is violence. He's old Fae. As old as Terran, and his kind always drained any mortal lovers of their blood as they took them. At least, when they didn't just eat their heads first."

"Oh, sweet Jesus," I said, my gorge rising.

"Your Jesus is no good here," he said. "You have only me. At this moment, I am your god."

I barked out a laugh at that. "Any god that would care about me is a bastard, anyway," I said. "So it's such a small switch from Him to you."

"Tough little bird," he said. "But are you tough enough to go against Ferranus should it come down to wiling your way into his bed in order to kill him?"

His face burrowed into my neck and shivers moved the length of my spine as his breath washed my skin.

"My job is to prepare you for the moment he has you splayed out the same as I do right now, his teeth on your neck, his hands roaming your thighs." At that, his free hand whispered over my pants and I felt each inch so acutely, it nearly had me shrieking in impotent frustration. His hands, his hips, every part of him that touched me echoed his words so intimately, my skin raged.

I hated myself more than him in that instant. Because I'd let myself get fooled. I should have known by his scent alone that he wasn't Stone. Stone smelled of caramel. I'd known that and ignored it. Blade, the bastard, reeked of cinnamon.

"Take your hands off me," I ground out. "Or I'm going to kill you." I omitted the fact that I was going to kill him later, anyway. My mind ran amuck with images of slicing his throat as he slept.

He chuckled darkly. "You weren't fast enough for me," he said. "Remember that, big bad hunter. You aren't strong enough, either. If you want to survive to save your sister, you need to be ready when the king decides to strike. Because strike he will."

My cheek was starting to hurt from the pressure against the wall, but I wouldn't give in. "I am ready. I don't need seduction. I can kill him in a heartbeat long before he decides to try to rape me."

"Try?" he said, laughing. "If this is all you've got, he'll do more than try."

I gave it one more attempt to peel myself out of his grip, wrenching in every direction, seeking some weak spot in his hold to either throw him or jab him in the voice box. Pinned against the wall, I didn't have many options.

Even so, for some reason, he let go.

I spun and lunged. The movement was less graceful than I'd hoped, more like a nearly toppled sprinter, as I pulled away. Pivoting blindly, hastily, I faced him because I would not let him grab for me again. The line of my scar burned where he'd touched it. My fingers went to it automatically, and he watched the instinctual movement with interest burning in his gaze.

"You never answered me," he said, his eyes narrowing to slits. "Who did that to you?"

"You're a made-Fae with centuries of experience in violence, and you want to know who might have nearly killed me?" I huffed through my nose in dismissal, using the distance to get control of my erratic heartbeat.

"Nearly killed," he echoed in a voice so heavy with threat and rage that prickles of dread spidered up my spine.

I tried not to show him my unease. No good ever came from showing your enemy discomfort. Instead, I laughed. If it sounded fake, I didn't care. I just needed the emotional distance.

"It was forever ago," I said. "I don't owe you my life story."

He prowled toward me, backing me up from the alcove and out into the suite proper. "Stay away from me," I growled. "Or I'll kill you."

"You told me Stone informed you of just how brutal I can be," he said as he advanced, ignoring my threat. "You think you know brutality because you face monsters in the mortal world?" He shook his head and let go a chuckle. "You know nothing about me. Stone knows nothing."

I butted up against the bookcase that edged the fireplace. And he licked his lips as he watched me. I was trapped again like a bug. There was no denying he was dangerous. But I was dangerous too. Just he wait and see, come closer and try.

I smoothed down the front of my T-shirt, grounding myself with the feel of something familiar.

"Give me my knife," I said, "and I'll show you how I face a monster."

It was a challenge I thought he'd refuse, but then, with a short laugh, he reached behind his back and extracted my karambit from a sheath beneath his shirt. He held it out to me, much the same as Stone had, butt end first. I noted he didn't try to avoid touching the metal of the blade itself, just casually handled it as if it were a piece of wood.

"Game on, lover," he said with a wide grin. He cracked his head from side to side, and spread his arms out. "Let's see if you can take me."

My next moves, I knew would mean life or death. I had no illusions about Blade's strength or his ruthlessness. It was the fact that he was goading me into making a mistake that bothered me most. As though he thought I would do something stupid and endanger myself at this early stage.

He was a warrior, but he was also a fool if he thought that. I had no intentions of dying right there, not at his hand.

"You must think I'm stupid," I said, my gaze settling on my blade. I wanted it. My fingers itched to hold it. But I was not going to fight him for it. I'd been through one test already and I didn't have to prove anything to him.

"What I think," he said, "is that you know you're in over your head. What I think is that the Iron King will swallow you whole."

He flipped the knife around in his grip so that the blade was no longer tucked along his forearm, but pointing toward me, with its curve closest to me, its most harmless hold.

I would not take the bait. Crossing my arms over my chest, I stared back at him, watching the way the muscle in his jaw feathered until the hinge turned white. I considered turning my back on him, dismissing him, but I wasn't quite that brave. Instead, I tapped my foot, suggesting I was tired of his bullshit.

After a time, he snorted. "I knew you were weak," he said. "Like the rest of you mortal women, all you're good for is a quick roll in the hay."

I knew my teeth clacked together. All the ire I'd been holding at bay, pushing through the best of my willpower. But I doubted he'd seen it because he made the mistake of turning his back on me.

I took the opportunity and leaped for him then, aiming to accomplish no more than get close enough to do some damage. Make him drop the knife. If I got the chance, I would kill him.

But it was a critical miscalculation. By the time I was within range, he spun around, so quick he was no more than a blur. He elbowed me in the chest, and my lungs gave their air the bum's rush. I fell backward from the force, but because I'd been standing close to the table, the edge of it connected with the back of my hips.

I staggered to my balance point, on my toes, putting some elasticity in my thighs and low back. I regrouped. Then I raced for him.

His dodge and weaving reactions seemed to slide from him like hot oil. Each movement was fluid and almost mesmerizing. He might have been dancing with me, so easy and greased were his movements. He was a fighter. Not a brawler or a scrapper. A true, honest to goodness warrior. He'd known battle in his lifetime, and if I'd thought him merely brutal before, I understood the difference then.

One misstep and he would be on me in an instant.

We circled each other warily, both looking for an opening. I made a sudden lunge, aiming a swift kick at his midsection. But Blade was too quick, sidestepping my attack and delivering a sharp punch to my side.

I gasped in pain, but managed to keep my footing. The next time I made a move, it was to fake a high kick before dropping down and sweeping my leg out to catch him off guard. A laugh almost slipped free of me when he stumbled, but it was a reaction that came from nerves alone. I had time to recognize the dump of adrenaline before I let it loose.

Clamping down on it, I followed my foot sweep with a blow to his forearm, finding the little frog-jump muscle in his forearm perfectly. The karambit fell from his grip and clattered to the floor. I swooped in. Grabbed the handle. I was pulling it back when a sudden spark leaped over my fingers and traveled up my arm.

The blade slid from my grasp and fell between us, both of us crouched in a sprinter's position.

I felt an undeniable pull of something that made me look at him.

His palms lay flat on the floor in front of him, just inches away from the blade. With a shock, I realized he was watching me with shuttered eyelids. A flutter of muscle in his cheek came and went. Tension coiled in the air like a wire about to ground.

He was waiting, I realized. Measuring me, taking stock. I'd not taken him down at all; he'd faked it. I knew that as suddenly as a light being switched on in a pitch black room. The knowledge all but blinded me. What I didn't understand was what he was waiting for.

For the first moment since I'd landed in Fae, I felt real, true terror. I'd been brash before, thinking my skills would be enough, believing in myself with a cocky arrogance that Gideon always said would get him killed. And he was right. Except this time, it would be Kit's life on edge, not Gideon's.

This moment, more than any other proved I knew nothing of the capabilities of the creatures in this realm. I had no idea how much magic they could wield or bring to bear beyond what I'd seen, and right then, I feared what I didn't know. More than that, I realized I was indeed woefully unprepared for what might meet me when I faced the king.

For several long moments, we crouched there, caught in a moment of tension, but then, as quickly as it had come Blade pushed himself to his feet and kicked the karambit toward me. Without another word, he pivoted on his heel and those long legs devoured every inch of space between us and the door.

The click of the lock sent a shiver over me and I fell to my butt, my legs splayed out over the floor.

Once my eyes spied my blade, I plucked it from the floor and pulled it to my chest. With the pad of my thumb, I tested the edge.

Sharp. As sharp as when I'd brought it to Fae in the first place. I swallowed down the knot of adrenaline that tightened my throat. We'd been playing for keeps in those moments, and he'd known it.

With my heart pounding in my chest, I too got to my feet and zombie-walked to the table where I laid the karambit down with great care.

I couldn't shake the feeling that something had shifted between us. I just had no idea what it was.

CHAPTER 17

THE MOMENT I REALIZED I'd somehow dodged a burly, near-rabid bullet, my heart started to pound so hard in my ears that my head began to hurt. I looked at the closed door Blade had just gone through. Why he'd left, I had no idea, but I suspected it had something to do with the erection that hadn't deflated the entire time we fought.

I scrubbed my face with my hands. Fighting always raised lust of some sort. I was no stranger to the sensation, nor was any other hunter I'd met. Most times, we used the primal drive to channel the blood-lust needed to take out our quarry. Sometimes it was just focused into a pure, old-fashioned lust for survival.

But lust was lust, and many times, Gideon and I had punished each other in the most delicious ways after a difficult but successful hunt. Like beasts, we thought only of one thing and be damned if anyone was within earshot if we sated each other in an alleyway several blocks away or in a bathroom stall if we managed to get to a bar.

My throat ached at the thought of a bathroom stall, and an image of myself peering through a crack at Blade and Jasmine flashed through my mind. For a second, my eyes closed, and I weaved on my feet at the memory. Just days ago, I told myself. Maybe a week. That was how long it had been since I'd found myself in the Velvet Boar as Blade and Jasmine moaned and sweated on the other side.

I sank into a chair, letting my legs splay out. Jasmine. Despite giving herself so whole-heartedly to a Fae she trusted, he'd killed her at an order from his boss. No argument. No protests. Just death.

To think that the lust I felt right then was anything but desire for his death would mean I was as depraved as Blade was.

And I wasn't. My fingers trailed along the arm of the chair and found my jacket. With a start, my neck snapped as my gaze flew to the pocket. A week at least, I thought. It had been a week since I'd come to Fae.

But I wasn't wholly unprepared. I still had that inhaler filled with Bloodmist. In a world where magic was as autonomic as breath, I needed an edge, not a weapon.

I chewed the inside of my cheek thoughtfully as I stared down at the inhaler in one hand and the karambit in the other. Blade had seemed to show no worry about touching the iron of the karambit. I thought that strange when Stone had been careful to avoid it. He'd warned me that Ferranus did not share other Fae's vulnerability to cold iron. The karambit would be about as useful a tool here in Fae to assassinate the king as a needle, I realized. But now, looking at the karambit in my grip, I began to wonder if it was actually my knife.

It felt like my knife. If it was, it might be best to cut my way through the entire cartel right now, use the vulnerability of fae to iron to my advantage. Rampage thorough the halls until I found Terran and his sons. I'd have to kill my way through, slice through every soldier I encountered as I went, but it wouldn't be impossible. A blast of Bloodmist would help. Hype me up, make me feel invincible, add to my strength and agility.

I knew how it worked and I knew, like Gideon no doubt had, that it could give me the edge I needed. He'd probably expected me to use it as a last resort, something to keep me on my toes and push the envelope enough that I could actually carry out an assassination on a Fae king in a realm of magic I didn't understand.

But all that depended on knowing if my karambit was the real thing. And right now, rolling the inhaler around in my palm, I couldn't think of anything else. Because what if I did take the hit? What if I did rampage through the castle thinking my karambit was the real thing when all it turned out to be was a whittled stick glamored to look like my knife. Stone had said the family possessed that sort of magic.

I chewed my lip. My entire mouth flooded with water at the feel of the vape in my grip. My thumb played over the deploy button, stroking the surface and feeling the grooves of it like the wrinkles of a lover's face.

I could take a hit anyway. Use the blast to drive me storming my way through the castle and let happen what would. If I didn't survive, it would be their own fault. Maybe Kit would be a useless pawn then, and they'd abandon the notion of harming her. As leverage, she was no good if the assassin was dead.

It wasn't like my life was worth much anyway, and taking the risk that the soldiers would kill me before I even got to Terran wasn't the issue.

My head dropped back, and I sighed. The fight with Blade had shown me just how difficult it might be to head an all-out front-ended assault. I wouldn't even make it to one head of the hydra, and if I was going to do that, I wanted a shot at one of them. Hopefully, Terran or Blade.

The thought of the hellhound made me uneasy. He'd been fast and strong and if I was truly honest with myself, he could have mopped the floor with me. The only way I got in one strike was out of trickery.

Knowing I was so powerless here made me feel desperate in a way I hadn't felt in years. In those days, I'd self-medicated my way out of that emotion with whatever I could find. Booze and drugs and even mindless, emotionless sex tossed a heavy canvas tarp over the gaping chasm, allowing me to pretend it wasn't there.

Gideon had brought me out of that, giving me purpose even if I'd had to dog him for years to finally agree to train me. Becoming a hunter had at least built a ladder from the hole and given me a reason to climb out. Even then, it had taken years and a lot of bottoming out to finally ascend. The chasm was still there, though. The tarp at the surface secured by tent pegs waiting for a buffeting wind to either blow it away or yank the ropes taut.

That wind had come, it seemed. I couldn't meet this challenge on my own. Now was the time to test the security of those pegs. I was years away from that time in my life. Surely, I was strong enough. And if I wasn't, it wouldn't matter. I'd be long dead before the withdrawal kicked in.

With hands that trembled, I brought the vape to my lips. There were two mechanisms to the inhaler. I could suck in the hit, inhaling it into my lungs or use the button that deployed a tiny needle beneath my tongue. It would take mere seconds that way for the magic to slither through my veins and spread throughout my body.

It wasn't until my cheeks tightened with excitement that I realized I wasn't just talking myself into using. I wanted it. And by then, I'd already deployed the button. The corner of my eyes pooled with tears. I told myself it was just once. Things weren't going to be the way they were. The ache to use was just an old cell memory rising to the surface, and that wasn't going to matter in a few moments.

A sharp sting dug itself soundlessly beneath my tongue. For a second, I just stared ahead, unable to do more than watch the door as the drug greased my muscles, my brain, and my adrenal glands.

With a sense of belated euphoria, I found myself sliding down the chair until my butt met the floor. Some part of me thought this was odd, that the hit shouldn't be this strong. Maybe I'd taken too much, or the pen hadn't been calibrated correctly.

My head dropped back as some part of me floated to the ceiling. The hum of fragrant air brushed against my skin as a spot of dirt on the wall caught my attention.

I was still staring at it when someone waved a hand in front of my face.

I blinked. Then again because the first one felt far too long, and I wasn't sure I hadn't fallen asleep for a moment. It occurred to me that I wasn't just sitting on the floor anymore with the chair behind me, propping me up. I'd collapsed to the side and had sagged onto my ribs. A puddle of drool lay beneath my cheek.

Most decidedly not my usual high. But it was clear that at some point, I'd either passed out or zoned out. Whichever it was, the result was that I'd not been aware enough to know when someone had entered the room. I didn't even know how long I'd lain there. And that made all the alarm bells clang at once. That was not the Bloodmist I was used to. For a second, I cursed Gideon, thinking he'd dosed me with something different, a new drug, maybe even a regular old dose of heroine or something.

I moved jerkily to get up, sliding my hands beneath me to roll onto my knees, the peculiar, yet familiar, sensation of smoke roiling through my veins had begun at the very core of my body. So. Bloodmist after all, even if the effects were a bit late in coming.

I teetered on weak knees, swaying back and forth at a rate that had me grappling for the wall to steady myself.

"She wakes," Terran said to someone standing just out of my view.

I grimaced toward the floor so that he wouldn't see the rage in my eye. My chest burned with it so hot I knew he'd feel scorched from it. My heart rate had already sped up. The magic in my system threading its way through my veins like roots from a weed, fast and invasive. Anticipation flowered in my chest, that I wasn't completely at a disadvantage here anymore, that I might be able to stand up to him, stand against him, bring him and his cartel the fuck down.

Relief, too, that I'd not taken a hit of something that might put me completely out of commission. I just had to get up first. Then they'd feel my wrath.

"What did he do to her?" came a second voice, one that stopped me dead.

Stone's voice. I swiveled my head toward it. His hands were crossed over his chest and he was peering down at me with an expression of concern.

I stomped down on the rising adrenaline that begged me to fight and fight now. I wasn't about to waste the hit on Terran when I wasn't sure how strong the alliance with Stone was. And I was still trying to focus, dammit. What in the hell had Gideon put in the Bloodmist?

"I'm fine," I said.

I attempted a wave of dismissal, but neither of them, not the hard-faced Terran nor the furrow-browed Stone gave any indication that they believed me.

"Really," I said. "I'm fine." Were the words slurred, I wondered, or was it just that my hearing had grown muffled, because that was not a side-effect.

The muscles near Stone's earlobe whitened. "You should have told Blade not to hurt her."

Terran's arm shot out so fast, I barely caught the blur of motion before Stone arched backward from the force of it on his cheek. The sound of it striking him was loud enough it made me jump.

"When you are Don Sidhe, you make the decisions," Terran growled. "Until then, do not question me. At any rate, this is not Blade's work," Terran said. "Your mortal, it appears, has done this to herself."

I lifted a hand in the air, waggling my fingers at Stone. "The mortal is right here," I said. "She can hear you."

Terran leaned over, his eyes glinting like chunks of ice. "Can she, now?" he asked. "Can she also get up?"

I sucked the back of my teeth. "Just you watch."

By then, the magic had indeed unfurled into my muscles. With a swift movement, I flipped over and onto my feet, somersaulting to stand in front of him, grinning like an idiot at how smoothly my body worked. An uncommon grace had taken hold, one I knew well, a preternatural keenness of senses that made him look almost too bright. Much better. Now, that was the Bloodmist I knew and loved.

Oh, they lived on borrowed time and had no idea. I was already imagining the multiple ways I was going to kill them. Each play behind my eyelids pulled the stupid grin upward higher.

Terran's eyes narrowed as he scanned me. "What magic is this?"

I shrugged. "Nothing but the magic of wanting this to be over."

I blinked. This time three times. Everything in the room was too sharp. The lights were too bright. My mind began roaming through strategies like a machine, too fast for me to keep up and I had the feeling my eyes were ratcheting like a woman suffering the effects of vertigo.

But along with the glaringly powerful senses, came a thousand different scenarios, and I sorted through them in record time to find one that seemed most promising.

The cursed objects. I'd forgotten them in the fray and the chaos.

I gathered my feet under me. Let them make of me at the moment what they wanted. Better to show them the real Ava Ashe, the one who could give a shit about her own life, who was afraid of no one, who was so excommunicated from her family that they wouldn't even take a simple phone call from her.

That version of Ava wasn't afraid to take a risk. She knew her skills, what they were, how to use them, and they didn't lie in seduction.

That version, unlike the pathetic creature who went along with a ridiculous Plan B was good at Plan A. She knew how to kill. It was the thing that salved her wounds and helped her sleep at night. What did it matter if it was a king or a kraken? Fae king or Fae warlord?

And there was one other thing in this realm that could give me an edge besides the Bloodmist. An equally magical edge that might even the playing field.

"I want the dark objects," I said, addressing Terran. "I know you have them." I thought of the mirror he'd used to show me Kit. I knew that was the least of the magics contained in that pouch.

His eyes narrowed. "And why would I give them to you?"

I cracked my neck as I regarded him, the drug making me bolder than normal. "You want the king dead, don't you?"

He brushed at his trousers too fastidiously. "It's why you're here, but I fail to see how giving a mortal access to black magic can accomplish that task."

With a shuttered gaze, I watched his reactions. Something bothered him about those objects.

"You said you needed the king to commit violence. There's no way he's going to do that if he knows the magic will backfire on the perpetrator. Those things I took from Lilah are regular items, are they not? He'll never know what sort of violence he's doing until he triggers the curse."

I almost had him. I could sense it the way a hound senses a rabbit nearby.

"You don't need to give me all of them," I pressed. "Stone can educate me on what they do, see if any of them will be useful, and I can find a way to put it into the king's possession. Surely one of them has the sort of magic needed to kill." I thought of the ring that made the poor grade school kid try to kill his teacher. "At least let me look at them. If none are worth pursuing, we can drop the issue and go with your Plan B."

And I'd get a good cataloging of the magic so I could bring down the whole damned cartel. But I didn't say that. I barely let myself think it, just in case one of these bastards could read my mind.

Terran's jaw ticked sideways. He wasn't used to being ordered about. I thought he was going to protest, so before he could speak up or decide I needed to be punished again for my insolence, I pointed at Stone, steeling my spine and hoping for an ally.

"What harm can be done in me looking?" I went on, pushing just a little harder. "He'll be right there with me."

Oh, the glory of Bloodmist's invincibility.

Both Terran's and Stone's eyebrows climbed to their hairlines. I waited, wordless until Terran rolled his shoulders with authority. I all but smiled to myself at the expected reaction. He was a cliché I'd murder like a writer murders her darlings the moment I got the chance.

In the end, Terran eyed me up and down with a ruthless assessment.

"Stone has become too soft," he said, implying I was the reason his son had lost his edge. "I'm not sure he can be trusted to keep his ladle out of the soup when things get too hot." He grinned with both extended canines showing. "And since my boys take after me physically in that department, I'm not sure he'll have enough brain power to reason his way out of any trouble."

It was such a ridiculous and awkward attempt at euphemism that I couldn't help snorting. "I'm guessing since you can reason well enough to run an entire crime syndicate, that you don't get much action in that department." I cocked my head at him. "I'm sorry to hear that."

His mouth twitched, and I thought he was going to lose his steely cool, but then he laughed and slapped the table before turning that cold gaze on me once more. I felt the regard powerfully enough to hasten to fill the silence.

"You already showed me what would happen if I double crossed you," I said. "I'm not going to take the chance. I just want my sister safe and I want out." I cut the air with my hand as I drew it across my chest.

Terran shook his head. "The objects are not up for discussion."

I ran a hand over the back of my neck, drawing his eye to the scar that snaked its way around my throat. "I'm sure Blade has already informed you how well the seduction went."

"You're acting as though this is a negotiation, Ms. Ashe," he said. "There is no request on the table. Just an order."

I ran my hand over the back of my neck where it had gone clammy. "Plan B is a ridiculous strategy when the assassin is more killer than seductress. It's best I use Plan A if possible. Like you wanted in the first place."

This last said so he'd feel as though I'd grudgingly given him some respect.

"You want this done right, you'll give me the objects. You're the one who said we need to create opportunity." I could almost hear Gideon's voice in my head as I pressed forward, my neck clammy and wet. "Give me what I need to make sure nothing goes wrong."

I took a step closer. It was a risk. One step might appear threatening or confident. It was also a test. Did they trust me or would they react?

My breath caught in my throat as I waited to see what the Don Sidhe of the Shadow Court would do to me.

Chapter 18

MAGIC CHARGED THE AIR like a distress signal, surging through my veins. Someone was going to die here, was my first thought.

Instinctively, my fists clenched tightly at my sides, my entire being attuned to the minute details of the moment. The caress of air against my cheeks, the distinct scent of Terran's breath, the subtle tensing of Stone's shoulders—all of it glided through my consciousness like well-oiled gears spinning with an almost frantic speed.

In the charged air, a profound silence settled between us, brimming with tension. I'd lost. Whatever reasoning I had, a credit to the Bloodmist coursing through my veins wasn't enough. Not here. Not with beings who wielded magic like mortal lungs used breath.

Then, the incredible happened. Just when I thought the magic would crackle through me, punishing me for my insolence the way it had in the cellars, a weary sigh escaped the Don-Sidhe's lips.

A sign, a glimmer of hope that I had almost swayed him. I couldn't let that flicker fade away.

"If you trust Blade more than Stone in this case, then let your dark enforcer handle them," I said, attempting to infuse a casual tone into my voice that belied the turmoil tearing up my stomach. "It doesn't matter to me. As long as I find out if their magic can help me do what you need."

Terran tapped the sides of his legs with his fingers, his eyes narrowing as he considered my words. He glanced at Stone again, his expression caught between contemplation and hesitation.

The silence dragged on, stretching like a taut string pulled to its limit. And then, with a deliberate slowness, Terran nodded. It was a subtle movement, almost imperceptible, but it carried a world of significance. Relief flooded through me, mingling with a tinge of apprehension.

"Go ask Mica to retrieve the stash," he said, his voice laced with authority. "And while you're at it, fetch Blade as well. I want to know exactly what he did to our assassin that she'd rather trust a black object's magic than her own cunning."

His gaze bore into mine, holding a challenge and a warning. The intensity of his scrutiny sent a shiver down my spine. I had the feeling that whatever he planned to ask of Blade, it would have been preferable for me to have just tried to seduce the dark enforcer.

As Stone exited the room, the space between Terran and me crackled with an electric tension. Time slowed, suspended in the charged atmosphere, until Stone returned, trailed by a younger fae.

Mica, with his ash-colored hair and piercing gaze reminiscent of Terran's, entered with a guarded demeanor. Unlike the others, his frame was lean and lithe, lacking the bulk of sinewy muscle. His eyes, dark as obsidian, flickered in my direction while his body angled subtly, showcasing the ornate golden embroidery adorning his shirt.

He stood out like a relic from a medieval tournament. His clothing adorned with an array of jewelry, each piece emitting a delicate tinkling sound as he moved.

Stone approached, his arms cradling a chest made of oak wood. He carefully placed it on a nearby table. A sizable blacksteel lock held it securely shut, far more substantial than necessary for its dimensions. After all, I'd carried the whole kit and caboodle in a small pouch from Lilah's lair.

The room hummed with an undercurrent of anticipation.

"I had to ask Stone to carry the chest, Father," Mica explained, his hand resting atop the lid as he faced Terran. "It was too heavy for me."

Terran's exasperation was palpable, punctuating the sharp glare he directed at his son. "By the gods, Mica, it's not a block of cement; it's a simple box. I would have thought you could handle it."

Mica visibly shrank beneath his cloak, and a surge of protectiveness welled up within me. I longed to lash out at Terran, but I bit my tongue, choosing silence instead. No good could come from getting involved with fae family drama when I had my own to deal with. Even so, that crestfallen look seared itself beneath my eyelids.

Terran cast a meaningful glance towards the door, his irritation evident. "And Blade?" he asked in an impatient tone. "Where is he?"

Stone shrugged, as if to convey his lack of control over the dark enforcer. Terran emitted a disgruntled hum from deep within his throat. "If he wasn't so damn useful, I'd be inclined to punish his insolence."

His attention shifted to the chest, then, almost as if he'd already decided Blade was too far gone to consider berating and that the chest was more important than wasting his breath on the dark enforcer. With a swift jerk, he ran his palm over the lock and yanked back the lid to peer inside. I couldn't help but flinch at the abruptness of his movement, feeling as though I stood in the presence of a fragile bomb in the hands of a bomb disposal team with a death wish.

"We'll make sure the trove is returned to the pouch we took it from so it's easier to transport," he said, inclining his head toward the door as a shadow invaded the outline. "Took you long enough," he remarked.

Though he attempted nonchalance, a deep swallow betrayed his true emotions—a subtle gesture that I alone seemed to notice amidst the tension-filled room. I slid my gaze to the dark enforcer. Blade seemed to note Terran's reaction with the tiniest pull of his lip toward the left side. He crossed his arms over his chest, his gaze darting to me and back to his father.

"I was busy," he said in a clipped tone.

I expected Terran to comment, but instead he jerked his chin toward Mica.

"You have training to tend to," he told the young fae. "Go do it. Your natal magics need honing."

Mica pouted like a teenager, but he finally shoved his way sullenly past Blade, whose gaze followed him from the room like an indulgent parent. The moment the dark enforcer saw me watching him, he straightened his spine and pulled down a neutral mask over his expression.

But I'd seen. He cared about that boy. My mouth twitched in thought. Ammunition, perhaps?

Once Mica had distanced himself enough from the room, Blade exchanged a subtle nod with Terran, indicating that it was now safe to speak. So. One more bit of intel. That boy was not part of the cartel.

Terran cleared his throat. He regarded the box with his hands in his pockets for a long moment. No one in the room moved. I wasn't sure anyone was even breathing. I know I held my breath, and not just because I was afraid of what the boss was going to say.

Those objects had been held securely in a leather sack the whole time they'd been in my possession. There had been a lot of them, too many to hold in one small pouch, and yet they'd fit. It led me to suspect that the sack itself had been enchanted, potentially safeguarding their magic and preventing any unintended consequences.

I'd not seen them up close. I didn't even know how many there were or what their specific curses were. Terran's willingness to handle them indicated that he either possessed knowledge about them or possessed a remarkable recklessness towards self-preservation that could only come from a man confident he possessed more power.

I doubted he was foolish enough to unleash them so recklessly, but I braced myself just the same.

After he delved into the box and rummaged around for a bit, he pulled out a familiar-looking bit of material, holding it up by the golden strings as he shook it at me. I couldn't help blowing out a breath of relief when nothing more happened than a bit of dust cascading to the table.

He passed the sack to the dark enforcer. "Blade will explain what each of them does. He knows the magics of each item." He fixed me with a long, hard, cold stare, then. "I'm sure I don't have to remind you that Flint has become very familiar with your sister."

Familiar. Meaning he knew her every move. My jaw tightened as I tried to answer without showing the full force of my hatred. I held his gaze until he rolled his shoulders beneath the expensive suit until I could school my tone into something appropriately submissive.

"I'm pretty sure I got the message when you had your enforcer murder my friend."

He grunted, but didn't reveal his thoughts through any shift in expression. "We have no more than a couple of weeks before the End of Days Endowment begins," he said, raking me with a naked look of assessment before turning to Blade. "If we are going with a mix of Plan A and B, then she'll need to get fitted." When he eyed me again, it was with a look of displeasure. "Our glamor will not be enough to cover that."

I peered down at my tank top and yoga pants, the boot toes looking clunky against the parquet floor. I didn't feel the least bit offended. If I was less than his idea of a seductress, then that was his problem. It even gave me a bit of satisfaction to think he was disappointed.

I maintained a stoic gaze, devoid of emotion, as he pointed towards the armoire.

"I highly doubt that anything hidden within our closets possesses the power to transform you into Cinderella," he said. "No matter how potent the enchantment may be."

"I was under the impression you needed a chick who could use a glass slipper to slit the prince's throat," I said coolly. "Not fuck him with it."

A short, darkly indulgent chuckle came from Blade's direction.

"We might have need of a chick who can do both," Terran said, putting emphasis on the echo of my words as the corner of his lip curled back to suggest how he felt about the crassness of my comment. Satisfaction settled into my belly with all the pleasure of a warm chocolate chip cookie that I'd been able to get under his skin.

A quick, half-smirk played over Blade's face and disappeared. "Erachne," he said with an air of finality, as though that one word possessed incredible power.

It didn't seem to strike Stone as a solution. Instead, he made his doubts known with a snort of disdain. So loud every eye in the room turned to him.

He met each gaze with a shrug. "You've all lost your minds if you think Ava should go to Erachne."

The crimson serpentine patterns in Blade's irises resurfaced as he retorted, "You have a better suggestion?"

Stone looked to his father, who was thumbing his lip as though contemplating something dicey. I watched it all with mounting curiosity.

With a somber tone that sent a shiver down my spine, Stone turned to his father. "Allow me to fetch Erachne here," he said.

His father put three fingers to his forehead and rubbed his hairline thoughtfully. "Erachne is not fetched, Stone," he said. "Not by anyone or anything. You should know that."

"Bribe her then," he said, inching closer, as if proximity alone could bridge the distance between their opposing suggestions. The comment was a shuddering echo of a Godfather line that wrapped a clammy fist around my chest and squeezed.

Terran fixed Stone with a lingering gaze, his hands interlacing behind his neck, elbows pushed forward. A sigh escaped his lips, carrying an air of resignation that failed to thaw the chill in my core.

"You don't lure a spider with honey," he remarked, his voice carrying the weight of experience. "You trap her with flies. Ava must go to her."

"There's no need to send Ava on the Shadow Trail when there are plenty of quality seamstresses right here," Stone said, and his expression was an example of complete composure so absolute, I knew he was mastering any small twitch that might give away his thoughts. But I saw the way he grazed the side of his trousers with a curled fist, and I knew that in his way, he was fighting for me.

A snort came from Blade's general direction. "Hell of an assassin you picked, Stone, if you can't trust her to ride the Shadow Trail."

I held my tongue, morbidly curious to know what dangers he thought a seamstress might pose that would make him butt heads with his boss. Stone fixed his gaze on Blade with a look that froze my blood.

"You and I both know the Shadow Trail is not for the faint of heart, Fae or not. And it's certainly no place for mortals. She'll be dead before she can even begin."

Chapter 19

BLOOD ROSE TO MY cheeks, flushing them with anger at Stone's words. Just how weak did he think I was, anyway? I had the vague thought that the rage was coming from the sudden fuel of the Bloodmist, and that if Stone was worried about this Shadow Trail, then reason suggested I give him a listen. But it was too late. I was already storming toward him, fully intending to get in his face and argue that I most certainly could travel wherever the hell I wanted. I was no weak, shy, wilting petunia.

"If you don't think I have the balls, Stone," I ground out with the stupid drug ratcheting up my pique to far past cocaine level aggression. "Then maybe you should have black-mailed Gideon to do your dirty work."

Oh, the Bloodmist was roiling now. I actually hoped Stone would try me. The three of them were right there. I'd have to take out all three, sure, but—

Blade scooped me neatly by the elbow as I sped past him, holding me back from Stone. Terran fixed his attention on the dark enforcer's hand on my arm and his mouth twitched to the side. That infuriated me more.

I snapped my elbow back into the dark enforcer's stomach. For an instant, I tasted the smug tang of satisfaction, but that quickly soured as my bone met rigid muscle. I smothered the wince of pain and fixed my gaze on Stone because I did not want to see Blade's face right then.

Stone simply shook his head. "You don't get it, Ava." He directed a hateful look at Blade. "He suggested Erachne because he wants to get rid of me, even if it takes you out in the process."

Blade laughed, a humorless sound. "You flatter yourself that I care what happens to you."

Stone turned to Terran. "You know we've lost high Fae on the Shadow Trail."

"It's the only way to get to Erachne," Terran countered. He crossed one ankle lazily over the other.

"Would you let Blade sabotage this plan, Father?" Stone said, his voice low. "Let me fetch Erachne here to us. I'll use whatever means we have to convince her—"

I snorted. "Meaning blackmail."

He pinched the bridge of his nose. "You don't get it, Ava—"

"I'll go."

The words clung to the air with nails of iron and it took a few seconds for everyone to realize it was Blade who'd spoken them. All eyes turned to him.

He shrugged, a lazy moment that didn't match the unearthly glint in his eyes as he raked me head to heel in a way that made my spine tense up. "I'll take her."

As surprised as I was to hear this solution, it seemed to enrage Stone. His eyes flashed with a mix of anger and frustration. The cords in his neck were rigid columns of granite as his throat worked to form what I presumed was going to be a hot retort. Didn't matter. I wasn't about to let him stand up for me. I didn't need it. Not from him. Not from anyone.

"Wherever the hell it is, just send me already," I said, without a hint of false bravery. "I can hold my own."

Stone fixed me with a steely, angry glare. "You have no idea what's out there, Ava. Magic is part of the equation here. It will always be. And you don't have it. Hell, if you'd have been able to hold your own against a group of Fae with even a little bit of magic, you'd not be standing here."

"You know why I'm here," I ground out.

"Enough," Terran said, cutting Stone off. "Erachne needs to see her to fit her. She's going."

When Stone's eye landed on me, they softened with what appeared to be sympathy. "But she can't ride, Father."

"I can ride better than he can."

Terran canted his head at me thoughtfully until Stone cut the air with a flat palm, indicating I shouldn't argue.

"She's talking about riding a motorized contraption. Not horseback." He measured me with a studious glance. "I don't think she's ever sat a horse."

Terran ran a hand through his hair. "Admittedly, that will make things more difficult." With one hand shoved into his pocket and the other held in the air, thumb running over his fingers thoughtfully, he began pacing the room. "She needs to go. The Shadow Trail can't be done on foot." He pivoted sharply to skim me with a final glance. "She'll just have to ride tandem."

Stone's face paled. Whatever bothered him about that scenario also made Blade's cocky grin grow wider. "I see where this is going," the dark enforcer said and leaned against the door frame, hooking one foot over the other as he regarded Stone with a cool eye.

I blinked, realizing with horror what was about to be suggested. "You're not about to ask that I ride with Blade? On the same horse?"

Terran cut me off with a glare. "I'm not asking anything," he said. "I'm telling you. If you can't ride on your own, then you'll have to travel with the dark enforcer. And if you can't ride at all, you'll ride with him. We don't have time to dawdle with a novice rider. Plus," he went on. "Blade is better equipped to face the dangers of the trail than Stone, and I'll not have my Consul risking himself and my entire cabal for a mortal woman's safety."

The suggestion in the words was clear. Stone was indispensable, while Blade was not. I stole a peek at Blade to see his reaction, but he merely unhooked his ankles and straightened his spine, stretching along the door frame like a serpent uncoiling.

Stone caught me watching and tried once more to protest. Terran cut him off before he got more than a single syllable out. "It's done, Stone," he said. "Blade will guide her along the Shadow Trail to Erachne's cottage. They will find a gown befitting the opening gala, and they will return. If she survives, we'll know she's well-suited to her task. If not…" He let the rest trail away and didn't need to fill in any detail.

I was still trying to find a good argument to side with Stone when Terran turned on his heel and headed to the door. Stone followed close on his heels as though he intended to argue the point further. He paused, however, as Terran crossed the threshold and his fingers curled around the blacksteel knob of the door handle. With a gaze that slid from my face to Blade's in a pointed expression, he said, "Be on your guard, Ava. The Shadow Trail won't be the only danger you face on the road."

In a rush of movement that was all air and darkness that even the Bloodmist couldn't see through, Blade had Stone pinned to the wall by his throat. I was sure I heard the sound of Stone slamming into the wall before I saw him being propelled into it. A dip in the plaster haloed his head and crackled the wall at least a foot in each direction.

I'd not seen the dark enforcer move, just felt a brush of air and the swallow of shadow. No one but me moved at first at the sight of Stone's booted feet dangling a foot from the tiled floor. His face was suffused with red.

The only part of Blade that showed was his back and a knot of muscles at the base of his neck that indicated the force of the strength it took to hold Stone in the air.

"You all but gave her to me just hours ago," Blade growled into Stone's face. "You expected me to take her and use her in ways no male should, just to see if she could withstand it all long enough to drive a cursed blade into my throat." He hoisted Stone higher along the door.

"That's what you expected, isn't it, brother? You thought she'd kill me for you?"

CHAPTER 20

I should have been horrified by the words, but I wasn't. All I felt was the pounding of my heartbeat racing away between my ears as I watched Stone struggle to breathe beneath Blade's grip. His hands grappled for Blade's so ineffectually, he might have been a worm squirming beneath a raven's claw. I tried to tell myself rage was responsible for the increased pulse but with each kick of Stone's heels into the door, I flinched. My hand went to my neck. A sudden wash of black shadow wiped into my vision from the sides. I felt altogether too clammy.

It took an effort of sheer will to push back against the panic. I dropped my gaze from Stone's ever-widening eyes and said, "I don't need to feel threatened to want to kill you," I said to Blade. "I would happily cut all your throats."

A sound came from Stone that drew my eye to him. Sadness met my gaze. Sadness and something that spoke of sudden and unexpected loss. I thought I knew what it might be, and the realization nearly floored me.

"Oh my God," I said. "You bullied me into coming here and expected me to deliver my pussy to some age old Fae who, according to Blade here, would be as happy to chew my head off as drive his dick inside me." I barked out a harsh laugh. "You hold my sister hostage and threaten her life, and you think what? That I'm going to go all Patty Hearst on you and fall for that bastard?" I pointed at Blade.

Stone sagged against the wall, Blade's grip loosening, it seemed, just enough for him to speak.

"I don't know who that is," Stone said in a tight, constricted voice. "But we aren't all the bastards you think."

"No," Blade drawled, leaning in close enough to Stone's face that he could have bitten his nose off. "Just me, right? The black sheep. The hellhound shifter who takes mortal lovers and then tears their throats out at the Don's order."

Blade looked back at me over his shoulder and what I saw in his face actually did horrify me. He barely looked like a man, let alone a Fae male. I took a step backwards in reflex before I realized what I was doing. Seeing it, something moved in Blade's eyes again, and the feral look softened. He snorted, and dropped Stone to the floor.

"Too fucking cowardly to admit what you wanted," he said in a voice laced with disgust. "Some things never change."

He turned all the way around, putting his back to Stone in a way that suggested he had zero fear of attack from behind. Maybe he was even hoping Stone would try something. Whatever his intent, my eyes fixed on him, curious and horrified at the same time because the drug weaving its way around my veins was telling me I'd missed something, something that made Blade's reaction to Stone even more shocking.

Stone stumbled and caught himself by grabbing the door handle and I was sure his knees buckled. Just a bit. Enough that when his gaze flicked to mine, and he knew I'd seen it, he lifted his chin. Defiant. My own hand ran to my neck and whispered across the scar that reminded me just how difficult it was to hold fast to belligerence when you couldn't breathe.

Whatever I thought of him then, it wasn't cowardice. I knew it down to my marrow. Blade seemed to sense it because he wouldn't let it go. Like a dog with a meaty bone, he kept gnawing away, as though he wanted to show everyone just how nice a chew it all was and couldn't imagine we didn't want a taste.

"It seems your vanilla Fae lover didn't think you would endure my affections, Ponytail. In fact, it seems he was hoping I'd try to rape you."

I caught Stone rubbing at his neck with his hand and staring hard at the back of Blade's head. The bald hatred in his face was enough to make me furrow my brow. Something wasn't right here. I just didn't know what it was. Hatred that deep and pure should propel Stone at Blade, not have him standing there rigid and brooding.

Blade ran his thumb across his throat in a slicing motion. "He wanted you to kill me. He thought even though my father was clear in his orders to merely teach you what to expect from the king, Stone here thought

I'd bully my way between your legs." He prowled the room toward me, his eyes steadier on me than Stone's were behind him. "He thinks I'm an old-fashioned Fae, don't you Stone?"

"I think you're a bastard," Stone said in a strangled voice, his gaze never wavering from that spot on Blade's head. "She would never let you touch her. She'd die first."

"Were you that ready to sacrifice her, brother?" Blade said, his gaze hooded as he regarded me. "Do you hate me that much that you would offer your pretty mortal to me, hoping she had the balls you don't?"

I blinked. Canted my head. The words roiled about my mind, collecting into the bottom of the sieve like gold nuggets.

"Brother," I whispered, trying to sort through the entire cache without losing one piece.

Blade's eyebrow arched. "Oh yes, Ponytail. Brother. I'm surprised it took you so long to see the resemblance."

Stone flinched at the term, and I knew it was true. Impossible as it was, they were brothers. My mind reeled back to all the comments he'd made about family, trying to figure out if I should have figured it out earlier, but all I could hear in my memory was him confessing to having three brothers. Mica. Flint. He'd never named the third.

"Oh my sweet fuck," I said, inching away as I did my best to hold on to all the information without losing one bit to shock.

Blade met me step for step until I edged into the back of the table and halted. He stopped just short of touching me. The heated scent of cinnamon coiled about me.

"Still think you escorting her to Erachne is a good idea, Stone?" he said, huffing out a chuckle as he watched every play of emotion I felt moving over my face. "I'm pretty sure, based on the loathing in her eyes that you'd never reach the outer markers before she slits your throat and runs for a portal."

I tried to shrug, to show a casualness about it all that would distract him from my very authentic desire to do just that to all of them. "Not to show favoritism here," I said, "but I'm not picky about who I kill at this point."

A smile tugged at Blade's lips. "I'm hurt," he said, leaning in enough to inhale. Deeply. "I had hopes you'd try me first."

I held his eye, even knowing…knowing he was taking my scent. With a swallow, I said, "Don't worry. I'll get to you all eventually."

"I don't doubt it, Ponytail, but what you fail to understand is that you are severely outmatched even with Stone. Much as I hate to admit it, he had the right idea testing you with me. I have very specific tastes in mortal women, and for him to offer you to me like a head on a silver platter…well, let's just say, he should be very happy you didn't try to slit my throat."

"You will die one day, Blade," Stone said, his voice unaffected by emotion, but I could see how tight his throat was by the way the veins stood out on his neck. "One day, you will do or say the wrong thing, and Father will remove you from this world and every other."

Blade smiled, a long, languid, terrifying smile. "Are you challenging me, brother? Because I would so love that." His shoulders squared. His head tilted not enough to lose its bead on my gaze but enough to indicate he would take up Stone's challenge if it was offered. Stone's fists uncurled as he gave a brief shake of his head. Blade huffed.

"I thought not," he said.

Stone's gaze flicked to me and back to Blade again. "Too much is at stake right now, Blade. Ava might be mortal, but she's nothing like the other human whores you favor in your mortal world. I'm sure you've noticed that already. She'll fight you like a hell cat."

Blade studied me, the heat in his gaze making me feel more naked than if I was nude. "A more perfect match was never made, then, I'd say."

His gaze fell to my throat, and it was entirely too intense. I wanted to squirm beneath it, like a bug on a hot plate. Just when I thought I might give in to the urge, he waved his hand at Stone in dismissal.

"We'll try her on Nutkin," he said. "Make sure the stable boy has him fed and watered. I'll tack him myself. If she can stay seated without him killing her, we'll travel by road instead of the Shadow Trail. Does that satisfy you?"

Stone said nothing, and the tension mounted until it was a knot in the air, squeezing so hard I had to get away or lose my breath. I had too much information already to process. So much, my brain was short-circuiting trying to unravel it all and sort it into bite-sized pieces. The Bloodmist was making my skin itch.

"I need a drink or something," I mumbled, and Blade gestured toward the bathroom.

"Go," he said. "But make it quick. We set out in ten minutes."

I fled to the bathroom without feeling the least bit ashamed for running. Standing before the massive gilt mirror, my arms hanging at my sides, I examined my reflection.

I looked the same. My black hair fell over one shoulder. Several frizzy looking knots here and there were testament to the fact I'd not had a chance to comb it properly. The scar on my throat stood out as ugly as ever, maybe even more so. Here in Fae, it had taken on a worm like quality instead of its regular road rash appearance.

But I could see the glint in my eye, the spark that told me something was going on inside my mind, something I might not have let slip by if my misted brain hadn't been so busy taking in everything in an effort to assess a threat where there was none. An overload of data that would need processing at some point, the most important coming to the fore and the rest buried beneath a shroud of linen for later unwrapping.

Stone and Blade hated each other. That wasn't any newer information than I'd gained since the moment I'd first seen them together. What was surprising was that I sensed something else in that information that the mist had stored away because, while it wasn't an immediate threat, it was most definitely a threat.

I blinked and kept my eyes closed, wiping out all visual sense as I filtered through all the bank of information. It took a moment, but it was there, hiding behind a rock nestled over the opening of a dark cave in my subconscious.

I wasn't surprised that Stone had used me, thinking Blade would assault me and that I'd fight back because I was a hunter and that would be my natural inclination, even if I had no chance of winning. I actually felt pretty chuffed that he'd presumed I had the ability to take on the dark enforcer at all.

And as shocking as it was to check the basket of the filter and discover the two were brothers, that wasn't the thing that caught the Bloodmist's attention, because it wasn't something that would register as a threat. I'd also known that Blade enjoyed mortal women. I'd seen it with my own eyes in the bathroom of the Velvet Boar. Jasmine had trusted him. She'd liked him enough to offer herself to him, and yet by Blade's own admission, he was an old Fae. Had she known old Fae treating their human lovers like the mates of a preying mantis or a black-widow spider? Would she have given herself to him so easily? I'd never know.

What I did know, and what was truly itching the skin beneath my scalp, wasn't that Blade loved mortal women, or devoured them when he was done.

It was that Stone knew this.

He'd made it clear that he loathed that quality in Blade. When he'd compared it to the king's penchant for human women, he'd indicated it was a perversion. He was disgusted by it.

And yet, he'd given me every impression that he was attracted to me. That he wanted me.

And if he thought that was a perversion, then he was faking that interest in me and my safety. Making a grand show for his father's sake. For Blade's. And if he was willing to do that, then whatever machinations he was moving about like pawns on a chess board when even his own father wasn't aware he was manipulating things, then he was more of a threat than Blade.

Chapter 21

If the thought of traveling the Shadow Trail was supposed to frighten me, I was horrified by the sight of the ride we'd be taking. With a broad nose and hooves the size of a Clydesdale's, I might have thought I was on a mortal farm, standing in front of a workhorse but for the fire red eyes that danced in their sockets as they sighted me.

Facing a beast so big was frightening enough until I stood next to it and it reared back, rolling its eyes at me as though I'd planned to slit its throat. Which was impossible. I didn't think I could reach its shoulder, let alone lay a blade against it. Not that I wouldn't have tried after it nearly scared the ghost out of me.

Moments before Blade had led me to the monstrous beast's stall, I'd donned the duster jacket and pocketed a bit of soap from the bathroom in case I needed to wash my hands of blood or grime along the way. Smoothed out my hair. I didn't know what Fae bled, but some monsters I'd met had noxious fluids that, if ingested, acted like poison. I felt the lump of that soap against my ribs as I squared my shoulders and promptly headed to the door of the stable. Out of reach of that massive beast and the hellhound shifter tacking him.

The city sprawled out around the paddock. Gardens and dirt roads petered out and turned to flagstone and smooth stone buildings all the way to a thick cluster of cottages surrounding a large wall, and beyond to a glistening white castle atop a sharp hill. I was sure I could follow the sight of the huge white castle hemmed in by glistening white stone without having to climb up on a horse. Presuming that's what the beast was. I had my doubts.

"Where are you going?" Blade said from behind me, the first words he'd spoken directly to me since Stone had left and we'd packed for the journey. A few apples and pears and a large loaf of hardy, crust-laden bread wrapped around a hunk of ripened cheese. A few raisins and a large skin of wine.

I ignored him. If I couldn't kill him, I certainly wasn't going to make idle chitchat. The flash of image of the things he'd done to Jasmine still shot through my eyelids when I closed them too long.

"I asked where you were going." A bark of a command that made me spin around. My lip curled with revulsion as I realized I couldn't keep my mouth shut after all. A glob of manure smeared beneath my boot. Pursing my lips to keep from cursing, I gestured wildly past the stable door to the city beyond.

"If you want to know where I'm going, then track me," I said. "You're a hellhound."

It was petty, but I didn't care. I scraped my boot on a chopping block and then pivoted in the straw. I made for the door without looking back, showing him the full span of my back.

He was behind me long before I sensed him there. "I could track you," he drawled. "But I'm fresh out of your blood. Care to offer some?"

A brush of warm air washed over my neck as his nose roamed the side of my throat. Without thinking, my elbow shot into his stomach in a reactionary movement that I regretted the moment it met hard muscle. I tried not to show my surprise when he barely let go a short exhale.

Even if I could have stopped him from grasping me by the shoulders and spinning me around, I wouldn't have had time to do more than kick at him. Which I did, lifting my knee with a thrust that came as instinctive as the original elbow jab. I didn't hold back one bit.

But he somehow avoided the knee to the crotch and managed to wrestle me into a hold that pinned my hands behind my back and arched my chest forward. Awkward and totally off-balance to kick at him again.

My gaze skated over his frame, looking for evidence I'd hurt him. Not one sign. I pushed against him. "I'm sure you have plenty of blood from your work in the cellar."

Backing me up, he forced me against the wall by the door. With one hand…one massive and strong hand holding mine behind my back, he then placed the other palm on the door frame, penning me in.

"That wasn't my work," he said shortly, his nostrils flaring.

A bark of bitter laughter escaped me. "I seem to recall you cutting me to ribbons at the orders of your boss. I call that work."

"My father," he said, correcting me in a voice tinged with some emotion I couldn't name. "You might as well say it." He leaned into his palm, lowering his face so his mouth was near mine. A muscle in his jaw clenched. "And I seem to recall healing each scratch as soon as it broke your skin."

I glared up at him, both surprised at the revelation and angered by it. "And when you punished Jasmine for your boss, did you do the same? Were her screams just really good acting?"

His nostrils flared again, and that coppery serpent slithered around his irises again, wiping out the silver. He pushed himself off the frame of the door. Away from me.

"Get on the horse," he said. "Don't make me put you there."

"You take the horse," I said. "I'll walk."

He laughed at that. "The gods take me. You plan to walk twenty miles?"

"Twenty miles?" I stomped to the door and looked out over the city where buildings of all sorts checkered the landscape, growing closer until they reached the white stone wall that encased the castle. "It's right there. I'll take a cab."

His black eyebrows arched over the bright green and silver of his eyes and I crossed my arms over my chest.

"You're not in Manhattan now, Ponytail. You're in Fae. We aren't beholden to cold iron or technology."

"More's the pity," I said and shoved past him into the open air. I breathed in the smell of the city, so much like a mortal metropolis I could close my eyes and imagine I was home. "Seems you could use a bit of modern technology in this backwards realm."

His hand snaked out and closed around my elbow. I pulled back, automatically going into a fighting stance, hands up, eyes wide.

"There she is," he said, a glint in his eye. "The fighter Stone thinks will save us all." He chortled and crossed his arms over his chest, the muscles moving beneath his sleeves like puppies wrestling. His gaze roamed my body from top to bottom, lingering on the empty karambit sheath strapped to my thigh.

"I've been ordered to take you shopping and take you shopping I will." His eye skimmed my clothes. "Can't say I disagree with Don Sidhe. You look like an assassin."

My arms flew out to my sides, and I shot him a sarcastic glare. "Right?" I said in a mocking tone. "Imagine that."

He pivoted in the straw, gesturing over his shoulder, beckoning me back inside.

"We're not going to the city shopping. The image that the Iron City is just outside this paddock is an illusion, a twist of magic that lets us see what's happening while remaining invisible. The City of the Dead, where the safe house is located, is on the fringes of that realm, balancing there on a fulcrum so sharp it could teeter off if not leveraged with a constant stream of blood."

I stored that information, remembering my stint in the cells and understanding finally why I'd not heard any noises or that no one saw me inside the open window.

He strode to Nutkin and checked the tacking. "This stable, this paddock, it will slide back into the realm of the Iron City as smoothly as if we were already there. No one will be the wiser. If I hadn't told you, you would never notice."

I wasn't sure why he was giving me so much information, but I held it like a gem. I waited, hopeful he'd divulge more, but instead he gave a yank on the lashings of Nutkin's saddle and turned to me.

"I'm taking you to Erachne's. It's at least a day's ride. Which means two by the time we get back. There's a tavern much like the Velvet Boar right around the halfway mark. We'll stop there on the way back. You'll blend in. You'll rest and eat. We'll set out again at first light."

I was starting to feel like I'd wasted the Bloodmist. I could feel the effects surging through my tissues, and I knew the swell of the magic would evaporate soon and leave me with a hangover that would make this miserable trip even more miserable.

My very marrow was restless for a fight, and I was getting exhausted with all the data my senses kept gathering and storing and making me sort through.

My fingers roamed the pocket of the duster jacket and fell upon the inhaler. Maybe I didn't have to suffer. There was plenty of drug in the vape for a full week if I used it to just even out the effects. Keep myself topped up. Just in case. And still have some left over to take out the cartel. Once I figured out how to do that. My gaze sought the cursed object's pouch. Blade still hadn't educated me on what was in there or how to use them. We'd gotten side-tracked. But when he did—

"Tell me again why it has to be you taking me to the seamstress?" I asked, eying the horse. "And why can't it just be some shop in the city?" I ran my palms down over my pants, feeling for the karambit out of habit and finding the sheath empty. Right. They'd taken that back. "I mean...I thought we were in a hurry. Surely, an off-the-rack dress will be fine. Or something from that closet in the suite."

He tossed a blanket over Nutkin's back. "Because we need something special. And because Erachne only caters to certain clients."

"You mean Shadow Court clients?"

He dropped the saddle onto the horse's back. "I mean people she trusts. You'll find a broad selection of gowns and haberdashery to choose from."

My lips pursed at the thought of gowns and ribbons, but I was more amused at the thought that he'd used the word haberdashery.

As I watched the way he adjusted the saddle so tightly, pondering why the seamstress would trust Blade and not Stone, I caught a flash of a pink fingernail partnering the other nine fully black ones. Maybe the notion of haberdashery and gowns wasn't so foreign to him.

He finished tacking the horse and stepped aside, giving me a long, pointed look. The horse was massive, at least a head taller at his back than Blade.

"I'm not getting on that thing. It's not a horse." I pulled an elastic from my pocket that I'd found in the suite's bathroom and smoothed my hair into a bunch, twisting the elastic around it.

"Get on," Blade said as said horse swung its doe eyes to mine and dug its hoof into the straw. "Before he stomps you flat."

I started to back away, but Blade snagged my arm so fast, I didn't have time to see his hand move, let alone get out of range. "Get on," he said. "Before I stomp you flat."

"That thing isn't meant to ride," I argued. "You do realize that, right? You know it's a workhorse." I leaned sideways, out of sight of the beast, using Blade as a shield. For some reason, the thought of straddling Nutkin bothered me more than the notion of facing the Iron King.

"Get on, Ponytail, or I will throw you on."

I made a grab for the saddlebag before he could toss it over the horse's back. I'd watched him stuff the apron of dark objects in there and I wasn't leaving without it.

He yanked it back out of my grip. Maybe a little too forcefully, and I wondered if I'd actually hurt him earlier and he was no longer going to misjudge my strength. Or maybe he was just pissed.

"You realize we'll never make it in time if you walk and I ride." His chin dipped meaningfully. "Your sister's safety depends on you riding."

His tone dripped with sarcasm, but I didn't need more reminding. I got the point. A heavy sigh escaped me as I ran my gaze over the beast. It had the shape and smell of a horse, but there was something else, something 'other' about it.

"It's not going to leech my will or something, is it?" I asked with a wary eye on the way its skin seemed to shiver over its bones as it swatted a fly with its tail.

Blade rolled his eyes as he stuffed the apron of dark objects into the rucksack hanging from the beast's saddle. "He doesn't have that sort of natural magic." A half grin played with the corner of his mouth. "But I can't promise he won't throw you off."

That did it. By the time he finished and turned around to adjust the rucksack, I was already walking back toward the stable door and out into the paddock. The odor of manure and earth mixed in my nostrils, making them flare. He hadn't suggested which direction Erachne's would lie in, but I figured I had to at least clear the city gates, so I headed that way.

It must have taken him a short while to realize I hadn't just auto-obeyed him, because I had put several dozen paces behind me before I heard the sound of horse hooves pounding the dirt of the road.

CHAPTER 22

I HALF-EXPECTED HIM TO halt the horse and order me to get on, and I fell back, deciding to let him lead the way and I'd plod along behind or beside him. Because there was no way I was getting onto that monstrosity he called a horse.

That was not what happened. He scooped me, mid-step, from the ground and tucked me like a sack beneath his arm. An embarrassing squeak of surprise escaped me and when I heard it, I started to fight. I kicked back like a donkey and he leaned in the opposite direction automatically, evening out the balance point.

Infuriated and humiliated, I throttled about in his grip, sputtering all the while despite my best intentions to curse at him like a real lady.

"Fuck off already," he growled after I struck a particularly good blow to his kidney with my knee. "It's impossible to get you seated with you fighting like that."

"Then you've got the point," I said through gritted teeth. "Put me down."

With a curse, he dropped me. I fell to the ground at least half a dozen feet. My knees struck before my hands and luckily, I rolled to avoid the hard slam that could have broken both my wrists.

"I'd say it's your funeral," he finally said, urging Nutkin forward when the horse paused as I'd fallen. Almost as though it understood what was going on. "But it won't be. It will be your sister's."

From the ground, I slid him a long side-eye. He looked down at me from over his shoulder as the horse moved along, leaving me in the dirt.

"You're implying I won't make it," I said as I pushed up onto my knees.

He shrugged, and reined in Nutkin, guiding him to swing around so he could look at me.

"You won't," he said flatly, and jerked his chin at me. "At least, not on foot. I've never known a mortal to last but an hour."

"I won't be alone," I said. "Remember? You're escorting me. You. The big bad dark enforcer for the Shadow Court."

One hand planted itself on his thigh as he regarded me. "Escorting you implies we'll be going at the same speed."

I glared at him. "So slow the hell down."

He rolled his eyes, and I was sure I saw Nutkin do the same. I was getting to my feet when Blade began plodding back in my direction, heading toward the paddock.

"Where are you going?" I asked.

He dropped his head back. "As much as I hate to admit it; Stone was right. You don't have what it takes to travel the trail. You'll be dead before nightfall."

"I'm made of stiffer stuff than you think," I said and renewed my fantasies of slitting his throat while he slept.

He turned around in the saddle to face me. "If you were, you wouldn't be whining about sitting a horse."

The gall. I heard myself splutter out a dozen syllables before my tongue decided on a few words. "That's not a horse," I said. "I've seen horses. That is a beast."

His shrug came with a snort as the two clomped back toward me. "Yes, you've said that already," he said in a dry tone. "Of that, you're half right," he said when he was close enough for the toe of his boot to nudge me in the chest. "Fae horses do have several differences that would make them stand out against horses from your world. Horses in your world have lost their wild souls. They've become slaves to your ideals of decor and dance. None of them are war horses like Nutkin."

I sucked the back of my teeth. "Stupid name," I said.

"If you want to keep from being thrown when you do get on," Blade said. "I'd suggest you apologize. The old boy picked the name himself and won't take kindly to your insults about it."

I halted and adjusted the strap that held the empty sheath to my thigh out of habit. "Alright," I said. "I'll take the damn horse."

The horse nickered at my head and I had the pre-science to duck as it decided to try for a bite of my ear.

"Nutkin," Blade corrected. "He doesn't like to be objectified."

I pinched my nose. "Nutkin, then. I'll take Nutkin."

Blade made a sound deep in his throat. Half thoughtful, half displeased. "Then, do, by all means, get on, Ponytail."

"You know, a vampire once taunted me with a made up nickname. I hacked his head off with a dull hatchet."

"I'm surprised he didn't put up a fight," he said. "But then, maybe he was already dead."

It was a taunt, and I knew it, but still, I toed the dirt, managing to get a hunk of black earth stuck to the toe of my boot that had a decidedly shitty color to it.

With a look that could have scored paper, I said, "He was in no position to fight anymore by then. I'd already tied him to a cross I made out of oak boards and doused with holy water."

"Barbaric," he drawled, unimpressed.

I shrugged. "Only if you think it's OK to burn him alive, which I would have if Gideon hadn't intervened."

"Spare me the tough girl stories," he said. "I'm not interested. If you think you can handle this nasty business, then just get on."

I stared at him. "You want to sit behind me like the big spoon in a drawer? " I snorted. "Nothing doing. You're fast. You can walk. I'll ride the horse."

His black eyebrow lifted once again, this time with humor. "You don't even know where you're going. And besides, I said I'd get you safely to Erachne's and back. If I leave you one hour alone with Nutkin, who will protect you when he gets a good whiff of that sex pheromone you're giving off like perfume."

Reeling back, I stared at him. "If by pheromone you mean hatred, then I'm quite sure he'll leave me alone."

He rolled his eyes. "Go ahead and delude yourself. I know a sex pheromone when I smell it. I'm a hound at heart, and I know a bitch in heat. If it's not a hard-on you have for the horse, then you want to fuck me."

I gagged on my disbelief. "I want to fuck you up, but that's not the same thing."

"Where I come from, sometimes that's the same thing. I won't leave you alone with him. It wouldn't be prudent."

"I don't need protection, and certainly not from a horse."

"You say that now. But Nutkin has deflowered a few mortal women in his day. It's kind of his kink."

"You can't mean—"

"I mean, one of the differences between your horses and Fae horses is their wont to shape shift. With the right encouragement, they will slide free of the equine form and take that of a man. Well, except for the one place where it really counts." He waggled his eyebrows. "Some women rather like that."

"You're a monster," I said with a curled lip.

He canted his head and pressed his lips together. "I never claimed to be anything but, Ponytail. Now, what will it be? Ride with a monster or take your chances of getting fucked by one?"

I eyed the saddle, measuring it mentally and noting that it was big enough for two but not by much. Still, it was useless arguing, and it was so unlike me, I wanted to kick my own ass. Get shit done, that was me. I didn't complain or try to weasel out of things. That I was even acting out was testament to how much he was getting to me.

So I smothered down my rage and held out my hand with a beleaguered sigh.

In response, his hand snaked out with lightning speed and hauled me in front of him as though he'd reached down and grabbed a hat from someone's head. No effort. Not even a grunt. And when his massive hand curled around my waist to guide me and adjust me to the seat, I felt the strength in them coursing through his arm. The same strength that had held me beneath his arm like a bag of laundry.

As awkward as it was, it was a good chance for me to gage just how strong he was, and seeing he wouldn't be overpowered easily, only made me realize I had to rethink my plan to merely muscle my way through the cartel with Bloodmist and a few weapons. I had to be cannier than that.

We settled together, his hips moving against my backside as he guided Nutkin along. The city evaporated under the glory of a bright blue sky. A few sheep munched on grass and the occasional dog ran along the road with us. Once I thought I caught sight of a large bird with leathery wings, but at the same moment, Nutkin chose to step into a pothole and jostle my vision away and by the time I looked again, whatever it was had gone. I wasn't sure, but I thought he'd done it on purpose, and when Blade chuckled to himself, I was sure of it.

The trees grew less scant and larger, and every so often, I caught sight of ancient-looking ones with branches that moved like arms on the breeze and dressed with a glittering silver instead of green.

I hated to admit it, but we moved much faster than if I'd stayed on my feet and walked. The only trouble was the rocking motion and the heat of Blade's body made me drowsy. Exhaustion overtook me in no time.

I came awake with a start, realizing I'd dropped my head back against his chest. His gaze dipped to mine and held it silently for what seemed an eternity. The silence was like nails on a chalkboard.

"What?" I prodded. "Are we on the trail?"

"You thrash about in your sleep," he said. "Damn near kicked me right off Nutkin."

I ran a hand over the back of my aching neck. "There's no off switch on the hunter instinct, I guess," I said. "My subconscious knows a monster when she's sitting next to one. Riding along peacefully instead of trying to kill you must have its alarm bells ringing like crazy."

"I'm sure of it," he said, conversationally. Too conversationally. Even the tone of his voice was less of a barking order and more of a pensive, friendly tone. "We entered the Shadow Trail an hour ago."

"Something's wrong," I said in a hiss of a whisper.

His mouth touched my ear, and a shiver went through me as his breath brought one word to me. "Yes. Something very wrong."

In the next instant, a cacophony of shrieks rent the air and Nutkin reared back. Several horrendous looking creatures dropped out of the sky all around us.

I had time to utter one curse before Blade punched my karambit into my palm and his massive hands encircled my waist. The next second, he dumped me onto the ground.

Right in front of three wendigos.

CHAPTER 23

WE WERE SURROUNDED. WHAT I thought were three wendigos were really two groups of three. I crouched low in front of the trio before me, taking a second to let my muscles reacquaint themselves with my brain.

The creatures stood at least seven feet. Emaciated and gaunt, with elongated arms jutting from their skeletal forms at odd angles, as though their creator had fixed the balls of the shoulder sockets without ensuring a good fit. Ashen skin made their eyes look like hollow abysses rimmed by fire. They swung massive antlers side to side, black ivory racks that protruded far enough in front of them that it would make straight on attack difficult.

In the time it took for me to count them out in my mind, the wendigos circled around me. "Are wendigos fae?" I asked aloud.

"Cryptid," he answered. "Not wholly fae. But they'll die beneath a blade the same as any creature if you stick them right."

"That's all I needed to know," I said and raised my fists to my chest, blocking my throat so I could get my bearings before they came at me. The karambit was a solid, welcome weight in my hand, but I doubted I'd get close enough to use it. For that, I'd need a god-damned broadsword.

Without swinging my head, I took in everything I could. The lay of the land, the trees with their branches reaching for us. I noted where large boulders made a sort of bedding beneath one rowan tree and edged out of range so I wouldn't topple over them. I needed a clear battleground: I couldn't risk knocking myself unconscious should I slip and fall.

The air had grown thicker, as though someone had poured oil into the breeze. It grew harder to breathe. I wasn't sure where Blade was, but Nutkin had already begun charging for one cluster. My peripheral vision took in three clusters in all, a horde, I believed Gideon called them. Horde. Sounded right. I certainly felt as though there were far too many for two combatants to take on.

I was edging sideways, thinking to bolt behind Nutkin to give me time to assess more of the threat when three of them came for me.

A second pair closed in on Nutkin.

I'd fought one wendigo once, back when Gideon had unleashed it on me in the training room. At first, I'd thought it a joke, that he wanted me to fight a gaunt, emaciated-looking creature that might blow over if I blew on it with so much as a draft of coffee breath.

Not so. He'd wanted to present me with an opponent in a safe way so I could fully know their capabilities. And what it was capable of made me very happy I had never met a wendigo in the field. The thing was dastardly powerful and fast for all its pale thin skin showed each movement of muscle and bone beneath.

I'd only beaten that wendigo with help from Gideon who had briefed me on the details of its nature, details that had long flown out the window since, and that I struggled desperately to remember now as I edged out of reach of the trio in front of me.

One thing that came back to me was that they worked in a horde whenever they could, acting as though they used one brain when they attacked. That quality was evident now as the three closed in on me.

I recalled Gideon telling me the wendigo I'd fought would have eaten me piece by piece, tearing my skin from my body in ribbons, that its gaze would hold me fast if I looked in its eye so it could mesmerize me to the point that I'd offer myself to its jaws as though I were offering it a tray of crudités.

How could you fight something if you couldn't look it in the eye and know its moves before it made them? Fighting that wendigo back then took all my cunning and two blasts of Bloodmist, and it still had barely been enough.

With my synapses using the last of the Bloodmist to separate all my senses into a machine that process multiple inputs of information, I darted forward. I feinted with my left hand as one lunged for me, before throwing a hard right hook to distract it.

I used the surprise of a full frontal and immediate attack to reach for my karambit.

The wendigo dodged easily, then lunged at me from the side, its great rack of antlers blazing a trail through the air. I sidestepped and leaped around it, landed a swift elbow to its back, then followed up with a kick to the back of its knee. The creature stumbled.

That was my chance.

The karambit slid into my grip, as smoothly as melted butter. I sliced as I struck another blow, letting the blade hiss its way through its flesh.

The Wendigo howled in pain, rearing back with its antlers swinging back and forth in an attempt to catch me. A small victory, I knew, one I didn't have time to relish. I could sense its companions closing in, hear the gut-wrenching sound of their low-throated chattering to each other like bones being shaken in a wooden jar.

I spun to face them, keeping low, throwing a flurry of punches and kicks that kept them at bay. But for how long? I wasn't a good low-level fighter. I needed the thrust of height and weight if I was to get anywhere. Hunkering down to avoid the antlers was tiring my muscles fast. Lactic acid was building up, making them burn.

And just where in the hell was Blade? Was that awful whinnying sound Nutkin going down beneath the horde that attacked it or was it a victory cry as the massive horse stomped them into dust?

I had three on me, and I had to be singular. I had to focus. One thing at a time.

At close quarters, instinct and training took over. I was a fluid mass, moving like water, eyes wide to gather every detail, ears pricked for each sound. Without having to think, I followed up the initial kick with a spinning back-fist that carried my blade straight across the creature's throat.

The Wendigo stumbled backwards, dazed and dying. Brackish colored blood ran from between its fingers as it clutched the wound. Two down, my mind counted in wordless thought. One to go.

A dark chuckle rose to the air around me, slowly shifting to a guttural growl, as though whatever had made the sound was moving through completely different vocal cords.

A grunt, a howl. Another wendigo behind me shrieked in pain. So. Blade must be fighting. Or Nutkin. I found myself grateful for the size of the horse then, hoping he was doing his share of fighting.

I launched myself at the wounded Wendigo. My breath came in hard shallow gasps, rationing my air as the adrenaline drenched me and demanded every ounce of energy my body possessed. Long hours of training meant I wasn't out of breath but my muscles burned just the same. With a fierce yell, I launched myself at the last of my opponents. A sharp jab with the karambit. A roundhouse kick that caught the creature in the ribs. A sharp crack carried its way to my ears as the Wendigo staggered backwards.

I closed in, slicing mercilessly, punching in alternate rounds. Blood sprayed over my face, wetting my lips. It seemed an eternity before the Wendigo lay motionless at my feet.

I allowed myself one long breath of refuel before I pivoted, karambit raised, eyes so wide they hurt. Everything came into sharper focus then. Nutkin trampling the carcass of one long dead wendigo. Five others littered the ground around the massive hellhound. Blade in his beast's form was covered in blood. His muzzle dripped the brackish fluid onto the legs of the one at his feet. He stomped, once. Twice, making the body beneath him bounce and rebound.

When he swung his gaze to mine, the blazing color of his eyes burned through me. He was gone. No trace of man or Fae lay within that gaze.

A shudder took my spine. Here was a beast to be reckoned with. A thing of such horrific strength and power that it sent waves of energy through the air to all but curdle my blood.

But there was something else in the air. A pheromone, a scent of lust and rage that made my knees weak.

Predator, my mind whispered. My fists went up again automatically. I braced myself, the sharp edge of my blade facing the dark enforcer, and I sucked in a gust of heated air as he aimed himself toward me.

"I'll kill you," I warned. "Back off."

A growl moved through his throat, shifting subtly at first as his huge paws ate the distance between us.

Each step, he became less beast and more man, but the transformation, slow as it was, did nothing to lay the hairs back down on my neck. They strained ever more fiercely toward the heavens. The adrenaline, the expectation of violence, made my skin hum.

I fell into a fighting stance. Waiting. My breath was a hiss in my ear.

"I swear," I said. "If you come any closer, I will kill you or die trying."

He came anyway, his growl changing to that same dark chuckle I'd heard quilting the battle air in those moments I was taken with the fight. That chuckle thick-ened as he approached, and by the time he stood within a foot of me, my chest was heaving and he was fully human.

He was laughing. Laughing… And completely naked.

CHAPTER 24

"Do try to kill me, Ponytail," he said. "I would enjoy wrestling your body beneath mine and feeling you squirm when you realize just how powerless you are."

Every inch of him was hard muscle. My eyes trailed down his body, taking in the small and intricately inked and linked brands all the way to his…

Oh, my god. Was he ever naked. Some primal instinct bade me take one more step backward but when I did, Nutkin's nickering chortle reminded me we weren't alone. This wasn't some ancient post-war scene where the women became spoils of rape and assault. I was a hunter, a fighter, with training of my own to take down anyone who attacked me.

I'd watched the way he carried himself these last days. I'd watched them all. Noting how he moved when he reached for a piece of fruit. Measured the reach of his arms, the curl of fingers. When I sat against his chest, feeling the motion of Nutkin beneath us, I took record of how taut the muscles were, how quick to play about in their dance of core work. I knew his breathing pattern because I matched it with my own.

So when he came at me, I was ready. A swift dodge and I was out of reach, the Bloodmist still firing in my veins. Another swing for me, and I was behind him. I kept my footing for three long, agonizing moments.

And then he had me.

"Not bad," he murmured against my throat from behind. "Most mortals don't last three seconds. Most Fae either."

The way his breath moved across my skin sent shivers down my back. Legs that had been stiffened by adrenaline now washed out from beneath me with the sudden receding of its tide. The drug peeled back like the tide from a murky shore.

He spun me around to face him, and I didn't have the energy to resist.

"That was something, wasn't it?" he said in a hoarse voice. When he peered down at my face, those irises flared bright and died down. "I've never seen a woman fight like that. Not mortal. Not Fae."

For a moment, my heart squeezed at the unexpected compliment. Kit always complained about my fighting long before I'd found Gideon because it caused her trouble. Gideon only pressured me to be more, be better, be faster. The monsters I killed only showed appreciation by their deaths, and that was a silent, unsatisfying commentary.

I almost smiled for him. But then the shutters came down over his expression and he released me.

He turned away, showing me his back and the flex of his powerful glutes. Strong thighs moved him to a pile of tattered fabric lying on the ground. He stooped and plucked the material and held it against his chest.

"You weren't naked before," I said, not knowing what else to say. Gratitude and pride were uncommon strangers.

He looked back at me over his shoulder. His throat was tight, the muscles corded from jaw to clavicle. "What's that?"

My eyelids went to half mast, remembering. When he'd transformed at Terran's command in the cellars, he hadn't lost a single stitch of clothing.

"Before," I said. "You weren't naked when you shifted in the cellar."

He pivoted to face me full on then. One tiny quirk of his eyebrow as he ran his hand through the pitch black of his hair. Then I blinked and watched as clothing began to slide over his body as though pulled from an invisible closet by a valet dressing his king.

His arms spread out at his sides, accepting the sleeves of the jerkin. His legs shook to let the trousers wind around his legs. It was a slow, almost methodical process, as though he wanted me to see every second of the event.

All the while, he watched me as though I was taking off my own clothes one by one. It felt so ridiculously sexual that heat crept up my neck. I had to drop my gaze to his hands to avoid the searing look in his, and when I did, I noted he still held the torn trousers he'd retrieved from the ground.

"You have glamor," I said, realizing that the pants he held were the real thing and that the ones on his body had to be magic.

They'd obviously torn as he'd shifted, leaving them unwearable, which meant when he'd shifted in the cells of the mafia's safe house, those had torn as well. But I'd not realized he was even naked then. He'd been dressed the entire time.

"You glamored clothes for yourself after you shifted in the cellar. Otherwise you would have been naked then too." I narrowed my gaze at him, overlaying the Blade of the moment with the one from that.

He stooped to pick up his torn shirt and clutched it at his side. "We all have some glamor," he muttered as Nutkin ambled over, his snout and fore-quarters misted with blood. Blade laid his hand on the horse's nose and scratched off a clot of black fluid. "Some have more than others. The base Fae can't access theirs and the low Fae can barely use it at will. It's why they grant their magic to the king."

I didn't dare interrupt lest the flow of information dry up, so I held still, barely breathing as he ran his palm over Nutkin's back, scooping up palmfuls of blood and flinging it to the forest floor. Each time he did, it made a sickening thwacking sound that made me flinch. I was used to violence and bloodshed, but the sight of the wendigos and their skeletal figures stretched out along the forest carpet, with their gray skin soaking in black blood made me nauseous.

It took an effort of sheer will not to look when he flung a blob of blood at one of the carcasses.

"We need to get going," he said, as his hand met the lacings of the saddlebag. He stuffed the clothes inside, and as he did so, I caught sight of the pouch filled with those dark objects.

I was relieved to see them, but there would be plenty of time to talk about those cursed things later. Right then, I wanted the truth more. I was tired of feeling at a disadvantage.

"You took your God-awful time glamoring your clothes just now," I drawled. "It didn't seem to take that long in the cellars. I didn't even know you were really naked back then."

I carefully omitted the fact that it had happened when he'd sliced through my flesh at his father's order because I did not want to seem vulnerable. Not when I'd just kicked ass in front of him. Not when I'd shown I wasn't a damsel of any sort. For some reason, that was important to me.

He patted Nutkin's rump and planted his hand on his hip. I tried not to let my gaze trail to where his fingers tapped lightly, knowing that the glamor could go away if he willed it.

"Why, Ponytail," he said in a light voice. "Are you complaining that you didn't see the whole package the first time around? I would have thought you were too occupied to care, but I can give you another peek now to make up for it."

My face felt like I'd got too close to a fire.

"What I'm complaining about is how long it took now," I countered. "What I'm saying is that I'm beginning to think your power isn't limitless." I grinned at him with a hard satisfaction because I knew I was right.

He'd used up too much of the stores shifting and fighting, and he couldn't just glamor himself as effortlessly as before. I was beginning to understand why the Shadow Court hired a human assassin. First, the vulnerability to cold iron in the face of a fae who could wield it, and now to know the magic wasn't limitless. Humans might be more frail, but they had their advantage. "You need to re-energize."

He snorted as if I was completely off base. "Maybe I wanted to reward you for killing those beasts so beautifully." He dropped his hand from Nutkin's rump and started to prowl toward me. "Did you like what you saw, Ponytail? Because you really did earn it."

He wasn't fooling me then with his arrogance. He was trying to distract me, make me uncomfortable in order to deflect. I knew the tactic well.

I'd hit on something useful and he knew it. The magic had limits. Hope flared in my belly, deep down and almost imperceptible, but hope nonetheless. If the king's waned over time, and he was their most powerful, then what happened to those with less power? Even the city of the Dead needed constant blooding. Maybe it wasn't so impossible to kill a fae. Or several of them. Or even an entire cartel.

With a grunt, he heaved himself up onto Nutkin's back and swung his leg over. "We're almost there," he said with a glance at the bodies littering the forest floor. Already, the stink of them had changed from mank and murk to rot. I wouldn't be disappointed to leave it behind.

He pulled a rag of shirt from his saddlebags and leaned down to swipe it over my face the way a mother might, first pouring water from his water skin on the corner then swiping it over my cheeks. He stared at me for a long moment, then barked out an order. "Get on."

Lips pressed together thoughtfully, I gripped his hand. The callouses on his palms and fingers married mine, lighting some electrical shock that ran up my arm. No doubt the bastard was doing his best to keep up the pretense, so I would think he had a massive well of power to draw from. And because I knew better, because I felt victorious in the face of his pathetic attempts at distraction, I settled onto the saddle in front of him and let him put his arms around my waist, pinning me to his chest.

With my entire body humming, I clamped my mouth shut and stayed silent, because there was no way I was going to comment on the fact that every inch of his naked body clung to mine.

After a long time of quiet that was both relieving and filled with tension that something else might jump out at us, we broke into a small clearing.

"We're here," he said shortly.

He slid off Nutkin and looped the reins over a boulder, leaving me atop the horse. Immediately, the stone bloomed upward into a granite hitching post that formed a copper ring around the end of the rein. When he strode toward a rotten looking stump in the middle of the glen, I tried to slide off too, but discovered my legs were frozen in place.

Dismayed, I rapped at my thighs to wake them up and said, "Why would a seamstress live so far out of the city?"

"You expect a tree sprite to hole up in some city sapling?" he answered over his shoulder. "Not enough natural magic there and too much song of stone and mortar to provide adequate housing."

He halted in front of the stump and knocked on open air.

Three sharp raps echoed over the field like thunder. I might have jerked in response, except I was too busy rubbing the numbness from my thighs.

With my legs tingling, I slid from the saddle and promptly fell on the grass.

Sucking back a hiss, I rolled onto my hands and hoped he hadn't noticed, then whatever dismay I felt at my awkwardness evaporated into wonder as the stump rose up sharply to the heavens.

It spread inch by inch as though a canvas was being painted in front of me. It put me in mind of Jasmine's fairy paint. A pang of loss struck me that ached enough to make my jaw clench as I relegated it to the realms of dark mental storage.

As the tree grew in front of my eyes to an ever-green whose trunk held the kind of circumference that would take five men to encircle with their arms, I climbed to my feet, favoring the leg that seemed to be the least asleep and was fussing at me with sharp tingles every time I moved.

Blade stepped back as a circular doorway carved itself into the trunk. Several porthole-shaped windows peppered the surface, each with glittering, gauzy material fluttering as though an unseen breeze was dancing with them.

When the door opened, a short, rotund woman wearing a kerchief smiled brightly out into the glen. Snappy black eyes roamed Blade's face with the scrutiny of a judge.

For his part, he stood immobile, letting her assessment run over him like water. With my legs finally feeling normal, I took a step toward them, intent on getting the whole charade over with.

Her gaze flicked to mine at my movement, and that friendly, rotund, and fresh-faced visage disappeared beneath a wolfish jaw with long canines.

In the next instant, she charged me.

CHAPTER 25

I was about to be eaten by a tree sprite. With no knowledge of what the creature could do, I backed away a safe distance as fast as I could without looking like a coward. For all I knew, she could levitate or fly, and I wanted to be out of harm's way before finding out.

Just as I'd stumbled over a stump that hadn't been there before, Blade chuckled, swinging his gaze to me as he spoke to the sprite.

"Don't worry," he said. "She's just some assassin I'm supposed to turn into a Galatea with your wonderful magic," he said, shaking his head.

The sprite, for her part, halted mid-step. She canted her head at me the way a small dog might investigate a new surprise, then she giggled in a coquettish way that put a smile on Blade's face. A smile that seemed surprisingly authentic.

She gestured at us to enter, disappearing into the shadows of her tree trunk bungalow.

Inside, the home looked far larger than the trunk's circumference, and it had a more octagonal feel than circular. The mossy carpet closed over the soles of my boots, cushioning any sound I made as I moved, and it felt so soft I fought back the urge to stoop and run my hands over its surface.

With walls made of smokey colored bark, the scent of forest permeated the space and gave a feeling of being held within the heart of an ancient, wooded glen. Above us, several teardrop shaped lights hummed with a soft glow.

Fabrics of all sorts draped themselves over workbenches and wooden looms. Several stools made of oak but covered in tapestry were scattered through the chamber. I thought I spied a cat darting between a sofa and a chair, skittering off into a different room.

The circular windows I'd spied outside were larger from the interior, letting in beams of natural light that fell on a bookcase filled with leather spines that stretched far above me to the third floor. A ladder rested beside a shelf she had obviously been filling because several books lay open on its steps.

Drapes of silk in all colors hung from a garment hook so large it looked more like a hoist. But it was the material closest to the window that caught my eye. The gauzy beauty of it drew me to it.

"That's spider silk," she said, coming up behind me. "I have one gown made with it. Tricky to work with and very expensive because the material takes so long to spin." She flashed me a smile of tiny pointed teeth. "But it is the most stunning material I own. I will only sell it to the right woman."

I got the message immediately. I wasn't that right woman. Beyond her, Blade was running his hand over a gown cut so low it would reach the navel of the woman wearing it.

I tried to smile at her, but the feeling of being unworthy coupled with the sense that Blade was tuned to my reactions made me wary and nervous, and my attempt ended up more of a grimace.

"I understand," I said. "I was just admiring it." I crossed my arms over my chest, acutely aware that I was covered in black blood. "I'm not sure what I'm looking for," I confessed after some thought.

She canted her head at me. Those jet-colored eyes blinked three times in rapid succession as her smile revealed those tiny points again. "That's fine," she said. "I know exactly what you want."

Taking my arm, she pulled me in the direction where Blade had begun to shake out the abominably indecent gown. In an uncharacteristically feminine movement, he stuck his leg out and up into the skirt of the dress, examining the length. If Erachne was worried about the dirt and dust and sweat of fighting and riding that was thick on him despite the clothes he'd glamored over his body, she gave no indication.

In fact, judging by the beam of pride on her face, she intended to show me the same one, and whole-heartedly approved of his measuring.

I shook my head, aghast at the thought. "Not my style."

Blade looked askance at me, flicking his gaze up and down my body with the efficiency of a good tailor. "Yoga pants and sweatshirts won't work for this."

I cut him a look that very clearly told him to stay out of it.

Uncrossing my arms, I said, "Do you have something more…" My gaze roamed the room and landed again on the spider silk gown. "Something more demure. Less…" I flapped my hands against my legs. "Showy."

Before the sprite could answer, Blade tugged the gown from its hanger and splayed it over his arm. "Showy is exactly what we're going for." He winked at me, but it looked more like a leer.

My lips pursed so tightly it was difficult to grate the words out. "I'm not wearing that."

"Try it on," the sprite said. "It is made to flatter the wearer. I assure you, you'll love it."

She ran her gaze along the cut of its shape and I got the feeling she wanted to touch it.

"Fine," I said and grabbed the dress from Blade's arm. "Where do I change?"

"Nowhere till you wash first," she said and pointed to a small chamber where a suspicious-looking bit of modern plastic peeked out from the room like the tail of a mouse. "Wash in the stall and then get dressed. I'll be in for adjustments in a moment." She canted her head at Blade, and some silent communication ran between them.

With a sigh of resignation, I headed to the shower, a narrow grated floor in a corner separated by a ring of floral plastic.

With a groan, I began to peel off my clothes, noting a large splotch of brackish earth covering my backside and a smear of blood that ran the length of my neck. The vape nudged against my fingers as I shrugged out of the duster jacket. My mouth flooded with water and I had to drag in a deep inhale.

This was not the time. Maybe before we set out again, so I'd have shaken off the peculiar coma I'd suffered the last time and be good and grooving if we came upon more wendigos or whatever else awaited us in these woods. I couldn't risk falling asleep now.

The shower head, no more than a funnel attached to a tube that disappeared into the ceiling and scored with holes, ran to body temperature. Enough stream trickled over me to clear away the dust and blood coating my skin and hair. As if it knew when I was clean, the water shut off by itself.

I stepped out into a room that looked vastly different from the one I entered. The shower behind me disappeared and before me was a bank of tri-angled mirrors, giving me a full 360 degree view of my body. For an instant, my gaze sliced up to my throat, where my scar seemed all the bigger in the mirrors. I swallowed hard and squeezed my eyes closed. A soft mewling sound from a few feet away drew my attention. The cat sat on a plump brocade chair, watching me.

"Not pretty, is it?" I asked it. The thing stood and stretched, her little fangs flashing as she yawned and settled back down, turning her back to me.

There was just enough time to yank the dress up over my legs before the sprite entered, and I was glad I'd decided to wait on the Bloodmist. She closed the door behind her softly and approached with such small steps I wasn't sure she'd make it across the room before the month ended, but in seconds, she stood in front of me.

Her smile flashed at me again. The tiny points seemed even longer as the mirrors reflected light back at her. An echo of the cat's grin.

"He wants this one, so I'm afraid whether you like it or not, it's yours." A quick hand moved across the bodice and, with one fluid movement, it slid up and over my body like a wash of hot water.

I stood there, wooden, as she made small adjustments. I did not want to look in the mirror and see the scar on my throat on clear display, so I let her fuss, only barely holding it together because soft and sexy was so not my forte and I dreaded seeing the end result.

I had the horrible feeling I'd look like a man in drag.

At last, she made a satisfied sound. "It's exactly what you need but for one thing." She pulled the elastic from my hair and fluffed it out. The locks fell onto my shoulders and dipped over my collarbones. A bit of air tickled the top of my head and she grinned, this time, so wide she showed a set of pointed fangs on each side of her mouth.

"Perfect." She spun me around to face the mirror.

I gasped at my reflection. All evidence of blood had disappeared. The scar was still evident, but it had turned colors and looked like a vine tattoo sprouting leaves that dipped and moved on my skin as I turned. My hair looked lusher than ever.

"It's magic," I murmured, twisting and turning to admire the way the vine inking ducked from my throat to cover the bruises I always had on my skin from hours of fighting and training, the nicks in the skin that had turned silver. "I look—"

"Gorgeous," she breathed.

I did. I looked gorgeous, and that wasn't a word I ever used to describe myself. Gideon always said I would be beautiful if I wasn't so hard-edged, but in Erachne's gown, I looked soft and roundly feminine.

I did not look forward to the task ahead, but I was so surprised and pleased that I wouldn't look like an old mare dressed up in fancy ribbons that I clutched her hands tight and held them against my chest.

"Thank you," I said.

She pulled my hands to her lips and gave them a quick peck. She lingered over them for a moment, inhaling, maybe rubbing them a bit too much with her dry fingers. Our eyes met over the clutch of our hands.

"It's not magic that you are beautiful," she said. "But even so, the right man will see past the glamor of the dress to the woman beneath. Be careful who you show yourself to, lest you find yourself laid bare when you don't wish to be."

Confused, I was just getting to ask what she meant when Blade rapped on the door once before he burst into the room.

"Time," he growled. "We are running out of time. Tell me you're ready."

Erachne shoved me in front of her and stepped back. "She is ready," she said as she let go of my hand in a way that made me twirl on my feet.

The way the gown moved around my body, swirling around my legs, made me feel like an expert dancer instead of the princess she no doubt tried to make of me, but I doubted any princess would show as much cleavage as I did.

"Tell me you've never seen a fit so good on a woman mortal or fae," the sprite said in a tone that crowed the pride she felt in her creation. "The hair complements the gown, don't you think?"

His gaze ran the length of the dress, repeatedly returning to my throat where the vines hid my rope burn scar. I watched him swallow. I saw the tic in his eyelid.

"I prefer the ponytail," he said in a brusque tone and then swirled on his feet to slam the door behind him.

I was left to gape at the door, feeling utterly ridiculous.

"He was never one for haberdashery," she fussed and began stripping me of the dress. "Part of his nature, I presume, like mine. Prefers the rawness of natural materials."

It took her slight fingers touching my throat as she peeled away the bodice to realize how woodenly I was standing, and I closed my eyes to the mirror. The transformation back to hunter and assassin wasn't something I wanted to witness. Best to leave the soft woman behind and open my eyes again to what I really was, as though nothing had happened to make me feel differently.

Only when I felt the coolness of nudity did I turn my gaze back to the sprite, who was busily bundling up the gown.

"Will it look that good when I put it on?" I asked. "I mean…will the magic work?"

I had no idea if the magic that had transformed me would work without her ministrations, and something told me I needed that magic if I was to complete the task set before me. Otherwise, why bother trying to dress the old nag in ribbons for the fair at all?

"You will look the same," she said, giving me a strange look. "The dress is spelled to bring out the natural beauty of the wearer." She snapped her fingers. "Pull it on, and just like that, you are what you need to see."

"Like a glamor."

She put a wrinkled hand to her breast, insulted. "Certainly not. I told you. The gown has no special magic except to show what's there." She winked. "Some women might look like crones in the dress. Why do you think I show it to every High Fae lady who comes here looking for a gown? I want them to see what they really are."

She chuckled to herself as she finished wrapping it in a supple bundle of birch paper with a wide ribbon made of the same sorts of vines as I'd seen on my neck. When she'd finished, she passed it to me.

"When you are finished with it, put it in the same wrapping and leave it beneath the nearest tree with this spell." She passed me a slip of paper with symbols on it that were indecipherable, but that were obviously some sort of language. "It will return to me. This is a loaner, not a gift."

I nodded, feeling very much like Cinderella, and clamped down on the manic laugh that wanted to slip free as I thought of my words to Terran earlier.

With the nervous laughter successfully smothered, I followed her out into the main boutique. Silently, she took Blade aside and while they were murmuring some secrets, I strained to listen. Whatever they had to say to each other, they kept cloaked from my ears. Since I wasn't welcome, I strolled out to the sunshine and stood there watching the trees move in the breeze until he stormed out of the boutique and, glowering as though he'd been chided like a child, and climbed atop Nutkin.

"We have five hours until nightfall," he said, looking down at me as I reached up for his help. "I would rather not run into more wendigos or worse before I've had a chance to rest. We'll have to push Nutkin hard."

We rode as he said, fast and hard, and I was breathless by the time we made it back to the little town where the tavern made its home. He lead Nutkin to a hitching post at the corner of a smokey stone building with a thatch roof as silently as he'd ridden the route.

The tavern he'd mentioned before setting out, I guessed. The one halfway back to the Iron City where we would rest and recover before setting out once more. Built two storeys high with windows shuttered by wooden slats, I imagined cold and damp quarters. The town around it teemed with life, and beyond, situated on a hilltop, the turrets of the Iron Castle rose above a lush green forest and rolling hills. The towers reached toward the heavens with glistening white stone hands and copper nails. Windows sparkled in the dying sunlight like diamonds backlit by a roaring fire.

Small humanoid creatures with transparent wings chased each other around the town's open air market as it closed down for the night. Streets went off in every direction, lined with colorful shops and market stalls. Goblins haggled over the price of shiny baubles.

Shoulder to shoulder, men and women of all shapes and sizes, dressed in regal attire, lined up along the walls. Carts and trundles and donkeys and horses alike, carried the aged and poor fae, who queued with the better dressed. The motley assemblage reminded me of a Peter

Jackson movie, and I had to blink three times to remind me it was all real.

Sliding from the horse, I stared at the sights, realizing that when I'd imagined Fae, it looked exactly like this.

I was still staring when, without a word, Blade pulled his clothes and the pouch of dark objects along with the gown from within the saddlebags.

The gown he stuffed into my hands without ceremony. "We have a room over the bar," he jerked his chin toward the tavern. "I'll have someone spell you a hot bath."

I noticed he was avoiding my gaze.

"And the dark objects?" I pressed. "What about them?"

"I'll bring them with me when I come back." He turned away, dismissing me.

My hands closed around the gown, feeling the softness of the material. I felt like I'd done something wrong. That old familiar sensation of disappointing someone haunted the fringes of my mind.

"What do you mean, come back?" I hated that I was asking. Hated that I cared.

He ignored me, busying himself with Nutkin's saddle. He obviously didn't think I needed to know, and I decided it didn't matter what he planned to do so long as I got my hands on those artifacts. Plus, I had to admit the thought of a bath tempted me. The shower at Erachne's had been brief and unsatisfying, a necessity rather than a respite. The grime under my armpits suggested I smelled worse than I looked.

Leaving him there to tack Nutkin with about as much interest as he'd shown me when he dismissed me, I trod the flagstones from the stables to the tavern proper.

For a moment, I lingered in the doorway, scanning the interior out of habit for a hint of threat or danger.

Several bulky shadows hunkered over the bar and a few more scattered around a broad fireplace, laughing and clapping each other on the backs and shoulders. No human women with fairy painted bodies. Just round faced and portly fae. The whole interior gave off a friendly, homey vibe.

The moment I stepped over the threshold, I realized exactly how exhausted I was. For the first time since entering Fae, I actually felt grateful. I couldn't have walked or rode one more quarter hour and I doubted I'd even remain awake long enough to take that bath Blade promised.

Inside, the heady fragrance of hops and yeast danced along wafts of savory herbs. The tavern owner looked suspiciously like Seamus. He took one look at me and directed me to a room with an efficient nod and a flick of his wrist. "Bath is ready," he said.

Quick and impossible as that had to be, I didn't question the news. Now that I'd set my heart on a warm soak, I couldn't get up the stairs fast enough. Weary, the climb might have been to my aching feet, I took every step with anticipation.

Unlike the Velvet Boar, there was only one room above this tavern. It possessed a rustic charm, with walls covered in faded tapestries depicting mythical creatures and sprawling landscapes. A single window allowed a sliver of dim light to filter through, casting long shadows across the worn wooden floorboards. The air carried a faint scent of dampness, mingled with the unmistakable aroma of ale and the lingering smoke from the hearth downstairs.

It was sparsely furnished, with a sturdy bed against one wall, covered in a patchwork quilt that had seen better days. A small round table stood near the window. Gouged in places, it was still clean and solid looking. A couple of mismatched chairs completed the meager seating arrangement. The requisite wingback chair kept its quiet counsel beside the fireplace.

Like the Velvet Boar, however, it possessed a fireplace that crackled cheerily, warming the room to bath water temperature. A copper tub the size of a small pool occupied the middle of the room. Draped over a standing copper hook a few feet away, a thick towel promised to wrap me in luxury when I did decide to climb back out. A washcloth and soap hung from the edge of the tub on a ledge made of pounded copper. A matching hand towel made a cushioned headrest.

I was already stripping down to my bare skin as I spied the tub, so I was naked by the time I reached it. I slung a leg over and dangled a toe in. A sigh of pleasure escaped me at the sheer gloriousness of it.

I sank into the water and took my time soaping up. Exhaustion and warmth made it tough to keep my eyes open. The bath, the room, the hard ride and fight with the wendigos sapped every bit of will to even try. I had the room to myself. There was no crime in letting them rest for five minutes.

A fact I was most sorry for when the door burst open and a glowering, sputtering Blade entered the room.

"Get out," he said. "Get out right now."

CHAPTER 26

THE HUNTER IN ME went to high alert. Naked or not, when someone bursts into a space growling like Blade was doing, his posture rigid and tense, instinct overrides humility. Every. Damn. Time.

I leaped from the tub, water sluicing down my body as I grabbed for any piece of clothing my hand fell on, which turned out to be the hand towel and not the luxurious bath towel beside the tub.

I was in a defensive stance before the water could puddle at my feet, but a hasty scan of my clothes on the floor proved my karambit was no longer tucked neatly into its sheath on top of my pants.

But I was ready for him, nonetheless. With a pivot that sent a splinter biting into the sole of my right foot, I faced him, my hands up, ready to punch out if he should move.

"You want blood?" I said. "Then come for me, you bastard. Just you come at me."

He did. And I wasn't nearly as ready as I'd thought. Even if I hadn't jammed a shaving of wood into my foot, I wouldn't have been ready. He was just that fast.

In less time than it took for me to inhale, he wrangled me into his arms, chest to massive chest. He arched me painfully backwards, and I was left peering up at the long fangs that had punched down from his gums. Not tiny pinpricks like Stone's or Terran's. Fully elongated, wolfish canines.

The last tickle of Bloodmist shuddered through me, sending a warning signal that came too late for me to react. I had nothing left of the adrenaline dump, or the magic. Whatever he planned to do with those teeth, we both knew I had nothing in me to fight it.

Ludicrously, I laughed. Just dropped my head back and gave over to the last convulsive drain of energy as though I wasn't staring up into a mouth full of dangerous teeth. As though his growl wasn't vibrating into my solar plexus and those teeth weren't already descending toward my throat. As though I wasn't just letting it happen.

But when the tips touched down onto the tender flesh, just a hair's breadth away from my scar, I knew I'd gone too far. The laughter finally died as a flash of pain radiated through my shoulder. I bucked, reflex and pain taking over where adrenaline and drug left a gaping hole. I thrashed in his hold, fully and completely taken by panic.

"You bastard," I wailed, both shocked and furious that he'd actually attacked me. "You weren't supposed to really do it."

In the next instant, the pressure of his bite receded and his lips moved over my scar like a caress. I had the insane feeling he wanted me to take a long breath, to inhale the scent of my own blood, to know…really know that he was a monster. No problem there.

Blood trickled toward my collarbone. I wrenched in his hold, ineffective and wooden, because some part of me was still dazed by impotent fury and shock. I craned my head toward his, thinking I could use the twist to peel him from my neck. I had time to see his eyes glaze over before he dipped his head toward me once more. Even as I twisted away, trying to get out of reach of his mouth, his tongue laved my skin.

Instantly, the pain evaporated.

He released me with a shove that left me staggering and clamoring to grab hold of something. I wasn't sure what had just happened, but it wasn't just aggression. I blinked at him, scanning his face for an explanation as did my level best to sort through the mixed messages blipping through the radar of my mind.

I managed, finally, to stand without shaking. "What in the holy, righteous hell was that?" I demanded. "You break in here like a hornet flew up your nose, and for what?"

Now that I knew I wasn't going to die a horrible death in the jaws of a hellhound, fear turned to anger. I dragged a palm over the bite, feeling for a wound and finding nothing but wet skin where the residual smear of blood had been. "What in the hell are you doing?"

His glower matched how I felt.

"Well?" I demanded.

"It seems pretty obvious to me what that was," he drawled. "You told me to bite you. I obliged."

Inspection proved my hand didn't have any blood on it, just saliva. I winced and scraped my palm over my ribcage, muttering about the wonder of him suddenly acting as though I had a say in what went on at all. I thought I heard him muttering beneath his breath too and gave him a sharp look, suggesting he should shut the hell up.

The bastard had the nerve to tap me on the shoulder and calmly shove a bath sheet at me.

I snapped it out of his hand because I realized then that I was still wet and naked from the bath, and because I did not want to seem as though I was embarrassed by that.

"So how did I taste?" I spat out.

"Do you really want to know?" he asked with a cocky tilt of his head. "Because my answer might be very graphic."

I wrapped the bath sheet around my torso, knotting it beneath my armpit. Chest trembling with the effort to keep from heaving in rage, I stared at him.

"Graphic descriptions of blood aren't likely to make me squeamish," I retorted, my brow so tight with fury I could feel the furrows touch each other.

His only response was a single raised eyebrow, followed by a shake of his head that suggested I'd missed the point altogether. I side-stepped away from him, not putting my back to him for one second as I headed to the wingback chair by the fire. When I felt the armrest scuff along my arm, I took a long breath to swipe away the cobwebs of left-over spiked emotion.

"To be clear," I said dryly. "I did not want you to bite me. What kind of misfires go on in that brain of yours that you can't understand terror-filled rhetoric?"

He tapped his chest with his index finger. "Monster," he said, then he pointed the same finger at me. "Monster hunter. It doesn't take a psychic to figure out I was going to attack when presented with a chance."

My shoulders sagged, and I sank onto the chair. My legs splayed out in front of me, their chipped nail polish glinting in the firelight. A quick glance upward showed he'd taken up post along side the tub, watching me. His arms were crossed, that same painted nail winking at me with the same sort of worn chipping as on my toes. I sighed and tightened the knot in the towel as it had started to loosen. Along with the drain of adrenaline, so went my energy. I was tired of being on high alert all the time. Even as a hunter in the mortal realm, I got to enjoy a shot of mezcal every now and then. Kick back. Breathe.

I dropped my head back on the chair, spent. If we were going to be doing this together, we needed to come to some sort of agreement about privacy. Or failing that, we needed to at least have an understanding that we didn't try to kill one another.

"So, are you going to tell me what had you rampaging in here like a bear with a sore ass?" It was the best conciliatory sentiment I could come up with.

His right eyebrow lifted. "So full of colorful analogies."

"Fuck off," I said. "Is that colorful enough for you?"

His gaze flickered over me, taking my posture in with a dismissive glance before returning to my face.

"Fucking wasn't exactly what I had in mind when I rampaged in like…a bear with a sore ass, was it? But I could be convinced otherwise if that's what you're intending by parading about in a towel."

I shot him an upturned middle finger. "You could have passed me my clothes instead of watching me try to cover myself with a handkerchief."

Surprisingly, his eyebrow inched up even higher. "And when would I have done that, exactly?"

I lifted my head off the back of the chair. "Maybe before you came at me like—"

"A bear with a sore ass," he said, cutting me off and waving his hand in a get on with it gesture. "Right. I get it. Except you should have known better than to taunt a predator."

"Why are you here?" I asked.

He sighed. "The raiment. Where is it?"

Blinking stupidly, I tried to wade through the dump of adrenaline toward the path of least expected concerns. "The raiment?" I asked, confused.

He prowled toward me, and I had to struggle not to quail under the ferocity of the air that moved ahead of him. "It was in my saddle bags. It's gone."

I hung over my thighs as I looked at him. "That's the reason you roust me out of the first decent bath I've had in days? To ask about that damn itchy scrap of lace?"

It took his gaze dropping to my thighs for me to realize the towel had started to gape open. I yanked the edges closed again and stood up to search for something more secure.

"That itchy scrap of lace, as you call it, is the only thing that will keep you disguised from the king's guard.

I'm assuming you don't want them chasing you into the mortal realm when this is over. So where is it? Where did you hide it?"

"I didn't take it." I spied my filthy clothes across the room and hitched up the towel once more so I could retrieve them without baring more skin than I needed to. I wanted those clothes on. Now. There was no way I was continuing this or any other conversation with him behind a veil of fidgety terrycloth.

Holding onto the knot, I stood and strode smartly to where the pile rested on the floor near the tub. Even though it went against every grain of training, I put my back to him, a far preferable view to show him as I yanked my pants and drawers from the pile. I shook them out with a snap so I could pull them on beneath the towel.

I felt his eyes on my back so acutely, he might be burning me with the lit end of a cigarette. "Don't stare," I grumbled without turning around. "It's not polite."

"Monster," he repeated as though I'd forgotten, and I imagined him tapping his chest again. "And this monster is about to lose his shit if you don't tell him where you hid the raiment."

"What does that matter?" I asked, yanking on the material and cursing beneath my breath as it stuck to my wet skin halfway up my thigh. I cursed like a construction worker as I tried to wriggle around the fabric.

His footfalls started to move toward me. "I told you why it matters," he said. "You need a disguise to avoid the guards."

I almost laughed out loud. He was pretty good at keeping up Terran's ruse of making me think I would survive this ordeal. I had no illusions that I was going to get out of Fae alive, and we both knew it.

"I wish I did steal that damn corset," I grumbled as I undid the towel and let it slip to the floor. "I'd yank it over your head and turn you into something I could stomp on." With my bare toes, I shoved the material aside so I could make room to pull up my pants. "Then I'd send the damn thing to Kit so she can disguise herself as a hunk of rock, so Flint can't find her. Then this stupid problem would be solved and this would all be over."

There was a long silence during which I believed he might have either left or turned his back on me. Then, I felt him so close, the hairs on the back of my neck strained upward. A tingle moved through my belly.

"The way I hear it," he drawled, his breath whispering over my skin in a feather stroke of heated air, "Is that your sister would never take your call."

That was too low a blow. Even for the monster behind me. I spun around with my shirt in my hand, too angry to care that I was still naked from the waist up. Before I could think it through, my fist shot out.

He caught it long before it struck his stomach. Then he grinned at me. Actually grinned, the bastard.

"I will kill you," I ground out. "When this is over. I'm going to drag my karambit over your throat while you sleep and feed you your own blood."

"Do give it your best shot, Ponytail," he said, with a hooded gaze and a low, throaty voice. "I might enjoy the way your hands roam my body as you try to get that knife from me." His gaze dipped to my chest, where it lingered suggestively, and my eye twitched at the gaze.

"Not that I'm overconfident," he said, "but I dare say you'd enjoy the wrestling match, too."

I glowered at him and clutched my shirt over my chest, putting the distance of a fist between us. "Damn straight I'll enjoy it," I said. "But not for the salacious reasons you infer."

He canted his head. "Such large words for a monster hunter," he said. "Very polysyllabic of you."

"Fuck you."

He didn't respond to that; instead, he stepped back and spun on his heel. As he prowled the room, he lifted objects one by one, as if inspecting them when we both knew he was just doing it to annoy me. "Did you know Ferranus keeps trophies from his human lovers?"

"You don't say," I drawled, trying to decide if I should take the risk of yanking the shirt down over my head while he was distracted so I could at least have the distance of some thin fabric between his intense gaze and my sense of dignity. I hated being left blind for the moment the material draped over my face—he was so damnably fast.

"it's true," he said. "He even has a sash made completely out of nipples."

"You're lying."

He aimed his feet toward the fireplace without showing me his face, so I could tell if he was indeed making up a story to shock me. "I'm Fae," he said. "We don't lie." He lifted the poker from the scuttle and angled it sideways, looking it over. It was made mostly of thick wood, but the hook at the end was made of blacksteel. I wondered just how tough that magical alloy was. Maybe it would have just enough heft that I could whack him over the head with it.

I inched toward him as he tapped it in his hand. It certainly sounded like it had weight.

"If you didn't hide the corset," he said thoughtfully as he dropped the poker over his shoulder. "Then someone in the tavern did." He sighed. "I really hate to have to tear through an entire tavern before I've even had a drink." He spun around to face me. "Are you sure you didn't take it?"

I halted mid-step and shook my head, trying my best to look like I wasn't planning to attack him. "Even if I did, do you think I'd want to be remembered as a pixie?"

"Ah," he said. "Our dear Captain of the Guard. He has no imagination. But the truth is the glamor changes depending on the viewer. Our captain wanted to see a helpless creature, and so he did."

In a heartbeat, he'd closed the distance between us again and plucked the shirt from my hands. His fingers brushed over the skin of my knuckles, creating a buzz of electricity that hummed along in every direction.

I jerked away, surprised, and the curious arch of his eyebrow made me think he'd felt the same thing. Not that he'd comment on it, and since he wouldn't, I decided to pretend it hadn't happened.

Just as quickly as he'd taken the garment from me, he jammed it over my head and hauled the neck hole down to my shoulders. Shocked, and blinking stupidly, I backed up way too late and his mouth hitched at the corner for a second before it disappeared. He took another step, closing the distance I'd put between us once more. There was a peculiar look in his eye as he peered down at me, and for a second, I thought he knew all along that I wanted to take that poker from him and crack him over the head with it. I swallowed nervously.

"Do you know what looked back at me when I first saw you in the raiment?"

CHAPTER 27

MY CHEST FELT ENTIRELY too tight. I couldn't speak to save my soul, and if I had I doubt he'd have paid any attention because his gaze was so intense, so churning with that wild-looking serpent that I was sure he read every motion that ran through my mind as I imagined how to attack him. Except, he wasn't angry. It was something else entirely.

His voice devolved to a rasp. "I saw a mortal who can be reckless, who refuses to get close to anyone because she thinks she isn't worth loving. A woman who hates herself as much as the monsters she kills."

I was so stunned at the assessment that I stood there seething, letting him adjust the strap of my tank top.

"Not exactly flattering," is what I said.

His gaze dropped to my mouth. "You don't think?" he said. "I'm sure I know others would find that sort of woman interesting. But do you know what I really saw?"

I tried not to look interested when I said, "Oh, do enlighten me as to what a monster like you might think of me."

He grinned in a smile that bared his teeth. One more step and he was close enough that I could almost taste his breath, and I knew it would taste of cinnamon.

"Oh, I saw you, Ponytail. A human woman with a long black ponytail tied by a worn elastic left in her hair so long it had gathered several knots. A scar marked your throat. I thought right then that it was a battle wound. Some monster nearly got you, didn't they? But that's just the physical you, isn't it? Inside there's a woman who'd go to great lengths to protect others, any mortal in fact, except herself. Someone who holds a deep belief in humanity as a noble ideal, yet struggles to see herself as worthy of being a part of it."

My throat ached at the bald assessment. Despite standing there dressed in filthy clothes, with the damp of water soaking them into a chill and water still beading on my arms, the room had grown far too small and hot.

"You're wrong," I said through the tightness in my throat.

His eyebrows quirked and his head dipped lower to capture the gaze I'd dropped as I'd all but ducked out of his view. Ever so cautiously, he laid his cheek against mine. And for some reason, some ridiculously tormented reason, I let him.

"Am I?" he murmured with his lips at the corner of mine, fluttering against my skin in a way that made the base of my spine tingle. "Tell me where I'm wrong, Ponytail?"

My hand came up between us, pressing on his chest. I meant to push him away so I could escape the bald look of some expression I couldn't name on his face, one that made every inch of my skin hurt with shame.

But when I felt his heart hammer beneath my palm, I found I couldn't exert any pressure. I swallowed. Hard. Words burbled up despite my best intentions to keep them contained.

"The monster who put the scar on my neck was human," I said, "and it wasn't a fair fight. He nearly killed me. It was Kit who saved me." My voice choked off at my sister's name and it took an effort to finish the sentence. "My sister was the only one who thought I was worth saving, and now she could care less if I live or die."

I almost choked on the last words. The pain in my voice was humiliating. I had no intention of letting the rawness of that admission flay the air between us, but there it was. My hands shook at the confession.

His eyelids shuttered and his expression went carefully blank. He gripped my arms around the biceps as if I was a child trying to evade questioning.

"I asked you before who did that to you. Back in the suite when I came to you as Stone. You didn't answer."

The memory played at the fringes of my mind. I'd lost sight of the fact that it hadn't been Stone who'd asked it because just moments later, the male who asked it of me also attacked me. My mind swam now at the recollection. It wasn't Stone who had asked me, whose voice had been thick with fury. Not Stone. Blade. Blade had asked that of me. Dizziness swam behind my eyes and yet he still kept talking.

"You wouldn't confess the origins of your scar to Stone," he said in a low voice. "And yet you give it freely to me now. What does that say about you, Ponytail? What does it say about us? Do you keep trophies too? After you kill your monsters, do you take something from them?" he asked, and his grip tightened on my arms.

I shrugged him off, surprised he let me go. I retreated toward the tub, and he followed me step for step until the backs of my thighs dug into the rim and he had me caged there.

"Tell me, Ponytail," he said in a voice that rumbled deep in his chest. "And don't lie to me; I'll know. Do you take trophies?"

The sound of the metal clinking against the tub made me look down to where Blade held my karambit and where he was clenching it so tightly, his fingers had gone white.

I didn't dare lie right then. It felt as though I was being asked to swear on the blade that had saved my life so many times it was as good as a rosary. I just couldn't do it.

"Small ones," I whispered in confession. "Insignificant stuff. Like a strip of clothing or a ring." I hung my head. "Sometimes a tooth."

That last hurt to say because my mind flashed me several images all at once of me using the karambit to dig into mouths of monsters and vampires alike to dislodge molars or canines. It wasn't a pretty picture. Gideon didn't even know that about me. I didn't think he'd understand. I didn't think I could stand for him to know the real heart of who I was.

I watched the hand gripping my karambit clench tighter around the handle. It trembled, ever so slightly in his fist. If he heard the deadly way my heart was pounding in my ears, so loud it made me wince, he didn't remark on it. Just stood there, looking at me, that piercing gaze roaming my body with an intensity that made me feel exposed.

A long hiss of air fled his lungs as he finally relaxed, a decision made.

"Whether you wear Erachne's gown or the raiment, others will see what they want," he said in a rasp that was barely audible and the air between us went electric. "But I see you the same as I did at the witch's house before you knew I was the hellhound who trailed you. The same way I saw you at your mentor's. It's your truth I see. What you truly are. And I know by that, we are the same."

At that, he began to unbutton his shirt, and I nearly bolted, realizing that at some point, he must have dressed for real and that he planned to disrobe and attack me again the way he had in the suite of Terran's safe house.

Instinct bade me dodge for the karambit, but he held it up at the same moment he must have seen the intention flare in my gaze. The flat edge of the knife faced me, without threat. One finger scored the air above it, signaling me to hold back.

I did. For the love of a hateful god, I did. Even as my stomach bottomed out and I hated myself for the reaction, I waited like a pinned hare beneath an eagle's gaze.

Then he pulled his shirt back off his shoulders, letting the fabric gather behind his mid back and puddle at his elbows. The knife hung tip downward, an inert thing in his grip.

Naked, his chest revealed a strength and power I'd only seen in one other being in all my time as a hunter. Stone had come close to Blade's physique but where the Consul looked thickly solid like a chunk of hard wood, Blade was all hard sinew and muscle.

With that same lightning speed he'd displayed time and again, his free hand snaked out to grip mine before I could resist. He lifted my palm to partner his along the handle of the knife. A tingle moved over my fingertips. His eye caught and held mine. Inviting me to take the blade from him or surrender to the way his index finger twitched against mine, inviting my touch higher. To the long muscles of his forearm. Beyond it to his chest.

A challenge, that gaze said.

I didn't have much in my miserable life, but I had my pride. I took that challenge and I watched the path of my hand as it traced along a series of raised skin, brands on his chest and arms that meant something.

I distanced myself from that touch, might as well have been watching someone else's fingers hover over each worm of scar branded into his body, the ones that had me so curious the first time I'd seen him in his towel at his apartment door. I forced myself to go numb at the feel of them, told myself I hadn't already memorized them.

But I knew better. Each one felt familiar. When I swallowed it echoed behind my ears like a waterfall.

The symbols weren't large. Each about the size of a thumbnail, they lined his flesh in such an aesthetic way, it was as though an artist had put them there. I touched each one almost as if my fingers were moving across braille, reading the story of a man's confession. His body went tense beneath my exploration, and I was sure he was holding his breath until he spoke and made me doubt the evidence of my own hand.

"I keep brands of my fiercest kills," he said in a low voice. "Symbols that remind me what I am and what they were to me."

It was a strange admission for a violent man like him. Like he wanted me to know the depths of his depravity and was checking my stomach for the deviance I might feel beneath my fingertips. A test. One monster to another.

In a motion so swift, I didn't have a chance to resist. His fingers splayed over the small of my back and he pulled me close enough to drop his nose to the crook of my neck. It was so sudden that at first, I gave in with such ease that it took a waft of cinnamon rising to a cloud around my head to realize just what had happened. Even then, despite my brain screaming at me that this wasn't right, this wasn't done, he was a monster, my eyes closed on their own. Confusion and indecision created a thick muddle of paralysis.

Even as my legs turned to sodden teabags, as my brain rat-a-tatted out a Morse signal for me to get the hell out of there, I did nothing when his lips moved against my skin. Did nothing like a stupid teenager as he inhaled the very air that rose from my pulse.

A curling heat began to worm itself into my core then. He inhaled as though memorizing my smell, and I had to pull in a gasp of air because everything in the room had suddenly gone claustrophobic.

It was an effort not to melt into that embrace. I'd seen what he'd done to Jasmine. I knew his brutality. And even while I struggled with my own traitorous need, his voice cut through the war inside like a flare going up in the darkness, a thick, strangled tone that made the back of my neck tingle.

"What I am is too much, even for those who use me for their own ends," he growled. "I know what it is they see when they look at me. What I want to know is what do you see, Ponytail?"

The question held more demand than I could bear. It pulled images from me that had no business flashing before my eyes, strobing in the glow of that crimson flare.

This wasn't right. I knew it. I was not some stupid teenager. I was a hunter. I knew monsters. I knew the compulsion of vampires, the irresistible pull of sirens and incubus, that every monster had their own allure. And they used whatever means they had within their nature to get what they wanted. What they needed. The question was: what did Blade want, really, from me?

I knew he wanted me physically. As reluctantly as that realization crept upon me, I felt it in his body. I heard it in his voice. I knew his kind even in the mortal realm. Sexual beings who took what they wanted and used it to slake their thirst, willing to do, to say, to pretend what they had to in order to pull that quenching drink of water toward them.

I know because I was that sort, too. I'd used Gideon, trying to get him to fit into that cock-eyed shape in my soul that even hunting couldn't fill. I'd used so many others since then. Used drugs. Used hunting and killing. Nothing fit.

That meant he was right: we were the same, because God help me, the monster in me saw the monster in him and it responded. It wanted to take what it craved, the way a hit of Bloodmist called to me. Consequences be damned.

But I thought of Gideon and all those men I'd used. I thought of Kit. I thought of Jasmine and I reminded myself that the consequences here in Fae were nothing like the mortal realm. Blade wasn't just a man I picked up at a bar.

He was the damned dark enforcer of the Shadow Court and if I for one moment thought I could bed this beast and walk away unharmed, I only had to recall the woman he'd torn apart at his father's command. I just needed to recall that first, gaudy moment I'd taken smoked my first hit of drugs that snaked a path toward my parents' death, to the hit of Bloodmist that had me writhing and sweating on a mattress far and away from the only world I understood.

And that was the thing, finally, that allowed me to gather myself. I pushed against his chest with my palm, and even though I moved him about as much as I might move a mountain, he released me.

With a pivot of my heel so sharp, it nipped at my ankle, I faced the tub, out of reach of his penetrating gaze.

"I think you should leave," I mumbled, my fingers trailing to the rim of the bowl and clenching the copper so tight my knuckles blanched. "And if you touch me again, be prepared to brand another scar into your body."

A long moment of silence stretched itself out between us like an elastic. I felt the pull of its tension and wanted desperately to find some slack. I just couldn't. I kept hearing Jasmine's screams. I kept seeing him hoisting her onto that sink in the Velvet Boar and in my mind she was a ragged and bloody mess as he thrust into her.

I thought I would be sick. When I clutched at the tub, I was ashamed of how white my knuckles were.

"I'll give you ten minutes," he finally murmured.

I nodded, mute, and waved at him over my shoulder. I felt him there, hovering for a minute before his boots scuffed the floor. A moment later, the door closed, and I knew I was alone.

My legs let go, then. I collapsed onto my haunches, my hands till clinging to the rim of the tub, my head between my arms.

Chapter 28

Ten minutes passed and Blade still hadn't returned to ask about the corset again. I wasn't sure if I was relieved or angry at being rushed out of the tub, only to have him take off like a dog off leash for the first time. By the time a sharp rap sounded on the door, I was ready to spit fire.

I yanked the door open, fully prepared for the argument I was running through my mind. But it wasn't Blade at all. It was the Seamus look-a-like standing in the hall holding onto a bundle of material that looked suspiciously like the linen tunic Terran had forced me to wear in his dungeon.

"For sleeping," the rotund Fae said with his gaze lingering on the way the dried blood made my shirt move stiffly as I reached for the garment. "I can have those washed and laid outside the door within a couple of hours. Blade says to sleep now. It will be a long day's ride on the morrow."

"Blade can go fuck himself," I said, but I pulled the tunic from him and let it lay against my leg. I was exhausted and ramped up and hungry all at the same time. "You be sure to tell him that."

The little Fae bobbed a bow and turned tail to leave me staring at his back as he retreated down the stairs. The din of laughter and the murmur of several conversations, some loud, some hushed, warbled up from the main level.

I shut the door, hoping to drown it all out. God only knew where Blade had gone or what he was doing, but if we weren't leaving till morning, I knew I'd not have to see or talk to him for hours.

For whatever reason, the thought of that freedom just made my mood more sour. All the things I wanted to say and yell roiled around in my mind until I slammed my fist into the wall.

I'd sleep in my clothes, bloody and dirty as they might be. And I'd lie on the bed, not under the covers. And if he or anyone else came into the room uninvited, I'd be ready. With a toss, the tunic got flung across the room. I watched it sail toward the chair and miss by an inch.

Boots on, I sagged onto the mattress, testing its comfort. The pillows smelled of lavender when I laid back, and I tucked my head sideways to inhale. The fireplace crackled too cheerily from its side of the room, the snapping of the dried wood a chatter of recriminations that I never seemed able to escape once my eyes were closed.

My eyes trailed to the peg behind the door where I'd hung the duster. I could make out the bulge of the vape hanging from the inside pocket and thought it strange that it seemed so large and noticeable. I had to drag my gaze from the lump and, so to distract myself, I considered changing. After all, there was no need to foul the bed by sleeping in my filthy clothes.

The puddle of material sat where I'd thrown it after the tavern owner delivered it to me. A wordless suggestion from Blade no doubt to remind me of the threat Terran had delivered in the dungeons.

If I closed my eyes, I could still see the bald look of desire on his face. I could feel the way he reacted to me pressed against him. The way his eyes held mine, like he did really know me, like he was searching for something, made the small of my back tingle. My arms splayed out beside me on the mattress, and my boots swiveled back and forth and tried to shut out the memory.

It was no use. As soon as I closed my eyes, that image came back full force. Like an ear worm rick-rolling through my brain.

With a sigh, I flopped to my side and stared at the door. The duster was still there, of course, but this time, it seemed to take up so much space against the wood. I couldn't even see the peg it hung from anymore.

Something was wrong. That door, that peg, was clearly visible just a moment ago. It wasn't just the growing shadow in the room as night fell through the window. I hadn't even turned down the oil lamps.

I heaved myself from the bed and clomped over to the door, thinking that if something was there, it would move when it heard my boots.

Nothing.

I looked askance at it, cocking my head, straining to see through the shadows of material. With a lifted hand, I brushed my fingers along the garment. Ran my palms beneath it. Felt the wood of the door and the peg and folds of leather, but nothing more.

My fingers met the hardness of the vape inside the pocket, and curious, I pulled it out. Blinking down at it, my throat started to ache. I had to swallow multiple times before the water would go down.

There was more inside than I thought. And here I was in a strange tavern with all manner of magic-wielding creatures below and the threat of an ancient and powerful fae with the scent of my lust in his nose. Would there be a better time for a hit?

The decision wasn't really a decision. I bit down on the nozzle and pressed the plunger. Sucking back hard, I felt the sizzle of magic as it coiled beneath my tongue and spread into my cheeks.

Everything became too much, then. The heat of the room, the fire crackling too loudly. Even the splinter in my foot stung more. My clothes felt too tight. I couldn't stop picking at the caked blood on the front of my shirt, so I decided to watch the door to make sure that powerful fae didn't decide to come back in and do to me exactly what he'd started in Terran's suite.

I was still chewing the insides of my cheeks, staring at the door when sleep claimed me.

I woke to full-on darkness, curled in bed with someone spooning me. It took several seconds of confusion and punching through the mist of magic before I realized I was naked. As was the stomach and legs of the person spooning me.

Out of instinct, my elbow snapped back hard and met with something equally solid.

"Fuck," came Blade's gritty, sleep-fogged voice of pained surprise.

His arm, slung over my belly and gone unnoticed till that moment, lifted off me as he cradled his nose behind my back. Thus freed, I scrambled from the bed like a fire had caught the sheets. I ran for my duster, where it hung on the peg of the door all the way across the room. My feet pounded the floor with soft fleshy treads, stopping short when I reached the door and the peg I'd hung it on.

It wasn't the duster I wanted, or the vape. I'd spied my karambit hanging in its sheath above my jacket. That was what I wanted. I no sooner had my fingers on the duster jacket when he closed his fist over my hand.

"If you're thinking of using that knife on me, you might consider how things went the last time you tried to slit my throat."

I twisted beneath his arm. In the time it had taken me to race across the room and touch down on the strap for my karambit, he'd already turned up the oil lamp and jaunted over to me to stop me from pulling out my blade. Now the play of the lamp's light combined with the firelight did something peculiar to his face. He looked…weary.

"Just how fast are you?" I asked, measuring how much quicker he would have had to move to pause to turn on the light and still get to me before I pulled out the blade.

"I can be as fast or slow as you like, Ponytail," he murmured with his eyes hooded. "Ladies' choice."

A sense of horror sped through me as I noted just how naked we both were, how tightly we'd been wound together. My mouth went dry.

I dropped my hands, covering my boobs and groin in the same motion. "Sweet Jesus," I said as full, humiliated horror seeped into my chest. The Bloodmist. Oh, the horror. "We didn't just…"

He chuckled in a low, dark tone as he swept a hand over his hair. "If we had, you'd be missing your head, wouldn't you?"

He dropped his arm as well and stepped back, giving me room to breathe because I obviously needed it based on the hyperventilating I was doing.

"Take your time," he drawled, watching me suck in air. "It's a lot to process, considering you've been zoned out the last few hours."

My gaze snapped to the bed. "Hours?" I'd never lost myself to Bloodmist like that before. Was it the exhaustion or that the magic of the realm was doing something to the magic of the drug? My lips pressed themselves together as I fought through the miasma of possibilities, all of which boded more ill than I thought I could stand.

He ran his palm lazily over his chest as he eyed me and my obvious state of panic, and I found my gaze drawn to the movement the way a cobra might be tempted to uncoil from its warm basket. I was so damned distracted by it that I had to squeeze my eyes closed to ground myself to the here and now, and the very real embarrassment I felt at spooning him in my sleep.

"Please," I said, waving a hand in his direction. "Get dressed." I spun around, showing him my backside instead of the front as a compromise I could live with for the moment. "And where the hell are my clothes? And why? Why in the name of fuck am I naked?"

Because I'd most definitely been dressed. I completely remembered pulling my pants on, and him…and him yanking my tank top down over my head. And yet, I didn't have a stitch on now.

My scour of the floor and surrounding area turned up nothing to cover my bare skin. Even the damp towel was gone. The fireplace chattered its taunts at me even as it bathed me in warmth.

"Here," he said from a few inches behind me.

With a sense of dread, I looked over my shoulder at him to see him dangling the night shirt.

I snatched it from him with a snap and pulled it over my head.

"Your clothes are getting washed," he explained, and his voice came through the material a bit muffled at first, but clarified once it was settled over my shoulders. "I could have dressed you in the tunic myself, but figured if you wanted it on, you would have put it on. And as to why you're naked, you tell me. I found you that way." He cocked his head at me. "I'm guessing my presumption that you might want to sleep in comfort instead of a splinter-in-the-ass trap of a floor was incorrect? That I shouldn't have carried you to the bed?"

My jaw seesawed back and forth as that image streaked naked through my mind. "And you were in bed with me because?"

He shrugged. "I thought since I was in Rome…"

"Fuck you," I growled. "If you're inferring I peeled off my clothes in anticipation of you returning, you are deranged."

"I wasn't the one who decided to take a long, naked nap on the floor. I am merely the gentleman who put you to bed free from assault. A feat, by the way, you might appreciate for its difficulty when a lecherous, blood-guzzling praying mantis such as me is snuggled up next to a naked, delicious-smelling bit of prey like you." He grinned, showing the points of his incisors. "I'm feeling peckish, Ponytail. Mind if I steal a wee nibble?"

My blood boiled. "You didn't have to snuggle up next to me."

He shrugged. "Hounds are pack animals. We love to curl up into a nice warm ball with our besties." He waggled his eyebrows. "But truth be told, Ponytail, you were the one who snuggled me. I merely did my best not to touch the nasty bits every time you shoved that hot, round ass into my hips."

"Get out," I said through clenched teeth.

He shook his head. "Oh hell no."

He prowled toward me, slowly, with deliberation, making me mark his every step before taking another. "I am going to sleep in that bed for the next…" he cocked his head, eyes slanted to the window as though assessing something. "Three hours. And you are going to lie there with me, so I know where you are, and we are going to get some rest."

I snorted. "Deranged doesn't cover what you are. I'll take my chances downstairs."

"Do you know what's waiting for you down there?" he asked. "Don't bother to guess. I'm quite happy to inform you. You might realize there are all sorts of violent Fae in this tavern as well as good, kind, base Fae.

You might know some of those Fae are the brutal sort like I am."

He stopped mere inches from me. "But what you can't truly appreciate is that mortal women are a sort of taboo here in Fae. Like anal sex used to be in your realm before the Internet trained every twelve-year-old boy to expect it from their poor teenage girlfriends. Many of us find the notion of indulging in such a taboo enticing. Some of us have very few scruples about abducting the kind of woman they want, using them however they want, and then selling them into a very lucrative black market once they find a newer model."

My nerves rankled at the thought of those nameless women being exploited and discarded that way. But I wasn't forgetting where I'd first noticed women just like that.

"Like in your tavern," I said, the clench on my teeth no lighter in pressure. "Like the cartel you work for."

He raked his hair with both hands. "My human whores are well-cared for and are all quite consenting. The ones Stone acquires for the cartel, however..." he let the sentiment trail off, all the while holding my gaze. "Well, let's say my father makes a great deal of money on that front because of his counsel. He's an industrious little bee, even if he leans more toward the vanilla tastes."

I snuffed a draft of air out my nostrils. "OK," I said. "So you're all monsters here. You've made your point." I paced toward the door. "But I'm a big girl. I kill monsters. I can handle myself."

He rolled his eyes. "We're not all monsters here. There are some very good fae in the realm. You just have been lucky enough to meet the worst of us." He seesawed his hand in front of his chest. "I'm guessing it's an occupational hazard."

By the time my fingers met the cold leather of the door handle, Blade had placed his palm on the door, holding it closed. The force of his hold, the angle of his arm, made me look up at him.

"I can handle myself." My voice, if not my hard gaze, held a threat I knew he noticed because his face lit up, the monster inside rising to the challenge.

"Is that the drugs talking or the weak girl underneath who needs it to kill those monsters?"

My jaw ticked and he must have noticed the reaction because he inched closer, the arm above me sliding down the door to rest on my waist.

"I know you're fierce, Ava," he murmured in a voice so confusingly gentle that I let him lead me back to the bed. "But let's not waste that violence on Fae who don't need the distraction tonight. Save all that delicious rage for the king."

That thing within his irises moved again, like flame coming to life as it circled the silver ring of his irises.

"I won't touch you," he said, holding his palm up while crossing his heart with his fingers. "I promise."

I chewed the inside of my cheek, thinking. Three hours. Three hours and we'd be back on that horrible horse. My thighs hurt just thinking about it. And to be honest, I wasn't feeling the same rush of adrenaline and magic the Bloodmist usually left me with. Obviously, I'd slept it off because I was too tired to utilize it.

I was bone-weary. Drugged sleep was never good, restorative sleep. I needed those hours.

I sighed as I glared at him. "Touch me again and I'll be the one tearing your throat out."

He smiled and two tiny points showed in his grin. "Not the right thing to say to a violent Fae like me if you're trying to keep my hands off you."

I clucked my tongue against the back of my palate. "I imagine it will be difficult to enjoy that excitement when you're struggling to breathe through the blood in your lungs. But please," I said, rolling my eyes. "Do feel free to test me."

I brushed past him and stalked to the bed. Without getting beneath the covers, I climbed over to the other side. "You take the spot nearest the door so you can protect my womanly charms from marauding Fae intent on exploiting what virtues I might have left."

I didn't wait for his reply. Instead, I sagged onto my side, so close to the edge, I had to hang my arm over for balance. I waited, breath captured in anxious lungs and trying desperately to make my chest move rhythmically. His dark chuckle floated over me, making my heart beat ratchet up even more.

Chapter 29

I woke alone. Wherever Blade had gone, he'd been quiet enough in leaving that it didn't wake me. I wasn't sure what to think of that, except I was glad I woke in one piece, unassaulted. The sun shone through the shutters in lines that reminded me of bar codes on a can of soup. First light had come and gone by at least an hour. Strange. I'd thought he wanted to get going early. I couldn't imagine him just letting me sleep. That sort of kindness wasn't his style.

Stretching, I dragged in a long draft of air and let go a groan. Every inch of my body ached from holding itself rigid so I wouldn't roll over into Blade through the night.

The sounds coming from below the floorboards indicated the tavern was roused and rolling. After swinging my legs over the edge of the bed, I tested my muscles slowly, rotating my shoulders, arching my neck. The soreness left swiftly, which was a good sign. I'd not hurt anything too badly in the battle with the wendigos or the hateful horse ride to and from Erachne's.

As my palm ran the length of the tunic I wore, I scanned the room, looking for my clothes. Nothing, not even the damp towel, turned up to my scrutiny. I guessed the tavern owner had come for my clothes after all, or maybe Blade had given the bundle to him for cleaning. Maybe that was why we were still here instead of hobbling along on the road with Nutkin farting every few yards. Blade was waiting for me to have something decent to put on to act as layers between us on the way back to the castle.

It was just as well. I didn't fancy strutting about in a tunic, or pressing my naked back against his chest, and the only other thing I could put on—Erachne's gown—was not the sort of thing a gal wore to sit atop a sweating horse for hours.

I cricked my neck one more time and stood, sighing out the last of the weariness. The fire had long gone out and was nothing but gray ash in the grate. Chill prickled my skin beneath the nightshirt. I considered pulling a blanket over my shoulders to ward off the cold while I waited for the laundress to return my clothes, but it seemed too much effort.

But I had nothing to do while I waited, and I found my gaze roaming to the peg on the door. If Blade had indeed given the little tavern owner my clothes, then what had he done with the Bloodmist inhaler? The mere thought of him rifling through my clothes and finding that vape sent me tearing across the room to scavenge for the thing. No telling what would happen if he tested it, and even worse…broke it and left me without a single hit.

I was already halfway to the door when a soft rap sounded from the other side.

"About time," I said and made for the handle.

Except…The back of my neck prickled as my fingers grasped it. I paused. Stared at the door. The rap came again, testing, a curious prodding to see if someone was within.

A sort of hairy-legged spider of nervous energy tickled its way up my spine as I narrowed my eyes at the wood frame. It was probably the little Seamus lookalike, cradling the bundle of my clothes. Probably. No need for alarm.

But I always trusted my gut.

And my gut was telling me to let go the handle and step back. I did, swinging my gaze about the chamber to find some sort of weapon because if it wasn't Blade or the little tavern owner, I did not want to be left empty-handed. Not in a place where Blade had inferred I might get my head chewed off.

I caught sight of the poker as it lay propped against the fireplace just as another, shaper rap sounded. Not so questioning this time. More like a battering ram demanding the door split open. I didn't hesitate another second. My lunge for the poker was almost panicked, and even then, I didn't get a chance to grab for it before the door shot open, cracking as it broke through its constraints. Of course, it wasn't the tavern owner or Blade standing there. Oh no. My luck was not that good.

A swarm of stinking, foul-looking, half-sized men stood in the hall. I counted eight, with hair matted so badly, I could barely see their eyes beneath the shag of unkempt locks. Not maids coming up to see if I needed more towels, that was for sure. I froze mid-step, my eye traveling to the poker and back again, trying to decide between bolting for it and slamming the door.

Too late, I opted for the door, because even if part of me wanted to tear them a new one, I wasn't a fool. There were too many of them, and while I might take out one or two, I'd never get to them all before they wrestled me to the floor.

They shoved back. Of course, they did, heaving themselves over the threshold like a phalanx.

I edged toward the poker with my hands out at my sides, buying time. Tension crackled through the air. "If you're planning a quick tumble, you should know I'm not affordable," I quipped.

One of them, a scar-faced male with rust-colored hair, aimed a punch at me. Rookie. I evaded the blow easily with a graceful bob, weaving under his reach as I spun into a backflip. My heart hammered in my throat, dragged into action too quickly after rising. The Bloodmist hit had long worn off, and I was feeling distinctly gnarly. Gnarly and logey, I realized, as I landed unevenly on my feet, paces away, but still too far from the poker to grab for it.

I had to run.

So I did. Reaching for the handle even before I was close enough to touch it, I caught a wink of light and shadow moving through the room. Silent. Not assassins by any stretch, but trying not to disturb the tavern below.

Everything slowed down as the makeshift weapon settled into my fist. Movement, the play of light, even the sound of a cricket caught in the woodwork of the window played fast and furious through my senses.

"I'm not a whore for hire," I said, trying one last time to distract them by acting like a poor, vulnerable mortal woman. "We purchased the room for the night." We. To indicate I wasn't alone. Just in case that helped.

It wouldn't and I knew it. I spread my arms away from my body, balancing, pulling in the gravity to use for momentum when I struck out.

"If you're hoping for a quickie from a mortal woman before her companion returns, then you're deadly wrong." I coated my voice with threat, just in case. I knew once I swung the poker, action would begin in earnest. I needed to delay that as long as I could, because where. The Fuck. Was Blade?

Rust-haired fae should have backed off at the mention of a companion. They all should have. But he just grinned, revealing his pointed teeth adorned with fae-styled grills, made of pewter or some other harmless alloy.

"Don't worry, sweetling," he said. "We aren't here for a quickie."

He signaled over his shoulder for his companions to rush me. Talk was off, it seemed, and violence was on. In the same instant that he lifted his arm to grab for me, I swung.

The poker cut a wide arc and struck him square in the throat. The hook caught him as securely as a gaffed fish. I hauled on my end, jerking the poker sideways to bring it back into play.

He staggered backward, gasping for air. The sound of his drowning in his own blood punctuated the sick thud of his knees as he fell onto the floor, clutching his neck. I doubted I had done mortal damage, but it was enough to give me a slight edge. Just one moment. That was all I needed to duck and weave and aim the poker at the next bastard who came at me.

"You picked the wrong bitch to bother," I said through gritted teeth.

One of them flashed me a smile filled with jagged points. My stomach clenched at the thought that if I didn't hold my own, my skin could well be torn to shreds by those teeth.

Every battle I'd ever fought, I'd fought with deadly earnestness. That was the meaning of my tattoo. It was no different now. I swung with deadly intent, not sparing an ounce of energy. Not holding back out of sympathy or pity. If I missed, I adjusted my stance, aiming lower, going for the stomach. Then spinning in a circle to strike out again, regardless of whether I had hit my first target. Someone howled in pain.

I sucked in a breath, and for a second, a thought nagged at the back of my mind. Why was no one climbing the stairs to investigate? Why didn't the tavern owner care that someone was going bat-shit crazy against several brutal creatures in his only paying room?

I remembered Blade's comments about the violent nature of those who patronized the tavern. Some Fae ate human flesh. Hadn't he teased me about losing my head? By their own admission, they weren't here for rape and assault.

There were so many, I couldn't waste one thrust by checking to see if it hit its mark. Instead, I whirled, ducked, and spun. A stab here, a thrust there. The dance took control of my limbs, like a heady rhythm takes a drummer. I let it go, confident that my body would know what to do.

I was near mad with adrenaline. My elbow snapped out several times, the crunch of bone reverberating through the air like fireworks.

Fluids of all sorts misted my face each time the poker came down, and I thought I just might win. I was giddy with the possibility, grinning like a fool because I had never taken on eight opponents alone before. Gideon would be proud of me. Shea would be jealous.

I kept on my feet and swinging for several moments. But in a flash of horror, I realized I'd overestimated the damage I'd done to the fae who had taken the poker to the throat. By the time I noted he'd stood back up, he'd already launched himself at my legs. He bowled into me with enough force to make me stagger. I slipped on his blood.

Three more dove for my legs as well. I side-stepped, trying to deflect their hands as they grappled for me. The instinctual pace to my right was my undoing. I had no where to go, no space to bring the poker to my defense again. My foot shot out, flat and stiff, aiming for a knee or a shin. The poker flew up as I kicked, knocked from my hand by a scuttle. My weapon clattered across the floor, clawing its way toward the fireplace with an end-over-end scraping roll that finished with a clank as it struck the bricks.

I had one or two seconds at most before they took me down. Knowing that, put the last surge of energy in me, and I raced for the wingback chair, aiming to grab for hefty logs of firewood.

I screamed bloody murder as I went down hard on my back. Bodies piled on top of me. They smelled of onions and musty earth. I felt the weight on my legs and arms, a suffocating pressure on my chest that I couldn't dislodge no matter how much I thrashed, how much I kicked.

"Get off me," I growled, my voice laced with a mixture of anger and desperation. I aimed my teeth at the one closest to my face as he tried to pull a hood over my head. I bit down hard, tasting the repulsive tang of sewer, and gagged as I tried to spit the revolting blood out. But the hood descended, enveloping my head, and the fluid dribbled out onto the fabric.

Next thing I knew, lights popped off behind my eyelids, and sweet blackness closed in on me.

The last sound I heard was the muffled laughter of my captors.

Chapter 30

My inventory of their injuries, once I woke and discovered they'd pulled the hood from my eyes, included several broken bones, a wound on the cheek that looked like a bite mark, and two smashed noses. I thought I saw a broken finger, but from where I lay trussed up by hemp rope on a cold earthen floor, I couldn't be sure. I just knew I didn't have the energy to do more than watch them catalogue the same injuries I was doing.

One Fae carried his ear in his hands like a baby bird and kept weeping over it as he sat crouched with the others around a guttering, smoky fire. All in all, not bad for a gal who'd been out-numbered by at least eight to one.

My own inventory was no less dire than the Fae who had decided to raid the tavern and haul my ass out of a comfortable room. Which was why I was still lying on my side on the floor of what looked like a cave.

I felt along my ribcage with probing fingers and wondered if I'd cracked a rib until a hard poke into the most offending of the hurts resulted in a wince instead of a blackout lance of pain. I knew I'd broken my nose by the way the wind whistled out of me in narrow, niggardly gusts. Each inhalation was like pulling air through wads of raw cotton, and the insides of my cheeks felt like they'd been shredded.

I tasted blood even now, hours after they'd taken me. Once I'd woken up, I'd watched the gang of them for at least an hour before I let them know I was conscious. A trick I'd learned from Gideon early on: gather as much intel as you could if you got caught.

Mind you, in all my years of hunting that had never happened, but Gideon wasn't one to leave things to chance. He'd locked me in a sort of escape room multiple times during my training, complete with goblins he'd paid to rough me up. I would have done anything for him in those days, and proving I could escape became a matter of pride.

This time was for real, and long before I'd opened my eyes more than a shutter, I stored every word I heard, felt around me to assess where I lay, and even ran my tongue over the ground to see if I could gather information that way.

My tongue told me I'd bled a fair bit. Probably from the nose.

After I realized where they'd put me was fairly dark and that they probably couldn't see me, I opened my eyes wider. That was when the firelight and moving shadows became my focus of attention. I peered silently through my lashes, letting my hair curtain my face. I kept my breathing even. I tried not to adjust my limbs, even though they screamed to move. Beside the fire, sat, my bundle of clothing. One of them held up my duster jacket, inspecting it in the light of the flame.

There were still eight of them, but one of them was perpetually hunched over and listing to the right with all the balance of a torpedoed warship. He was the one I'd stuck in the throat, was my guess, and while I'd not hit the carotid, he'd suffered enough damage to make it difficult to sit up straight.

I found it hard not to smile at that.

Instead, I made my eyes roam the space as much as it could without moving my head. Old-fashioned firelight torches had been stuck into the ground along the walls.

The glow flickered over rusty looking wall paintings that seemed to dance with a frenzy animals shouldn't be able to achieve. The creatures painted on those walls looked like they came straight from myth and were companioned by massively tall, winged beings. Several of them reminded me of the bawdy drawings in Pompeii.

So we really were in a cave somewhere. I knew the sensation of warmth, so wherever they'd taken me to was sheltered from the elements enough that the radiant heat from their fire could fill the space.

Just why these grubby little fae wanted me at all was still a mystery. They couldn't have been the ones to have stolen the corset or cursed objects or they'd be fondling them around the fire instead of the disinterested way they combed through my clothing.

And the realization that they had my clothing at all raised different sorts of alarm bells. Someone had given them my things, someone who had access to them. I tried to tell myself it was not Blade who had sold me out, that if he had some ulterior motive, he'd commit his own violence and it wouldn't leave me alive to sit here wondering why a group of filthy creatures were rifling through my clothes.

That moment between Blade and in the tavern was too electric to be anything but genuine. I tried to think of all the times I'd not trusted my instincts to my own detriment. And yet... I'd trusted Gideon. I'd trusted Stone. I didn't have a great track record when it came to men of any species. What if I was wrong? What if all I felt was my own complicated emotions running high on adrenaline and Blade's reaction to me was merely physical?

Trust was a razor's edge of danger. One to be walked by the foolhardy. The thought put a stitch in my belly that ached the more I thought about it, and sitting there watching those shadows move and mumble amongst themselves, gave me plenty of time to brood. Too much time.

So I set myself to a wiser path and roamed the area with a scrutinous eye, took in the way each one moved, what he looked like, the way his hands slid over my things, how much power went behind the thrust that tossed my clothes into the fire.

And that's when I saw it. My duster hanging on a guttered torch beside the fire, the leather getting scorched from being too close to the flame.

I winced as I noted the char marks on the bottom. Gideon was going to cane me for that. But it wasn't just the sight of it that excited me. No. It was the fat toad of a fae facing me across the fire. Those filthy grilled teeth bared in a grimace of confusion as he held my vape up to the light, passed it to a smaller fae with a wine-stain birthmark on his face that resembled a crow's wing.

My vape. A valuable bit of treasure, indeed. The swirling movement of the drug inside played faerie lights on the ceiling of the cave and sparked as the lights hit it.

My vape. My salvation. If I played my cards right, I might have a weapon within reach.

I coughed. Loudly. No one moved.

Louder this time, I managed another, rheumy cough, then curdled what breath came out in a rasp and a wheeze that made even me worry something was wrong.

I gagged on the words that worked past my tongue. *I was dying. I couldn't breath. Someone had to help me.*

As though some god had heard a silent prayer, the little Fae holding my inhaler turned in my direction. I thrashed on the ground, biting down on the pain as I moved. I managed to catch his eye and gawked at him, my eyelids wide.

I wanted him to see me, see my entire face. I took false breaths, like pulling hard on a straw stuck to the bottom of a glass.

"What in the gods is wrong with it?" Toad-face as he elbowed his companion. "Is it broken?"

"It's choking, you nonce," said another. "Do something so we don't lose the investment." He elbowed crow-wing, and all three peered at me with their backs hunched as they leaned forward, curious.

"I'm not going," said toad-face. His nose was crooked. The one whose nose I'd broken, obviously. I grinned to myself.

"I'm still picking dried blood out of my nostrils," he said, and as if no one believed him, he ran a thumb over the bridge.

"Well, if someone doesn't do something soon, we'll have nothing to sell." This from the one I recognized as the one who had been at the front of the phalanx when they'd come to the door at the tavern. Obviously, he was the leader. I remembered biting him at some point during the struggle.

That they planned to sell me, while distressing, at least indicated they'd want to keep me half healthy. Bully for them. I wheezed all the harder.

The leader pushed toad-face toward me. "God's own bowels," he said. "It's tied up. It can't do anything to you."

"My meds," I croaked out with enough effort that it took another good amount of coughing. "I'm asthmatic. I need my vape. Please."

The force of the shove sent toad-face nearly into the fire. He caught himself inches from the flame and teetered to his feet. With a glare back over his shoulder at crow-wing, he shuffled toward me, still hunched over.

"What are you asking for, woman?" he growled, keeping his distance.

I arched my neck, trying all while to appear as though I couldn't breathe. He looked back over his shoulder at the little fae holding my vape. "I think it wants that thing you got."

I bobbed my head as best I could, and he grinned, probably feeling victorious. "Yah, that's it," he said. "It needs that thing."

He waved crow-wing over and held his hand out for the vape. My chest went tight, hope a strangled thing in my lungs.

"What do we do?" the little male asked. "Just pass it over?"

"Hell no," Toad-face said. "That wild cat needs its nails clipped. I'm not untying it. Just drop the tube beside it."

The leader growled into the dark. "Both of you go. She can't take the two of you all tied up like that, and I'll be damned if I let this festering bite be for nothing. If we lose her, I'm taking it out of your pay."

The two facing me looked at each other for a long while before they finally approached.

"My mouth," I rasped out, just clear enough that they could understand without doubting me. "Then the button."

They were close enough that I could see their eyes peering at me with nervous energy. I opened my mouth wide and waited for one of them to put the nozzle between my lips.

I nodded encouragingly when the vape touched down and the little Fae hit the button. I nearly sagged in relief as I inhaled as hard as I could. I made a big show of breathing. Yes. That was it. I was all better now. I smiled.

They smiled back.

"Thank you," I said. "If I don't use it once a day at least, I won't be able to breathe. Do you think you could just slip it into my hand so I can use it as I need to?" My hands were bound in front of me, at least. I'd work out just how to get untied later. But first. The Bloodmist.

They looked at each other, then finally the little male stepped over me, his gaze watching me the whole time. He laid it on my lap atop the grimy and blood-covered nightshirt, then leaped out of the way and raced back to the fire. The other one watched me for a long moment. He scratched at his balls absently.

"Are you better?" he asked as he hunched down to catch my eye.

"Much," I said and meant it. While a small but sharp pebble was at the moment digging into my hip, and I was chilled beyond belief, I was indeed much better. He'd get to see just how much better very soon.

He grunted. "Good," he said, and I thought for a second I might regret killing him. Then he crouched down in front of me, his hands on his knees.

"You might want to sleep for a while. We'll be testing you out before we bring you to the Catacombs of Dread."

I had no idea what sorts of awful things would exist to give the place a name like that, but I didn't care. The magic of the drug was already tugging at my state of consciousness, and my stomach lurched as I realized it would quickly pull away all light and thought as it sent me into a comatose oblivion.

And what wrapped talons around my heart and gave it a hardy squeeze was the thought of what they planned to do to me while I slept the sleep of the drugged.

Chapter 31

Fear kept me awake for three entire minutes before the drug kicked in. Bloodmist wasn't a drug to take in the heat of battle. While the hit was quick, the actual magic mimicked the magic that put a vampire into a near-coma during their restoration sleep. In the mortal realm, that time was shorter and depended on the user. During the worst of my addiction, the coma stage was a few minutes, and I never lost consciousness.

Here in Fae, however, it was putting me completely under and taking me longer to come around. I fought to stay awake, desperate to stay alert, but as the sedative effect coursed through my veins, consciousness slipped away from me. I plunged into a darkness that felt as unfathomable as the surrounding tunnels. I didn't know how long I was out, but by the time light feathered its way into the fringes of the drowsiness, I sensed a presence nearby.

The drug awakened at the same moment, giving accurate measurement to how far from me that presence was. I could hear the swell of roaring heartbeats pounding with excitement and nervousness.

My eyes fluttered open, my vision blurry as it adjusted to the dim light of the campfire glowing over their shoulders.

Two of them hovered over me, their faces in shadow but for the glint of light in their eyes that caught the torches planted into the surrounding dirt. With my hands bound, I had very little options for defense, but the fools had left my ankles clear. If she who hesitates in the mortal realm is lost, then she who doesn't kick ass when confronted by several, lecherous looking fae, might as well ask them to paint fairy art all over her body.

With the surge of magic borrowed from the drug, I kicked out with all my strength, catching one of them off guard, grunting with the effort of putting all my force into the blow.

He stumbled backward, a startled yelp escaping his lips. Tied and awkward, I gave the fight my all. In a roiling mess, with me using my legs for leverage, rolling where I could, kicking when I couldn't. Once or twice, I was lucky enough to bring my fists down onto someone's back. More than once, I was able to kick and scoop for their feet. I missed several times, but once or twice, I landed a solid blow.

I might have bitten one of them.

After a decidedly brutal head-butt to one of their skulls, a blow that took considerable power and hurt more than a bit, the two of them backed off.

Blood trickled from a cut on my lip, mingling with the sweat that drenched my brow. But at least if they came at me again, they'd know to expect a fight. And they didn't look like warriors. So that was something, at least.

I waited, eyeballing each one until they slunk back to the fire, muttering and nursing their wounds. The drug boiled in my veins, making everything too sharp, too loud. All of it was a waste if I couldn't get untied.

Around the crackling fire, their gazes met mine.

"If you come at me that way again," I hissed, my voice laced with threat. "Then you best come at me with the intent to kill."

The firelight flickered, and I knew by the way they eyeballed me that it cast a menacing glow over my face.

The rusty-haired fae snorted. "You're human," he said. "We'll do with you what we will."

A bitter smile played at the corners of my lips. "Then for your sake, I hope your will includes castration."

He recoiled, confidence crumbling beneath the taunt. They exchanged uneasy glances, the weight of my challenge hanging heavily in the air. The power dynamics had shifted, not enough for them to release me or give up on whatever intentions they had for me, just enough that they'd approach me with caution next time.

They found uneasy spots around the fading embers, then, and I sat with my legs bent, arms wrapped around them, the length of the shirt pulled over the knobs of my knees. The Bloodmist pumped through me in waves, stronger, it seemed, than before. By the time they all heaved themselves from the fire hours later and began to pack, I worried things were going to change for the worse. When three of them approached me with a long hunk of petrified tree branch, I was sure of it.

"I need to relieve myself," I said to the one closest to me. Toad-face again.

"Then do it," he grumbled. I noted he wouldn't get too close.

"What? No privacy? No bucket?"

He shrugged. A long, heaving sigh escaped me as I realized there would be no wiggle room, no quarter given. Not now. Not after the resistance I'd put up. I looked him over, contemplating how badly my bladder was aching, feeling the rage building with each spasm.

"I can hold it," I said. injecting as much reluctance in my voice as I could while I lifted my bound hands up to chest level. "Do whatever you need to. Just get me the hell out of here."

He smirked, the bastard, and motioned for someone to help him tie my hands to the branch. Crow-wing was the one who came forward. He avoided my gaze like he was ashamed. He looked young, with barely any whiskers on his chin and a smoother complexion than the others. I held my wrists out, waiting for them to attach the leash to my bonds. I suffered an instant of pity for the poor boy, but pushed it aside. They were all bad guys. They all deserved to be treated the same.

When they were both within close range, I planted my feet as far apart as I could manage. It didn't take much coaxing to bring my bladder to the fight. The splash back of urine as it struck the floor between my legs sprayed over both of them. They cursed and leaped back.

I shrugged as the ghost of a smile tugged at my lips. "Sorry. Guess I couldn't hold it after all."

Standing tall, I swept my gaze over the walls and faces as I straightened my spine as much as I could. The fae who had bound me clenched his fists, seething with rage while the little one swiped at his breeks.

"It's more trouble than it's worth," Toad-face muttered under his breath, the words barely audible. "We should just get rid of it already, Slavin."

The one I'd pegged as the leader, Slavin, cursed. "I didn't give up an ear for nothing," he grouched. "Get a stick. We'll prod it the rest of the way."

The flurry of footsteps scuffling about suggested someone had gone to find one.

"Best make it a long one," I said through gritted teeth.

It was already evident these were what Stone and Blade called base Fae. Creatures with magic but unable to wield it. Fae who needed brute violence and gang assault to survive. While it might have been smart to fight back to show them I wasn't just a compliant human, there was no way they were going to just let me go. I'd just given them a reason to stay clear of me. And clear of me meant they weren't going to untie me. Not smart.

Yet I couldn't find it in me to regret fighting back. Some part of me knew that fighting was what I did best. I'd just have to pick the right time. Judging by the way crow-wing ran back in from the front of the cavern with a long thick branch, holding it with both hands, I guessed that wasn't going to happen any time soon.

Slavin took one look at the length and grunted. "Whittle it down to a point worthy of a vampire's heart," he said. "Let's see how it fares against the threat of a stake."

I chortled to myself at the comment as I waited, hands in front of me, fingers tapping my stomach. I felt like a kid with ADHD high on a dose of sugar. Ants crawled up my spine, begging for a release of all the energy. So, despite my best intentions to wait for the right moment, when they came at me again with a long hemp rope attached to that sharp, pointy stick, the Bloodmist raged until I ended up fighting like a cornered beast.

But it was short-lived. Even if two of them went away with fresh bites on their arms, they succeeded in tying my ankles together with enough rope to give me an awkward, short-paced step. Then they formed a tight circle around me, brandishing the stick. It was clear they intended to use it to prod me deeper into the cavern, like a reluctant beast being herded along.

As two remained behind me to prod me forward, and the others leading the way deeper into the caverns by way of torches they held high above them, their conversation drifted toward what they hoped they'd get for me and where they'd take me first. None of it sounded good. Talk of Dark Enclaves and indenture, suggestions of becoming fodder for baser creatures than they. Far worse things got suggested and shot down, mostly because it seemed the fae were lazy. Slavin's comment that he didn't want to go too far into the caverns was more about getting rid of me quickly at the taprooms than it was fear of facing something called a hoar beast who was likely to eat them as buy me.

I remained silent, considering the fact that my attacks might not prove quite so defensive if they decided to give up the compunction to keep me as unmarred as possible. Then, I brooded over ways to get free enough to kill them and dance in their blood. I imagined taking Slavin's front tooth and using it to gouge out his eyeballs while he watched his friends die.

Manifest what you want, the 'woke' contingent of humanity always chanted. Well, I manifested that fantasy at great intensity for the entirety of the journey as they continued to discuss their options, each suggestion more chilling than the last. Their laughter echoed through the cavern, mingling with the sound of their footsteps and the occasional prod of the stick against my back.

One bright spot was that they hadn't seen it necessary to take the vape from me. Crow-wing even fished it from the floor of the cavern after I'd dropped it in the fight and gave it back to me. It was still in my grip as I staggered on.

The longer and farther they pushed me deeper into the dark recesses of the cavern, the more I realized escape would take more than a bit of magical drug. Even with a good sense of direction, I'd already lost my bearings in the gloom.

Eventually, the chalky walls of the cave started to show parts of broken bones embedded into small alcoves in the stone walls. I kept trying to figure out what they were, but if I paused too long, the fae either poked me from behind or yanked on the leash, making me stagger or flinch. Dust rose up from the floor with each step to coat my feet and toes with ash colored grit. I started holding my breath every five or six inhalations to keep my lungs clear of the ash and dust.

By the time the walls of the catacombs were lined with fully skeletal remains, meticulously arranged in intricate patterns that made my spine crawl, I had started to recognize some of the shapes. Most of them were human. But some seemed born of myth and legend. I was pretty sure I saw a mermaid, her tail fused and curved around what appeared to be a centaur.

It could have been beautiful if it wasn't so macabre. But my escorts—they seemed oblivious to it all, and the further we trod through the tunnels, making turns that I lost count of despite my best attempts to memorize the path, I realized the truth.

Even if I could escape the clutches of the Fae who held me, I wasn't getting out of the caverns alive.

CHAPTER 32

I was still working through the realization that I was lost without these Fae to guide me back out, when the passage turned yet again and branched off into tunnels that led deeper still into the caves.

The air was thick with an ancient scent, a blend of damp earth and rotting meat. My heart pounded in my chest as we continued. The caverns formed a labyrinthine maze of twisting tunnels and jagged stalactites. Shadows danced upon the rough-hewn walls, casting eerie silhouettes that seemed to mock my every step. As I trudged forward, my captors flanked me on all sides, just out of reach of attack.

Yet, despite my resolve to maintain calm, a shiver ran down my spine as we plunged deeper into the darkness, and my skin prickled with an unsettling anticipation. The scent of damp earth mingled with an underlying hint of decay. A sickly sweetness clung to the air.

As we plumbed the ever-thickening darkness, the sounds of distant murmurs and echoing footsteps grew louder. My heart pounded, matching the thrum of voices that rose and fell in a swell that indicated we'd found some sort of civilization at last. The residual effects of the drug still gathered in pools within my veins. The sounds of their feet as they shuffled along, the feel of the ropes against my skin. It was agony to have it all so clarified without being able to act on any of the sensory load that came at me. My feet ached as though they were nothing but raw wounds. The claustrophobia of the passageways was made worse by the swelling of my broken nose.

Around us, soft flickers of ethereal light danced about. Dread climbed my spine like a spider when they winked out and on, moving with trails of light that suggested whosoever or whatever it was, it was most eager to see why a human was in their midst.

We wound deeper into the catacombs. The passageways expanded and twisted until it opened up to a vast chamber, its ceiling lost in the darkness above. As if we'd somehow reached into the past to an old wild West town, the area presented a cluster of rough-hewn buildings erected like a town square. Torches and gas lamp posts lent the village light, while polished copper columns placed strategically into the darkest crannies cast that light back. The effect was one of early morning light, with a lovely sun-warmed glow.

The acrid scent of burning wood fires and the thick, fatty aroma of open-fire roasting drifted on the stale currents of air coming in through natural vents in the rock. I was hanging my head back, studying those vents, looking for evidence of an outside exit, when the stick poked into my back. I jerked as the sharp point of it scored into my spine.

"Move," said Slavin, who had taken control of the poker from the little fae. "We're going there." He pointed to a massive closed-in gazebo made of rough-hewn timber and gave a short nod to one of his comrades. "Go get it registered." It. Meaning me. I was getting used to being referred to as a thing. Couldn't say I liked it much.

From ahead of me, the little fae began reeling in the rope at his order, and I moved along with it, my heart in my throat as I recognized a Gideon-esque opportunity about to open up. One more step and I could lift my bonds up over his head. Strangle him and use him as a hostage for my freedom.

But he stopped coiling the rope too soon, and I was left several feet away from the chance to strangle him. My fists clenched at my sides as disappointment dropped a stone in my stomach. The vape in my grip felt cold and hard. I tightened my fist around it, determined not to let it drop, no matter what happened.

I raised my eyes to the wooden sign hanging above the broadly arched entrance, lit by some magic to show runes and words carved into its surface. "Skin and Teeth Auction" it read.

The sign squeaked like a rusted weather vane in an invisible and unfelt breeze. More magic, I supposed, meant to enhance the aura of mystique surrounding the place.

My gaze dropped to the environment surrounding the framework of timbers that arched over a circular platform at the heart of the gazebo. Beyond the platform, from deep into the shadows that swallowed up shape and form of any sort, a motley group of base Fae gathered in a cluster of noise and waving arms.

If I concentrated and strained to hear just one thing through all the murmuring and conversations, I could make out the sounds of argument cutting the air as they harangued each other for placement in the bidding queue, explaining in wheedling tones that their items were far more important than another's.

As I watched, a blast of light pierced the darkness, lighting up the gazebo platform and clawing its way into a chamber just beyond it in the way a cut of lights suggests the start of an arena rock show. So. Not all fae here were unable to access their magic. Someone inside had enough power to wield light. And it was enough that it revealed at least ten more creatures of all sorts, along with a dozen humans. They stood rigid against the inspection of a host of High Fae. All of them shackled to the stone walls by blacksteel chains.

"They're about to start," hissed Slavin. "Hurry. Before there isn't any time for it to get checked over by the high bidders."

Trolls paraded back and forth like soldiers, stopping now and then in front of a creature pointed out by a High Fae. An inspection, I realized. The High Fae patrons then prodded at the merchandise with magic instead of invading fingers. I watched mouth after mouth open as if yanked by some invisible force. Saw several snakes of light coil around a throat. Nausea rolled through my stomach and twisted my bowels. I tried to remember Erachne's comment that not all fae were brutal, violent creatures, but it was difficult to imagine here.

I swept a glance at the seven who still surrounded me. They were all watching the same thing I was, no doubt waiting for their scout to return and tell them he'd acquired a place. The look of outright greed on their faces as they regarded the High Fae milling about, the pouches they carried in cupped hands, made me want to yank out every grill and shove it up their asses. Not for the first time, I twisted my wrists in the bonds and cursed the scraping of the rope that bit into my skin.

Suddenly, the holding area went dark, and the platform lit up. Beside me, Slavin groaned. A sudden craning of his neck drew my attention back to the holding area. It had gone dark again, but two trolls had emerged, and between them, my little fae captor fairly capered along. He was excited. Waving at us.

So that was that, then. My time was quickly running down. With a sigh that I kept buffered beneath my breath, I scanned the rest of the space, doing my best to ignore the steady path the trolls and my little captor were taking toward us. There was an escape route somewhere. There had to be. An opportunity. Something missed that most waking merchandise didn't notice.

As my eye took in the audience sitting in chairs that fanned out around the platform, I realized there were more than just High Fae here. I recognized a few demons and mortal looking women who were no doubt witches. One black-haired woman caught my eye. She looked vaguely familiar, but by the time she started to turn from profile to full view, my captors had yanked on my bonds.

I lurched sideways and cursed him soundly.

"Shut up," he growled. "Or I'll give you away to the first witch I see."

"That's not much of a threat," I told him. "Considering the last witch I saw, I killed." I grinned at him, confident he'd fully comprehend the issue I'd present to whoever purchased me.

The little fae returned with the trolls, clutching a paddle with a blank slate. "Lot twenty two," he said.

Things sped up then. Slavin bit down on my shoulder hard enough for his grills to dig into my skin. I flinched at the sudden violence, but too late to back away. He drew blood, the bastard. In a flash of movement, I recognized by now as a sort of fae speed, just slower than Blade's, he grabbed the paddle and spat a mouthful of my blood onto the surface of the slate. With an awkward hand that indicated he was unaccustomed to writing, he drew out a rune. My lot number, I supposed, marked in my blood.

They relinquished me then to the trolls, and I was ushered to a small, elevated viewing area at the back, where several cages lined the walls. Five other captives were already confined. Four of them were human, all of them male. One looked to be a young base Fae with round eyes and an innocent face. He was bound by his feet, with his hands in some sort of sack. He hunched on the floor with his arms around his knees, staring ahead at nothing and responding to no stimuli. He was either in shock or so far into a state of PTSD that he couldn't do more than keep his heart beating, his breath moving.

It was the look on his face that made my heart ache. A flash of image ran through my mind, of a boy chasing his teacher with a bloody pair of scissors, and my lip curled back in revulsion. These were all victims. All the kinds of people I'd vowed to protect, and now here I was among them. It was hard not to struggle as I was tied to the wall between two ragged looking men with heavy beards. A flurry of activity seemed to take over the patrons as they realized a late entry was added to the roster, but in the end, only one fae approached me. A tall, wiry-looking male, but not High Fae, though he was well dressed in a silver-threaded garment of good tailoring. Instead of the luminescent quality I'd noticed in Blade and Stone's skin, his had a jaundiced cast.

"What is she?" he asked the troll, who directed him to a paper stuck to the wall above me.

Apt to be violent if given quarter, it read. *but can be controlled by withholding the instrument clutched in her hand. She needs it to live and will acquiesce to any demand if threatened with its removal.*

The fae made a thoughtful sound deep in his throat, and his glance went to my curled fists.

"Are you violent, female?" he asked. "You speak the English, do you? Not some guttural noise that I can't understand."

"I understand you," I said.

"Then are you prone to violence?"

I shrugged as best I could with my hands bound. "Untie me and see," I said.

With a deep-throated chuckle that sounded more benevolent than the kind of nefarious sound I expected to hear from him, he said, "They often put those disclaimers up to attract certain bidders. A sort of bait and switch as you mortals would call it." He canted his head at me. A blink, and a membrane slid down over his eyes.

"My name is Castor," he said, and then his hand went up in front of his mouth as though he'd said too much. "I mean, my name is John." He laid a finger over his lips. "We don't give our real names to just anyone here in Fae."

"You think I care?" I countered. "To me, you're a nameless monster." I didn't need to reiterate that I killed monsters. It was written above my head.

He shrugged, unimpressed with my insult. "Everyone has the face of a monster beneath the comely visage they present to the world. It just takes the right circumstance to remove the mask."

Edging closer, he leaned toward me, conspiratorial. "But I suppose now that you have the power of my true name, you might use it against me." He smiled, a mirthful movement of his mouth that sent up a red flag in my hunter's heart. Protect, the flag said. Innocent. I ignored the warning. No one here was innocent.

He waited, as though he'd said something important and I wasn't catching it. Then, finally, he sighed. "I suppose it doesn't matter now," he said. "Since you likely won't be alive long enough to wield that power. How very fortunate for me." The membrane slid down over his eyes again and flicked back up.

He held my eye so boldly, I began to feel the way a piece of chocolate cake might moments before it's devoured.

"I'd bid for you," he said, "but I'm not interested in wasting my magics on taming a violent helper. But I do wish you well, human."

"Ava," I said, not sure why I confessed my name, but there it went. I marked his face, memorizing every feature. My gaze dropped to his fingers as they moved like birds over his chest. Each finger sported a tattoo that phased in and out as he gestured.

"Goodbye, Ava," he said, finally. "And good luck." He strolled away and out through the door toward the gazebo. The lights of the platform blazed beyond it for a long moment before it went dark again.

"They'll be starting soon," said the man beside me.

I dragged my attention from the blackness where Castor had disappeared to the man beside me. His face was scarred and weary-looking, a man who had unspoken tales of hard use.

"Is there a way out of here?" I asked.

His chortle was a rasp of hopelessness.

"Yeah," he whispered. "Death."

CHAPTER 33

HIS WORDS SENT A chill down my spine. "Have you tried to escape?" I asked in a low voice, my eye on the trolls as they shambled over to a man who hung from his bonds. The way the man's shoulders bowed in made it clear he had no energy in him left to fight.

My companion's voice was laced with resignation as he spoke, and a dark, humorless laugh fled his lungs.

"There is no escape from Fae." He nodded at the space where I knew the platform waited. "This is the way out. You've entered a realm of shadows here. No one will find you. No one will come. Whatever happens tonight, at least I'll be done with Fae, finally, whether I take my own life or they do it for me."

I leaned closer to him. "But there must be a way out. A weakness in their defenses. Something you just didn't see."

The look he sent me held a mix of sympathy and skepticism. "You're new to Fae if you think there's a way out of this damned place. It's the dregs of the world. No one comes here unless it's to commit acts that even Fae find horrendous. You can't break free, and even if you did, the horrors that lie beyond these caverns... they will consume you. The best we can hope for is a quick death."

I met his gaze, my voice unwavering, frustration mounting within me. I sucked the back of my teeth. "You give up too easily."

His shrug suggested he thought otherwise, and I didn't have the heart to press him more. I knew despair when I saw it, and it made my stomach feel like a lead weight had been tossed into it as I studied him. What had happened to them all to make him feel as though this was his escape? That the thought of what happened beyond this auction would be preferable to fighting for his freedom?

I watched the parade of Fae leaving the room to find seats beyond the platform. Patience was becoming a liability by this time; opportunity the likes of which Gideon would say should present itself waning so thin it might never appear.

And just as I was considering the thought that we might all end up on the auction block before good fortune could intervene, the man the trolls had been examining was released from his bonds. He shot me a glazed look, seeking my eye and holding it. I hadn't thought he'd been listening, but the intelligence, the clarity in his gaze, was evident in that look.

This is your chance, it said through the dull shine of despair. Take it.

He started to struggle, thrashing in the troll's clutches with what had to be the last of his strength. I could tell by the way his muscles appeared all knotted and lumpy that he didn't have much power left. He was giving me the last of the energy he had.

His struggles infuriated the troll, and with a growl, the huge handler began pounding on the man's back. The poor soul fell beneath the blows. On his knees, the man curled up into a ball, tucking his head in, holding his arms over his neck.

A growl tore from me as the Bloodmist rose like smoke in veins, amplifying my own anger, calling out to the last vestiges of adrenaline in my own glands. I kicked out and twisted in my own bonds. Shouted. Roared like a beast. "Monsters," I yelled. The sound of my shouting echoed back at me. "Bastards."

The human beside me grabbed my arm, his eyes wide with fear. "Idiot," he hissed. "They'll kill you."

I turned my gaze to him, my eyes narrowing as I tried to sort through my disgust at his surrender to see through to the man who had probably already done everything he could, to no avail. I tried to see the victim, not the coward. Tried to remember what it was like to be a champion of those who didn't have the strength to fight back.

I spared a thought for Kit as I contemplated my next move. For her, I'd come to Fae. For her, I'd gone to war for a battle she didn't even realize she was fighting. To keep her safe, I'd accepted the role of killer instead of protector. But if I moved to save these poor men, would the Shadow Court realize I'd been abducted from the job they'd set on me and not deserted it? In the end, when I was gone, would anyone know and stay their hand when it came to my sister?

I might be sealing her fate in the next moment. One decision, one heartbeat away from the point of no return, and I knew I couldn't hold back.

This was what I existed for, all I'd ever be. A killer. Just as Lilah had said, just as Stone had said. Killing was all I was good for. And Kit was a world away. These men didn't have to die. Not here. Not this way.

I could do something about it. Or die trying. And that had to mean something.

"According to you, I'm dead anyway," I hissed. "But I'm not going down without a fight."

Another dull thud sounded. A huff of expelled air amid a groan of pain. My stomach lurched at the sound, and when the troll landed another blow on the fallen man's back, my stomach recoiled automatically in sympathy.

"Fuck you," I shouted at the troll. "You revolting mountain of limp dick. Take on someone with some spit and fire left in them." I yanked on the bonds, straining against the immovable weight of them. "Or are you a coward? Afraid you don't have the guts to go against someone who isn't nearly dead already?"

I was barely aware that the gazebo beyond the holding room had gone quiet, that the audience was on their feet. I just knew the troll paused, his foot aimed mid-air at the fallen man's midsection. He swiveled his head in my direction. Eyes way too small for the size of his head, and too narrowly set to be anything but myopic, panned over me. Anger settled over the deadpan expression.

The man next to me kicked me in the shin. "Keep quiet," he ground out. "They'll come for us next."

I panned him with a long, pointed look. "That's the plan," I said.

My gaze shifted to the torches lining the walls. An idea formed, one borne of the possibilities the Bloodmist flickered through at a speed I could barely keep up with. "Fire," I said. "I've never met a monster who wasn't scared of it."

"You haven't met a demon then. Or a fire-wielding fae."

I tilted my head at him. What did he know of demons, I wondered. In the suffocating heat of the holding pen, with a man's life hanging in the balance, I supposed it didn't matter. What mattered was how I could use him. How I could make his sacrifice count?

"Help me distract them," I whispered to him. "That's all I ask." That was it. That was all I had time for before I started to thrash against my bonds, kicking out, screaming at the top of my lungs curses that would make a hardened general turn rosy red from shame. The man next to me started to rattle his chains. He yelled, cursed. Then the man next to him.

I felt like Spartacus in that moment, and I had no doubt the others felt similar. We weren't going to go gentle into that dark night. Not one of us.

By the time the guards closed in, annoyed and irritated at the bothersome noise that was drawing the wrong sort of attention from their patrons in the audience, I was ready.

They came for me first, raining blows that I dodged and ducked thanks to the play in the blacksteel links and shackles. That drove them mad enough to yank on them, pulling them from the stones in an effort to strike at me. The sharp bite of the blacksteel on my wrists as the chains tore from the wall sent a jolt of pain singing its way down my arm to my wrists.

But that was my moment, and I took it. I pulled hard on my end as I swept out with my feet, dropping the troll to his ass in surprise. His release of the chains was automatic as he tried to catch himself before he thudded with force to the floor.

By the time any of them realized I was free, my feet were already aiming for the nearest torch.

Three steps. That was all I gained before they understood what was happening. Three steps that tore the oxygen from my lungs as I dodged and twisted, trying to keep myself from being caught up by strong arms.

By sheer luck, I was able to duck to avoid a roundhouse punch to the jaw. Cheers rose around me. Shouts of encouragement from my fellow captives. The other captives, those not beaten into silence, stomped on the cavern floor, creating a symphony of noise that drew more attention from the gazebo, enough that the auctioneer himself barged into the holding chamber. If his gaze fell on me dodging and weaving my way to the torches, I didn't see it. All I had eyes for was that flame.

When the moment came, I saw it. A small gap between two meaty looking trolls that showed a large flame roaring with fire. What Bloodmist still snaked its way through my veins was enough for me to smoothly execute a shoulder roll between them. I came up in a snap of hot energy. Grabbed the torch from its holder, its flickering light clawing its way into the darkest recesses of the chamber.

The wood of the gazebo was old, I knew. I could smell the dryness of it. I could have tossed the torch at the framework, lit the entire place afire, sending the bidders running for freedom.

But I wanted the bastards running the place. I ran for the auctioneer. He was too arrogant, too blinded by the results of hundreds, maybe thousands of auctions before this, to realize what was truly happening until I was within a foot of him. I felt the whoosh of air behind me as one of the trolls lunged for me and missed.

The other captives shouted louder. They rattled their chains. The din grew and grew until the whole of the holding pen was nothing but an electrified swell of air that tightened its energy like a vise.

A grin stole my lips. A moment. That was all I needed. One second and I would have the fire shoved up his ass, and I'd buy the prisoner's freedom with his death.

I could feel the trolls at my back, their slow gait hammers on the stone floor that were too powerful and too heavy to keep up with me.

But the auctioneer...he was fast. I suspected at first he was high Fae by his delicate skin, but a high Fae like Blade would have been too quick for me to corner. This Fae was not high Fae. Caught somewhere in between, he had magic all right. But not enough to move like Blade or wield his magic unconditionally and without consequence.

I cornered him. His eyes flashed at me as he backed up against the wall. The eyes of a hundred bidders stung my back like bees. The silence of the room and the platform and arena behind me felt vacuous.

And then the arena broke out into applause. As though this was all part of the show. With the audience jeering behind us, I flattened him against the wall with the torch at his face.

He flinched. I raised the torch high, the flames illuminating my face and warming my brow as I held it between us.

"I should kill you," I said in a low voice. "I should raze this place into ashes."

He held up his hands in the space between his chest and mine. "I'll let them go. Just drop the torch."

Something danced in his gaze that made me pause as he raised his hand, gesturing over his head. "Guards," he said in a very low voice. "Let everyone go."

Long moments of indecision swelled the air as the trolls thought through the command, but then finally, they heaved sighs so loud their breath wafted over me. It took an effort of will not to wince at the stench.

I held the auctioneer at bay as a stampede of bare feet rained around me like a long-awaited storm on arid ground.

I waited, wanting to be sure the captives had gained some distance before I made my move.

Because there was no way I was letting the Fae in front of me live. Because I knew one thing about myself now: I was a killer. Not an assassin who picked off targets from behind walls or glamored corsets. I was a hunter. I killed monsters. And he was a monster.

I must have waited a moment too long.

In the same instant my brain decided now was the time to attack, someone grabbed me from behind, grappling my wrists and wrenching me sideways. The torch fell from my grip onto the stones in a spray of sparks.

I hadn't heard him, the troll who had approached. There had been no movement in the auctioneer's eyes, no signal that anyone stood at my back. It was as though he'd popped in from thin air.

"You took your time," the auctioneer drawled.

I tried to extract myself from strong arms, but whoever had me, had me so tightly I could barely expand my ribs for the stretch he was giving my shoulders. I gave a half-hearted attempt at a flip, but his feet were solidly glued to the stone floor, and there was no moving him. I ended up flailing in his embrace.

The auctioneer whistled and the other trolls shambled forward, shoving ahead of them, the group of Fae who had abducted me in the first place.

A brief, unproductive haggling session ensued while the monstrous thing holding me breathed hot air over the top of my head.

After a time, when my shoulders had gone numb and the pins and needles in the tips of my fingers had stopped firing in the wake of a cold numbness, the auctioneer somehow insulted my Fae captors. Someone spat on the stones. One of the trolls shoved at the leader. The next I knew, I was bound once more while the troll held me immobile beneath the little fae's ministrations.

Slavin came face to face with me, his hands planted on his hips. "I should leave you here," he said with a glare at the auctioneer. Then with a jerk, he tugged the ropes taut, and the thing released me.

It was only as I looked back over my shoulder, once we were several paces away, that I realized the thing holding me had been a Boggle, raised from the mountain earth itself, and that the chains around its neck sizzled with magic.

The rune on his forehead read 'Mhet'.

Dead. That's what the word meant. Dead, but still enslaved like a zombie. With no way out and no freedom even from the grave.

The word whispered through my mind for the entire trek as my Fae captors led me deeper still into the catacombs.

They tried to sell me half a dozen more times, testing out the smaller markets and the taprooms. I fought every time each and every time someone came to inspect me. I fought and made my sale a living hell for anyone who dared come near. I lost time and marked the passage by the number of fires they made in deserted parts of the tunnels where natural vents in the mountain pulled the smoke up and away from them, leaving me to cough in the darkness at the vestiges of ashen smog that trailed my way.

Those fires cooked stinking and rancid meat they found in the tunnels. Rats, probably, or worse. And it chased away the chill enough to keep me from shivering myself into a broken jaw.

Without sunlight or moonlight leaking in through the depths of the caverns, it was impossible for me to tell when one day began and one ended on my own. But the little Fae gathered around in a cluster, like a pack of huskies, and went to sleep three times. I took that to mean the passing of three days. Those times, they tied me to a stake they drove into the ground, bent, and drove the other end in.

At least, they gave up trying to accost me. I counted that as a win even if they only fed me sporadically, supplying me with scraps of bone with little meat, and crab apples from their stores, a hunk of moldering strong smelling cheese in a leather pouch that they slung over my neck because they didn't relish coming close to me more than they had to. By that time, I didn't care if I ate. I lived on hits of Bloodmist and waited for the moment I could take advantage.

By the time we entered what Slavin called, the last tavern, one low fae, a squat figure with straw-colored hair, had the nerve to slip his fingers between my thighs. I had just enough energy to bring my knee up to his nose.

We fled amid a shower of rotten fruit and stones. An hour of shuffling later, we stopped. All of us were exhausted.

This time when they tied me, it was to a tangle of underground tree roots. My vape was empty. They refused to feed me while they munched on whatever they'd managed to catch in the dark passageway.

"Let's just sell it to Lucifer and be done with it," said one as he spit a bone at the fire. "He is always looking for a mortal who can withstand the rigors of his menagerie." He sent a long hateful glance my way. "It's proved that at least, and no one will miss it when he breaks its body."

"Maybe you don't fear the trip to Hades," said the one sitting next to him, "but I would rather kill her myself first than go there. The bitch is not worth the price of that admission."

Slavin stretched as he fed another piece of wood into the smoking fire. "She might be a good fit for the Kennel if we could get her out of the catacombs and through a portal. Errol could put her in the cage to fight the witch born. I'd gladly take a loss to see the sorceress carve her heart out with a bolt of magic." He shivered. "Except with Maddox gone, the portals have been impossible. She might not make it through alive."

"Would that be so bad?" another said, and they all turned to me and studied me for a long time. It wasn't difficult to see the eagerness and relief in the stares. They wanted to get rid of me, but were not willing to give in just yet. I half-expected them to grumble or argue more, work through the logistics of taking me to a realm through malfunctioning portals.

So I wasn't surprised when Slavin ran his hand over his face, scrubbing his skin as though he were washing himself of responsibility. A fae Pontius Pilot.

"We have one last place we can take it," he said, and the sharp inhales of the others made my skin crawl.

Wherever it was they planned to take me, it terrified them all.

CHAPTER 34

I WAS WALKING TO my death, and I knew it. As we tramped deeper into the darkness, every current of air a whisper of dread that hissed in my ear.

I took no satisfaction in knowing I might have made my fate worse by struggling. Some small part of me wished I'd not fought at all. If I'd just been compliant and submissive in the first tavern we'd visited, I might have escaped by now. And had a hell of a lot shorter distance to run if I did escape. I blamed the Bloodmist.

Now, advancing even further into the passageways, I doubted there was a way out even if I did manage to escape. I'd had precious little sleep and now stomping along on aching feet, with my hands bound at my sides this time, I was left to weave and sway, doing the best I could to keep my balance as I trod over the dank and damp earth of the curving passage.

My feet ached where they weren't broken and chafed. In the places where cuts and abrasions scored the flesh, enough dirt had embedded into the wounds that it thankfully made the skin numb. In the back of my mind, I knew I should be worried, but the greater part of me, the part that knew I wouldn't live through this latest parade into the catacombs, was grateful for the reprieve.

I stopped avoiding mucky puddles that gathered where condensation dripped brackish fluid onto the floor. If infection took me out before lockjaw did, I'd not complain.

My skin hummed with the magic from the last residue of drug. Every sense tingled as I noted every hair on the backs of their necks, every sound of their footfalls on the stone floor. My thigh muscles burned. Scratchy eyelids rasped down my eyeballs with each blink. While my senses were heightened, my energy stores were almost non-existent, the result of constant and repeated adrenaline dumps.

I was thirsty, too. And somehow, that seemed worse than all the rest.

After what seemed an eternity, torchlight flickered along the stone walls toward us from somewhere in the distance in purples, greens, and orange hues. The glow cast eerie shadows that danced with an otherworldly radiance against the walls of the catacombs. With the respite of light, I could see that the walls were not smooth and polished stone, nor were they lined with bones the way the earliest parts of the cavern walls had been.

Now, they appeared distinctly serpentine, with scales of stone and rock weaving over and under each other in a pattern that might have been beautiful if the dread wasn't already riding my spine like a jockey.

The heat that wafted back from the chambers ahead felt like a kiln, and in the bleary exhaustion of my mind, I thought we'd somehow descended to the very core of the earth. I thought of Lilah the witch, then remembered my battle against her kraken when she'd plunged me into the depths of its belly, and I even considered the possibility that we'd somehow traversed into the stomach of a dragon. She'd tried to warn me, I remembered, and I'd laughed at the thought that I could ever be afraid to die.

Voices rose in the distance above the dripping noise of condensation, the footfalls of my captors striking the ground in near unison, my own shambling, shuffling footsteps. As if the fae with me also knew this was the end, they picked up their pace. Some murmurs ahead of me suggested they considered turning back. The way Slavin halted, canting his head and holding up his palm to the rest of us, certainly indicated he wasn't sure if he should continue.

Like hell. I was almost there. I wasn't going to turn away from my death now. Not when I was so close to ending this misery. If it took the last of my energy, I was going to finish this.

"What's the holdup?" I demanded, my voice a rasp that sounded like I'd swallowed a wad of sandpaper. "You pussies changing your mind?"

With one last bracing breath, I forced myself to shoulder my way past the three fae ahead of me as they lingered at a bend in the passage. And I gasped at that sight that greeted me.

"Oh fuck me," I said.

The fae male next to Slavin, the one holding my bonds, dropped his side of the leash and hunched over himself, vomiting a splash of bilous coffee and chunks of cheese onto his boots.

Two crosses, one on either side of the passage, just where it curved around, stood at the entrance. They stretched to the ceiling of the tunnel several feet above us. It took an effort to let my gaze linger on the forms of whatever those crosses bore to make out that they'd once been humanoid through the cloister of maggots and flies.

How flies could find anything this deep inside the mountain and below ground was beyond me, but there were enough larvae and flitting black insects to know these…these things had been dead a long time.

My feet shuffled me backward before I was even aware I was moving. I bumped into one of my captors, stepping on his foot and sliding to the side as I lost my balance at last.

"No," I said, aware that my head was shaking back and forth, that I couldn't stop it. "Just kill me now." I sent a long, pleading look to Slavin. "I won't fight you." I sliced my hand along my throat. "Just end it. Right here."

I saw the male swallow, the skin of his throat bobbing as he struggled to keep his breakfast from spilling free.

"We go on," he managed after a few moments. He nodded, as though convincing himself he'd made the right decision.

A flat thwack sounded and echoed in the cavern as he back-handed the male who stood nearest, swiping his sleeve across his mouth. The stink of sick rose like a cloud of acid. "We go on."

So we went, amid the smell of vomit and rotting meat, the buzz of flies and the sound of growling in the darkness, surrounding us, shrouding each footstep as we advanced into the catacombs.

No one spoke for a while as we tramped along, quieter now. It took a steeling of the spine and nerves to continue as those crosses snaked along the passageway, leading us still deeper into the mountain. After the sixth cross, a fresher one with what looked like a goblin hanging by his wrists and sagging into the chamber with a bloated belly and legs torn free of the cross, I realized the growling was coming from smaller animals, not larger, predatory ones. Scavengers protecting their bounty. I saw the eyes of one blinking out from behind the goblin as it bit down on his calf. Eyes blinked out. Blinked on. Savoring the taste of a fresh meal over the rotting ones from earlier in the line.

"What is this place?" I dared ask.

The little fae male brushed against me, almost as though he needed comfort. I couldn't say I blamed him.

"It's the Bone and Blood games," he said, leaning in to whisper the words. Fear, that's what I heard in his voice. Real fear. I felt him trembling.

"I'm the one up for bid." I jerked my chin toward the next cross, where a fat fae male hung beside a thick-necked mortal man. The mortal was dead. The other nearly so. He groaned softly, caught in his own misery and pain, unaware we were passing by. "I'm the one who should be afraid."

The little fae kept his eyes down, wrangling my arm onward with him as he skirted the crosses. "Those who bring subpar bounty to the games also forfeit their lives. It's how they assure their patrons that only the best are pitted against each other."

I wasn't sure if I should be flattered or terrified. "The best?" I said in a small voice, realizing that those victims on the crosses were probably fighters of high caliber. My gaze ran to a burly goblin with hands the size of plates, and for the first time, I realized that not all the wounds were from the crucifixions.

My steps halted as I scanned the rest of the line, searching for more evidence that these victims had gone through some sort of battle and weren't just sacrificed out of deviant desires. The sudden stop yanked hard on the little fae as he kept going while I stood still.

He paused and looked back at me, his brow furrowed. Several lines, etched at least an inch deep, ran all the way to his hairline. I half-expected him to yank on the bonds, but he didn't. Instead, he came toward me. When he spoke, it was in a conspiratorial hiss.

"You want to live through this?" he asked. "You'll come along quickly. We'll find you a good opponent. One we might win against."

I shrugged. I'd already decided I wouldn't go meekly to anything, and judging by the crosses and their inhabitants, I wanted to be good and sure I didn't live long enough to suffer. If I went down, so would they.

The others kept going, and I suspected they were so caught up in their own thoughts and worries that they didn't realize we'd lagged behind.

"What does it matter to me what happens to you all?" I asked in a low voice. "Maybe I want to see you suffer." I narrowed my eyes at him, giving him every indication that I just might throw whatever fight they put me through. "Maybe I won't measure up." I skimmed my chest and hands with a bald stare. "I'm certainly not in prize fighting condition anymore."

He blinked. Looked back toward his companions who had slowed their pace and begun inspecting the victims on the crosses, men and women and creatures who breathed still. Their assessments not long past but their suffering far from over.

"If I let you go," he said as he leaned in. "If I let you go, will you take me with you?"

Chapter 35

I almost laughed at the ludicrous suggestion I escape with the little fae on my heels. But I swallowed it down. This was one of those Gideon-esque opportunities. I wouldn't waste it.

"Can you find the way back out?" I rasped, edging closer and lifted my wrists up, just enough that he could cut through the bonds if he liked. Quick. He had to be quick or the others would see.

"They'll take the weakest of us," he rasped out as he jerked his head in the direction of his comrades. "The games only require one sacrifice. I have no illusions about where I stand with the cadre."

I glanced over his shoulder. "Cut me free," I said. "And we'll run together." Just how far he thought we'd get, with me all but lame, I had no idea, but I was willing to let him think I'd run like hell and fight for him if need be. I'd promise anything so long as he cut me loose.

For a moment, I thought he'd go for the small knife I saw on his hip, a tiny prick of a blade I'd seen him core an apple with or cut a few hunks of cheese. I tried to prod him by inching even closer, aiming my right side toward him, giving him every opportunity to slice through the bonds and let the hemp free.

But just as his hand went to his hip, Slavin snapped an order at him that he was taking too long, and the moment died. The little creature dropped his head back and grabbed me by the arm to guide me the rest of the way.

I wasn't sure what I could have said or done to hasten his decision, but that was all lost now. Heart in my stomach, we turned the last bend and the chamber ahead spread out like the gaping maw of a leviathan.

Every fae in the party fell silent. The air, hot as hellfire, was sharp as razors each time I took a breath.

An arena made of stone benches and earthen floor took up the most of the chamber. This was the end of the line. The last horror the catacombs had to offer. With one passage in and out, stretching back behind us, lined with the groaning, stinking bodies of the unfortunate.

Roman style columns and arches rose in a semicircle around one half of the oval arena. A dome of greenish light flickered, reminding me of a neon sign phasing in and out. The whole building might have resembled the Roman coliseum but for the runes and elvish lettering ringing each column. I found myself wondering where the animals and prisoners were kept when the tiers of seating went down into the ground instead of rising to the ceiling of the cavern.

The cadre's leader looked back at everyone over his shoulder. "We split the earnings 50 to 50," he said, eyeballing the males clustered about, shuffled one foot to the other. "Does anyone have a problem with that?"

The little fae in charge of my bonds drew back as though he wanted to hide behind me. Poor thing. I actually felt bad for him. No others in the party had reason to worry about me measuring up. If I wasn't found worthy, the little fae would suffer and the rest would be free to leave unharmed.

"Untie me," I hissed at him under my breath. I might not care if he lived or died, but I did care to screw these bastards out of living. "I'll block their way till you're all the way down the tunnels."

His brow furrowed, a line of confusion seaming his features. "I don't understand."

"Just do it," I said. "You want to end up on one of those crosses, or do you want someone else to?"

We both knew where this was going and how things would end up.

"My name, my real name, is Hueil," he rasped. "If you survive—"

I laughed and choked on it. There was no way I was going to survive, and he knew it.

"Just go," I barked, hurting my throat with the command. "Now."

He didn't hesitate then. With a swift movement and a soft crunching sound, his little blade flicked up through the bonds. I felt them release and fall to the floor of the cavern. Without a look back, he bolted past me into the passageway behind us. I felt the rush of his movement as it breezed along my arms and caught the whiff of warm butter and yeasty bread that he left in his wake. The sound of his treads echoed the beating of my heart.

Gone. He would make it. My chest sunk in as I closed my eyes, listening to the sound of his footfalls fade into the darkness. I'd die, and I knew that, but I'd die with the sound of his escape in my ears. And soon one of those who remained would fill my hearing with the screams of their torment.

A hunter couldn't ask more than that.

It took the rest of the cadre precious moments to register the sound of Hueil's escape. It was some sort of blessing that the torchlight showed me each one of their faces as they all realized their scapegoat was gone. I savored those looks as they understood that the game had shifted. Any one of them could be the one to be sacrificed now if I didn't measure up to whatever opponents waited in the arena. And I wouldn't. I had nothing left to fight with.

A deep, belly-moving chuckle fled my lungs on a rasp of overheated air. "Might be a good time to change your minds," I said to none of them in partic-ular.

A storm of rage clouded Slavin's expression. Three of the others, realizing too late that they could be on the literal chopping block, shrank back, no doubt imagining themselves in Hueil's place, high up on one of those crosses, watching the rats tear at their feet.

Not a chance. I slid smoothly into the way, spreading my now-freed arms out to my sides, showing them I was free, inviting them—daring them—to try to get past me. Although both limbs felt like I was hefting concrete blocks, my arms trembling with the effort, a grin stole my mouth just the same. The tightness of dehydration split my lips. I tasted my own blood.

"You still have time to reconsider," I said, knowing there would be no reprieve for me. They would never change their minds. Not now. Not after they'd trekked so far.

They considered it, though. I saw it in their faces. I saw the weighing of their odds teeter in their gazes as they flitted over my shoulder to the tunnel behind me. Hueil's footsteps were already fading near nonexistence.

When they did race toward me, I knew they weren't coming for me but aiming for that dark tunnel behind me, desperate to get hold of Hueil before he escaped their clutches forever. I wasn't going to let that happen. It took effort, but I lashed out with a flat-palm, heel connecting with the chin of the poor male who didn't stop in time to avoid the blow. Bone crunched. The drug sighed in my veins. A stutter of the energy, then a full stop.

Gone. Truly gone. I was alone with my human frailty now. I couldn't find it in me to regret using it up to save the little fae.

Fully spent, I pivoted sharply to watch two of the males race several yards before giving up. Numb and feeling the creep of ice through my veins, I swayed on my feet, letting the rest of them wrangle me back into their grip. It was over. I'd done what I could for Heuil, done what I could for myself. All that was left was to hope death would be swift in His claim.

They herded me onward toward the arena without a single struggle from me. Each step was leaden, but supported by the fae, we tramped all the way to where a weary looking fae with blonde locks curled and styled in a Victorian wig fashion adorned a pinched and narrow face. Not high fae, I didn't think. He was far from beautiful even if he glittered at the edges with a soft, buttery light.

With bleary vision, I regarded the male wielding a feather quill like a weapon as he took me and my captors in with a sharp eye. I thought I saw some sort of ticking close down over the corneas and then disappear.

"She isn't healthy enough to fight," he said. "This isn't some fight club in the townships and cities. This is the Dread Catacomb." The feather stroked beneath his chin. "Those who make the journey do so because they can't get the kind of sport we offer just anywhere."

Slavin of the cadre puffed out his chest and I rolled my eyes. "We know what we have," he said. "She just needs a bit of broth and rest."

"You realize what will happen if the combatant is sub-par."

A slap of a fat, grimy hand on the overly large book balanced in the registrar's hands. "We know what we have." He angled his chin to the light so the registrar could take note of the missing teeth and abrasions he sported all over his face, neck, and chest. The rest of them did the same, unbidden. "You must have heard about the blacksteel lady of the flesh and bone auctions."

It was the first I'd heard myself called anything of the sort, and the pride in his voice as he gave the title out like an honor surprised me enough that I straightened up unwittingly.

A grunt from him, then, as my shoulders squared. Another scrutinous look at me, as though he couldn't believe what he was seeing beneath the blood and grime. "She's Spartaena?" he said in a musing tone. A long pause. He poked into his cheek with his tongue. A scratch of the quill on the pages of the book without him so much as looking down at them.

Slavin noted the shift in the clerk's demeanor immediately. Canny, crafty thing that he was. "You've heard of her, then?" he said, his eyelids shuttering to half-mast. He postured just a bit, showing the worst side of his face where I'd bitten him and left a sizeable bruise.

He knew damn well news couldn't have traveled that fast ahead of us about a mortal woman fighting her sale, or that anyone would even care. But he bandied the information about as though it had weight. It took all I had not to snort right out loud.

I couldn't imagine any good salesman or clerk wanting to reveal what he might or might not know if it meant paying more money, so it was a shock to hear the butter-aura fae volunteer the next words.

"Everyone this side of the catacombs has heard of that damnable woman. She all but ruined the last house. Several indentured mortals fled and killed the overseers because of her rhetoric." He gave me a long look of disgust, coupled with a hefty dose of greed.

"I'll give you fifty dragons for her," he finally said, drawing out the moment the way a good actor might, putting elastic into the tension.

"One hundred."

"How do I know it's even her?"

All Slavin did was wave at his companions, all sporting some sort of injury.

"Eighty." The feather scratched across the surface of the vellum, and the registrar refused to look up or hold anyone's eye. I had the feeling he couldn't keep the excitement from his features and didn't dare look up lest he end up paying far more than he wanted for a woman who couldn't even hold her own water.

I looked down at my feet. Apparently, that thought was a literal one. Ammonia rose in a waft around me and I side-stepped out of the puddle. Humiliation was for those who would live to be embarrassed, but it didn't stop me from stealing a glance at Slavin. My heart sank to my bare feet at the way he shot a look of victory my way.

Each seam in his aged, brutal face looked like it was grinning. My captors all shifted from foot to foot, their eagerness to be the ones to get their hands on that money barely able to keep them still. They knew the change in circumstance as well as I did.

"And the other fee?" Slavin asked in a low tone, and I knew he wanted to hear what he'd already suspected. "Surely delivery of such a fierce mortal, the bane of all the houses this last week—broken and subdued by my gang, I might add--is as good as a gift to any house in the catacombs. We'll take the eighty dragons," he went on. "But we want the other part of the payment waived as well."

The clerk flicked the feather back and forth several times as he weighed the decision. "Fair enough," he said in a crisp tone. "I'll notify the game master that no further payment is needed since she won't be fighting."

Wouldn't be fighting. That was all I heard and was still trying to process exactly why, blinking like a wet-eyed milkmaid as the clerk counted out several coins from a pouch tied to his waist. They clinked together as Slavin held out his palms and they fell in one by one.

He counted them aloud, like a new reader would pronounce words in a child's book. Numb, defeated, still reeling from the thought that I wouldn't be dying just yet, I watched him slip his share into his pockets.

By the time I was tossed into a holding area, alone, caged on all four sides by a buzz of magic that let go with a wave of a fae guard's hands and sprang to life again with another, I began to wish I'd taken Heuil's knife and plunged it into my throat.

Chapter 36

THERE WOULD BE NO broth. No rest or respite. It wasn't needed if I wasn't going to fight. They left me to lie there as my former captors were shoved aside to let a tall fae male pass. He was someone important, judging by the way the clerk glowered at Slavin when he didn't move aside fast enough to let the male through. With a quick check of the pages the clerk held open, the male nodded and jerked his head toward me. Some chatter that I couldn't hear lit Slavin's face, and he turned to me as well, that smug look bloated to full victory.

So. whatever the clerk and the game master planned for me, it made Slavin very pleased. Dressed in long robes of blood-red satin edged in black-matted fur, this new male turned and headed to the podium that stood on the precipice of the pit. Claws and talons clacked along the hem of his robe as he moved. Each step left a viscous stamp the same shade as his cloak in footprints with six toes.

Blood, I knew. Somewhere along the way, he had stepped in a pool of it. A shudder wracked my core as he took his place behind a black granite podium. The others around me herded toward the back as the game master raised his hands and light crackled from his fingertips to shoot up over his head. A cascade of falling stars lit the entire chamber with enough light that it showed several groups of fae males, similarly dressed, eddy out from the darkness of the outer walls. They all gathered beside the podium while the stars—lights I could see now, drawn and tugged upon by some magical force—fixed themselves into sconces all along the chamber.

Now, every seam and crack of stone and face was on display within the chamber, and I could make out every nuanced twist of rock and stalactite that clung to the ceiling. They looked for all the world like claws driven into the ground above us by some gargantuan beast and poked through to the cavern below its feet.

And the chamber walls were smooth, an obsidian blackness that went round in a semicircle, much like the inside of an amphitheater. On one side, the half of chamber I stood in with the clerk, a holding pen of every sort of fae male gathered together in a holding cell made of the same vinalyia I'd seen in Terran's dungeons.

Ahead of me, a drop of black space hollowed out from the obsidian stone was lined with tiers of seating made up of reclining lounges in a Roman fashion, set sideways with lush cushions for elbows to rest upon. The entire set up meant that each patron had a lounge area with small braziers and bottles of greenish wine. No two areas were the same, and in all there might have been space for two hundred where there might have been seating for a thousand if made of benches.

But I had the feeling this entire spectacle had little to do with mass interest or with getting as many bodies in seats as possible. This was a specialized, elite arena, one that meant any death here would not be swift.

At the moment I realized just how set up for spectacle the place was, a blaze of light flashed purple, then green, then red, slicing through the air with the precision of a laser, drawing attention upward. In no more than a breath, I stood alone with the game master on a dais high above the center of the pit. Magic, either by design or by order, had transported me to stand next to the game master so close, I could smell the mulch and funk coming from his cloak. Whatever it had been, the hide still clung to the scent of its original owner strongly enough that I had to hold my breath.

"This," he intoned, loud enough to draw all eyes toward us. "This is a special occasion."

A murmur went through the crowd and he wasn't exaggerating about the uniqueness of the event. Every face I could see held rapt expressions of excited interest and curiosity. I stepped closer to the edge, feeling the press of magic shoving me back. But I stood there just long enough to catch a glimpse of the flagstones beneath the dais, to sense the buzz of magic holding it suspended over the pit.

Below, liquid black flagstone showed through in places, but mostly it was covered with what looked like peat, straw, and wood chips. A place of battle and death, if I ever did see one. At least the rushes and moss were clean of blood and bodies. Several pieces of equipment and devices littered the area below. A holding pen sat on either side of the semicircle, muscled men in loin cloths pacing like tigers as they stared at each other. I had time to wonder what the seesaw shaped device was before the game master beside me lifted his arms, swirling the magic between his upheld hands.

"Tonight," he said, drawing my eye back to him. "Tonight we have the Blacksteel Lady on the docket."

Silence. Even the game master's lungs stopped pulling in air as he paused to allow the weight of his words to settle over the crowd. Then a hiss. A shout. As one, the assembly bolted from their lounges, stabbing the air with their fists. A sizzle of impotent magic lifted to the air in a single cloud that hung over the entire pit like a noxious gas. Then it fizzled out with a long hiss of air, clearing like a thick fog being burned off in the sun.

"Bíogaithe Bord," they all cried. "Bord Bord Bord."

A crackling buzz sounded. A microphone of sorts, but not one made by any sort of human technology, lowered from some place above us. The hiss was too sentient, as if it was murmuring suggestions to the game master as it rocked toward us close enough for him to grip.

The game master swung his gaze to mine as he held onto the microphone, and I was shocked to see the sockets empty of flesh. "You see how they hate you?" he asked. "They can't wait to taste you."

Tiny wriggling white things playing about inside the empty sockets. I swallowed down the nausea long enough to hold his gaze, resolved to show no fear in the face of that horror. I tried to ignore the word taste, but it stroked along each fine hair of my body, making it strain upward in primal fear.

"Maybe it's your face they hate," I said, baiting him. "And you just can't see their disgust."

He sneered, his lips thinning out and stretching to either end of his jaw. A blink of fat teeth showed, then disappeared beneath a slug of a tongue that laved his mouth end to end. My stomach churned.

"My eyes were taken in service to the games," he said. "I work only to please the patrons. Even to giving them up for the sake of the spectacle." He tilted his head at me thoughtfully. "Much as you will do once the bid is won."

It wasn't fear or confusion that kept me silent at the comment. I knew the moment Slavin was told I wouldn't be fighting, that I would be auctioned off. I wasn't afraid of being sold. Not now. Now, I just wanted it over.

My silence was so that I wouldn't say something stupid to change that. A movement to my right drew my eye. My captors. All clustered around the sole entrance and exit, hanging around to see the result of their labors. Probably thinking they deserved to see my final sale after all I'd put them through.

But it was a stupid setup, I realized. Any human would know there should be multiple exit points in case of threat. Fire. Flood. Magic. Surely these fools should know they would have no escape if danger came to visit the chamber.

Then I realized the danger was probably within the chamber, not without. A fact that was reinforced when a roar of applause erupted from the pits, a din of throaty hoots of approval that suggested whatever the game master had promised, they were all in.

The microphone swung free of the game master's grip and descended into the midst of the tiers of seating, dangling there like a cobra's head, twisting this way and that. A thunder of Bord Bord Bord rang out again, filling the void until the crescendo was stilled by a single flick of the game master's hand.

"Bord it is, then," he said without aid of amplification. "Gather your bids, dear patrons, and maybe you will be the one to flay the first bites of skin from her flesh." He spread his arms out to the sides. "There is enough for everyone, but the killing blow and the heart belongs to the highest bidder."

A murmur of excited agreement ran through the crowds as everyone shouted Bord Bord Bord. A rash of goose-pimples rose over my skin. I shuddered violently as I realized the fullness of what was happening. Flayed. *Alive*.

My eyes squeezed shut at the thought. I swayed on my feet, barely registering the words of the game master as he explained what 'the Bord' was. A tasting menu of sorts. Not fighting. Not battle or indenture. I was to be the appetizer, main course, and dessert all in one.

I might have wanted to die on my feet, holding a weapon, but that chance was gone. *Flayed. Alive.* The thought was enough to make me dizzy. Panic razored through me. I wouldn't die this way. I'd rather take my own life than let it go like that.

My eyes snapped open. I could take my own life. Maybe not with a weapon. But I had feet. I could run. And run I did. Straight for the edge. I flung myself at the precipice, barely noticing that the game master hadn't moved an inch to stop me. His deep chuckle was the last thing I heard before a crack erupted in my hearing. A sizzle of pain coursed through me. And then I was…bounced backward.

I fell onto my knees and hands beside the game master.

"You can't escape the Bord," he said, and I craned my neck to look up at him. Arms still outstretched, he now held a lasso of light. He snapped it at me like a whip. When it lashed me in the cheek, I felt the hot run of blood long before the pain.

"Feel free to struggle, mortal," he said. "The Patrons do love the taste of fear in their meat, but some of us prefer to paper our sconces with human hide, and if you tear in places we don't like, we will have no choice but to hold back the killing blow until we find a smooth canvas."

I instantly went still.

As did every single fae in the chamber. The cavern felt like a crypt, hot and bloated with stale air. They were waiting, I realized. Penning in their excitement as they awaited the chance to bid. No one, it seemed, was willing to risk the chance of first bid.

The game master stood taller. He edged closer to me, ran the back of his hand over the top of my hair. That one motion was the one that released the smell from beneath his cloak. It stank of rot and mulch and things left to molder.

"Her hair is soft, patrons," he said in a soft voice that somehow still managed to swell around the chamber. A sharp, anticipatory inhalation as the crowd breathed as one. "Perhaps we'll offer her scalp first." He drew his hand away and as he did, I stood, not from my own power, but by his. Some magic lifted me to my feet, held me there, barely on my toes. Blackness threatened to puddle into my vision as the memory of a rope around my neck slithered out from the dusky chest I kept it in and into the light of consciousness.

I might have begged then. My mouth was moving even if I couldn't hear my own voice.

"Someone must want to be the first to bid," he said. "You'll not be blocked from bidding for skin or heart, patrons. Feel free to place as many bids as you like but don't let this lustrous black hair go to waste."

A cacophony then. One I could barely hear over the ragged, panting breath that razored through my lungs.

"The hair is mine," said a familiar voice as it rumbled through the chamber. Loud. Rasping. A growl in its undercurrents that made the hair on the back of my neck stand. It couldn't be. There was no way he could have found me here. Blade. All I could think was he hadn't betrayed me. Of all the emotions that rampaged their way through me in that moment, joy was the one that shoved all others aside.

The game master went up on his toes, trying to see into the tiers, looking for the source of the gruff voice.

"Brilliant," the game master said. "But the blacksteel lady's hair is no one's before the bid is won."

"You misunderstand me," Blade drawled, and this time, the game master had no problem picking him out from the crowd. He was the only one standing alone. Every other patron surrounding him was lying on their fainting couches, arms limp over the chaise-roll, their heads propped neatly on angled hands. I squinted. Something wasn't quite right with the angle of the arms and chin.

"What is it that I misunderstand, good Patron?" the game master said. "You will bid for her hair the same as the rest." At that, he stroked the top of my head again. A low, thunderous growl came from where Blade stood.

"The hair. The head. The breasts. The legs. All mine," Blade said in a growl that should have made the entire arena quiver in fear.

But the game master only cackled as he drew his hand away. Here, he had a ripe bidder, and that was all.

A roar went up from the crowd. Protesting. They all wanted a piece of me. All wanted a taste. The game master could see just how much money he was going to make in the next few moments if he played the game well.

He leveled his hollow-eyed gaze toward Blade. "I ask you one more time, good patron," he said. "What is your bid?"

At the question, Blade stepped into the light, all six feet three inches of him. His shoulders rolled with tension. Even from the distance that separated us, I could see his gaze flare with enough crimson to crowd out all the color from his irises.

It was at that moment, as the full light of the magic swung to him, as the microphone hoisted itself free of his face, as if it sensed the rage seething beneath his breath, that I realized what was wrong with the patrons surrounding him.

They were all dead.

"Blood," Blade said in a dark, deep-throated voice, strangled by rage and what I knew was a sort of mid-shift growl. "I bid lots and lots of blood."

CHAPTER 37

"Sweet gods of the underworld and innerworld," the game master said in a note so high pitched it screeched over the screaming. "It's the Hellhound of Stygiathalos. Run, Patrons. Run."

By the time Blade's full-throated growl shredded the darkness, I was already measuring the distance between the sound of it and my own skin. He wasn't coming to bid. I knew it and so did the game master. Fae of every sort, bound by the magic of the chamber, tried to flee. Each of them fell beneath the ferocity of the hound's attack as they came up against that muzzle and claws.

One exit, I told myself. One entrance. There was no way out, and they knew it. A bottleneck lay between the hound and their freedom. A bottleneck barred my way, kept me cowering on the dais that was even now moving on its own toward the farthest edge as the game master raced to his own escape.

By the time the dais lodged against the edge of the cavern the way a boat moors against the sudden and immoveable wood of a wharf, I knew no one would survive. It was foolish to launch the dais for its mooring. Foolish for the game master to even believe he could escape.

And despite the gut-wrenching horror, I was buoyed by the violence. They'd die. All of them. Somehow, Blade would take every last fae in this place and turn him into a puddle of bloody flesh. I didn't care what he did, so long as the rest of them suffered. So long as no one ever had to go through this charade again.

At first, I believed them bound by some sort of protective magic, an underpainting of protection given to the arena by the makers, to keep some sort of control over the events that transpired within, but then I saw some fae phasing in and out as they attempted to pop out of sight and realized they'd expended their magic somehow and were left with depleted stores.

I was no stranger to violence, but the things I saw as Blade tore through flesh and bone, as he tossed and twisted mangled bodies up and away from him, the way he bulled through the crowds, shredding as he went…it was too much.

I trembled all over. Somehow my arms had flung themselves around my head, trying to block out the noise. But the sounds of chaos, like fireworks to a soldier suffering the after effects of battle, leaked through just the same. Shell shock had nothing to the magnitude of fear I felt in that moment. All courage fled me.

It took several heartbeats to force my hands to the earth. To forge one knee ahead. To army crawl for the exit.

The exit. Oh, sweet Jesus. There was only one. And it was indeed plugged. Those fae who couldn't magic themselves out were clawing at each other to escape. God only knew what they'd wasted their magic on in this hope-forsaken catacomb, but they certainly had nothing left to save their sorry hides. I halted several yards away, afraid to get trampled, telling myself to wait it out, wait it out. I'd escape when all the violence was done. Or I'd die of terror.

The screaming and shrieking and pleading that went up then, was not for the faint of heart. The games master raced to the little clerk and in a puff of crimson smoke and blue light they were gone. Abandoning their precious patrons to the hellhound.

All sound evaporated then, drowned out by the hammering of my heart in my ears. Sitting on my knees, my head hanging back, my eyes panned the arena and the violence with a numb, leaden gaze. Devoid of any more live bodies to shred, Blade streaked for the clotted exit.

It seemed an eternity before I felt a muzzle nudge into the crook of my neck. Wet. Cold. Thick with what I knew deep down was blood. I smelled the copper on him, the sulfurous stink of magic, like ozone but with the underpinning of cinnamon. I couldn't move.

The muzzle...shifted against my skin and slid smoothly into oily flesh. "Ava?" One long drag of my skin before he pulled his nose away. I heard him shuffling about, trying to peer into my face as he crouched ever closer.

I clutched my knees tighter and realized I was rocking back and forth, my ass on the cold flagstone of the dais. I couldn't look at him. I couldn't look at anything.

"Ava, it's over."

My head shook back and forth of its own volition. Fool. It wasn't over. It would never be over. I stole a look from beneath the matted hair that curtained my face, toward the exit. Bodies lay to each side, creating a dry path of land between waves of blood and skin. That waft of cinnamon grew stronger, blocking out the stink of feces and death that had begun to coil around me like a python.

"Come with me, Ava," Blade said, his voice thick and strangled. "It's time to go."

Again, I shook my head, my gaze glued to the passageway. I did not want to look at him. I did not want to see the evidence of violence on his skin of my own near death. More than that, I wanted to see down that passageway, needed to see past the exit into the tunnels beyond.

"They got away," I said and barely recognized my own voice. It held no inflection. If my voice was a face, the affect would be blank and blanched.

"No one got away," he said in a throaty voice. He laid his hand along my shoulder, whispering his fingers toward the small of my back. I recoiled, and he sighed. "Two bought themselves time, but they did not get away."

I did look at him then. Covered in blood, I couldn't tell where he began and I ended, and I realized blood spray had reached me, had coated my hair and my skin.

"They got away." My lip trembled and my voice caught. A shudder of adrenaline flooded my core and wracked my spine. I couldn't stop shaking. My gaze went again to the passageway. It was empty. "They got away." For the life of me, I couldn't form another thought, couldn't put more words together.

"No one got away," he said, and a wicked gleam flickered in his gaze. "But not all are dead."

He turned his fierce gaze towards me. His eyes burned with an intensity that should have made my heart stop.

With a lifted chin, he held my karambit out to me and jerked his thumb toward the passageway, where a movement caught my eye. Slavin and two others. Tied to each other back to back, corralled against one side of the sea of bodies.

"Do with them what you will," he growled, his voice dripping with barely concealed fury.

My eyes drilled a path to Slavin. Before I realized I'd managed to even get to my feet, I was shambling toward him. The blade's handle dug into my palm. My knuckles hurt. My thighs felt like molten rubber.

But I pressed on. Bare feet sluicing through blood, leaving prints behind me as I advanced. I kept my eye glued to Slavin's, watched the fear turn to terror and then to panic. I saw in his face all the words he was bringing to bear to try to barter his way free. Every muscle twitch was one I marked, noted, and stored. I'd inspect it all later like shining baubles before I buried the memory so deep in a dark chest, I'd never find the trophy of this last moment ever again.

I was aware of Blade behind me, of a bleary-brained sense of comfort that he was there. If I couldn't do this, he would. He might even delight in it.

For me there was no delight. No glee. Just a sense of bald vengeance. No other creature, mortal or otherwise, would be taken by these cowards ever again.

Every step was one when my legs fought against the urge to flex and tense and retract. Sheer will was the only thing that kept me going. Five yards. Three. Two. One. I stood before them close enough to smell the ammonia from their bladders spilled on the stone carpet, the old cheese Slavin had refused to feed me the last day. My mouth watered. My stomach grumbled in protest.

The air crackled with something. Anticipation? Fear? I wasn't sure which. I just knew Blade stood directly behind me. Watching. Waiting.

"They're yours," he said.

And that was it. I felt no pity. There was just fury as I closed in.

By the time I stood in front of Slavin, only one small, miserable piece of me held back from gutting him right there. One piece of me frozen by conscience and impotent rage.

My fist clenched around the blade's handle. I hesitated. A small mote of conscience tried to shove its way past the anger. I trembled, keenly aware of the powerful fae standing behind me, waiting to see if he would have to take these lives, too.

Then, before I could stop myself, I slashed forward and to the side. Flesh tugged at the blade as I yanked it sideways, letting the arc of the knife zipper through textile and flesh. Again. And again. Until the thing that had dared take me was nothing but a quivering bit of flesh on the cave floor.

As the chamber grew silent once more, my gaze fell on remains of the Fae who lay dead in scattered pieces along the stones.

My breath was a ragged flame in my chest. My gaze sought Blade's and met it in silent acknowledgment. I spared a look at Slavin's body, broken and twisted on the floor and…I felt no sympathy.

I kneeled in front of him, the karambit held in a pincer grip as I angled the tip of the blade between the bastard's bloody lips. The grinding sound of metal against ivory crackled through the air. A pop. A small, almost significant expulsion of blood from a blackened cavity. And then my fingers curled over his tooth.

I closed my hand into a fist. The karambit clattered to the stone floor. I stared down at the open mouth and the gap at the front of his grin, and exhaustion began to worm its way through my battered body.

At last, it could rest, it must have thought. But I wasn't done. I had miles to go, dozens of tunnels to navigate. I wanted to feel the fresh air on my face. I needed to be free. I wanted to die in the sunshine.

But as I took a step toward the light, my legs, pushed far beyond their limits, finally betrayed me.

CHAPTER 38

I collapsed to my knees, mere inches from the dead fae's feet. The metallic tang of blood clung to the air, mingling with the stench of death that seemed to seep into my pores, marking me. In a flash, Blade was beside me. All evidence of the hellhound was gone except for the fiery gaze that narrowed with a peculiar, almost heart-wrenching concern.

I had nothing left, and I knew it. The itchiness of withdrawal was coming to claim me at last, crowding out the dump of adrenaline and complete exhaustion. I felt my stomach clench in protest.

Gripping my belly, I fell onto one hand and let the spasms come. They wracked me from the pits of my bowels to the joints of my jaws trying to bring up nothing but strings of bile. Every heave felt like a betrayal of my body—proof of my failure to keep going, to stay strong.

Oh, the wretchedness of having him standing there, watching me as I succumbed to a violence of my own making. The humiliation of it might have burned my cheeks if they weren't already stinging from bruises and cuts.

Watching me, Blade made a sound that must have come from deep in his chest because it sounded half human, half animal.

Trembling, I did my best to push myself back onto my feet. I couldn't let him see me this way. I wasn't weak. I was a warrior, dammit. I'd survived these catacombs, I'd freed slaves in that dread place. I'd gained a reputation that made them all quake. But here, now, every ache in my body whispered otherwise.

Sick as it was, however pathetic that victory, it was mine to claim. I'd struck down my enemy for Pete's sake, taken part of him to prove my victory.

But even telling myself all those things, I still felt the sickening press of nausea and a chasm widening somewhere in my solar plexus. I told myself that one last victory would be my leaving that place. That I wouldn't lose the last of my dignity inside its smothering chambers.

I eyeballed the opening to the cavern and I struck out for it, stubbornness my only companion in the smothering silence.

My march was a zombie's crawl, but I pushed on just the same. Ignoring the stink of bodies, the buzz of flies that somehow, even here, had already sought out and found flesh to nurture their young. At least, I thought I was marching.

It was only when I collided with the side of the tunnel that I realized I was staggering back and forth, side to side. A drunken motion that even my own eyes and brain couldn't sort through.

When I heard Blade's approach as he followed me into the passageway, I tried to wave him away.

"Leave me alone," I bit out. "I don't need any help."

His footfalls stopped. The space between us thickened, the air seeming to hold its breath. A wave of heat swept so fast up my neck I nearly passed out except for a clutch of the sweating cavern wall. As the heat receded and the blackness swam back to the furthest reaches of my vision, I stole a glance sideways.

He was naked, of course, his entire body covered in blood. But for those eyes peering back at me, lit from some fire within that reminded me of the heat of the cavern, I'd not have known he was even listening to me.

I found my voice, testing to see if I could even speak after all that. "You're naked."

His gaze shuttered in that infuriating way he had when he was going to argue with me or offer some sassy comment that would make my lips curl back.

"All the blood and gore you see around you and this is the thing that bothers you the most," he said in a tight voice. "What kind of monster are you, Ponytail?"

I had the feeling he had tried for light-hearted humor but the sound of his voice suggested the words had caught on several rashes of suppressed emotion on the way out.

I knew how he felt. But empathy was not on my mind right then. The pressure in my chest wasn't just pain; it was the weight of everything I hadn't said, everything I couldn't let myself feel. I glowered at him as I clutched my stomach. "A weary one," I said. "Now just leave me be. I can manage on my own."

His eyes narrowed. I expected him to argue or make some crass, arrogant remark. Instead, he kept coming, his movements deliberate yet filled with a simmering intensity.

Wordless, he scooped me off my feet, effortlessly hoisting me over his shoulder. A sack of grain, a swath of towel. A humiliatingly weak damsel being carried in the arms of the hero. I about puked all over his chest at the thought, but then I realized even that would take more energy than I had.

"Put me down," I said, my voice weak, the command nothing but a whisper.

His growl reverberated through the cave, vibrating against my body. It wasn't just anger—it was something older, deeper, primal in its force. But he didn't speak. Not one intelligible word. It was as though he was still caught somewhere between hound and man and had no ability to form language.

With each step he took, my resistance waned, replaced by a grudging acceptance. Every jostle reminded me of the broken pieces inside me, the ones I didn't have time to put back together. I couldn't have made it out on my own, and I had no idea how to even traverse the passageways. And it was a relief to give up, if only for a moment.

The cavern walls blurred as Blade carried me. I felt every muscle in his back tense and shift with precision, his strength unyielding, a silent reminder of how fragile

I was in comparison. My head lolled against his shoulder, the stubble along his jaw scraping against my temple.

"Where are you taking me?" I managed to rasp, though the words felt like they were dredged up from the bottom of a well.

His grip tightened, one arm banded around my legs, the other bracing my back. "Somewhere you won't get yourself killed," he muttered, his voice clipped. It was the voice of someone barely containing their anger, though I couldn't tell if it was directed at me or something else entirely.

The thought should have comforted me—being taken somewhere safe. Instead, it only stoked the fire of my frustration. "I told you, I don't need your help," I said, my tone sharper this time, but still weak.

Blade didn't respond. He just kept walking, his long strides eating up the uneven ground beneath us. The silence grew heavy, oppressive, like the weight of the entire cavern was pressing down on me, reminding me of everything I'd lost in that cursed place.

I might have slept, in fits and starts, my eyelids shuttering down as if weights of lead were attached. And in the semi-aware states I kept telling myself it didn't matter if his sweat mingled with my own, or the blood on both of us mingled in a greasy marriage of violent fluids that somehow seemed more intimate than any other. I was out. That was all that mattered. I was free.

And as Blade carried me onward through the high grass of the valley to the trunk of an ancient oak, his grip remained firm and unwavering.

By the time the faint glimmer of light revealed the last awful yards of the cavern, I wept silently. Tearlessly.

And the moment we stepped into the gloaming night, with the sounds of crickets in the grass, I could breathe again. The air was less stifling. Though the scent of blood still lingered like a phantom that refused to be banished, I knew it was the smell of victory.

Nutkin stood untethered and unsaddled, grazing on flowers that rose to his knees, pulling them into his whiskered lips with a long snake of a tongue before grinding his jaws sideways. Red and purple juice stained his mouth, a fact I was able to notice because Blade had angled himself to pull a blanket from the horse's saddle-bags, and my face ended up within smelling distance of its breath. the beast smelled of honey and lavender and the faintest whiff of manure.

Nothing ever smelled so wonderful.

Wordless, still, Blade yanked a blanket from inside the saddlebags. Nutkin watched it all with a sentient eye, whickering in what I thought were sympathetic noises as his gaze roamed my body. I imagined what I must look like to him, covered in grime, blood, and cuts. Smelling of God knew what.

"She's a fucking stubborn female," Blade said to the horse, and Nutkin's eye rolled back in agreement. "Fucking stubborn and violent and—" Blade's breath caught and he pivoted almost too sharply toward the tree. His shoulders shook but I didn't have the heart to look up to see what was in his face.

If he was laughing at me, taking pleasure in the fact that I had to be rescued, it would undo me.

But he said no more. Just snapped open the blanket on the grass beneath the tree. The whoosh it made as it took in air and landed made me think of summer nights and taking sheets from the outdoor clothesline, sleeping in air-massaged cotton. Winking myself to sleep with my father at the edge of my bed, watching over me. I heard his voice so keenly in that instant that my eyes stung.

I swiped the liquid that spilled away from my face before Blade could see it. I didn't want him to see me cry. Not now. Not ever.

And I didn't want to feel that awful sensation of nostalgia that would get me nowhere but into the sharp end of a vape full of bloodmist. Vape. God. I had no idea where it was now. I barely remembered the last time I'd felt it in my hand. The only thing I clutched was that tooth, and for some reason, I didn't even want that.

I imagined dropping it, thought about how it would sound when it fell with a light thwack to the ground. I couldn't do it. Instead, I squeezed my eyes closed, despondent and relieved at the same time at its presence, small and comforting in my palm.

He set me down with surprising gentleness, lowering me to the ground as if I might shatter if he moved too quickly. The scratchy fibers of the blanket brushing along the back of my neck, the cool grass whispered over my arms, grounding me in the present, though it did little to dull the ache coursing through my body. I

t smelled of horse and sweat and manure, and I breathed it in like it was the scent of apple pie. Then I instantly regretted doing so as my stomach whisked up the bile inside.

"Thank you," I said, biting back the pain and nausea. "For coming to get me. For not abandoning me." My voice broke on the last, and my eyes squeezed closed. It hurt, those words, and I wasn't quite sure why.

He made a low sound in his throat that might have been a growl. He dragged his gaze away from me and in that moment, the hellhound, the dark enforcer, returned to his expression.

"No one takes a bone from me."

The words were gruff and emotion filled despite the harshness of the sentiment, and I had the feeling he was holding something back as he rested his forearm on his knee. The green gaze with its silver lining had returned. The crimson serpent hiding behind the pinpricks of his pupils.

"You're the most stubborn mortal I've met, you know that?" he said, his voice softer now, though the edge hadn't completely disappeared.

"So I heard you complain," I shot back, stung by the assessment. But there was no real bite to my words. My strength was fading, and with it, my defenses. His lips twitched, not quite a smile, but something close. "You snore, too," he said. "If we're airing our complaints."

I wanted to argue, to push him away, but my body betrayed me. The exhaustion was too much, and I sagged against the trunk, my eyes slipping shut despite the protests of my pride. "It has come handy at times," I said, my voice draining away. Fingers skimmed my cheeks, drawing my eyes open to see him watching me, his eyelids half-shuttered. "I don't know how in the hell you managed to survive in the Catacombs of the Dread, Ponytail," he said. "But if I ever doubted your skills before, I know the truth now."

He beamed down at me, looking at me with a different gaze than I'd seen before in his eyes. If I wasn't so incredibly tired and achy all over, I might have taken a perverse pleasure in that gaze. As it was, I felt no victory. Just a hollow emptiness that ached like the hole where a sore tooth had once been.

"I wanted revenge more than I wanted to live," I admitted in a feeble voice.

"I know," he said with a short nod, then gave me a long look before he stood, knees cracking, to pull a canteen from the tackle. With a thoughtful look at my face, he returned, stooping to pour a small amount on a cloth he'd pulled free at the same time. This, she swiped over my brow, cooling my skin. Then he held the canteen against my lips.

"Drink," he said in a tone that brooked no refusal. "You're dehydrated."

I was worse than that, but I said nothing. Just chugged at the mouth of the canteen faster than I could swallow. The water dribbled cold and welcome over my chin and into the folds of my neck.

"You are a mess of blood and bruises," he said in a tight voice as he pulled the canteen away, giving me room to breathe, to see if I could keep the water down. "I don't know what's yours and what's theirs."

"Most are mine," I confessed.

That serpent of crimson peeked out from behind his pupils and coiled about his irises again as he looked down at me. I had the feeling he was reliving the attack in the caves and was enjoying each moment of recollection. It was as though he was taking a deviant pleasure in knowing the Fae who had abducted me were dead.

I knew the feeling.

With a tender touch that surprised me, he pried open my fingers and extracted the tooth. In his fist, it looked black and disgusting. The roots were crooked. A chunk of blacksteel clung to the top, a leftover piece of the bastard's grill.

Blade's swallow was loud enough as he eyed it sitting there in his palm to draw my eyes to his throat. So muscled. So tight with emotion. It made my chest ache to see.

"They're gone," he said in a soft voice. "All of them. Each and every fae in the cursed tavern paid in blood for what they did. Seems the owner was promised a princely sum to lure me away on the pretense of bringing you breakfast. He sent them to your room."

He looked up from the tooth to hold my gaze, almost in a dare. "He's dead now too," he said in a flat tone.

I had the feeling that whatever demise the Seamus lookalike had suffered, it wasn't enough to satisfy the dark enforcer.

He wanted me to challenge him, I thought. To complain about the death of an innocent, but I couldn't. I felt no sympathy for the fae who'd sold me out.

His hand brushed against my temple, calloused fingers surprisingly gentle as they tucked a strand of hair behind my ear. "Rest," he murmured, his voice a low rumble that seemed to vibrate through me.

It was an order, but there was something else there, something softer, as if the word itself carried a promise of safety. But one thing I'd learned in Fae, was that safety was an illusion. Like everything else.

"I'm fine," I insisted, trying to elbow my way up off the blanket and failing. He skimmed me with a pitying look.

"I said rest. You need time to…" He coughed in a most uncharacteristic way before continuing. "You need time." A pause as he laid his hand on the saddle seat. "I'll keep watch."

"Watch for what?" I asked, my knees already trembling so much I had to pull them up to my belly and roll onto my side.

His eye went to my ribs as they quaked uncontrollably. "Wendigos," he said shortly. "You're in no shape to help me fight any that might come our way, and while I'm not in my best fighting shape at the moment either, I have a feeling I'd fare better than you."

Right. So we weren't off the Shadow Trail after all. The thought of facing those nasty creatures did nothing to salve the deep-rooted anger still coursing through my intestines.

Or was that withdrawal?

Of all the things I'd faced in those catacombs, that was the thing I feared the most. Because it would come, and there was no power in this world or any that could keep it at bay. Death would have been so much easier.

A movement, the barest of sounds, and he was by my side again. Squatting next to me, watching me with those bright green eyes. The serpent swallowed its tail within his irises as he regarded me. My stomach fluttered, a reminder that I'd not eaten. A blessing, probably, in light of what was stalking me.

To distract myself from the gnawing in my stomach, I asked, "How did you find me?"

"Your blood," he said and wouldn't look me in the eye. "There was enough left in the magic of my hellhound's brain that I was able to use it to track you. By the time I made it to the Bone and Skin Bazaar, I'd lost what was left."

He shifted in the grass, imperceptibly turning away from me. "Luckily I met an ugly little trow with a birthmark on his cheek. He told me where to find you. He suggested I hurry or there would be no 'you' to recover. I let him live, but only because of the sense of urgency in his voice. But for that, he'd be dead right now."

"Heuil," I said, thinking of the little fae. He'd saved my life twice, it seemed. "I guess I owe him a debt."

One black eyebrow climbed half an inch. "And my payment, Ponytail? What do you think a hundred lives are worth?" There was a gentle tease to his voice, such an unfamiliar sound that a soft chuckled escaped me.

"Oh, I have a horrible feeling your payment is coming."

It was a dark bit of humor that I doubted he understood. No matter. He'd get the joke in a short while. Once the withdrawal took me over completely. The thought of it made me groan, and he eyed my stomach again, his gaze trailing from where my hand was holding it steady, to the rasp of scar on my neck, to the pulse that was hammering away like a carpenter on double-time.

"Or maybe we won't be moving at all," he said. "Maybe you need more than a few hours."

My eyes flicked to the horse over his shoulder, afraid to hold Blade's eye because I didn't want him to see the desperation in mine.

"I might need a beat or two, yes," I said. "Will it be safe if I sleep? Just for a couple of hours?" I hated the undercurrent of hope and weakness in my voice, but the thought of moving superseded any sort of ego I had left.

His gaze shuttered as his hands found mine. Something softened in his gaze.

"You're safe, Ava," he said and that red snake moved in his gaze again. "I have a feeling you're about to suffer the worst part of your road yet—And when a warrior travels that road, facing her most terrible enemy in that realm of shadows, she shouldn't do it alone. I'll be here for you."

Realm of Shadow. That's what the poor mortal man in the catacombs had called the auctions. A shudder of energy moved over me, moving my hair like a fresh breeze that smelled of cinnamon and cloves and brushed a cool current along my brow. I knew what that whisper of energy meant. A vow. The most ruthless fae in the Shadow Court was pledging to protect me.

I nodded, silent, accepting it because I had nothing left to cling to. There were worse things, I supposed, than trusting the Dark Enforcer. And I did feel safe with him despite the shivering advance of withdrawal. The soothing touch of grass that dipped and waved at me held my attention as the the moth-winged hues of twilight fell around us. Nutkin grazed nearby, the rhythmic sound of his chewing a strangely comforting backdrop.

For the first time in days, the tension that had kept me strung tight seemed to loosen.

Blade watched me, a flicker of concern in his eyes as I clenched my fists around the edges of the blanket, but I managed a faint smile, if only to lessen the storm in the depths of his gaze as he studied me. I didn't want to imagine what he might be thinking of me right then, realizing exactly what had kept me going in that horrible place, the things I'd had to endure and do just to survive.

My addiction was a shameful thing, a dirty habit that took my sister from me. And yet, in those dreaded catacombs Bloodmist had saved my life. It was hard not to feel the sticky residue of irony.

Better to shift my attention to the waning of light as darkness encroaching the expanse of horizon. I let myself savor the way the sun dipped below the tree line, the way the stars winked at me from the velvet sky as they roused from sleep.

Because as the sliver of day's last light edged Blade's body with the same glimmer of crimson that edged his irises, a dull ache began in my limbs. Slowly pulsing, growing warmer, sharper, until it felt like fire had lit itself beneath my skin, that ache reminded me of the truth that lay beneath that seeming salvation of addiction and drugs.

That despite the loveliness of a dusk sky far removed from the horrors of the catacombs and the hard, beautiful edge of Blade's jaw in silhouette, before the night was done, I'd be begging him to kill me.

★ ★ ★

Special Thanks

I have many people to thank for their help and support on this one.

Debra L. Martin: a stellar romance author you should check out, whose comments sparked a very special scene in the catacombs. Thank you, Debra.

Caroline Jenkins and Denise Sherman who beta read early copies and helped in finding all my grammar oopsies.

A special thanks to Julie Pederick, who fed me her excitement and knowledge of fae culture during the beta read stage. So many plot holes and strategies were massaged and clarified with her help.

www.ingramcontent.com/pod-product-compliance
Lightning Source LLC
Chambersburg PA
CBHW020643120726
47906CB00001B/100